THEN SINGS MY SOUL

Doreen L. Hatton

(With Leslie and Hal Briggs)

ISBN 978-1-64140-941-4 (paperback)
ISBN 978-1-64140-942-1 (digital)

Christian Faith Publishing, Inc.
832 Park Avenue
Meadville, PA 16335
www.christianfaithpublishing.com

Printed in the United States of America

For Mason

ACKNOWLEDGMENTS

1. Based on an article copyrighted 1999–2010 by the Independence Hall Association, dated July 4, 1995.
2. Articles by Laurie Strauss and Dolores Steele.
3. Wikipedia (online)
4. Text: Sabine Baring-Gould; Music: Joseph Barnby
5. Lowrie M. Hofford and Harrison Millard
6. Luacine Clark Fox
7. Article on Christopher and Dana Reeve Foundation on the Internet entitled "Exercise and New Function - Spinal Cord Injury"

CHAPTER ONE

Overhead, the clouds were dark and ominous. As if on cue, just as Bishop Brown stepped forward to begin the graveside service, the sky ripped open, and the rain poured down upon the mourners, stinging their legs and arms under their umbrellas. The funeral directors had covered Lily and her children with a blanket to keep the water from soaking them, as they sat together under a canopy set up in the graveyard.

The April rain drenched Lily to her very soul. The scene before them had a sense of unreality to it. The shiny bronze casket before her held the body of her husband, Samuel. Samuel, so sweet and loving, so full of life, lay before them in that hateful box. *Oh, Samuel, this just can't be happening!*

The graveside service was about to begin. Lily tried to concentrate on what was being said, but her thoughts carried her back to the last time she saw her husband alive.

I love you. I'll be back soon. Those were the last words Samuel had called out to her as he headed across the street to Widow Payne's. Mrs. Payne, a small silver-haired woman in her eighties, was having some problems with a clogged sink, and Samuel had gone over with his tools in hand to help her. He was good with his hands. Even though he wasn't a plumber, he knew how to fix things. It was a natural talent he had. As her home teacher, he often helped the widow whenever he could. He was happy to serve her once again.

But it was different this time. As Lily reflected upon the events of that horrible night and the instant that would change their lives forever, she felt a deep sense of hopelessness.

After finishing the repairs, Samuel had headed back across the road to their home when he was hit by a boy driving too fast in the dark. Samuel was killed instantly. The police told Lily he had been struck by fifteen-year-old Aaron Turner. Aaron only had a learner's permit and should not have been driving alone, and at night.

Lily tried to turn her attention back to the bishop, as he spoke words of comfort to the mourners there in the graveyard. He was saying something about Samuel, how kind he was, how popular he had been as a priesthood teacher. He mentioned Samuel's natural leadership skills.

As the bishop continued to speak, Lily's thoughts carried her back to the day she had first met Samuel. He had just returned home from the Italy, Milan mission. They were both attending Brigham Young University in Provo. On this particular day, Lily was standing just inside the door of the Wilkinson Center, where the BYU students congregated, waiting for her girlfriend, when Samuel walked in. He was carrying what was obviously a heavy box. She had walked over and opened the door for him. He smiled and nodded his thanks as he passed her.

Who is this tall blond-haired, good-looking guy, Lily had asked herself. *I must find out. He's really cute.*

Lily was wearing a royal blue dress under a white sweater. The blue of the dress matched her dark blue eyes. Her dark hair curled naturally to her shoulders. Lily had one of those classic oval-shaped faces. Her tall, slender figure showed an inbred grace. As her short blonde-haired friend, Paula, walked through the door, she looked at Lily admiringly, "You look nice, Lily."

"So do you," Lily returned the compliment. Paula was wearing a pair of green slacks and white blouse with a matching green sweater. Lily grabbed Paula's arm and pointed to the handsome man who had just walked past her and asked, "Do you know him by any chance, Paula?"

"Sure, that's Samuel Langston. He just got home from his mission. He's from my hometown. I'll introduce you to him. Hey, Samuel," Paula called to him. "Come and meet my dear friend, Lily Wright."

Samuel had placed the heavy box down on a table near him and was about to walk away when he heard Paula call him. He turned around and walked over to where Paula and Lily were standing. "Hi, Paula. It's good to see you."

"Samuel, I would like you to meet my friend, Lily Wright."

"Lily Wright, thank you for opening the door for me. I should have stopped and introduced myself when I walked past you, but that box of books was so heavy I had to hurry and find a place to put it down." Samuel shook Lily's hand warmly.

That was how they met. Samuel was as smitten with Lily as she was with him. It was love at first sight. From that day on, Samuel bragged to his friends that *that was the day I met Miss "Right"*.

Samuel had studied to be an accountant, while Lily earned her degree in education. She wanted to be an English teacher. From the moment they met, there was no one else. They were married in the Provo temple a year later and graduated together three years after that.

As the graveside service continued, Lily glanced at her children. Rose was sobbing quietly. Bonnie and Suzie on each side of her had clasped her hands in theirs. Suzie's curly blonde head rested against Lily's shoulder. As she struggled to listen to what the bishop was saying, her mind raced back to when their sweet Rose was born. How happy they were when their children came to them. Rose was born shortly after they graduated, then Bonnie two years later, and Susan two years after that. Life was so very good.

As the children grew, Samuel worked as an accountant, and Lily stayed home to raise them. They were active in church callings and in their community. As Samuel and Lily got to know each other, they discovered that each had special musical talents. Their lovely voices blended beautifully together, and they were often invited to sing at church and community functions. Samuel would accompany them on his guitar, and Lily on the piano. As the children grew, they were added to the group. First, Rose sang with her parents, and then Bonnie, whom her daddy called Bon-Bon. Even though they were very young, their voices were strong and true. Samuel had a fine tenor voice, and Lily sang in her lovely alto.

Eight-year-old Susan, Susie Q to her dad, had been added to the group when she was six. Their voices melded together beautifully. They were asked to sing somewhere nearly every week. Besides singing in their church services, they often performed in hospitals for sick children and in retirement homes. They loved to blend their voices in songs of praise to their Heavenly Father, and they also loved to sing the old classics. Family Home Evenings were filled each Monday night with music. After the lesson was presented, the family loved to stand around their mother at the piano and sing together, with Samuel playing the guitar and singing there beside them. Then they would kneel in prayer, afterward ending the evening with a delicious snack. Samuel, Lily, and the girls took turns giving the lessons, saying the prayers, and preparing the snacks. *Life was good, perhaps too good,* Lily thought as she sat listening to the rain pelting the canopy. *I should have known it was too good to last,* her mind choked on the thought.

*****

The funeral had been beautiful. Bishop Trenton had conducted the proceedings. He had also made arrangements to have the program recorded for the family. Later, Lily and the girls could listen to it and feel its comforting messages in the privacy of their home.

After Bishop Trenton said "amen" at the end of the graveside service, Lily and the children were escorted along with other family members to the waiting hearse and vehicles. Soon, the family and mourners were back at the church building where the ladies from their church congregation were waiting to feed them.

As the mourners came through the church doors, they closed their umbrellas and shook off the water from their raincoats. Some took off their shoes so they wouldn't track the water any further than the foyer. They then walked into the recreation hall in their stocking feet. The tables were lined up with white tablecloths on each one, and everything was in readiness.

Rose took the hands of her grandfather and grandmother Langston and escorted them to their seats at the head table. Bonnie did the same for Lily's parents. Susie clung to her mother. As the food was being served, Lily visited with the dear people who had come to the luncheon. There were tears and hugs. Several shared with Lily and her family experiences they had had with Samuel. He was much loved in the ward and community. They would miss him terribly, they told her. Some pressed checks and cash into her hand as they hugged. Finally, they said their goodbyes, and all headed home. Lily and Samuel's parents came to stay with Lily and their grandchildren for a while, and then they headed home, promising to come back the next day.

"The police chief wants to visit with me tomorrow morning at ten o'clock," Lily said.

"We'll be over at nine-thirty to stay with the girls while you go and visit with the police," Samuel's parents told her.

"We'd like to come with you when you see the chief of police, honey," Lily's mother remarked.

"That would be great, Mom and Dad. I could use your strength when I go talk with him."

The grandparents hugged Lily and the girls and were gone.

*****

For supper that evening, Lily managed to open a can of tomato soup. Rose got out crackers, while Susie and Bonnie set out bowls and spoons. It was all that Lily could think of to fix, but it was enough. None of them felt like eating anyway. It was Friday evening of a nightmare week.

The preceding Monday had been perfect. It had been a lovely warm spring day. After the children had gotten home from school, they sat around the kitchen table doing their homework while Lily fixed roast beef, mashed potatoes, peas, and a tossed salad for dinner. Samuel came home from work as usual at five-thirty, and then, after hugs and kisses all around, the girls had finished their homework, set the table, and then sat down to eat their delicious meal. Bonnie said the blessing. As they ate, each one got to tell what their day had been like.

Samuel had been helping last-minute clients, *the procrastinators* he called them, finish their federal and state taxes and get them sent off. Tax season was a stressful time for accountants, and he was glad it was almost over. "Now, Susie Q, what did you do today?" Susie liked to have her dad call her that.

The eight-year-old bobbed her curly head up and down as she giggled. "My teacher asked me to clean off the chalkboards, and Johnny asked Teacher if he could help me. We had fun." She giggled again. She got out her homework book and showed her dad and mom how well she was doing with her writing.

"Good work, honey," her dad said. "Bon Bon, it's your turn."

"Well, I didn't get to clean the chalkboards with my 'boyfriend,'" Bonnie emphasized the word *boyfriend*. Susie kicked her sister under the table. "Ouch," Bonnie yelped. Everyone chuckled. "We had a spelling bee. I was the last one standing on my team. Mrs. Carlson says I'm a good speller."

"Wow," Lily said. "I used to be the last one standing on my team too when I was in school. You must be taking after me."

Samuel laughed. "Yeah, but she has my good looks."

"Well," Lily conceded, "she does have your pretty blue eyes and blond hair." With that, Lily planted a kiss on the top of her husband's head.

Rose piped up. "It's my turn. We got to work on our computers today. Our assignment was to write an essay on one of the Founding Fathers. I chose Benjamin Franklin. His history is amazing. We have a week to finish the assignment. I can't wait to learn more about him."

Samuel leaned over to give Rose a kiss on her cheek. "The Founding Fathers of our great country were some of the greatest men who ever lived. They risked all they had to found our great nation and create the Constitution. I am happy to hear that you are studying about them in school, Rose."

Rose had asked her dad one day why he never gave her a nickname. He had told her, "The rose is my favorite flower. It is one of God's most beautiful creations. How can I possibly improve on that? I love you, my little Rose." Happily, that had satisfied her. It made her feel special.

"Now," said Lily, "I have some news. The school superintendent called me today and asked me if I would be willing to do some substitute teaching. Now that Susie is in school, they wanted me to use my degree and get some teaching in and possibly work into a permanent position in the next year or so. I would be substituting for the English teachers in whatever grade they needed to use me. I told him I would discuss it with you guys and let him know tomorrow. What do you think?"

"Mom, that would be great," Rose said. Her sisters echoed her sentiments. Samuel hugged his wife. "I agree, honey. Go for it."

*****

Lily shook off the memories of last Monday, their last evening together. Following their meager supper, Lily and the girls picked out a movie to watch until it was time to go to bed. Unable to concentrate, they sat staring at the little screen holding hands in silence, an occasional sob from one of the girls punctuating the quiet behind the dull drone of the television. Lily had not shed a tear. She knew the tears would come, but for now, she was just numb.

"Mom, can we sleep with you tonight? You have a big bed, and we can all squeeze in it. Can we, Mom?" Susie pleaded with her mother.

"Just this one night, then," Lily answered.

After teeth were brushed and clothes changed to pajamas, they knelt around the king-sized bed and said their prayers. Then they got under the covers and lay there in the dark trying to coax sleep to come and blot out the sadness, at least for a while.

Lily lay awake thinking of that Monday evening, the night the unthinkable happened. They normally do nothing on Monday evening except what they do as a family. It is a special night, a night to be together. The world is not invited in on Family Home Evening night. However, this particular night, Julia Payne had called to ask Samuel to help her get her sink unclogged. He had told her he would come over at 8:00 p.m. He knew she was on a tight budget and could not afford a plumber. He was happy to help her.

It was Rose's turn to give the lesson on that fateful night. Even though she was only twelve, she did a remarkable job. It was on forgiveness. She talked about how the Savior had forgiven the woman caught in adultery and confounded those who wanted to stone her by telling them, "He who is without sin should cast the first stone." They left one by one, and the Savior told the woman to "go and sin no more." She rounded out the lesson using other examples. It was a very moving lesson. Lily and Samuel were proud of her.

After the closing prayer was given, Samuel picked up his tools, and with a hearty *I love you* and an *I'll be back soon,* their handsome husband and father left, closing the door behind him. The special dessert Bonnie had prepared would have to wait until their dad got back.

"So what should we do now?" Generally they practiced their musical numbers for a while after Family Home Evening was over, but on this night without dad being there, they questioned what to do with the rest of the evening.

"I know," Lily said. "We'll have a piano recital. Susie, you go first."

"Mom," Susie laughed, "I just started taking piano lessons."

Bonnie said, "I'm sure you can think of something to do. I hear you plunking on the piano every time you go past it."

"Yeah," Rose piped up, "plunk us something for our recital."

"Okay, you asked for it." Then Susie stood up, walked slowly. and with great exaggeration to the piano, carefully sat down on the bench, spreading out her skirt, and began to "plunk" out a number that had her audience begging her to stop. Susie got up from the piano, bowed down low, and to cheers and clapping walked regally to her seat beside her mother.

Bonnie was next. She got out her music book and played a simple rendition of "I am a Child of God," then, mimicking Susie's deep bow, sat down to appreciative applause.

Rose played something by Beethoven, which Lily thought was very good, and then she too milked the applause by bowing low. Now it was Lily's turn. She got up and mimicked the girls by walking with exaggerated steps to the piano. She sat down, adjusted her skirt, and played a lovely Chopin piece. The girls clapped appreciatively, as she too bowed down to her audience.

Samuel had not come home yet, so it was decided that they would go ahead and have Bonnie's dessert. Afterward, it was time for bed. The children changed to their pajamas, said their prayers, and went to bed. After kissing each child good night, Lily had gone into the kitchen and poured herself a diet soda, turned on the television in their family room and watched a movie she had recorded earlier. She settled down on the couch to wait for Samuel to come home.

Lily had awakened to a knock on the door. *That's odd,* she had thought, *Samuel would have just walked in.* The door was unlocked. She glanced at the clock. It was eleven-thirty. She must have fallen asleep soon after the movie started. She stood up and walked to the door. She opened it and saw two policemen standing there. "Mrs. Langston, we have some bad news. May we come in?" Lily stepped back to let the officers in. "It's your husband. He was hit by a car. I'm afraid he didn't make it. He was killed instantly."

Lily was caught by one of the officers as her knees buckled under her. He helped her to the couch and knelt in front of her. There were tears in his eyes as he spoke. "We are so sorry. He was hit by a fifteen-year-old boy who should not have been driving at night. We are so very sorry."

She stared at him. She was trying to make sense of what he was telling her. *Samuel dead? Samuel's not coming home?*

The officers were telling her that they would call Samuel's parents and her parents if she wished them too. She nodded. After they had gotten in touch with both sets of parents, the policemen stayed with her until they arrived to be with Lily.

Now, as Lily lay in the darkness thinking of the events of that dreadful night, she couldn't help thinking that if he had turned down Mrs. Payne's plea for help, he would still be alive. After all, they never went anywhere on family nights. But she couldn't get mad at her dear friend. She was their longtime neighbor. A tiny woman with white hair, Julia Payne, and her husband had been unable to have children of their own, so she had mothered the youngsters in their ward and they, in turn, had loved her back. Lily and the girls often took treats to her. She was one of their favorite people. She was so kind. Often, Mrs. Payne was called upon to give a lesson in Relief Society, the ladies' auxiliary in their church congregation, when the regular teacher was not going to be there. She was truly special, and everyone in their ward who knew her loved her. She was devastated to hear that Samuel was killed walking home after he had fixed her plumbing problem.

And Samuel was the first to help when there was a need. He would encourage and help a young scout with his Eagle Scout project, or go to see someone who was ill in the ward, or visit in the hospital. And, of course, there was their music. He loved to play his guitar and sing with his family whenever they were called upon to perform. How could she be angry with him for doing an act of kindness.

The parents had come soon after the police had called them. From then on, everything had been a blur. Lily was numb. The girls were inconsolable. Lily's parents took over the arrangements for the funeral and worked with the ladies of their congregation in planning the meal after the funeral and all the other arrangements that had to be done. Lily appreciated all that her parents had done and all the others who came to help and comfort them.

The week was like something she had seen in a movie. She was watching from the sidelines as it had unfolded. She went through the motions, but her mind could not comprehend it. She was like a sleepwalker.

Now Lily lay in bed wide awake as her children finally slept beside her. She prayed. Somehow, she knew that they would get through the nightmare. Somehow, some time.

CHAPTER TWO

Lily arose early. There was no sense trying to sleep any longer. She got up as gently as she could so as not to wake up her daughters. She was thankful that they could sleep. She went into the bathroom and took a shower, dressed, and then sat down at the kitchen table. It was covered with flowers and plants of all kinds. There had been so many flowers that she had requested the funeral home take most of them to the hospitals and care centers so that others could enjoy them. She also asked the dear ladies from the ward to be sure and take some flowers to Mrs. Payne. She was heartbroken about the accident. Lily wondered if she should get up and water them. Not right now, she decided.

Instead, she got her purse and took out the cash and checks she had received at the luncheon after the funeral. Then she took pen and paper and began to list the names and addresses of those who had given them checks. The cash was a big problem. She could not remember who had given her the money. She would send thank-you notes for the checks and the flower arrangements and to all the wonderful people who had helped, but she was at a loss as to who had given her the cash. After she listed the checks, she counted the money. There was just over $800. It would help them until she could receive the insurance money from Samuel's policy.

Funny how things happen, Lily thought to herself. His policy was for $100,000. She and Samuel had discussed getting a larger insurance policy just last week. Term life was relatively inexpensive, and since Samuel was a healthy thirty-eight-year-old, they could probably afford to carry at least half a million on him. Samuel was going to look into it this very week. Lily sighed, *Too late now.*

She would need to apply for Social Security benefits. Also, she fervently hoped that the Turner boy had insurance on his car. She would have to make the decision as to whether or not to pay the mortgage off on their home. So much to think about. She would have to gather up what moneys were owed by Samuel's clients and pay off any bills they had. It was all so overwhelming.

Lily thought about the Turners. She didn't know much about them and was anxious to visit with the police and find out just how the accident happened.

She started to sob. She sobbed the tears of loss and heartache. Finally, she dried her tears and went into the bathroom and splashed cold water on her face. It would not do to have red rings around her eyes when she went in to see the police.

She then walked into her bedroom and sat by the bed. Her precious girls were just beginning to wake up. Susie's curly blonde mop of hair would need to be brushed. She and Bonnie had their dad's blue eyes and blond hair. Rose had her mother's dark hair and deep blue eyes. Lily thought her daughters were the most beautiful children in the world.

"Hi, sweethearts, did you sleep well? It's time to get up so we can have breakfast together, and then you will need to shower and dress before Grandma and Grandpa Langston come to be with you while my mom and dad and I go to the police station." Lily tried to smile at them, but she wasn't sure she succeeded. She knew she had to be strong for her children or her whole family would fall apart. *Keep things light,* she thought to herself.

"What would you like for breakfast? You have the choice of cereal, milk, and juice, or juice, milk, and cereal."

She smiled when Bonnie said, "I think I'll have milk, juice, and cereal." She appreciated the ladies from the Relief Society for bringing the leftovers from yesterday's luncheon over for them. They would eat well for a few days before she had to go shopping, something she really dreaded doing.

After breakfast, the girls got their showers, brushed their teeth, dressed and combed their hair. Susie needed a little help with her curly mop. Just as Lily was finishing with Susie's hair, the doorbell rang. Though the Langstons and the Wrights had come in separate cars, they arrived at the same time.

Lily dressed in a blue dress and had her lovely dark hair fastened with a barrette at the nape of her neck. She managed to apply enough makeup to erase the dark circles under her eyes. But, try as she might, she could not erase the sadness in them.

Her in-laws settled in with the girls, and Lily and her parents gave each of them a hug and then headed up town to the police station.

Captain Snowden of the Provo, Utah Police Department, met Lily and her parents at the door and ushered them into his office. He was a middle-aged man, tall with graying hair. He had a kind face, which this day showed a deep concern. "Hello, Lily. Thank you for coming down here this morning. It's nice to see you again, Mr. and Mrs. Wright. I am so sorry it has to be under these terrible circumstances. Please come and sit down over here," indicating an overstuffed brown couch on one side of his large office. After shaking the captain's hand they sat down. "We have a lot to talk about. As you are aware, your husband was hit by fifteen-year-old Aaron Turner. How much have you learned from the newspaper and television coverage of the accident?"

Lily answered, "Not much. We haven't watched the news or read anything in the papers. It was all we could do to get through the funeral and greeting people who came to visit with us. We do know that he hadn't been drinking. That's really all we know."

Captain Snowden nodded and then began to fill in the events of that evening for them. They listened intently. "Aaron lives with his mother, Connie Turner. She is bedridden, except for a wheelchair, which was recently given to her, and he has been her primary caregiver. There are some neighbor women who come in nearly every day to check on things while Aaron is in school, and a home health nurse comes in two or three times a week to bathe Connie and make sure she is taking her medications. What happened last Monday evening was extremely tragic for several reasons." Captain Snowden paused. "There is nothing that I can say that will soften the pain you and your family face at this terrible time, but before we decide on the appropriate charges, let me tell you what happened."

Lily nodded. The captain continued, "Earlier in the evening, Aaron was giving his mother her medicine. It is in liquid form, and as he was pouring her dosage, he dropped the bottle. It shattered. They were not able to save any of it. The medicine is critical for Connie. It was then decided that if Aaron was very careful, he could probably make it to the pharmacy and buy her some more. It is just a few blocks to the store. Her prescription is kept on file at the pharmacy, so Aaron could just drop over there and get some more.

"On his way back from the pharmacy, it was dark, as you know, and raining some. Your husband was wearing dark clothes. Aaron didn't see him and hit him. He was going too fast for the conditions, and it is against the law for a fifteen-year-old, even though he had his learner's permit, to be driving without an adult in the car, and never at night. So he will be charged with vehicular manslaughter. He will also be charged with reckless driving, driving without an adult in the vehicle, and driving at night. He is in serious trouble.

"I know Aaron and Connie Turner. They live just on the next street over from my home. Aaron is a very good young man. He has never been in any trouble. He goes to school and, by the way, has good grades. After school, he goes straight home to take care of his mother. He has never had a chance to play sports and do a lot of the things that teenage boys get involved in.

"He plays a mean guitar. His mother wanted him to have something he could do that would give him some pleasure in his hard life. He and his mother had talked about what he might like to do that would not take him out of the home too much. He had always had an interest in guitars. He enjoyed watching musicians play their guitars on television. It was decided that it would be the perfect instrument for Aaron to learn to play.

"Connie was able to find a used guitar that was in good condition through a friend of theirs who works in a music store. The friend also helped them find a teacher who would come to their home to teach Aaron to play. It was also discovered that Aaron has a remarkable singing voice. He has become very accomplished with the instrument."

Lily thought, *Like my Samuel.*

"He often gets a chance to play and sing for school functions and has become quite a popular young man in the school, although he, for obvious reasons, does not have the time to socialize like other young people of his age. He has to be home to take care of his mother every day after school." Captain Snowden continued, "In the evenings, after dinner dishes are done and homework is finished, Aaron sits down and entertains his mother. She tells me it is like having her own miniconcert every night. It is really the only real pleasure Connie has in her life right now.

"What I would like is for you to go home and talk with your family members about what they feel would be the proper punishment for this young man. He has never been in any trouble. Though it is largely going to be up to the district attorney's office how they will handle this tragedy, I know he will value your input."

Lily and her parents stood up. The captain shook their hands. "Give me a call, Lily, after you have had a chance to visit with your family, and let me know which direction you want us to go. Aaron is in custody, and we are arranging to have a preliminary hearing a week from next Monday. Mrs. Turner, Connie, has been placed in a nursing home for now."

"We will talk over what you have told us, Captain, and I will be sure and call you." Lily and her parents walked toward the office door.

"Thank you, Lily, and Mr. and Mrs. Wright. I look forward to hearing from you. Take what time you need."

On the way home, they were silent, each thinking about what Captain Snowden had told them. Finally, Lily's mother spoke up, "I don't think Aaron should go to jail, Lily. He didn't mean to hit Samuel." She burst into tears. "He should be allowed to be with his mother."

"I've been thinking that too, Mom. Let's talk it over with the Langstons and the girls and see what they have to say about it." Lily pulled into the driveway and turned off the engine.

*****

There were hugs and tears all around when they went inside. Lily said, "It's lunchtime. Let's eat and then we will tell you what Captain Snowden told us." Lily went to the fridge and got out the leftovers. Rose and Bonnie set the table, and Susie went to sit on her Grandpa Wright's lap. Fred Wright was a bald man with brown eyes over which he wore horn-rimmed glasses. He hugged her tightly in his somewhat chubby lap. Her small frame snuggled close to him.

There was ham, fruit salad and a tossed salad. And there were the delicious funeral potatoes that they all enjoyed. Lily thought about other funerals she had helped with and for which she had made her share of funeral potatoes. There were dinner rolls and real butter. She got out milk and sodas for them to drink.

After they finished eating, the table was cleared off, and the dishes put in the dishwasher to be washed later. They then went into the living room and sat on the couches and easy chairs. Lily began to tell her children and her in-laws about the meeting they had had at the police station. Lily's mother filled in some of the details, wiping tears away as she spoke.

After reiterating everything the captain had told them about Aaron and his mother, and how Aaron had happened to be out driving on a dark rainy night, Susie was the first to speak. "I don't want Aaron to go to jail. He needs to be with his mother."

Grandpa Langston replied, "But, Susie, what he did was careless in the extreme. They can't just give him a slap on the wrist and a warning. What do you think should happen to him, honey?"

Where Fred Wright was of medium build, bald and wore glasses, Matt Langston was tall, slender, with dark hair and dark eyes.

Bonnie spoke up, "They can give him probation and community service hours, can't they? The captain said he was a good boy. Do you remember the lesson Rose gave in Family Home Evening? Gee, was that just last Monday? It was on forgiveness. She told us what

Jesus taught, that we had to forgive as He has forgiven us for all our sins. I vote for that."

Grandfather Wright shifted his position so he could place a hand on Bonnie's arm. He said, "We may not have much say in what punishment he receives. What do you think, Lily?"

"I got the feeling when Captain Snowden was talking to us that he wanted to know how we felt about his punishment, and that he would listen to any suggestions we had. How do the rest of you feel about giving Aaron probation? He has never been in trouble before. Even though he probably would be placed in a youth detention center, it may harden him. He may come out a different person. He made some mistakes that led to our terrible tragedy." Lily wiped away the tears streaming down her face. "Like Rose said, we are to forgive. Everyone. Period. I feel that is the right thing to do."

Lily's mother got up from her chair to come sit by Lily. Julie Wright was five feet six inches tall with her daughter's dark blue eyes. Like her husband, she too was pleasingly plump. "I raised a wonderful daughter. I had a feeling that you would feel that way. Two wrongs don't make a right. We won't have Samuel while we are here on earth, but we all know that Samuel will be with us after we are resurrected. We will be together as a family for all eternity. We can take joy and comfort in that knowledge. If they put Aaron in prison, he may never have a chance to be the person we believe he can be. What a waste that will be and for what reason? After all, it won't bring Samuel back. I agree with Bonnie that probation and community service would be punishment enough for Aaron.

"Yes, yes, tell the captain how we feel, Lily," Samuel's mother cried out, wiping at her tears and blowing her nose. Dallas Langston was tall and slender like her husband. She had blue eyes and light-brown hair. Together they were a strikingly handsome couple. The only one who had not expressed an opinion was Rose. All turned toward her, anticipating that she would agree with the others. What happened next was not what they expected. Rose stood up and angrily blurted out, "Aaron killed my dad. He needs to go to prison. He killed my dad." She covered her face with her hands as she sobbed.

Lily quickly stood and put her arms around her daughter. "Rose, I am so sorry you feel that way. The Savior wants us to forgive as he has forgiven. You taught us that lesson. What do you think we should do now?"

Rose looked at her mother and the others. "Do what you want to do. I just don't want to be a part of it." With that, she ran out of the room.

After Rose left the room, the others sat in stunned silence. Finally, all agreed that Aaron should not serve jail time. Lily dialed the phone and asked to speak to Captain Snowden. When he answered, Lily expressed the wishes of her family on Aaron's behalf. Captain Snowden cleared his throat and thanked Lily for calling back so soon. It was clear from the tone of his voice that he was hoping the members of Samuel's family would feel that way.

"Lily, would you and your family be willing to come to the hearing a week from next Monday? It will be held at 11:00 a.m. in the court house. You know where that is?"

Lily said, "Yes, I do, Captain. We will all be there." She looked at her parents and in-laws who nodded their heads in agreement.

After her parents and in-laws left, Lily went in to Rose's bedroom. Rose was lying on the bed sobbing. She didn't want to talk to her mother, but Lily stayed until the sobbing stopped, and Rose looked up. "Rose, what happened just now is so unlike you. Do you want to talk about it?"

"I hate Aaron Turner for what he did to Dad. How could he have been so careless? He shouldn't have been driving anywhere."

"Rose, it is not in you to hate anybody. Nothing you have ever been taught would lead me to believe you could hate anybody. Please, Rose, think and pray about what you are saying."

"Well, I do, Mom. I'll go along with the probation thing if you want me to, but I want nothing to do with Aaron Turner." With that, Rose turned her face into her pillow and began sobbing again. Lily padded Rose's shoulder, told her how much she loved her and quietly left the room.

*****

Aaron Turner sat on the bed in his holding cell. His world had spiraled downward since that terrible night just over two weeks ago. Why had he been going so fast? He should have turned down one street before he did, but he had missed his turn. What was to become of him now? *Oh, Mother, Mother*—he sobbed—*I am so sorry,* he thought bitterly, *what will become of you now, Mom? I won't be able to care for you if I am locked up. I love you so much.* His slender frame shook with his sobbing.

"Aaron, it's time for your hearing." The jailor unlocked the cell door and escorted Aaron to the room in the courthouse where the hearing was to take place. He looked around. He knew his mother wouldn't be there. There were some people he didn't know and a few of his neighbors.

And then he saw Lily and her children and two older couples who, Aaron supposed, were Mrs. Langston's parents and in-laws. He had not expected them to be here. They looked like they had all been crying. It made him want to cry too, but he stubbornly refused to shed any tears in front of the court.

Everyone stood up when the judge walked into the courtroom. He nodded his head, and everyone sat down. The district attorney then addressed the court, "Your Honor, I have been visiting with Samuel Langston's family, and we have come to a consensus in regard to what punishment should be given Mr. Turner.

"If it pleases Your Honor, we wish to offer Aaron Turner probation and community service. The community service will replace time in a youth detention center for Mr. Turner and will last until he is twenty-one, a period of six years. We will decide on the community service in the next week or so, but for now, we feel that he needs to be at home taking care of his mother and going to school. How does Your Honor feel about this?"

Judge William Thomas looked over his horn-rimmed glasses at Aaron, who was very pale under a shock of reddish-brown hair. Aaron and his attorney, Jacob Manning, stood up. "Well, Mr. Turner, I would say that you are a very lucky young man. The Langston family has pleaded for mercy on your behalf. I am inclined to agree with them. You have never been in trouble, and you are needed by your mother. So I am allowing you, for now, to be released in the custody of your attorney. Mr. Manning will take you to the nursing home where your mother has been placed, and then he will take you both home and make sure you have what you need in the way of food, etc.

"In the next week or so, it will be decided what community service you will be given. It will probably be something you can do on Saturdays, so it won't interfere with your schooling and taking care of your mother. Your attorney is going to see if more help can be assigned to your mother's care. Be grateful that there are still good people in the world, young man. Court is dismissed."

Aaron was stunned, relieved and happy all at once. He turned and caught Lily's eye. He said a silent, *thank you.* She mouthed, "You're welcome."

CHAPTER THREE

Jacob Manning turned and placed his hand on Aaron's shoulder. "We need to go to the clerk's office and sign some papers to have you released from the youth detention center. They will place you in my custody, Aaron. After we get the paperwork done, we will go get your mother and get you both home."

Aaron had tears in his brown eyes as he questioned his attorney, "Why did Mrs. Langston and her family do that? I figured I would be locked up in a juvenile facility. I was so scared. What I did was truly awful, but I saw forgiveness in their faces. How come?"

"Because Lily Langston and her children, and I suspect the grandparents, are true Christians in every sense of that word. They are going to suffer greatly over the loss of Samuel, but they recognize having you incarcerated in some facility will not bring Samuel back. They truly want what is best for you and your mother. That is the Christian way of doing things. It's going to be all right, son." Jacob gave Aaron a hug.

After the paperwork was filled out and signed, Aaron and Jacob headed over to the nursing home where Connie Turner was waiting. When they walked in the front door, they noticed Connie sitting in her wheelchair near the front desk. She embraced Aaron as tears flowed down her cheeks. "Mr. Manning, what can I say? I know your helping Aaron was because you were assigned by the court as a pro bono case, but I thank you just the same." Connie took Jacob's hand and squeezed it between her own cool hands. "I got a call from the clerk of the court who told me what the outcome of the hearing was. Words cannot express how I feel," she choked.

"I did very little, Mrs. Turner. You can thank Lily Langston and her family for the outcome. And you have some very good friends in high places. I am speaking of Captain Snowden. He was hoping for this outcome, as I am sure you probably suspected."

"He is a dear, dear friend. He has been like a father to Aaron," Connie replied as tears rolled down her cheeks.

"Well, you two, let's get you home." Jacob and one of the nurses at the home wheeled Connie to the car and gently placed her in the front seat. Connie was a small woman with short dark hair and hazel eyes. It was easy for Jacob and the nurse to lift her into the car. The wheelchair was folded and placed in the trunk. After she was safely buckled in, Aaron got in the back seat. Jacob drove to the Turner's home and got Connie settled on her bed. He turned to Aaron and said, "Make a list of groceries you want me to pick up, and I will run and get them now. Is there anything else you need? Are the utilities all up to date?"

Aaron looked at his mother. Though she couldn't walk, she could still pay the bills and do any other chores that didn't include walking. Shortly after her accident, kind friends and neighbors had donated the money to buy Connie her wheelchair. It helped her get around very well. "Yes, they are all paid up to date."

"Good, do you have that list, Aaron?" A few minutes later, Aaron handed Jacob the list. "Okay, I'll be back in about an hour."

After the door closed, Aaron leaned over and hugged his mother. "Mom, somehow I need to make this up to Lily Langston. What she and her family did was unbelievable. They gave me my life back. Somehow, I have to make it up to them."

Connie hugged her son back. "Somehow, I think the time will come when you will be able to repay their kindness. Now, son, will you get out your guitar and play for me? I would love that."

Aaron got out his guitar and tuned it and began to play for his mother. He played and sang some of her favorite songs. She lay back and closed her eyes. The tears that flowed were no longer tears of sadness and fright, but tears of relief and joy. Her son was back. Because of the Langstons and their forgiving nature, she would have her precious son with her. *Thank you, Heavenly Father, thank you for your goodness and love, and for precious people who follow your commandments to love and forgive one another. Whatever happens now I know is in your hands.* Connie opened her eyes and smiled at her son.

Neither Connie nor Aaron heard Jacob Manning come through the door. He didn't bother to knock. As he set the groceries down on the counter, he heard Aaron play and sing for his mother. He was touched by the beauty of Aaron's clear tenor voice, and he could clearly play that guitar of his. *Wow, I am impressed,* he thought.

Quietly, Jacob put away the food where he thought it should go. The cool stuff went into the fridge, of course, but if he couldn't find where the soups and other foodstuffs went, he left them on the counter for Aaron to put away. Then he moved closer to the bedroom so he could hear the music better. After a while, Jacob let them know he was there.

"Don't stop, Aaron. I have never heard someone as young as you play and sing like that. You are truly talented," Jacob complimented him.

"Thanks, Mr. Manning."

"Oh, call me Jacob. I need to leave in a few minutes, but I would love to hear you play a couple more songs, okay?"

"Sure, here is one that I composed myself."

And he composes too. I really am impressed, Jacob thought to himself. A few minutes later, after assurances that Connie and her son would be fine, Jacob left to go home. His own son would be getting home from school soon, and he wanted to be there for him. James turned ten last month in March. He had wanted more children, but tragedy had struck them, as it had the Langston family. Jacob's wife, Trudy, was hit by a car. James never got to know his mother. The accident happened just after James turned one. She was hit by a car while she was crossing the street in a bad snowstorm. The driver didn't see her, just as Aaron hadn't seen Samuel Langston.

As Jacob drove, he thought back to that night and the horror of the accident and the aftermath. Nine years ago, he had been inconsolable. It took many months and years before the pain lessened. Jacob's parents helped with the baby. In fact, they were kind enough to move into his big house and be there for both him and baby James. They were still there, and Jacob loved having them close. His parents often go out of town to visit his two sisters and a brother, along with Jacob and James, when he can get away to go. But they make their home with Jacob. Having his parents in his home to take care of James while he is at work is godsend.

As the years passed by, it became more and more obvious that James had problems. After going to several doctors, it was finally determined that his son was autistic. Having his parents in his home to take care of him while he is at work was truly a blessing.

As Jacob drove home from the Turners, he thought about the women he had dated over the years. Finding someone to spend the rest of his life with has been more difficult. *They were all so nice, and pretty too,* Jacob mused. But no one as yet has really clicked for him. *Perhaps, I am just too picky.* Jacob Manning glanced up at the rearview mirror. His dark eyes thoughtfully glanced back at him. *Gee, what's not to like.*

When Jacob and Trudy married, it was for time and eternity. They married in the Salt Lake Temple. Jacob never thought for one moment that his life with Trudy would be cut so short here in mortality. At times, he found the loneliness he felt almost unbearable. But his wonderful boy and his parents have helped to soothe away the emptiness he still sometimes feels.

As he drove, he thought of Aaron and his mother. He wondered at her illness. What had caused her disability? Would she ever be able to walk again? What kind of community service would the court give Aaron? It would be great if somehow it could be centered around his amazing talents. Perhaps he could put a word in with the judge when he went to court in the morning. *I'll do just that,* Jacob decided.

Jacob arrived home to the smell of freshly baked bread. Hmm, is there any smell on earth more heavenly than that smell? He realized he was hungry. *I forgot to eat lunch today,* he thought. *No wonder that smell is making my stomach growl.*

"Hi, Dad, I beat you home." James walked toward his father and gave him their special hand sign. "How was your day? You had the Turner hearing today, didn't you?"

"Yup, and it went well. Thank you for asking, son." With that, Jacob smiled warmly. James was small for a ten-year-old. He had brown hair and his mother's lovely large dark brown eyes.

"Smells like your grandmother has done it again. Boy, am I hungry. Hi, Mom, it sure smells good. How soon can we eat? I'm starving." Jacob saw that the table was already set. That meant that dinner must be almost ready.

"Thanks for making bread, Mom." He gave his mother a big hug, his six-foot-two frame totally enveloping her much-smaller one, and then he helped her put the food on the table. His silver-haired father came in from the patio with a plateful of steaks, and they all sat down and said the blessing on the food.

As usual, James took one item of food at a time. He did not want his food to touch. If it was up to him, he would have skipped everything but the dessert. However, his grandmother talked him into starting with his vegetables. That was a real challenge, but finally, the compromise was no veggies, no dessert. After eating two or three bites of corn, he got up from the table and scraped the rest into the trash can. Grandma Manning rolled her eyes but said nothing. James sat back down and helped himself to the mashed potatoes. After finishing them, he was given a small piece of steak. Finally, apple pie and ice cream.

As they ate, Jacob recounted the day for his parents and James, especially the Turner-Langston hearing. "It was remarkable," he said, "Lily Langston and her family did not want Aaron going to a youth detention facility. The judge then gave Aaron Turner probation and community service. The community service will be decided in a few days."

"Aaron Turner is a very talented young man," Jacob told his parents and James how he had come into the house with the groceries for the Turners and had heard Aaron play his guitar and sing for his mother. "I was totally blown away. What a wonderful talent he has. I am going to ask the court if we can figure out a way for him to use his talents as part of his community service."

"What a wonderful idea, Jacob," his mother replied.

"I agree," his father told him.

"Me too," James added.

After they were finished, James folded his napkin carefully, laid it on his plate, and then placed his knife, fork, and spoon on top of the napkin, the bottoms of the three lined up perfectly in a straight line with each other. This he did every night. Then he looked up and smiled.

Later, when it was time for him to go upstairs to bed, he would place his right foot on the step and then the other one before advancing to the next step. As he slowly climbed the stairs, he counted each one. Because it would drive Jacob and his parents crazy to climb the stairs with him, they waited at the foot of the stairs before following him. When James reached the top of the stairs, he would turn and smile. This was their signal to follow him upstairs. The routine never changed.

CHAPTER FOUR

Lily hung up the phone. The call was from Mona Thompson. She worked for the Hunter Cancer Clinic as their public relations manager. Soon there would be a big fund-raiser for the clinic, and Mona asked Lily if she and her girls were up to singing a couple of songs for the benefit. It was to be in two weeks. "Do you feel like performing so soon after your husband's death? Could you be ready by then?" Mona asked her. Lily did not commit right then to doing it, but said she would discuss it with the girls and get back to her. Mona thanked her and hung up.

Mona had been with the Hunter Cancer Clinic as their "chief go-for do-for person" as she liked to call herself for some years now. She was thirty-eight years old on her last birthday, a good-looking tall, slender blonde lady by her own impartial judgment.

Lily looked at the calendar. It was one month to the day that Samuel was killed. It was May 15. The nights were the most difficult. Most of them found her crying herself to sleep. Someone had told her that if she placed a pad and a pen next to her bed, she could make notes about things that were troubling her or those she needed to do the next day. That way, she could clear her mind and hopefully get some sleep. She did find that it helped.

Susie sometimes would come and crawl into bed beside her mother. Lily felt that the time would come when Susie would no longer feel the need to be by her mother's side in the night. But for now, Lily appreciated her youngest daughter's small warm body next to her. One night, when Lily lay sobbing, Susie's little hand found hers under the covers. So sweet. So comforting. Lily hugged her little daughter to her as she finally fell asleep.

After talking with Mona, Lily worked on paying the bills and calling the last couple of Samuel's clients who had not paid in full for the work he did on their taxes. Both promised to have checks in the mail by the end of the month. She also finished up the last of her thank-you notes.

The girls had returned to school the Monday after the funeral, one week after their father's death. The first few days at school were difficult, but it became easier as the weeks went by. Rose's teacher told Rose that if she didn't feel like completing the assignment she had given her on writing about a Founding Father, she would average her grade without it. Rose insisted she wanted to find out all she could about Benjamin Franklin and would get the assignment done as soon as she could. Her teacher smiled at her, pleased that she was going to complete the work.

Lily had received the $100,000 life insurance payment on Samuel's life. She had also sat down with Aaron Turner's insurance people. Her attorney and friend, Bill Green, attended the meeting with her. What resulted from this conference was a very nice settlement for Lily and her girls. Not only was theirs a one-time payout, but the insurance company would also pay for Rose, Bonnie, and Susie to go to the colleges of their choice when the time came. Bill thought the insurance people were being very generous. Lily thought so too, and so documents were signed attesting to the settlement, and copies were given to Bill and to Lily for safekeeping.

This settlement from the insurance company allowed Lily to pay off the mortgage on her home and her other bills. She was now completely debt-free. Bill helped her find a trusted financial planner who set up investments for her, one that was held to build equity, and one that would pay out each month to help with their living expenses.

Bill was working on the probate of Samuel's estate. Thank goodness, he had a will and a trust agreement. While Bill was working on the probate, he had Lily come in to make her will and set up her own trust agreement.

Lily had started doing substitute teaching. She was loving it. She taught two or three times a week where she was needed in the Provo public school system. With her teaching money and the money coming in from the annuity, plus the children's Social Security benefits, Lily and her daughters were financially set. She paid her tithing faithfully. She knew that she was being helped by a loving Heavenly Father. She felt Him often. She missed Samuel terribly but there were times when she had the comforting feeling that Samuel was close.

Before her girls came home from school, Lily went out into the backyard and pulled weeds from her flower beds. Her yard was lovely. All of them had worked in the raised garden over the years until it had become something of a showplace. Trees surrounded the yard, and in the center, Samuel had built a raised platform where there was a place for the barbecue and tables and chairs and a couple of outdoor couches. This was covered by a gazebo-like top to keep out the sun but still let in the breezes on a warm summer evening. They often had get-togethers with family and friends. They were always special times.

Around the edges of the platform were their raised flower beds. They had planted perennials over the years, and every spring, they filled in between with annuals such as petunias, pansies, and marigolds. Lily would need to get these planted soon.

"Mom, where are you? Oh, there you are. The flower beds are looking good, Mom." Rose came down to stand beside her mother. Nothing more had been said about Rose's outburst the day they had gotten together and discussed wanting to keep Aaron out of jail. Perhaps, she has had a change of heart and doesn't have those bad feelings against Aaron anymore. The outburst had been so out of character for her precious Rose.

"Grab that digging fork over there and help me finish getting the weeds out, okay? I just have a few more feet to work on and then they will be banished from our garden, at least for now," Lily continued to pull weeds as she spoke.

"Mom, I finished my essay on Benjamin Franklin. Teacher gave me an A++. Can you believe it? She said it was the best in the class. I love Benjamin Franklin," Rose finished.

"How about reading it for us in Family Home Evening next time?" Lily hugged her daughter. "Remember what your dad said about the Founding Fathers, that they were some of the bravest and most stalwart men who ever lived?"

Just then, Bonnie and Susie came out into the backyard. "Hi, Mom. HI, Rose. Can we help?"

"Of course, but we are nearly finished. Dig in, and we will be finished more quickly." Lily looked around. "It's time to mow. I talked to Bill about hiring Joshua to come and mow it for us every week. Josh was excited. He will come on Saturday mornings and do it for us each week."

"Good, I like Josh," Susie said. "I like Tom and Margaret and Lucy too. We need to go on another outing with them this summer." Lily felt she wasn't ready for that. It was too soon. As they finished their digging and went into the house to do homework and get supper ready, Lily and the girls talked about the times when the Greens and the Langstons had gone camping around Utah. Their home state was awash with wonderful sights to see. From red rock canyons to tall mountains, to deserts where special treasures could be found in nature, it was full of interesting places to visit.

The Langstons and the Greens would take their campers out into the desert, sometimes following the Pony Express trail. They would stop at Simpson Springs or the Dugway geode beds and look for geodes. They traveled to Topaz Mountain and looked for crystals.

One time, they drove down to southern Utah to the Escalante area and found moqui marbles. These could be small as marbles or as large as baseballs. It was said that Indian children used them to play games and throw them back and forth like baseballs to each other.

At Antelope Springs, they found trilobites, and along the trails, they found pieces of obsidian that are called Apache tears. The Langston and the Green children saved their treasures. These were magical times. If and when they were to go on another of those fantastic trips, Lily supposed that Tom Green, Bill, and Mary's oldest son, could help her drive her motor home. He was now seventeen.

Utah has five national parks. The Langstons and the Greens loved Zion National Park and Bryce Canyon. "Bryce Canyon is especially lovely," Lily said. "I love the red rock formations. They are spectacular."

Susie said, "Bonnie, do you remember when we went to Topaz Mountain looking for crystals? You and Rose went up the hill a little ways, and when you were digging, you loosened a rock, and it came falling down the hill and landed right at my feet? Thanks. It's the best rock we found that day. It's full of crystals."

"How can I forget, Susie? You keep it on the top of your dresser. I think it should have been mine. After all, I loosened it." Bonnie smiled at her little sister.

"Well," Susie piped up, "I do let you come into my room and look at it once in a while, don't I?" They all laughed.

After they had finished eating and the dinner dishes were washed and put away, Lily said, "Come, girls, we need to make a decision together. Mona Thompson called me this morning asking if we felt like singing for the Hunter Cancer Clinic's charity event. It is going to be held in two weeks. How do you feel about it?"

Rose was the first to speak, "Dad would not want us to sit home and mope. He loved the times we performed. I think we should do it. We are kind of rusty since we haven't sung since Dad died, but I think it is time."

Bonnie said, "I vote yes."

"Me too," Susie quickly chimed in. "I want to sing for it."

"That's settled then. I'm glad you all feel that way. We need to get back into the groove of things, even though I really don't much feel like it." Lily could not keep the tears from welling up in her eyes. The girls held their mother in a group bear-hug.

"Now, because your father is no longer with us, we shall have to practice without his part. Tomorrow I will go to the music store and find pieces of music for women's voices only. For now, I think I will get trio music rather than quartet. That way, Susie can sing soprano or the lead part with Bonnie. You sing the second soprano part, Rose, and I will sing the alto." Lily found herself getting a little excited in spite of herself.

"Our homework is done. Let's go practice some songs before we go to bed, okay, Mom?" Bonnie asked. Lily and the girls practiced some scales and sang some of the church hymns until it was time to go to bed.

Clothes were changed into pajamas, teeth brushed, and family prayer was said. Then kisses and hugs were exchanged all around, and Lily tucked her girls into their beds with a "Good night and I love you," answered by "me toos" all around.

Before Lily herself went to bed, she called first her in-laws to let them know about the singing engagement and then called her parents. She told them of her busy day of working in the yard and about the upcoming charity event for which they were going to sing. Her mother and father were pleased, as were Samuel's parents. They told her they would certainly be there to support her and the kids. After talking to her parents, Lily got down on her knees, turned off the light, and said her own private prayer.

In her prayer, Lily thanked Heavenly Father for her many blessings. She thanked Him for her darling daughters and for her parents and Samuel's parents. And she thanked Him for Samuel. She told Him how much she missed her precious husband. She asked Heavenly Father for the strength she would need to get through the difficult coming months and years without him, *Help me to be strong and stalwart, to be a good mother, and teach my children to love thee and keep thy commandments.* She asked Him to bless all the precious people in her life, her dear friends, and all who have been there and continued to be there for her and the children. She asked Him to help them prepare the music for the upcoming fund-raiser for the cancer clinic, *And please bless and protect Aaron Turner and his mother.* She ended her prayer, "In the name of Jesus Christ, amen." Lily lay down in bed and quickly fell asleep.

CHAPTER FIVE

Aaron Turner stopped mopping the hallway on the third floor of the Hunter Cancer Clinic to watch a nurse wheel a child toward him in a wheelchair. The child looked to be about six or seven. She had blonde hair and blue eyes. As they passed Aaron, the nurse acknowledged him with a nod and a smile. The child waved and called, "Hi."

This was his third Saturday to be working at the hospital. He had been assigned to the janitorial staff to work out his hours of community service. He didn't mind the hard work. It was actually therapeutic. He mopped floors throughout all the hospital. That took most of the eight hours he worked. He had breaks morning and afternoon and an hour at lunchtime. Aaron took his breaks and lunch hour in the janitors' quarters.

Jacob Manning had also arranged to have Aaron entertain the patients and staff during the last hour of his workday. Aaron looked forward to his time performing for the patients when the hour came. Because his learner's permit had been suspended for the duration of his probation, Aaron rode his old bike to the hospital. Since the hospital was only about a mile from his home, it was no big deal. He liked riding it. He strapped his guitar on his back and off he went, with a big hug for his mother and a wave goodbye. Their neighbors took turns looking in on Connie. Also, she was just a phone call away if she needed anything. With her wheelchair, she could get around the house pretty good now, even get herself lunch or snacks. She could tell that her son was enjoying the work at the hospital, and especially the time he got to perform for the patients.

On the first Saturday Aaron worked, he sang and played his guitar for the patients on the first floor. The second Saturday, he played on the second floor of the hospital. He would keep rotating each week. Today he was going to play for the children who were patients on the third floor. He was through his mopping duties, and after washing his hands and combing his hair, Aaron sat down before the youngsters to play and sing. There were children of all ages, from babies to teenagers. *So many sick kids,* Aaron thought.

For the next hour, he played for them. He played and sang songs that children would know, primary songs, Disney tunes, funny ones too that he could remember. The children responded with clapping and smiles and laughter. Several raised their hands and requested special songs they wanted him to play and sing. After he was finished, and he played longer than the allotted hour because the children did not want him to stop, several raised their hands to ask him questions or to tell him about their illnesses.

One little boy said, "I have leukemia, but I'm in remission. I'm going home soon. This is my mom." The boy pointed to the pretty dark-haired woman sitting next to him.

"That is wonderful, young man. Nice to meet you, ma'am," Aaron told the lady, smiling at the boy and his mother. She smiled back.

There were several more children who wanted to talk to Aaron. He was patient and listened to everyone. He enjoyed talking with the children. They seemed so bright and happy in spite of their reasons for their being in the hospital.

"What is your name?" This from the little girl who had passed him in the hall in her wheelchair.

"My name is Aaron, Aaron Turner. What is yours?"

"My name is Grace. I have cancer. I'm going to die." Grace's mother was sitting next to her. She was holding Grace's hand as the tears came streaming down her face.

Aaron was speechless except for a mumbled, "I'm sorry."

Grace smiled, "That's okay, Aaron, I'm ready."

He couldn't bring himself to answer any more questions. Aaron got up, told the children he would be back soon, and walked out of the room, his own tears running down his cheeks.

When Aaron got home, he told his mother about his day. He ended by telling her about Grace and how what she had told him had hit him smack between the eyes. "Mom, she was so calm and matter-of-fact. It was like she was telling me what they were going to eat for dinner. I saw acceptance in her, like she personally knew the Savior and was happy she was going to be with him soon. Is this even possible?" Again, Aaron's eyes filled with tears.

"Yes, Aaron, I believe it is true. Children, especially, have the kind of faith that brings them in tune with the Savior's love. You know how Christ, when He came to the people on this continent after His resurrection, gathered up the little children and blessed each one individually. He held them in His loving arms. He wants us to be like the little children. That means He wants us to have that kind of faith and trust in Him. Grace has that kind of love for Him, so she is not afraid."

Aaron pondered what his mother said to him for a while and then he said, "Mother, would it be all right if I went to visit Grace after school on Monday?"

"Of course, son. I'll be fine."

CHAPTER SIX

It was Monday evening, time for Family Home Evening. Rose was going to give her presentation on Benjamin Franklin. Dinner was through, and the dishes cleaned away. They had practiced their songs for the fund-raiser they were to sing at in a few days. Lily had picked out several trios. After playing and singing them, the girls had chosen three that they liked a lot. One was a sacred number, one a show tune, and one had a patriotic theme. They liked all three very much. They were to sing two numbers. Perhaps they would be asked to sing an encore. "We will be prepared, just in case," Lily told them.

Susie said the opening prayer. Bonnie picked a verse from scriptures to read, and then it was Rose's turn. She got up, brushed a dark stand of hair out of her eyes, and began: "Benjamin Franklin was born in Boston on January 17, 1706. In his family, there were seventeen children."

"Wow, that's a lot of children," Susie remarked, noticeably impressed.

Rose smiled at her younger sister and continued, "Benjamin's father wanted him to become a clergyman, but because the family could not afford to send Ben to school long enough for him to become a full-fledged preacher, he instead helped his brother James in his printshop. Benjamin helped him compose pamphlets and set type. Then twelve-year-old Benjamin would sell their articles in the streets.

"Benjamin Franklin became an accomplished writer, writing under the pen name of Silence Dogood while he was still working for his brother. His brother didn't know that Ben was actually Silence

Dogood because he slipped the articles under the door at night. The readers loved the articles, but James became angry and jealous when he found out Ben was the author.

"Benjamin and his brother James became unpopular with Boston's very powerful Puritan preachers because the Mathers were in favor of inoculating the population for the deadly disease smallpox, but the Franklins were against it because they thought the vaccine made people sicker. James made fun of the clergy, even though others of the clergy agreed with the Franklin's. Ultimately, James was thrown in jail for his views. While James was in jail, Ben kept the paper going. Ben thought his brother would appreciate it, but he was angry. After James harassed and beat his brother, Ben had had enough. He ran way in 1723.

"Benjamin found work as an apprentice printer in Pennsylvania. The governor of the state took note of Ben's talent and promised him that he would set him up in business. But, first, Franklin had to go to England to buy printing equipment. So Benjamin, being a trusted young man, did just that. However, the governor did not keep his promise. Therefore, Benjamin was forced to spend several months in England doing printwork until he could get enough money together to return to America.

"When Ben got back to Philadelphia, he went back to being a printer's helper. It turned out that he was actually a better printer than the person he was working for, so he borrowed money and set himself up in the printing business. He got so good, he began getting work to do for the government. He started to do very well in business.

"Some of his accomplishments included creating a newspaper that became the most successful in America. It was the first to print political cartoons, many of which Ben did himself. It was called the *Pennsylvania Gazette*.

"In 1733, he started publishing Poor Richard's Almanack. He didn't use his own name but called the writer Richard Saunders, a poor man with a nagging wife. The Almanack contained weather reports, recipes, predictions, and sermons. It contained clever observations and lively writing. It too was a big hit with its readers.

"He also started the Library Company of 1731. He had a terrific idea. Books were rare at the time and expensive. Benjamin Franklin gathered money from people he knew and pooled the money and bought books in England. This, then, became the first lending library in the country.

"Among other accomplishments, Franklin helped create the Pennsylvania Hospital in 1751. It was created to better help treat the sick. These two companies, the Library Company and the Pennsylvania Hospital are still running today, along with a learned group called the Philadelphia Philosophical Society.

"He wasn't through yet. He started a fire insurance company to help people who lost their homes by fire. This company helped the people buy fire insurance against loss. This company also is in business today.

"He invented the heat-efficient stove—called the Franklin stove—to help warm houses more efficiently. He refused to take out a patent on this stove because he invented it to help people make better lives for themselves. Franklin invented bifocals and even a musical instrument.

"Of course, his work with electricity when he did the experiment with his kite in the 1750s is legendary and brought Ben international fame. The world got the electric light bulb because of Franklin.

"At first, Benjamin Franklin considered himself an Englishman, but he soon felt that America would be better off becoming independent from England. Ben worked tirelessly for independence. His son, William, the royal governor of New Jersey, remained loyal to the English government. Unfortunately, this caused estrangement between father and son, which never was resolved to a happy conclusion.

"Franklin was elected to the Second Continental Congress and worked with five others to draft the Declaration of Independence. Thomas Jefferson wrote most of the document, but Franklin contributed a great deal to it. In 1776, Franklin signed the declaration and afterward sailed to France as an ambassador to the court of Louis XVI.

"The French loved Franklin. Ben was an ordinary-looking man who had extraordinary talents and accomplishments. He brought electricity to the masses. And he had a great sense of humor. In his late seventies, Benjamin Franklin became president of the executive council of Pennsylvania. He served as a delegate to the Constitutional Convention and signed the Constitution. One of his last public acts was writing an antislavery treatise in 1789. Franklin died on April 17, 1790 at the age of eighty-four. Twenty thousand people attended his funeral."

Rose ended by saying, "The great men who worked to bring us independence from England were very brave men. They risked everything they had for us as Americans to be free from tyranny. What they did was considered treason by England."

Lily, Bonnie, and Susie clapped vigorously. "Great job, honey." Lily complimented Rose.

Rose, obviously pleased with the appreciative response, smiled brightly as she added, "Like Dad told us, the men who fought for our independence from England were some of the bravest men who ever lived. They risked their lives, their liberty, and their property to make us free. Because of them, we have the greatest, freest country in the world."

"Yes, and I hope that Americans never forget it. We have so much to be thankful for, so let's have our family prayer together and thank Heavenly Father for this great land, this promised land that we should cherish with all our hearts." Lily clasped her young daughters to her.

After dessert, the family got ready for bed, said their good nights, and Lily tucked each one of her children into bed with a kiss and an I love you. She again was able to go to sleep after such a precious evening counting their blessings.

CHAPTER SEVEN

As soon as Aaron got home from school the next day, he went into the house to greet his mother, told her a bit about his day and listened as she filled him in on hers, and then he was off to the hospital on his bicycle. He made a quick stop when he passed the strip mall not far from his home and was at the hospital a short time later.

"Hi, Grace."

"Aaron, you came to visit me." Grace laughed happily and clapped her hands together. Grace's mother was sitting by her bedside reading a story to her.

"Aaron, it's so nice of you to come. If it's all right with you, let me just finish reading to Grace. I only have two more pages."

"Sure, go ahead. I like stories too." Aaron sat down to wait for Grace's mother to finish. She was reading from *Hansel and Gretel.*

After the story was finished, Grace's mother turned to Aaron and said, "My name is Hannah. I'm glad you came to visit." Grace's mother was a small, slender lady with brown hair and brown eyes. Grace had her mother's warm brown eyes. In fact, she looked a lot like her mom, except for the dark rings around her own lovely eyes.

"I have something for you, Grace." Aaron brought his hand around, the one he was holding behind his back.

When Grace saw the doll he was holding out to her, she squealed with delight. "Oh, Aaron, she's darling. Thank you so much. I love her already," Grace lifted her arms to give Aaron a hug. The doll had blonde hair and blue eyes. She was dressed in a pink dress and pink bonnet with pink underpants and had on white ankle socks and little black shoes. She was twelve inches tall. Grace hugged the doll and sat her on the bed beside her.

"Well, Grace, how is your day going?"

"Much better now," Grace laughed. "Thank you for coming to see me and for bringing me this sweet doll."

"What are you going to name her?" Aaron asked.

"Well, let's see. Oh, I know. I am going to name her Hope. That's it, Hope." Grace picked up the doll and hugged it again.

"How is your day going, Aaron?"

"Much better now, now that I am here with you, Grace, and your mother," Aaron laughed too.

"Do you have any brothers and sisters, Grace?" Aaron asked.

"I have a younger brother. His name is Bobby. He's four. And I have a little sister, Jennie. She's two. Daddy takes care of them so Mommy can be with me in the daytime."

Hannah said, "My husband, Peter, is a night watchman. He comes home and sleeps for a few hours, and when I am ready to leave to come and be with Grace, he gets up and takes care of the younger children. Then, in the afternoons, he puts the children down for naps, and he can sleep then for a couple more hours. When I get home and after dinner, Peter comes to the hospital to spend some time with Grace until he needs to be at work. Its working out pretty well right now."

"I'm bald, Aaron. This is a wig," Grace then pulled off the brown wig to show Aaron her bald head.

Aaron told her, "You are beautiful even without the wig, Grace. You are one very special young lady."

Grace smiled at Aaron, "My daddy tells me that too."

Aaron, Grace, and Hannah continued to chat together until Aaron stood up and said, "I need to go home now and get some dinner for my mother and me. She's in a wheelchair, so I help her as much as I can. Her name is Connie. I think she'd like to meet you, Grace, one of these days."

"When are you coming back? Can you come again tomorrow?"

"I tell you what, Grace, I'll come tomorrow evening and bring my guitar and teach you some fun songs. Then when I come back on Saturday, if you're feeling up to it, you can come up to the fourth floor and help me sing for the patients on that floor. What do you think about that?"

"Okay, I'd like that a lot. I'll see you tomorrow then, Aaron." Hannah stood up and shook Aaron's hand, thanking him once again for coming.

Aaron replied, "It was my pleasure, Hannah."

*****

The next afternoon, Aaron brought his guitar, and they sang songs with which Grace was familiar, songs from *Sesame Street* and some Disney tunes. Hannah even sang along with them on some of the songs. They sang and laughed and talked for some time, and then Aaron had to leave.

On Saturday, Aaron came to the hospital, and after his shift was over, he and Hannah pushed Grace in her wheelchair to the elevator up to the fourth floor. The patients were gathered in a large homey room, some in wheelchairs, some in walkers, and some were wheeled in on their hospital beds. Most had tubes in their arms and oxygen tanks. Aaron's visits to the patients were becoming the talk of the hospital. As he did his janitorial work, the patients often called to him if they happened to see him in the hall. He would chat with them a few moments and then go back to his mopping. He had some patients whom he considered friends. It was hard when some of them passed away. He had to remind himself that this was a hospital, after all. Not everyone was going to get well, he knew that.

Grace had become his favorite. Having her there while he put on his miniconcert was special. He introduced her to the patients on the fourth floor. He said, "This is Grace. She is an escapee from the third floor. Her mother and I sneaked her up here. Shhh, don't squeal on us to the nurses." Then he winked at the nurse standing next to Grace. She rewarded him with a sweet smile.

Aaron began to play his guitar and sing. Some of the patients joined in if they knew the songs. Most just listened. For an hour, the lovely music flowed into the room. Grace sang some of the tunes with Aaron in her sweet seven-year-old voice. After a while, it was obvious that she was becoming tired, so one of the nurses helped Hannah wheel Grace out of the room and back to her own room. Grace waved to Aaron. He waved and threw her a kiss.

That night as he and Connie got ready for bed, Aaron said to his mother, "I'm being punished for killing Samuel Langston, but somehow, it doesn't feel like punishment at all. Sure, I work hard every Saturday for seven hours. But then, I get to do what I love to do: make people happy by singing and playing for them. I played one song of my own today, and the patients seemed to enjoy it. I can't help the feeling that somehow I am doing some good in the world." As Aaron spoke, he gently raised her head and shoulders, plumped up her pillows, and settled her back down.

Connie smiled her thanks, "Yes, my precious son, I believe that. Often, good things come out of bad things. One day, even Lily Langston and her daughters will find a silver lining in their storm. It takes time, but one day there will be happiness for them. They are a strong family, and they have a lot of faith. And you, what great joy you bring to people with your talent. You are a good son, Aaron. I am proud of you. Your future is bright if you will just continue to work to bring joy to people. You sure bring happiness to my soul."

Aaron reached over to give his mother a big hug and kiss. "I love you, Mom. You are the best mother in the world."

"I love you too, son," Connie whispered.

After Aaron went to bed, Connie thought about him and how he had come into the world. Connie was very young when she got pregnant with Aaron. She was dating a young man whom she thought might be husband material. She dated him for a few months, and then one night, they made a mistake, and she ended up pregnant. He told her to get an abortion. This was absolutely against all that she believed in, so she had refused. He left. She did not name him on Aaron's birth certificate, as she was determined that Aaron would never know who his real father was. As far as Connie was concerned, he was a total nonentity in her life.

After she got pregnant, her parents were wonderful. They made sure she got the prenatal care she needed. They stood by her through everything. With their encouragement, she finished high school and graduated in the top third of her class.

To Connie, Aaron was the best thing in her life. Before the night that he ran into Samuel Langston, he had never been in trouble. *His probation is going to be long. Six years seems like an eternity. But so far, he is handling it very well,* thought Connie.

Her thoughts turned to her accident, the accident that changed her life and her son's. Connie's parents were babysitting him so she could go skiing with some friends. She hadn't gotten out much since she had had her baby boy. It was only when her parents could take him that she was able to get out for some recreation. Her parents were good to take Aaron when they could, but they both worked odd-hour jobs, so it was difficult for them to get a few hours to volunteer to babysit. Also, they were tired from working so much in those days. This day, though, her mom and dad were both going to be home so they told Connie to go and have a good time on the ski slopes with her friends.

They decided to go to the Alta ski area not far from Salt Lake City. It was a bright sunny day, and the skiing was spectacular. As they were skiing in the late afternoon, Connie missed a curve, fell, and slid into a tree. Her lower back hit first. Though she remained conscious, the pain was terrible.

Her friends called for help. Though it was only minutes, it seemed like an hour before the ski patrol came. One of them knelt beside Connie and asked her where she was hurt. "My name is John, what's yours?"

Through the pain she managed to blurt out, "Connie. It's my back. I hurt my back."

The gentleman noticed her right leg was twisted under her, so he and the other three patrol members who were with him gently moved her leg so that it was extended out in a normal way.

"Did you feel that?" John had asked her.

"No, I didn't feel it," Connie was crying.

"We are going to lift you onto this board. It will stabilize your spine. We will tie you to it so you won't be able to move. Hang in there, Connie. We will soon have you in the life flight helicopter and headed to the hospital."

After the ski patrol had Connie carefully strapped to the board, each took hold of the board and headed down the hill.

Later, as she lay in her hospital bed, it became apparent that in all likelihood, she would never walk again. The injury to her spine was severe. Over the years since the accident, the doctors who treated her told her there was a slight possibility down the road that something could be done to restore her ability to walk. She kept up with the new technology as best she could. Some little glimmer of hope would be written about in journals and then would peter out. Still, she kept hoping.

Her mom and dad took care of Aaron until he was old enough to go to school. They kept in close touch until Connie's mother passed away, and then, a short while later, she also lost her father. Her mother died from breast cancer and, a few months later, her father died of complications after a severe bout of pneumonia. Connie was devastated. As she lay there thinking about the aftermath of her accident, she thought about the sisters in her church congregation who came forward to help her. Several of them still do. *I love those ladies so much. I could never have made it through those years without them.* She wiped away a tear.

In her wheelchair, she could get around and take care of some of the chores that need to be done in an ordinary home every day. She could help get dinner and load the dishwasher and even do some light housekeeping. The dear neighbors still came and checked on her almost daily, or at least called her to make sure she is all right. The home health nurse came a couple of times a week to bathe her and make sure she is taking her medications. She would also help Connie get in to see her doctor on appointment days.

Connie wondered as she fell asleep how she could ever afford to pay for an operation if a medical breakthrough did happen.

CHAPTER EIGHT

"What are we going to wear to sing, Mom?" Rose asked. "We better start thinking about it."

"You're right, Rose. Do we want to dress alike? I think that would be fun. At least let's see if we can find dresses that complement each other. Let's go shopping for dresses tomorrow after you girls get home from school," Lily suggested. "Wow, the concert is in two days. We had better get a move on if we're going to get new dresses for it." They had practiced and practiced until they knew the music by heart.

"Oh yes, let's do," Bonnie said.

"Yes, let's do," Susie echoed.

The next day after school, Lily picked up the girls, and they went shopping. After searching through two or three stores, they found a dress shop that had just what they were looking for. It was almost like the dresses were made just for them—dresses that complemented each other but were not identical.

Rose's dress had a navy blue skirt, a white top, and a matching navy blue and white-checked short-sleeved jacket. Bonnie's dress was white with navy blue and red trim on the collar and a matching red and navy blue belt. Susie's dress was red. Lily's dress was navy blue. She had several pieces of jewelry at home with which she could trim her navy blue dress that would coordinate the red and white of the other dresses. They stood before the mirror at the shop and looked at the lovely picture they made. "They're perfect together," the pretty blonde clerk told them. They agreed unanimously.

"Now we need shoes." Lily and her daughters went to the shoe counter and picked out shoes to complement their dresses. "All right, let's go. You still have to do your homework when we get home," Lily said.

"Mom, we don't have any homework. It's Friday," laughed Rose.

"Oh, right. Well, let's see, how about going to a restaurant for a sit-down dinner, then? We haven't done that since…we haven't done that in quite a while." Lily cleared her throat. She refused to let the tears come.

"After that, we can go see a movie. Okay, Mom?" Susie looked up at her mother with those big blue eyes. There's some good kid-friendly movies right now."

Bonnie chimed in, "Yeah, let's do."

"Okay, why not?"

*****

The charity concert was ready to begin. The announcer walked up to the stage and stood before the microphone. He raised his hands to let the noisy crowd know it was time to be quiet. When the crowd had sufficiently hushed, the announcer introduced Lily and her children to the overflow audience. There were loud cheers as Lily walked to the piano, her girls taking their places in front of the piano. They were all miked so they would be easily heard.

The first number they sang was called, "The Impossible Dream" from the *Man of La Mancha*. After they were finished, they bowed to the crowd. The crowd stood up and cheered; some people even whistled. Then the crowd quieted down, and Lily played the first notes of their second number, "Bless This House." Their voices were strong and sweet and clear; the harmony, lovely. Again, the crowd stood and cheered.

The announcer finally got the cheering fans quieted and then looked toward Lily and the girls who were now standing offstage. "Do you want them to come back for an encore?"

"Yes," the crowd shouted.

Again Lily sat down at the piano and began to play. And, again, the beauty of the piece brought cheers from the audience and another standing ovation. The song they sang was the patriotic song, "My Own America." There were others on the program, and they were also cheered and clapped for. It was a wonderful, successful evening by all standards.

"I think the charity is going to be a huge success," Lily whispered to her girls as they stood offstage.

"They liked us. It was so fun to be back singing again," Rose spoke what they all felt. Yes, it had been wonderful to be singing in public again.

"Mrs. Langston, thank you to you and your girls for the lovely songs. You were so great. The audience loved it. I loved it." Carson Hunter was holding Lily's hand in both of his. "I just can't thank you enough."

"You are very welcome, Mr. Hunter," Lily replied. "The girls and I love doing it."

Others quickly came up to the family to express their appreciation. Lily's parents came up and gave Lily and the girls big hugs. After a few moments, Samuel's parents managed to make their way through the crowds to embrace them.

"Wow, you bowled everybody over. You were wonderful. The concert was terrific. We could have spent another hour listening to all the beautiful music," Matt Langston told them.

Dallas, Lily's mother-in-law, echoed her husband's sentiments and added, grinning, "We just wrote out a nice big check to the Hunter Cancer Institute."

"That's great, Mother Langston," Lily replied.

*****

Carson Hunter was very pleased with the turnout for the charity concert, and he complimented Mona Thompson, who did most of the work putting the evening together. They would know by the next day how successful the drive had been financially. Carson mingled with the people and thanked as many as he could reach and wished them well.

As the crowd began to thin out, he found Jacob Manning. "Jacob, will you come in to my office Monday morning? I have another project in my mind I want you to carry out for me."

"What time do you want me in your office, Carson?" Jacob asked.

"How about 10:00 a.m.?"

"Good," Jacob answered. "I have a client at 8:30 a.m. and should be finished and able to be at your office by then." Jacob and Carson Hunter shook hands warmly, as dear friends do.

CHAPTER NINE

Jacob Manning opened the door to Carson Hunter's office and greeted Mr. Hunter. They then sat down, Carson behind his dark walnut desk, and Jacob facing him. The office was large and beautifully furnished. It was the office of a man who was very successful in business but who did not make a big deal of his great wealth. It was tastefully done but more functional than opulent.

Almost before Jacob sat down Mr. Hunter began speaking. "Jacob, I have another project for you." He held up a bag of coins and placed them in Jacob's hands. "I have had these coins for many years wondering what I should do with them. I have decided to give them to Lily Langston and her children. I have a strong feeling she will know what to do with them."

Jacob held the bag in his hands. He opened it at Carson's urging. There were ten uncirculated gold coins in the pouch. "These have to be worth a great deal of money," Jacob said.

With a twinkle in his eye, Mr. Hunter answered, "Yes, and let's make a little game of it. We will give her a coin each month. Hide it in plain sight in a place where she will find it but will be safe from other hands. I am sure she will find a good use for them."

Jacob Manning stood up and again shook Carson Hunter's hand. "I will get at it right away, sir. It will be a pleasure."

Mr. Hunter sat back down at his desk as Jacob closed the door behind him. His accountants had tallied up the earnings from the charity function they had held Saturday night. Carson was very pleased. They raised just short of $150,000 in pledges and cash. The money would be used to continue finding cures for the several kinds of cancer.

His thoughts turned to the first time he met Lily and Samuel Langston. It was shortly after their first child was born. Lily and Samuel were performing at a fund-raiser for a young boy who had been hit by a car. The youngster had run out between two parked cars and had been hit by a neighbor of the Langston's. The neighbor was devastated, of course, even though it was not his fault.

The boy had suffered a broken leg and bruises, as well as some internal injuries. He was going to be all right, but the family didn't have health insurance at the time. Lily and Samuel put the fund-raiser together themselves. They had the local radio stations advertise it and took fliers around the neighborhood, inviting people to come and donate toward the young family's medical bills. They even announced it in their church meetings.

Mr. Hunter was sitting in his office listening to the radio one day when he happened to hear the announcement of the fund-raiser. He called his wife and asked her to go with him. Carson and his wife, Kay, a handsome white-haired older couple, were very prominent in the state and well-known for helping in the community wherever and whenever they could. Their humanitarian activities were legendary.

A large crowd had attended the fund-raiser. Samuel played the guitar and sang duets with his wife. The Hunters were very impressed with the talents of the Langstons. Lily played a few lovely piano solos. The crowd loved the music and donated generously.

Afterward, Mr. Hunter went over to the table where the money was being donated. He told the individuals taking in the donations, "I will match whatever you take in. Here is my telephone number. Let me know, and I will write you a check tomorrow." The next day, Carson wrote Lily and Samuel a check for $12,500 to match the amount made at the fund-raiser. The family they were helping was delighted with the aid they got that evening. As well as thanking every donor at the fund-raiser, they sent a very nice card to the Hunters for their donation. The $25,000 would pay the ongoing medical bills until the youngster was completely healed.

Mr. Hunter called Mona Thompson to suggest she put the Langstons on a list of talent they could use for fund-raisers for the Hunter Cancer Hospital. "Of course, Mona, you will need to ask Lily and Samuel for permission to do that," he chuckled. Somehow, he knew they would be happy to add their names to that list. After that night, Carson kept his eye on Lily and Samuel. Over the years since that first event, they performed for several functions on behalf of the Hunters and their various philanthropic events. He and Kay became very fond of the Langstons.

As Lily and Samuel added the children to the group, the Hunters were delighted. It added a whole new dimension to their music. Now younger audiences connected with the music. When they performed for the younger groups, they sang and performed songs with which the youngsters were familiar.

Then the tragedy. What happened was unthinkable, painful in the extreme. Samuel gone just like that. The Hunters were at Lily's side as soon as they heard. They held each other. Carson knew things were going to be very tough emotionally for Lily and her family, so when Mona Thompson told him that Lily and her girls would perform for the fund-raiser, he was delighted. And their performance was as pure and beautiful as ever, even though Samuel was no longer with them. Somehow, they had pulled it together and made everything work.

CHAPTER TEN

Grace sat on her hospital bed as her mother placed her favorite wig on her small head. It had curls, which Grace loved.

"Mom, how much more time before Daddy, Bobby, and Jennie get here? I can't wait."

Grace's mother laughed. "Grace, that is the third time you have asked me that in the last five minutes. They will be here any time now."

"Do you think Aaron will come while they're here? Oh, I hope he does. I want him to meet all my family." Grace could hardly contain her excitement.

"You know he will be here, honey. This is the time he usually comes." Just as Hannah said those words, the door opened and in walked Aaron. He hugged Hannah and then went over to the bed to hug and kiss Grace. He couldn't help notice how thin she was. She was skin and bones. However, her smile was as radiant as ever.

"How is my favorite little friend?" Aaron asked. "Are you eating enough? Are you obeying the doctor's orders like a good girl?"

"I try to eat everything they give me, but mostly I don't feel like eating. But I'm doing my best. How is my favorite big friend, Aaron Turner? Are you being a good boy?" Grace echoed his words with a laugh.

"Absolutely, little one."

Just as Aaron uttered those words, the door opened and in walked Grace's dad with the two children. As Bobby and Jennie climbed up on the bed to be next to Grace, Aaron was introduced to Peter. Hannah said, "This is my husband, Peter. Peter, this is our friend, Aaron. I've told you all about him."

"Of course. Aaron, it is an honor to meet you. Grace talks about you all the time on the phone, and Hannah is pretty smitten with you too." The last remark was given with a wink in Hannah's direction.

"And these are Grace's two siblings, Bobby and Jennie. Bobby is four years old, and Jennie is two. Say hello to Aaron, kids," Peter said.

"Hello, Aaron," Bobby said. He held out his hand for Aaron to shake. Aaron was very impressed with this towheaded youngster. And little Jennie was the spitting image of her big sister. She reached up to hug Aaron. He hugged her close to him. In spite of himself, he could not help the tears welling up in his eyes. He quickly brushed them away. Tears were only for alone times, in the quiet of his room at night.

For the next half-hour, they visited together while the children played on the bed with Grace. Grace showed Jennie her doll, which she had named Hope. Jennie held the doll until it was time to leave. They didn't stay long because it became obvious Grace was tiring very quickly.

As they readied to leave, each one gave Grace a hug and kiss. There were "I love yous" all around. Hannah would stay a couple hours more, and then she would leave to go home and take over family duties, and Peter would come back to spend a little time with Grace until he had to be at work.

As the little family and Aaron closed the door to Grace's room and walked down the hall, Aaron asked Peter what the doctors were telling them about how much time Grace had left before the inevitable happened.

"The doctors give her a month, maybe less," Peter said quietly so the children could not hear. Hannah and Peter would have to sit down with their children and tell them what to expect very soon. Jennie was too young to understand, but Bobby would comprehend what they were telling him. It was very possible he already sensed that Grace would not be coming home. He was asking Peter questions. All Peter had told him so far is that his sister was very ill.

"I think it is time we tell him," Peter said simply.

Aaron touched Peter's arm, "Please let me know if there is anything I can do to help, okay? Here is my telephone number. Call me any time. I would be glad to stay with the children if you want to spend more time at the hospital, Peter."

Peter shook his head. "We have neighbors who will come and sit with the kids. Thanks, anyway. But I will let you know if anything happens in between your visits."

"I would appreciate that very much." With that, Aaron got on his bike, waved at the family, and headed home. When he got home, he filled his mother in on his visit with Grace and her family. Connie knew that Aaron was becoming very attached to Grace. She knew how hard it was going to be when his little friend would no longer be here. She could see the sadness in his eyes.

Oh, Aaron, she thought, *you are carrying so much heartache with you these days. There is the pain you carry for the Langston family. And now watching little Grace as she slowly dies. It has got to be almost unbearable.*

It was now summer. Aaron had asked Jacob Manning to ask the judge if he could work more days at the hospital with the possibility of shortening his probation. If they would figure the number of Saturdays there would be in the six-year sentence and let him work some of that time off on weekdays, he would appreciate it.

It was arranged, so now Aaron worked two weekdays and on Saturday. On Saturdays, he continued to bring his guitar and put on his miniconcerts in the last hour of the schedule. His concerts were a big hit. As often as possible, he and Hannah wheeled Grace to the concert and let her enjoy it until she got tired, and then she would wave to Aaron as her mother and a nurse whisked her away to her room.

On the other days, Aaron cleaned their house or mowed the lawn or whatever else needed doing. He would play and sing for his mother often. They would watch television together or just sit and talk. Connie wanted Aaron to cultivate friendships with young people his own age and vowed that when school began again in September, she was going to encourage him to join the school choir or whatever musical groups were available, maybe the school jazz band.

CHAPTER ELEVEN

Lily arose early. It was Saturday. The day was sunny and warm, a lovely summer morning. Today she was going to get out in the garden and plant her petunias and pansies. The perennials were coming along nicely, and it was time to get out and plant her annuals. Actually, they could have been planted a few weeks earlier. She couldn't bring herself to do it until now. She had gone out yesterday and purchased the plants, and now she was in the mood to go out and get her hands dirty in the warm black soil.

She quickly dressed in her jeans and T-shirt and pulled her dark hair up in a ponytail. After eating a bowl of her favorite cereal, she got her gardening tools, and out she went into the garden. She loved her backyard. With Samuel and the children, they had carefully planned every inch of the landscaping back there.

Josh Green had been mowing the lawn for them every week. It was green and lush and inviting. As Lily walked around the raised planters admiring the plants that were there, she spied something shiny in the dirt. "What could that possibly be?" she thought. She walked over to it and picked it up. It was a gold coin. Underneath it was a short note: "For Lily and her daughters." That was all. A gold coin. It was heavy and bright. It obviously had never been circulated. For what seemed to be a long time, Lily stared at it, turning it over and over in her hand.

Well, she thought, *this is a mystery if there ever was one.* After a few more moments, she put the coin and note in her pocket. *I had better get these plants put in the ground before I do much more thinking about the gold coin, or I will never get them planted today.*

For the next hour, Lily continued to plant, even though it was very difficult, as she could think of nothing but the coin. However, she finally completed her task. She stepped back to admire her work. *Lovely,* she thought. After gathering up the gardening tools and putting them away and throwing the empty containers in the trash, she went into the house to clean herself up and then went into the girls' bedrooms to see if the children were awake yet.

Rose was just waking up. It was shortly after 9:00 a.m. "Good morning, princess," her mother cheerfully greeted her.

"Hi, Mom."

"Rose, when your sisters wake up, I have something to show you all. It's a mystery. I want to see what you and Bonnie and Susie think of it."

"What is it, Mom?"

"You'll have to wait a bit. Oh, there you are, Bonnie. Is Susie up yet?"

"Susie, wake up. Mom has something to tell us." This from an impatient Rose. "Come into my bedroom. Mom has something to tell us."

"Don't you want to wait until after you've had breakfast?" Lily asked.

"No, no. Tell us now."

"All right." Lily pulled the coin out of her pocket, along with the note. The girls stared at it. It was so shiny.

"Where did you get it?"

"Well, that's the puzzle. It was in the flower bed. And there was a note. It just read, 'For Lily and her children.' It was obviously meant for us. But why and who could have put it there?"

"Oooh," squealed Bonnie, "I love mysteries. Do you think we will ever find out who put it in the flower bed?"

Lily replied, "Somehow, I think we are supposed to use it for something special. But what?"

"That's spooky." This from Rose.

"Yeah, that's spooky," echoed Susie.

Lily laughed. "Whoever put it there, I am sure, means us no harm. This may be their way of helping us get through our difficult time. We will keep our eyes and ears open and see if we can detect who might have placed it in our garden," she said in a conspiratorial voice. "In the meantime, we'll place it in the safe for safekeeping. Let's go get you some breakfast."

As it was Saturday morning, it was clean-the-house day. The girls went over to the cleaning chart to see who's turn it was to do which task. It didn't seem to be work when they did it together. Often, one would burst into song, and the others would join in, sometimes harmonizing. It was hard to be heard above the sound of the vacuum, but they just got louder and louder in an attempt to drown out the sound of the motor. And then they would laugh at the sheer nonsense of trying to sing as loud as they could. Sometimes, when the vacuum was turned off, they would still be singing at the top of their lungs, and then they would just laugh harder.

After the work was done, they could do what they liked. They took turns suggesting what they wanted to do the rest of the afternoon on Saturdays. Often, they went to visit the animals at Hogle Zoo, or they would go to the Clark Planetarium or travel to Lagoon to enjoy the rides. They liked to go swimming in the pool at Lagoon or some of the other fun spots around Provo and Salt Lake City. There were a lot of fun places to visit. Sometimes, they made a lunch and ate it in one of the parks in the area. They also enjoyed watching a live soccer game or their local baseball teams play in their neighborhood.

Since the evening they sang for the Hunter Clinic fund-raiser, they were inundated with requests to sing and play at various functions. Every day during the summer months, they spent some time working on new songs and brushing up on ones they already knew.

Sometimes they were paid for their gigs, sometimes they were for charity. When they were paid, they took out 10 percent for their tithing, kept some out for fun and treats, and put the rest in their investments.

Often, the grandparents came to the concerts. They thoroughly enjoyed what Lily and the girls were doing. They supported the charities as much as they could.

Lily was still having trouble sleeping most nights. She would often cry herself to sleep. But when she was awake, she tried her very best to put on a happy face for her daughters. Mostly, she was able to pull it off. She and the girls talked about Samuel every day. They talked about the fun they had had together. Someone would mention a special memory, and then they would all chime in one at a time with their own special memory of the same occasion.

The summer was going by, and with their music and other activities such as Family Home Evenings, their attendance at church services and her calling teaching her Sunday school class, Lily was able to keep her sanity pretty much intact.

One day, she mentioned to the girls that they should go together and visit Aaron Turner and his mother. She remembered that Connie Turner was an invalid. Perhaps they could do something to help her. Bonnie and Susie readily agreed, but Rose became sullen and distant when Aaron's name was mentioned. When Lily tried to talk to her about her feelings, she refused to say anything. Later, when Lily pressed her daughter, she would only say, "I am not going with you to see Aaron and his mother."

CHAPTER TWELVE

Aaron kissed his mother goodbye. It was a Tuesday morning, and he was headed to the hospital to do his janitorial work. As he rode his bike, he thought of Grace. She was getting weaker and could no longer sit for his miniconcerts. He thought of her family. *How hard is it going to be on them?* he wondered.

The first thing he did when he got to the hospital was to look in on his little friend. "Hi, Aaron, I am so glad to see you. Today I am going to heaven. There are angels waiting for me. I can see them, can you?" Grace smiled and held out her hands to him. "Don't cry, Aaron. The angels will take me to Jesus." Aaron lifted Grace's frail body and gently hugged her as Hannah sat with tears streaming down her cheeks. He carefully laid her back on her bed and turned to hug Hannah close to him.

"My daddy will be here soon. Bobby and Jennie are going to stay with our neighbors. Will you stay with me, Aaron? I would like that," Grace whispered.

"Let me go and change my work schedule with the janitors. I am sure they can find someone to replace me, and then I will be right back, okay?" Aaron bent down and kissed Grace on her soft cheek.

Aaron quickly left the room and sought out his boss. When Aaron told him about Grace, he was told to go back and be with her. Thanking him, Aaron was soon back with his sweet little friend. When he got back to the room, Grace's father was there.

Aaron shook Peter's hand and went to stand by the bed on the opposite side. Grace's doctor came in to visit with Grace for a few moments, and her nurses were in and out. They brought drinks in for Aaron and the parents. No one felt like drinking anything, but they appreciated the thought.

After a few moments, Grace looked up and smiled at someone unseen by the others in the room. Then she closed her eyes and was gone.

Hannah, Peter, and Aaron and the two nurses who were there in the room at the time stood together, not speaking. Silence filled the room and then quiet sobbing. It was some time before anyone could get enough composure to speak. Finally, Hannah turned to Aaron and hugged him and said, "Aaron, we would be honored to have you sing for the funeral. Will you?"

"Of course. When you are able to put the funeral arrangements together, Hannah and Peter, give me a call and tell me what you would like me to sing. It would be a great honor to do it. I loved Grace so much." With that, Aaron broke down sobbing. Everyone in the room was sobbing and hugging.

Aaron lost track of time. Finally, he left the hospital and rode his bike home. He told his mother everything that had happened. He told her about the angels and all that Grace had told them. He sobbed as he told her. She listened with tears in her own eyes.

"In God's eyes, children are perfect. He loves all of us, but children especially because they are so innocent, so trusting, so pure. She is in a beautiful place, Aaron, and I am sure she is happy there." Connie reached up to Aaron's face and gently wiped away the tears. "I love you, son, you are very special. Do you know that?"

"Thanks, Mom, for saying that. I needed those words." With that, Aaron bent down and kissed his mother on the cheek. "You are very special too."

"The next day, Peter called to let Aaron know when and where the funeral would be. He requested that Aaron sing "How Great Thou Art." Aaron readily agreed.

*****

The funeral was lovely. Grace was beautiful in her casket. Hannah told Aaron that she had thought of putting Hope, the doll, in the casket with her, but Jennie wanted it, so she gave it to her.

"Was that all right?" Jennie was standing beside her mother hugging Hope.

Aaron smiled at her and told her, "Grace would want her little sister to have her doll, I am sure of that, Hannah." He then gave Jennie a little squeeze. Jennie rewarded him with a smile.

The speakers at the funeral service talked about the Savior's love for each one of us, His children. They told of how Jesus came to earth to teach us that the way to true happiness was through Him. He showed us by example how to live to be happy. He took upon Himself our sins so that we would not have to pay for them if we repented. He died and was resurrected so that all mankind would be resurrected. It was His gift to all mankind.

They told us that Grace would live in the Celestial Kingdom because all children before the age of eight are perfect in the eyes of God and automatic heirs to the highest kingdom.

Aaron's song was lovely. He was determined not to choke up and managed to get through it with his strong, sweet voice intact. As he was singing, he held tight to his resolution not to cry, even though the whole congregation seemed to be in tears.

After the funeral and the graveside service, many came up to him and told him how much they loved his music.

His mother came to the funeral. Hannah and Peter had arranged to have someone from the funeral home bring Aaron and Connie to the funeral and graveside services. After the luncheon following the services, Aaron and his mom were taken home by the same kind people from the funeral home.

In the weeks following the funeral, Aaron continued to do his janitorial work at the hospital several times a week. Then he would go home and help his mother. The bright spot in his week continued to be his miniconcerts. He looked forward to them each week. For some time, he was lost without Grace, but slowly he began to develop other friendships, especially with the other children. The youngsters seemed to gravitate to him, and he found that to be very comforting.

CHAPTER THIRTEEN

Aaron opened the door to Lily, Bonnie, and Susie. Rose had refused to come. Lily was determined not to make a big deal of it. *She'll come around, in time,* Lily prayed that her daughter would soften her heart toward Aaron. "Come in, Mrs. Langston. It's nice to see you and your girls."

Lily let the girls go in before her, and Aaron shut the door after her. They walked over to where Connie was sitting in her wheelchair. "This is my mother, Connie. Mom, these are the Langstons."

Lily shook Connie's extended hand. "I am Lily, and these are my daughters. Bonnie is ten and Susie is eight. It's nice to meet you, Connie."

At Connie's urging, the three of them found places to sit on the couch opposite Connie. Aaron pulled up a chair for himself. "Aaron and I are happy you have come to visit us, Lily. We have thought about you often since the accident."

"I can't begin to express in words how horrible I feel about what happened to your husband, Mrs. Langston. If only I could take back that terrible night." Tears sprang up in Aaron's brown eyes. "In the storm, I missed the turn onto the street I should have taken and ended up on yours. I'm so sorry," Aaron repeated.

Lily replied, "Captain Snowden filled us in on what happened, Aaron. He is a good friend of yours, I believe?"

Connie nodded. "A very dear friend. He was almost as broken up about what happened as we were. Captain Snowden is like a father to Aaron. We have visited with the captain several times since Samuel died. He kept us informed on how you are both doing. That is why we wanted to come and see you today. We have a bond between us, even though it is a sad one. We wanted you to know that we hold no ill feelings. We know it was an accident."

"I am glad you don't hate me. I know you have a right to," Aaron spoke quietly.

"God would not want us to have ill feelings toward you. His gospel is about love. The Savior's whole teachings are about loving one another as He loves us. My girls and I have shed a great many tears in the last several weeks, but they are not bitter tears. We miss Samuel. But we manage to keep busy. In time, the pain of loss will diminish somewhat. Time is a great healer."

"That is certainly true, Lily," Connie replied. "Time is a great healer. And we know that the Savior redeemed all of us when He took upon himself our transgressions. He forgives us and wants us to forgive each other. How thankful I am to know of His love for us."

"Captain Snowden tells us that the staff at the hospital love you, Aaron. He tells me they are pleased with your work. You are always willing to go the extra mile to help wherever you are needed," Lily said.

Bonnie interjected, "He told us that you sing and play guitar, and that you are very good. Our dad could also play the guitar and sing. He sang and played with us all the time."

"We had so much fun when we sang together," Susie added.

Bonnie said, "Could you play for us sometime? That would be really cool."

"The captain told us that you play for the patients and nurses at the hospital every Saturday after your shift. What kind of songs do you play and sing?"

"All kinds. When I play for the children on the third floor of the hospital, I play children's favorites. Some of them sing along with me. Some are too sick, so they just listen. Even the nurses sing along if they know the songs. I love doing it.

"When I sing and play to the patients on the other floors, I pick out western music, gospel, popular songs, a little mix of all the tunes I can think of. The patients seem to like it," Aaron added.

"Did you know we sing together too?" Susie asked shyly.

"Yeah, maybe we know some of the same songs," Bonnie added.

Connie said, "Can you come back next week, and between you and Aaron, I can enjoy a little concert. We could have dinner together, and that would be fun. What do you say, Lily? You could get your heads together and see if you do know some of the same music. I would love that."

"Mom, how about Monday night, Family Home Evening?" Bonnie asked.

Lily smiled at her daughter. "What a great idea. How would Monday night be for you and Aaron, Connie?"

"Yes, that would be great. Mom, okay?" Aaron said.

"Of course. Let's make it early. How about five-thirty. Is that too early?"

Lily replied, "I see my girls are all excited about it so, yes, next Monday evening at five-thirty would be fine. We'll bring our stack of music and play and sing away the evening. The girls and I are singing the following Friday for Carson Hunter. He is having a special gathering of people in the medical field from other countries who are coming to Salt Lake City to tour the Hunter Cancer Center. They are interested in getting a firsthand look at the up-to-the minute innovations that make the Hunter Hospital facility so special. After the tour of the facility, Mr. Hunter will be hosting a banquet and wants us to sing as part of the entertainment afterward."

"Me too," said Aaron excitedly. "Mr. Hunter asked me to sing that night also. He liked what I am doing in his hospital and came to one of my miniconcerts. He said he was very impressed and asked me if I would be willing to have my name on his list of musical numbers for his fund-raisers and other festivities. Of course, I said yes. It will be an honor."

Susie said, "Yes, it's an honor for us too. It will be way cool to sing on the same program with you."

"Let us help with the food. What would you like us to bring? I make a mean tossed salad," Lily said with a laugh. "Or any other kind of salad you like."

Aaron said, "A tossed salad would be great. I'll make hamburgers and fries. Then we'll have ice cream and toppings."

"Super," Bonnie said. Susie echoed her sister.

"Okay, next Monday night it is then. We'll be back at five-thirty."

Connie and Lily shook hands. The girls gave Connie a hug, and then they turned and gave Aaron a hug, and then they were out the door and gone.

Aaron stood at the door for a few moments. "What just happened, Mom? Is this one of those miracles you keep telling me about? I just helped to bury my little Grace, and now the Langstons have come into our lives. And I am thinking that this is a very good thing for us. I have a strange feeling inside me like good things are about to happen."

"I have the same feeling, Aaron, like goose bumps on my heart. Wow, that is all I can think to say: *wow*."

Aaron hugged his mom. He then went and got his guitar and began to play and sing some of the songs his mother loved. He couldn't help notice the tears she wiped away, knowing they were happy tears this time.

*****

As Lily drove home with her children, she suddenly said to them, "I know what we are going to do with our gold coin."

Susie said, "It's something to do with the Turners, isn't it?"

"Yes, it is. Did you notice how run-down their house is? It needs a new coat of paint and some general fixing up. Bill Green is a pretty good handyman. We will see if he and his family want to help us paint and fix up the Turner's home for them. What do you think?"

The girls all chimed in in agreement with their mother. They began to talk of what colors they thought would look good on the walls, and what they wanted to do to decorate.

"Hold on now," Lily said. "It will be totally up to the Turners how and what colors to paint on their house. We will follow their suggestions to a T, okay?"

Bonnie said, "I can't wait 'til next Monday."

"Me too," said eight-year-old Susie.

Then, in a somber tone, Bonnie spoke softly, "What about Rose?"

"I'll talk to her," Lily replied. "If she won't join us, then we will have to carry on without her." Tears filled Lily's dark eyes and spilled down her cheeks.

"Don't cry, Mom," Susie placed her blonde head on Lily's shoulder. "Please don't cry. She'll get over whatever is bothering her. She will." Susie raised her head and nodded emphatically.

Lily removed her hand from the steering wheel for a brief moment and squeezed Susie's hand. When they arrived home, Lily called the Greens. After filling them in on what they had done and said at the Turners, she told Bill what they had planned and asked him to talk to Mary and the kids and see if they would be willing to help with the project at the Turners. It would probably take the rest of what was left of the summer to complete all that needed to be done.

"I will definitely talk to them, Lily. But I already know what they are going to say. It will be a big 'yes'. Find out next Monday, when you are there, what colors they will want to paint the walls and see when I can go over there to determine what needs to be done," Bill replied. He added, "Do you have money to get the paint and whatever supplies we will need?"

"I think we will be able to swing it, Bill. Thanks for agreeing to help us. It should be fun for our two families to get together on a project like this," Lily told him.

"You bet. I will talk to the family as soon as we hang up, and you call me as soon as you get the particulars. And thanks, Lily, for letting us be a part of this. Love you guys."

"We love you all too, Bill. Talk to you soon. Bye."

CHAPTER FOURTEEN

Aaron was just finishing setting the table when he heard the knock on the door. He quickly opened the door to greet the Langston family.

"Hello there, Aaron."

"Hi, come on in. Dinner is ready." Aaron stepped aside to let Lily and her daughters enter the room. They greeted Connie with smiles and handshakes. "Lily, you sit over here, and you girls find a chair behind the table there. Mom will pull her wheelchair up right here, and I'll sit on this other end. There, let me get the hamburgers and fries. Be back in a moment."

Lily set the tossed salad and dressing on the table. Aaron returned with the burgers and fries. The drinks, buns, and condiments were already on the table. After they were all seated together, Aaron bowed his head and said the blessing on the food.

"Rose didn't come with us," Susie piped up. "She's mad at you for killing our dad." Susie looked at her mother and saw the stern look on her face. *Oh, oh.* Susie looked down at her plate and whispered, "I'm not mad at you, Aaron."

"Neither am I," Bonnie quickly retorted. "We know it was an accident." She shyly put her hand on Aaron's. "We know it was an accident," Bonnie repeated.

For what seemed like a long time, they sat together in stunned silence. Aaron saw the look of sadness in his mother's eyes. He looked at Lily and then at Bonnie and Susie. He started to sob. He covered his face with his hands as his body shook uncontrollably. Lily quickly stood up and came over to where Aaron was sitting. She placed her arm around his shoulders in an attempt to comfort him. Susie started to cry, and then Bonnie.

Lily motioned to Susie and Bonnie to come over to her. Together they surrounded Aaron as he stood up. They each hugged him; he hugged them back. "It's going to be okay, Aaron. Rose will come around, you'll see. Now where were we? Let's eat, I'm hungry, and those hamburgers look absolutely yummy." Lily gave Aaron one last hug and then slid into her chair.

As they sat eating, the awkward moment past, and they began to talk about their interests. They found they had a lot in common, especially when it came to music. The meal was delicious. After they were finished, the Langstons helped Aaron clear the table and put the dishes in the dishwasher.

As the Turners did not have a piano, they would rely on Aaron's accompaniment to their songs. "We brought most of our music with us, Aaron. Which of our songs would you like to play?" Lily asked.

Aaron spent a few minutes going through the music and setting aside half a dozen pieces of music with which he was familiar. He got his guitar, tuned it, and began to play one of the melodies. As they listened, Bonnie and Susie began to sing along. Lily joined in. Then Aaron began to sing.

At the conclusion of the piece, Connie clapped her hands, "Wow, that was great. Your voices are fantastic together. Sing it again, okay?"

For the next two hours, the families lost themselves in the music. It was obvious that Aaron's talent complimented that of Lily and her girls. Ten-year-old Bonnie wanted to know if they could maybe sing together some time out in public.

Aaron and Lily looked at each other. "I have an idea," Lily said. "Let's pick out a couple of songs we can work on together. Then, if we are asked for an encore, you, Aaron, could come out and sing with us. It would be a surprise to Mr. Hunter and the organizers. What do you think, could we pull it off?"

Aaron laughed with the girls. "What a great idea. Wouldn't it be fun to see their reaction when it happens? Of course, it will all depend if there are requests for encores."

"Okay, whoever is first on the program won't let the cat out of the bag. After the last number we sing, or Aaron, if he is after us, if the audience wants an encore, we will announce that we are going to do a number together."

Susie jumped up and down. "Oh, I can't wait. Five days until Saturday. This is going to be so much fun." Bonnie echoed her enthusiasm.

"We will need to practice every day, Aaron. Will you be all right if he comes over every day for the next several days, Connie?" Lily asked.

"Yes, of course. Do you suppose I could come to the concert? I should love to be there to listen and watch the audience's reaction, especially Mr. Hunter's," Connie said.

"I am sure it would be fine. In fact, Mr. Hunter would be disappointed if you didn't attend. So would we." Lily smiled.

"That's settled then," Aaron told them. "What time would you like me to come over to practice?"

"Why don't you come about 10:30 a.m.? That would give the girls and I a chance to get our morning chores done."

"I'll be there."

Lily then turned to Connie. "Connie, my daughters and I have something to talk to you about. We have come into some money." Lily then proceeded to tell Aaron and Connie about the golden coin. Aaron sat down, and Lily and the girls returned to their chairs. We feel very strongly that we want to use the coin to help others. We have talked it over, and all of us want to do something for you and Aaron. We were wondering if you would mind if we bought some paint and freshened up your house a bit. Would you mind if we did that?"

Connie didn't say anything for a few moments. When she spoke, her eyes glistened with tears. "It would be wonderful of you to do that, Lily. For a long time, I have wished I could get out of this chair and fix up my house. Others have asked us if they could do it, but I guess I have just been too proud to accept the help."

Connie went on, "Aaron has been so busy with his schoolwork and coming home and taking care of me every night, it has made it impossible for him to do much fixing up. He has managed to fix some of the easier problems, but that is about all."

"We have a friend who is a very good handyman. He would like to come over and see what needs to be fixed. His wife and children would help us paint, and he would fix what else needs to be done to get your home in tip-top shape. His name is Bill Green. He is our attorney, and he and his family are our lifelong friends," Lily added.

"I'll help, of course," Aaron said.

Connie smiled. "I can wield a mean brush too, even if I'm in a wheelchair. I can paint the middle of the wall, and you smaller girls can paint the bottom of the walls, all right?"

"We'll come behind you and paint what you can't reach," Lily said.

"Bill Green has your telephone number, and he will call you in a day or two and come over to see what needs to be done. You and Aaron decide what color paint you want, and we will get it. We will begin next Monday after our concert for Mr. Hunter is over. We'll get that over first and then we can concentrate on getting your house refurbished. It will probably take most of the rest of the summer to finish, and that is fine with us."

"Thank you, Lily. You and your girls are very special. Aaron will be over to your house tomorrow at 10:30."

"We will see you next Saturday at the concert then, Connie. Bye for now."

As they drove home the inevitable question was asked. "What are we going to do about Rose, Mom?"

"We'll talk to her together. We really need her voice if we are going to sound good. When we get home let's say a prayer together, okay?" Lily suggested.

When they pulled into the driveway they closed their eyes and prayed for guidance to know how to get Rose to agree to sing when they sang with Aaron.

Rose opened the door for them. In spite of how she felt she wanted to know how their evening went. Susie was the first to speak. "We are going to sing with Aaron, Rose. You have to sing with us or it won't sound good. Please sing with us. Rose."

Rose looked up at her mother. "What is Susie talking about? I am not going to sing with Aaron, period."

"Come, let's go sit down, and we'll talk about it." Lily led her daughters into the family room, and when they were seated, Lily spoke, "Rose, honey, we had a wonderful evening. We wish you could have been with us. We got out our music, and Aaron played a few of the songs on his guitar. We started singing while he accompanied us, and then he joined in. It was magical. The only thing that was missing was your pretty voice." Rose sat with her arms folded across her chest and a scowl on her face.

"Please sing with us, dear." Lily then proceeded to tell Rose about their plans for surprising the audience after they had finished their own songs. "Aaron has also been asked to perform on the program. We think it will be fun for us to sing a number with him as an encore."

Rose did not speak but continued to scowl at her mother.

Lily smiled. "It is going to seem very strange, when the time comes to sing with Aaron, that our precious Rose runs off the stage and refuses to sing with us. And," Lily said playfully, "it won't sound nearly as good without you."

"Okay, I'll sing with Aaron, but I won't like it."

Lily got up and, as she hugged her daughter, smiled and winked at Bonnie and Susie, who both responded with a thumbs-up.

CHAPTER FIFTEEN

Lily rose early, as was her habit, and decided to garden for a while before the girls got up for breakfast. It was Tuesday. Aaron would be over in a few hours. As she went out into the garden, she spied something shiny in her flower bed. *Another coin*, she thought. As she again turned it over and over in her hands, she remembered the last coin she found. It was June 1. *This is July 1. A coincidence*? Lily thought not. *Okay, whoever you are, I know you come early, and you come on the first day of the month.* She looked at her watch. It was just past 6:30 a.m. She made a mental note of the time. When she went in after working in the flower beds for some time, she marked her calendar under August 1, "before 6:30 a.m." Lily thought, *We'll just see if you can sneak in here again without my catching you.*

When Aaron came in to practice with them, Rose refused to stand near him but stood on the other side of the piano. Aaron noticed, and his eyes clouded over. *Will she ever forgive me?* Aaron wondered. In spite of the initial strain, the practice went very well, and they were able to get a lot done. As soon as they were finished, Rose turned and went into her bedroom and shut the door. Lily, Bonnie, and Susie saw Aaron to the door. "See you tomorrow, same time," Lily called after him.

After their practice with Aaron, Lily drove uptown to a coin shop and sold the coins for what she considered a fair price. She then deposited the money and made a note in a notebook she always carried with her: the date, the time, and the amount with the notation "sold two gold coins."

Aaron had told them that he and Connie would like the house to be painted white on the inside. "We can decorate the walls with our pictures and paintings we have in the attic. It will be nice to have them on display again. Mom's aunt was a pretty good artist, and we have some of her paintings, most of them landscapes. And then there are some old photos that are framed that we can put up. I think they will look nice."

Lily had asked him what color they wanted on the outside of the house, that is, if they got that far before school started again. Right now, the house was painted a medium brown. Aaron thought it would be fine if they painted over the old paint with approximately the same color. Perhaps the windows could be trimmed in red, and the outside doors painted to match. He had seen a house trimmed like that once and had always thought that would be cool to do to his house if he ever got the chance.

"Yes, I think that would look nice, Aaron," Lily said.

The week sped by. Aaron made arrangements to go to the hospital to do his janitorial work after he left Langston's. Because he would be playing for Mr. Hunter's guests Saturday evening, the staff at the hospital made arrangements to have him do his miniconcert in the morning of that day. He had intended to just "bag" the hospital concert for that day, but the patients on the first floor would not hear of it. It was their turn to listen to Aaron, and they insisted he sing for them. He was fine with it. And that let him out of doing the janitorial work for that day.

The practices with the Langstons were going well, in spite of a sullen Rose who continued to leave abruptly as soon as they had finished. She would then go into her room and slam the door. Lily began to believe it was more for effect than because Rose was really angry. "She'll come around, Aaron. Just be patient." He felt better.

It was decided that Aaron would play his guitar on the encore music, and so that is how they practiced together.

The concert was to be held on July 5, one day after the Fourth of July holiday. Lily and the girls and Aaron tried to decide on the type of music they would perform. Most of the people in attendance would be from other countries, so they agreed to keep the music more mainstream. But they would perform one patriotic song if they indeed got to sing an encore together. They picked out "America the Beautiful" for that number. Not only would it be a surprise when Lily and her girls and Aaron got together to sing, but that song would knock the audience's socks off. They were all excited for the concert night to come.

Lily spent at least an hour a day practicing on the piano, and she and the girls would practice their songs together afterward.

*****

Bill Green knocked on the Turner's door. When he heard "come in," he opened the door to see Connie waiting for him in her wheelchair.

"You must be Bill Green, Lily's friend," Connie said. She guessed he was about forty years old, a bit over 5'9" tall. He had thinning blond hair and blue eyes. She took note of his kind demeanor and instantly liked him.

"Yes, I am. And you must be Connie. Lily has told me all about you and Aaron. It's very nice to meet you, Connie." Bill Green reached for her hand and shook it. Connie had put on her favorite pink blouse and even placed a pink flower barrette in her hair. Bill took note of how pretty she looked. "Now, with your help, I'd like to go from room to room and see what needs to be fixed. Let's start in the kitchen area and then we will go through the bathrooms and bedrooms."

For the next half hour, Bill and Connie went through the home to see what needed to be done. With her help, Bill made a list of the fix up jobs and a list of the materials that he would need.

When Bill was ready to leave, he turned to Connie and once again shook her hand warmly. "We'll get the materials we need and then get started, Connie. It has been nice visiting with you. See you soon."

"Thanks, Bill Green, for all you and your family are doing for us." With that, Bill waved at Connie and went out the door.

He had some of the materials already on hand at his house and would use those first. He called Lily and gave her a list. He also estimated how much white paint he thought the project called for. If they got the inside finished, then they could go buy the brown and red paint for the outside.

*****

The following day, after the music was practiced, Lily and her girls went up town and purchased all the materials to fix up and paint the inside of the Turner residence. They then decided to treat themselves to an early dinner at a Chinese restaurant.

As they finished their dinner, the subject of what to wear for the concert came up. "Well, this is a very important occasion for the Hunters and the hospital. Perhaps we could add some embellishment to what we already have," Lily said. "Let's see, we all have black skirts. Shall we buy some blouses to match each other? Do we want to wear the same dresses we wore to the last fund-raiser at the clinic? What do you girls think?"

Rose said, "Its summer. Let's buy summer dresses. They don't have to match, just look nice together."

For the next hour or so, they shopped for dresses. This time, they purchased the dresses at two different stores. They were not alike, but when they were standing together, they made a nice picture. They paid for the dresses and headed home.

Later, Lily took out her little notebook and marked down the amount of the items' cost for the painting and fixing jobs at the Turners and subtracted it from the money she got for the coins. There was still quite a bit left over. They would have plenty to buy the paint for the outside of the house.

When she and the children arrived home, Lily called Bill Green to let him know she had purchased everything on the list. Bill told her that he would meet Lily and the girls at Connie and Aaron's house on Monday at 9:00 a.m. and get the two families started painting the inside. Then, when he got off work, he would come and start on the fix ups. Mary and their children would be there to help.

CHAPTER SIXTEEN

They were seated together near the front of the stage waiting for the concert to begin. The Turners were seated at another table. Lily turned her head to see Connie looking at her and waved. Connie smiled and waved back.

The banquet had been delicious. Every kind of meat one could possibly imagine was served. The staff had taken into consideration the cultural differences of the guests who were invited to the festivities. Every person was given a menu and could pick any kind of food they wished. They were seated with a few couples from other countries. Most of them spoke English. Rose, Bonnie, and Susie were spellbound as they sat there. The guests were dressed elegantly. Lily had to keep reminding the girls to eat something.

One of the women at the table told the girls they were excited to hear them perform. This made them even more nervous than they already were. Lily smiled and thanked the woman and told her she hoped they would enjoy what they had prepared.

Carson Hunter got up and spoke briefly before the program began. He was handsome in his black tuxedo and red tie and silvery-gray hair. He said, "Ladies and gentlemen, it has been my honor to be your host for this very important day, a day when we can come together from all different parts of the world in a common cause. We at the Hunter Cancer Clinic have cherished this time we have spent with all of you. Thank you for being here." The guests rose and clapped appreciatively. "There are some wonderful advances coming forth for the curing of cancer. We as representatives of the medical community can help each other in continuing to advance the technology that is making the breakthroughs possible. We live in a remarkable age. It is only possible because of you here, and others who have spent their lives doing this research, that such amazing things are happening in our field. Bless you and thank you again."

Mr. Hunter looked down at his notes, "Now let the program begin. Here is our master of ceremonies, Mona Thompson, to get things started. Mona?"

Mona was stunning in her long black gown. Her blonde hair was piled on top of her head in a cascade of curls. She spoke, "I, too, would like to welcome you all to our country and to the Hunter Cancer Clinic. What an honor it is for us to have you all here in attendance at this great occasion. To begin our program, our first number is by the world-renowned violinist, Charles Campbell. Mr. Campbell."

After the lovely violin music was finished and the tumultuous applause had died down, Mona announced the next number and, following it, Aaron Turner was announced.

Aaron walked onstage and bowed his red head before the large audience. He then sat down and began to play. He sang three numbers to his guitar accompaniment. They were well-known country songs with which Americans were familiar. Although they were some of his favorites, he did not know how they would be accepted by those who were in attendance from other cultures, but he need not have worried. They loved him. After he was finished, he bowed down before the audience who quickly rose to give him a standing ovation.

After Aaron, there was one more number, and then it was time for Lily and the girls. "I'm scared, Mom. There's so many people." Susie clung to her mother. She wasn't sure she would be able to sing a note. Her mother put her arm around her and whispered in her ear loud enough for the other girls to hear, "Sing for your father, Susie. He'll be listening."

That was all Susie needed. The girls stood in front of the piano in their pretty summer frocks, and Lily sat at the piano. As they performed their numbers, the audience seemed to be mesmerized. After the first song, there was loud applause. They sang their second and third numbers, and when they were done, they bowed as Aaron and the others on the program had done. The guests stood up as one and loudly cheered. They continued to cheer wildly as Lily and her daughters waved to the crowd and left the stage.

When the crowd refused to let them go, Mona begged them to come back on stage for an encore. This is just what they were hoping for. They took their places again, and then Lily quieted the crowd down with her hand. "We have a surprise for you. We have been practicing with someone who performed earlier. Would you come up here, Aaron?"

Aaron rose and came back on stage. He was miked again and started strumming his guitar as Lily continued speaking, "We have become good friends with Aaron and his mother. We found out that our voices blend very well together, and so we decided to surprise you by singing a number together. Because yesterday was America's birthday celebration, we would like to sing for you 'America the Beautiful.' We hope you enjoy it."

When the number was finished, the crowd went crazy. "More, more." Aaron started playing again, and Lily and the girls and Aaron began to sing. They sang a song about home, and God, and love. It was a fitting end to an elegant program.

Afterward, many of the audience members came up and hugged them and told them how much they had enjoyed the music. All who had performed were congratulated. It was a magnificent evening, and Carson and Kay Hunter were delighted, as were all who had been behind the scenes working hard to make it the success it was.

For almost an hour after the concert was over, the congratulations continued. Most of the people with whom they spoke were strangers yet, just like family, but were bound together by a common cause. They were all part of a larger family, a family of scientists and educators and humanitarians who were dedicating their lives to the betterment of the human race. They were searching for cures for the different kinds of cancers and other diseases. Lily and the girls were humbled to have been able to do their part in making the evening special.

While the Langstons and the Turners were visiting together, a gentleman they had never met came up to them and introduced himself. He was a short, stocky man who, Lily guessed, had to be in his fifties. He was bald and looked at them over horn-rimmed glasses. "My name is Paul Strong. I am in the recording business. I would like to work with you, Aaron and Lily, and your lovely daughters, on making a CD. Will you come to my studio and visit with me about the possibility of such a venture? Here is my card." He handed the Turners and the Langstons each a card.

Lily and Aaron and Connie stared at one another, *He wants to help us make a CD. Wow.* Lily was the first to speak, "Mr. Strong, thank you for the offer. We will talk together and get back to you. For the next few weeks, we are going to be tied up doing some painting and fixing-up of a house, but after that—"

Connie interjected, "I think you should make an appointment and go see Mr. Strong as soon as possible. The painting can wait."

Lily replied, "But a promise is a promise, Connie. We have agreed to paint your house, and we will do it. However, we will take the time off to visit with Mr. Strong toward the end of next week. Would that be all right, sir?"

Paul Strong answered, "Let's make it Friday afternoon, say 5:00 p.m. That way it won't interfere with your house painting, except a little." He chuckled. "Would that be okay with all of you?"

The arrangements were made, and Mr. Strong turned on his heel and was gone.

As Paul Strong turned to leave, Carson and Kay Hunter came up behind Lily and Aaron. Mr. Hunter was the first to speak. With tears in his eyes, he shook Aaron's hand, embraced Lily and smiled at her daughters. "Kay and I were overwhelmed with your performances tonight. And when Aaron came up and sang with you, well, I nearly lost it. The pain that your families have gone through and are continuing to go through over the loss of Samuel, and then to come together like that, I was so moved…" Hunter couldn't keep the tears from flowing.

Kay Hunter quickly stepped up to Lily and Aaron to stand beside her husband and take his arm. Beautiful, statuesque Kay, whose eyes, like her husband's, were also full of tears, spoke for both of them, "Thank you, thank you. The evening was everything we had hoped for. And your singing with Aaron was the highlight of the evening. You are absolutely marvelous together. I hope we will hear much more of your music. That took a great deal of courage."

"Our guests were thrilled. People from all over the world came up to us and let us know how pleased they were with the program." Carson Hunter regained his composure. "Well, it's getting late, so we will say good night. And thank you again."

Lily and her daughters hugged the Hunters, as did Aaron and Connie. After they walked away, Lily turned to her girls and said, "It's getting late. We need to be getting home so we can all get some sleep. We have early church, and I still have to brush up on my lesson for my Sunday school class. We'd better be getting on home."

"I need to get my mother home too," Aaron said. "Her eyelids are drooping a bit."

Connie jabbed her son, "They are not. I am going to be way too excited to sleep. A recording contract. Who could have seen that one coming?" She turned to Lily. "My doctor told Aaron and I the other day that there is a slight chance that I may be able to walk again someday. There continue to be breakthroughs in spinal cord injury technology. He told us that it would be very expensive, and insurance wouldn't cover much, if any of it, because the techniques are experimental. But if Aaron can help with his music, what a wonderful blessing that would be to be able to walk again."

"Oh, Connie, we hope it will happen for you one of these days. How marvelous. We will be praying that it will happen." Lily put her arms around Connie. The girls followed with their own wishes and hugs. Susie bent and kissed Connie on the cheek. Connie was clearly pleased.

As Aaron started to push his mother's wheelchair toward the exit, the girls called, "We'll see you Monday morning with our painting clothes on."

As they were driving home, Bonnie said, "I felt Daddy there, did you?"

"Yes, he is our guardian angel. I know he was proud of us tonight," Rose added.

"Are we going to get to make a CD, Mom?" Susie asked.

"It sure looks that way. We will have to work hard and fast getting Connie and Aaron's house painted. With Bill and his family and Aaron, when he doesn't need to be at the hospital, I think we will be able to get the job done in good time."

"Yeah, and Connie said she could help too." This from Susie.

Lily laughed. "She is really a sweetheart, isn't she?"

CHAPTER SEVENTEEN

Monday morning, the Langstons and the Greens showed up on the Turner's doorstep ready to work. They were armed with all the paraphernalia they would need for their paint job: rollers, brushes, paint, drop cloths, masking tape for trimming purposes, gloves, paper towels, rags, etc.

Aaron opened the door and helped bring their stuff inside. Soon the drop cloths were laid down, and paint was open and stirred. It was decided they would begin in the kitchen. The cupboards and fixtures were covered with masking tape to keep them from errant paint.

Bill Green made sure all was going well before he headed to work. "I'll be back shortly after my last client leaves. That should be about 4:00 p.m." Bill gave his wife, Mary, a kiss and waved goodbye to everyone else.

Aaron got their stepladder and told them he would paint the top of the walls above the cabinets and the tops of the other walls. For a few minutes, they all tried to work in the kitchen, but there were too many of them, and they kept getting in each other's way.

Tom Green, the Green's oldest child, said, "How about if my family paint in one of the bedrooms and you continue painting here in the kitchen?" indicating Lily, Rose, Bonnie, Susie, and Aaron.

"Good idea," Connie answered. "But don't forget me. I get to roll the paint on the middle of the walls."

"Yes, Mom, that's your job." Aaron got his mother a roller and poured paint into a pan. He then set the pan on a sturdy chair that he covered with an old towel. Now the paint was within her reach.

"Go to it, Mom."

After Connie had worked on the middle of the wall for a time, there was enough space so the two younger Langston children could come behind her and finish painting the bottom part of the wall. Lily and Rose went in front of Connie and painted above her reach as high as they could. After Aaron was finished painting above the cupboards, he painted the top of the wall. When one wall was done, they stood back and admired their work. They were careful to smooth over the edges between the jobs done by each painter, so the work was seamless.

"I must admit," Aaron said, "it looks like it was painted by professionals. Good job, everyone. It looks like you got most of the paint on the walls and not on yourselves."

"Except for Susie, you have white paint in your hair," Rose teased her sister. Susie reached up and touched her curly blonde hair, getting more white paint in it.

"Well, it will have to stay there until we get finished for the day," Lily said. "Thank goodness, the paint we're using is water-based. It shouldn't be too difficult to wash out with a good shampoo."

The painting continued until lunch break. Then hands were washed, and chairs were placed out of the painting zone, and sandwiches were eaten with milk and sodas. Rose would not sit near Aaron but moved her chair away from the group. Lily looked at her sternly, but Rose just made a face at her and continued to eat apart from the rest. Lily sighed.

While they had their lunch break, Aaron got to know more about the Greens. Mary's hair, unlike her husband's thinning hair, was thick and blonde. She was his age, forty, had blue eyes and was of medium build. She spoke up, "My husband is an attorney. He has been the Langston's attorney for years. We have gone on some wonderful vacations together haven't we, Lily?"

"Yes, mostly in and around our home state here."

"Tom is our oldest son. He is seventeen." Aaron noted that Tom was slender, tall with brown hair and brown eyes. "He will be a senior this fall. Josh is fifteen." Josh was blond and slender with brown eyes. "That would be about your age, Aaron, wouldn't it?"

"Yes, I am fifteen. I will soon be sixteen, and I will be a junior."

"Josh will also be a junior. Margaret is thirteen and Lucy, eleven. They take dance lessons and are really very good. Tom and Joshua play basketball. Their being tall is a great advantage to their teams. They also play soccer."

Both Margaret and Lucy had brown hair and brown eyes. Aaron noted that they had the slender bodies of dancers. He also took note of how pretty they were.

Connie spoke, "I wish Aaron could have gotten into sports. He has had to come home after school to help me. I can get around and do a lot of things for myself, but he has continued to look after me. He has excellent grades in school. I am very proud of him."

"We are very blessed to have wonderful children, Connie, all of us. I am also very impressed with Aaron. And the Greens, what can I say? They have been like my own children. We are that close. Bill and Mary have raised a great group of kids," Lily commented.

"Oh, you are just saying that." Mary smiled. "Well, yes, they are pretty good, all in all, I guess."

With that, Tom leaned over and gave his mother a soft jab in the arm. "We are great kids, and don't let anyone tell you different," he said.

"Back to work, everybody." Lily stood up and cleared away the lunch clutter. When Bill came back just after 4:00 p.m., the kitchen and one of the bedrooms were almost done. Bill got out his tools and worked on fixing doors where the hinges had become loose. The families worked until the two rooms were finished.

They cleaned the brushes and rollers and folded the drop cloths and laid everything in an out-of-the way corner. By this time, it was after 6:00 p.m., and they were very tired.

"We'll be back tomorrow about 9:00 a.m." Lily said. "Will you be here tomorrow, Aaron, or will you be working at the hospital?"

"I told the staff at the hospital that I would just be working on Saturday this week, so I will be here to help with the painting the rest of the week."

"Good," Bill said. "The way we worked today gives me to believe that we should be almost through by Friday afternoon."

"Aaron and my family have a meeting with Paul Strong of Legacy Productions on Friday at 5:00 p.m. about the possibility of making a CD. We will need to be done and go home to get cleaned up before we go to visit with him," Lily added.

Bill nodded. "If we are not completely finished, Mary and me and our kids will finish up whatever needs to be done and get everything cleaned up. Right, kids? There are a few more fix ups I need to do, but they should be done by Friday, I think."

"We'll say good night, then, and be back in the morning." With that, Lily and the girls gave hugs all around. "Bye, everybody," Rose added.

That evening, they were tired but happy over what they had accomplished. "Let's just have cereal and juice for supper. I am so tired I don't think I can even lift a spoon," Susie sighed.

"I think we have some leftover meat and potatoes in the fridge. We can just open a can of green beans. Will that be all right for you, girls? Do you think you can manage to feed yourself, Susie?"

"I guess," Susie laughed.

The girls set the table while Lily warmed the food. After they ate their meal, they had their baths or showers and dressed in pajamas. After they were ready for bed, Lily gathered them close to her and said, "I know we are all too tired to have Family Home Evening tonight. So let's just say our family prayers and call it a night. Bonnie, it's your turn, I believe."

They knelt around Lily's bed, and Bonnie thanked Heavenly Father for their blessings and for the gospel in their lives. She thanked Him for their grandparents and all their relatives and friends. She asked blessings upon the sick and needy, the missionaries, and the men and women in the armed services, and the church and government leaders. She closed in the name of Jesus Christ, amen.

"That was a lovely prayer, Bonnie. Thank you." Lily took each one of them and held them close and kissed them. She then tucked them each in their beds, turned off the lights, and threw kisses. It was just after nine, but she knew they would all be asleep in short order.

She got into bed and was very soon fast asleep.

*****

For the next four days, the Langstons, Greens, and Turners worked hard, and by Friday afternoon, the inside painting was all done. Aaron got the pictures down from the attic, and the families had fun picking just the right places on the walls so that they would complement each other. When they were all finished, they stepped back and admired their handiwork.

Everything was done but the cleanup. Lily and the girls needed to leave as it was just after 3:00 p.m., and they needed to get home, get cleaned up, have a bite to eat, and be at Mr. Strong's office by 5:00 p.m.

"Susie, are you under that coat of paint somewhere?" laughed Bonnie. "It's going to take you an hour to clean all that paint out of your hair."

"You have some in your hair too, Bonnie. Right there on the back." With that, Susie raised her hand and touched Bonnie's hair, leaving a handprint.

Bonnie raised a paintbrush intending to do more paint on Susie, but her mother quickly grabbed her arm and took the paintbrush out of her hand. "I think Susie has enough paint on her already, thank you Bonnie. That will be quite enough."

"I'll meet you at Mr. Strong's office," said Aaron.

Mary added, "Bill will be here soon. In the meantime, we will start cleaning up, so go and good luck. We'll be pulling for you."

"We'll call you and let you know how the meeting with Mr. Strong goes. Bye, everybody. It's been fun."

Connie wheeled herself over to the door to say goodbye and thanked Lily and the children as they left.

CHAPTER EIGHTEEN

Lily and the girls met Aaron in the front office of Legacy Productions. It was 5:00 p.m. The front desk secretary was just getting ready to leave.

"Mr. Strong will be with you in just a few moments. Please have a seat."

Aaron turned to Susie and remarked, "Susie, you sure clean up good, honey."

Susie blushed. "Thanks, Aaron. You do too." They all chuckled at that.

Paul Strong came out of his office and motioned them all to come in. He had pulled together enough chairs for them all to sit in a half circle in front of his desk. After shaking hands with each one in turn, he then sat down on the front edge of his desk.

"I must tell you that I was blown away with your talents, each one of you. As I told you, I want to help you make a CD and market your music. The recording business has changed significantly since artists were signed to recording contracts. So much music is now sold online and uploaded on electronic gadgets such as iTunes, you will probably want to have your own attorneys present when we get around to working out all the logistics, that is, if you are willing and want to go forward with this.

"Some of the questions we need to discuss are: Do you want to make separate CDs and thus have separate contracts? If you want to be one group and create your CD together, then I would like to have some solo work done by Aaron, and a piano number or two by Lily, and the rest of the numbers by all of you as a group. Aaron, I understand you have written some of your own music. I would like to hear your pieces and see if we can incorporate one or two of them on the disk.

"Let's set up another time, next week, if you can. Bring your attorneys with you. And, Aaron, since you are a minor, your mother should be present. So how do you feel about working together on the CD?"

Susie piped up, "If I have a vote, I vote yes."

"Me too," chimed in both Rose and Bonnie.

Aaron laughed. "I think its settled then. When we come back, I will bring in my songs, and if you have the time, I could sing them for you. Would that be all right?"

"When would be a good time to make the appointment?" Paul Stone asked. "And I want you all to call me Paul."

Aaron said, "I need to work at the Hunter Cancer Hospital Tuesday, Thursday, and Saturday next week. If it's all right with Lily and the girls, could we make it Wednesday or Friday? I'll need to find an attorney and then check on when he could meet with us."

"Lily? What time will be good for your family?"

"Any day would be all right with us, Paul, so let's tentatively make it Wednesday morning, about ten o'clock. I will ask my friend and attorney Bill Green to come and meet with us."

"Good, let's make it 10:00 a.m. on Wednesday. Aaron, call me if you can't find an attorney, and we'll postpone it until you can." Paul stood up. "I really think this enterprise will be very successful. I can feel it."

"Thank you, Paul, we'll see you on Wednesday then." Lily shook his hand, and each one of her children then came forward to shake Paul Stone's hand, as did Aaron.

Aaron, Lily, and her daughters exited Paul's office and went out into the evening sunshine. It was now just prior to 6:00 p.m. Bonnie suggested they all go for pizza. There was a Pizza Hut on the corner, so it was decided they would eat there. Rose settled herself down at the other end of the table from Aaron. Aaron pretended not to notice. As they were waiting for their pizzas, Aaron called his mother to tell her he would bring her some pizza and would be home soon.

While they ate, they talked about the upcoming meeting, and they were all pretty upbeat about the possibilities. Aaron spoke about his mother's prospects of being able to walk again. "There is a lot going on in the field of spinal cord injuries. Mom's doctor seems hopeful that there will be some help for her in the future. It will be very expensive. Perhaps our CD will generate enough money that she will get her chance to walk again. That is why I really want this to work out."

"That is a wonderful reason for wanting to be successful, Aaron. We want to help her all we can too. How did you get up town, Aaron?"

"I took a bus."

"We'll take you home, of course." Lily and the girls dropped Aaron off on their way home. They said their goodbyes and Bonnie and Susie waved at him as they left his driveway. When Aaron got inside he told his mother about the meeting. "Who shall I ask to be my attorney, Mom?"

"Ask Jacob Manning. I think he would be happy to have you as a client. You seemed to get along with him very well. He appears to be a very kind man."

"Good idea. I'll call him first thing tomorrow morning, before I head to the hospital for my work. Hope he won't mind if I wake him up early on a Saturday morning."

*****

The next morning just after 8:00 a.m., before Aaron left for the hospital, he called Jacob Manning. "Mr. Manning, this is Aaron Turner. I hope I didn't wake you up too early."

"You didn't. It's good to hear from you, Aaron. How is it going with you?"

Aaron filled him in on what he had been doing since Jacob last met with him at his court hearing. Jacob knew a lot about Aaron's comings and goings because he was interested and had made a point of knowing what he was doing. He knew about Aaron's attachment to little Grace Summers and knew that Grace had died.

He also knew of his involvement with Lily Langston and her family. As attorney for the Hunters, he had attended the special evening Carson and Kay Hunter had recently had, where they had hosted the medical experts from the various countries.

Like the Hunters he too was impressed with the musical numbers the Langstons had performed with Aaron.

"The reason I am calling you this morning, Mr. Manning, is because a Mr. Paul Strong is interested in signing me and the Langstons to a recording contract. He is owner of Legacy Productions. We met with him this afternoon, and he suggested that I get an attorney to represent me. The Langstons are asking their friend Bill Green to be their representative. Paul Strong wants to meet us all again with our attorneys."

"When does he want to meet, Aaron?"

"Next Wednesday at 10:00 a.m. in his offices."

Jacob thought for a few moments and then spoke, "Aaron, I don't have to be in court that morning, so I will make a note of the time now, and when I get to the office on Monday morning, I will have my secretary rearrange my schedule. I will definitely be pleased to represent you. I will see you at Legacy Productions Wednesday at 10:00 a.m."

"Thanks, Mr. Manning. You are very kind to do this for me."

"No problem, Aaron. It will be my pleasure. Take care now."

Lily called Bill Green shortly after they arrived home and received the same positive answer. It was all set up then. They would meet with Aaron and his attorney at Legacy Productions on the following Wednesday morning.

CHAPTER NINETEEN

"Mom, Jacob Manning said he would be glad to represent me," Aaron said as he bent over to kiss his mother. "I'm off to the hospital now. Are you going to be all right? Here, let me help you get into your wheelchair."

"Thank you, Aaron, dear. Helen is going to come over about noon and bring some lunch with her. We will visit and watch some videos together for a few hours. I'll be just fine. I'm going to push myself into the kitchen and get a bite of breakfast now. You're a little late, so off with you. Love you."

Helen was their next-door neighbor who often came to be with Connie. They had become best friends. Helen was a widow and had no children. She was as eager for the company as Connie was, so they had bonded together as only two very close friends could.

Aaron entered the hospital and went to the janitors' quarters to sign in and get his mop and bucket. The head janitor greeted him with, "Hey, you're late. Glad to see you."

He replied, smiling at the old man, "Good to see you too."

Aaron was soon hard at work sweeping and mopping floors. By now, he was well-known in the hospital, both with the patients and the nurses and staff. Everyone liked Aaron. He smiled his way through the day, stopping now and then to chat for a few moments with a doctor or nurse.

He tried not to get as attached to the patients as he had to Grace. It was just too painful to love someone and have them die. He wasn't sure he wanted to go through that again. In the weeks following Grace's death, he had kept in touch with the Summers family.

They were still deeply mourning Grace, of course, and he wanted them to know he was thinking of them. He couldn't help shedding tears as he talked with Hannah. He could tell from her voice she was having a hard time of it. He included them in his prayers every night.

Try as he might, though, he just couldn't stay aloof. There were so many sick people, some of whom had only days to live. He didn't want to think about that. So he concentrated on his work and smiled when he met the patients.

It was harder for him on the third floor where the children lay in their beds or sat in their wheelchairs. As sick as they were, they smiled and waved at Aaron.

When the work was done for another Saturday, Aaron cleaned himself up and took his guitar to the third floor where the nurses and parents had gathered together the children for another hour of music and camaraderie.

After the music was over, Aaron sat and answered questions from the children. They wanted to talk about their illnesses. Aaron let them talk as much as they wanted. When it was time to wrap things up, he went to each of their beds and wheelchairs to acknowledge them with a hug or a pat, whichever was appropriate for the restraints—the tubes, the oxygen tanks—that surrounded them. Often, their small hands came up to touch Aaron's face.

Once again, as he left the hospital, the tears cascaded down Aaron's cheeks. Most of the parents hugged him as he left. He thought of a merciful God who had placed him in this position. Even though it was tough to see the suffering, he knew that somehow God had placed him here in the hospital where he could bring a little happiness to temper the sadness, perhaps a little hope in a sea of pain. He thought back to what his mother had said: "Often, Aaron, the Lord makes good things happen from bad situations." He was beginning to understand what she meant.

As he rode his bicycle home, he thought about the months since that April day when Samuel Langston died because of his carelessness. Now the Langstons were probably his best and dearest friends, along with Jacob Manning. And all because he turned down the wrong street on a rainy night and killed Samuel.

He was comforted in the thought, too, that he had been taught that families would be together forever in the hereafter if they were faithful to the covenants they made at baptism and had entered into a faithful temple marriage. He knew most of those whose family members were in the hospital believed this as well. Of course, that wonderful knowledge did not take away the pain of the loss of a loved one, but over time, there would be comfort and joy in the anticipation of families reuniting together again for eternity.

Aaron thought of Grace. Sweet, adorable Grace. She was automatically heir to the Celestial Kingdom. He felt strongly that she was happy with the Savior.

When Aaron arrived home, he made a snack for his mother and himself and then told her about his day at the hospital. Through his tears, he recounted the thoughts he had as he was riding home. His mother was touched by the things he shared with her. "Mom, Heavenly Father is blessing me. I can feel it so strongly. He is touching others through me. I am very humbled by this opportunity I am having to sing and play for the patients and staff in the hospital."

Thank you, Lord, Connie prayed in her mind. "We have so much to be thankful for, Aaron. I thank Heavenly Father every night and morning for my blessings, especially for you, my precious son."

"Mom, you don't talk about my dad. Please tell me about him. I feel so strongly that I need to know whatever you can tell me. Do I look like him? Did he have any musical ability? Was he smart? I think it is time I knew these things. This whole afternoon, I have been thinking about eternal families and where my dad fits in to Heavenly Father's plan."

"Aaron, your dad was indeed talented. He could play the piano beautifully. And he could sing too. You inherited his musical talent. And you have his red hair. All I can really tell you, dear, is that when he found out I was pregnant, we had a big argument, and he left. After he left, I missed him terribly, but we can't go back to those days. I wish I could. I think he joined the Navy. My mother and father took care of us. They were my salvation. They helped me through the tough times during my pregnancy and after you were born.

"And then, after my accident, they took care of us until you were able to take over my care. You, Aaron, are the best, most precious person in my life. I love you so much. I don't know how your father will fit in with us in Heavenly Father's plan, Aaron, but I have great faith that we will have all the answers beyond the veil."

Aaron held his mother close. "I love you, Mom. Thanks for telling me what you could. I have faith that all will work out the way it is supposed to."

CHAPTER TWENTY

It was Wednesday just before 10:00 a.m. in the offices of Legacy Productions. Lily and her daughters, Bill Green, and Connie and Aaron Turner with his attorney, Jacob Manning, were all together in the foyer.

Lily greeted Connie and Aaron and shook hands with Jacob Manning. "Nice to see you again, Mr. Manning. Do you know our attorney, Bill Green?"

"Of course, nice to see you, Bill. Bill and I have been on opposing sides on a few cases over the years. Looks like we'll be working together on this project. I'll enjoy that," Jacob said warmly.

Paul Strong entered the foyer and was introduced to the two attorneys. He greeted everyone and ushered them into the conference room adjacent to his office. "Thank you all for coming. We have a lot to talk about today.

"As you know, I am very interested in Lily and her lovely daughters and Aaron making a CD. As I told them the other day, the recording business has changed significantly over the past few years. It used to be that we would place the artists we wanted to represent under long-term contracts. It is no longer feasible to do that. The recording business has taken off in more than one direction. Now, not only do artists make CDs, but their music can now be downloaded via the Internet to electronic gadgets such as iTunes.

"What I would like to do is oversee the making of the CD. I have a sound studio for the purpose and it's set up with all the latest technological advances in the industry for making a top-notch recording. I will cover the costs of packaging and promoting it, as well as the use of my studio. In return, I would recover all the initial costs of the CD before Aaron, Lily, and the children would get anything. However, they would receive whatever proceeds come from the sale of their tunes over the Internet, less my 10 percent.

"Also, any proceeds from the CDs that are sold at the concerts or benefits they perform in would be the Langstons and Aarons to split fifty-fifty. As soon as the initial costs are recovered by my studio, then I propose a 30 percent cut for the studio on the sale of future CDs. There will be ongoing costs, of course, for packaging and promotion, etc., which will be about 20 percent, so Aaron and the Langstons would receive approximately 50 percent of every CD sold after the initial costs are recovered. They would split that between them.

"We wouldn't need to hire other musicians for background music unless you want to fill out an orchestra behind them. Lily plays the piano beautifully, and Aaron has magic fingers on that guitar of his. I can't see that we would need any more musicians. If we should decide to hire others then, of course, that would be an extra expense. These days, instruments can be added electronically later, so we won't need to worry about that now.

"I have been in this business for many years," Paul Strong told the others. "I have had great success in picking out exceptional talent to promote. I have no doubt whatsoever that if you are all agreed, this can be a tremendous success for all who are involved. How do you all feel about what I have told you? Do you want to talk it over and get back to me?"

Jacob Manning was the first to speak, "Is what you have told us the going rate for this type of business?"

"Yes."

"May we see your sound studio, Paul?" Bill asked.

"Of course. Come on, follow me."

Paul took them down the hall and into their sound studio. It was all decked out with all kinds of musical paraphernalia. To a lay person, it seemed to be very cluttered. But to a professional, everything was beautifully placed for maximum performance. Paul smiled. "Trust me, everything in this room has a purpose. We have one of the best studios in the business."

"When would you begin to record the music, Paul?" Jacob asked.

"I would like to get started next week if at all possible. We would need to pick out the music Lily and Aaron and the girls want to have on the recording and then practice the pieces before recording them. We want the acoustics to be just right."

Aaron spoke up, "I brought my music for you to listen to, Paul. I have three pieces here. When do you want to hear them?"

"I could listen to them now if you like, Aaron," Paul said. "I'll turn on some of the machinery, and we can get a feel for how they would sound on a recording."

"That would be great," replied Aaron.

Bonnie asked, "Mom, could we stay and listen to Aaron's music?" Even Rose, who at first was tempted to tell her mother that she didn't want to stay, decided she really would like to hear Aaron's songs.

"Yes, I think that would be nice," Lily said. She looked over at Rose and smiled.

After they were made comfortable in the guest area, Aaron was seated with his guitar before a system of microphones and wires. Paul Strong sat behind some kind of monitor or mixer and played with some knobs. When he was ready, he motioned to Aaron to begin playing. After Aaron had played and sang a few bars of his music, Paul stopped him. After doing some more adjusting, he then had Aaron begin again.

The songs were lovely. The first one he sang he called "Coming Home." It was about a young soldier coming home from war to the sweetheart he loved. The second one was more upbeat. He called it "Loving You." The third song he wrote for his mother. It was simply entitled "Mother." Connie was visibly moved by the music coming through the sound system.

After the little concert, everyone clapped. "Those are all beautiful songs, Aaron. We could use any one or all of them. Now, Lily and Aaron, let's schedule a time to get together and plan what music you will want to perform on your first CD. Is everyone in agreement about what I spoke of earlier? If so, I will draw up contracts covering just what we have agreed on today for you to sign with your attorneys present."

The attorneys agreed that what Paul Strong had proposed was fair. It was also agreed that the following Wednesday, they would get together and sign the contracts and then get busy picking out the music they wanted on the CD and which ones to make available on the Internet.

When Lily and her daughters got home, Lily called her in-laws and her parents and told them about the CD they were going to produce with Aaron Turner. Both sets of parents were delighted.

Aaron's mother was excited about the upcoming recording. She was also enjoying the newly painted rooms. Everything seemed so much brighter and sunnier now that there was a new coat of paint on all the walls. She enjoyed looking at the lovely landscape paintings her sister had painted. For too many years, they had languished in their attic. Then there were pictures of her parents and family members, and pictures of Aaron as a baby and as a young child. She pushed her wheelchair as close as she could get to each picture and let the memories of each one flow into her mind.

Over the next week, Lily and her daughters kept busy practicing their music. Lily got up early as usual and worked in her flower beds for a couple of hours every morning. She loved the morning hours in her garden. She felt close to Samuel when she was working in the yard they both loved so much. Josh Green kept the lawn looking like a showplace.

I should invite my family and friends over for a barbecue one of these evenings, Lily thought. She could show off her handiwork. But she just didn't feel like she was ready to entertain yet. She was managing to sleep most of the night now. When the loneliness overwhelmed her, she thought of her daughters. They were a great comfort to her. She longed for Samuel, but the music was helping to fill the void in her life.

Rose, Bonnie, and Susie were still asleep when she went back in the house, so Lily sat at the piano and played some of her favorite pieces. She loved the old classics by the likes of Beethoven, Mozart, Chopin, and others. After a while, sleepy heads peered around the door.

"Hi, Mom," a sleepy voice greeted her. "What's for breakfast?"

The dog days of summer began like this nearly every morning. "Good morning, my Susie Q, how about pancakes this morning?"

Rose and Bonnie followed Susie into the piano room. "Pancakes, it is," Rose echoed her mother. "I'll set the table."

Bonnie stirred up some orange juice. Susie helped her mother stir the batter and spoon the batter on to the hot frying pan. The pancakes didn't turn out exactly round, but no one cared. As Susie told her mother, "They taste just the same whatever shape they come out. Right, Mom?"

"Right," Lily dabbed a little of the pancake batter on Susie's nose. She then stepped away quickly so Susie couldn't retaliate.

Bonnie got the peanut butter out of the cupboard. Someone had turned them on to peanut butter on their pancakes. "Peanut butter and syrup, yummy," said Bonnie.

After they were finished eating, they all pitched in to clear up the breakfast. They then went to their rooms and dressed to do their morning chores with just a minimum of squabbling.

Now it was time to practice their music. They still hadn't decided what music they would like on their CD, so they practiced as many as they could before getting tired and needing a break.

Aaron came over when he could to practice the music they were to do together. His time was limited on the days he worked at the hospital, but he would spend hours with them on the days he was free.

On Sunday, Lily and the girls got ready and attended their church meetings. It then became a habit that they would spend Sunday afternoon at the Langstons and then at Lily's parents. When they went to the grandparents' homes, they would take with them their music and sing and play for their biggest fans. When Lily and her girls later arrived home, they sat on the sofa and just visited for a while before going to bed. It was a very special day for all the family. Then they would kneel together, hold hands, and say a prayer of thanksgiving for all their blessings. Afterward, there were hugs and kisses all around before saying good night.

CHAPTER TWENTY-ONE

It was Wednesday again. Lily and the girls drove over to Aaron's to pick him up for their day with Paul Strong. While there they went in to visit with Connie for a few minutes. Connie was happy to see them.

"Have a great day. Just imagine working on making a CD. How cool is that?" Lily and the girls laughed at Connie's use of the word 'cool.'

"Is there anything we can do for you before we go, Connie?" Lily asked.

"Nope, Aaron got me all taken care of. Go, and enjoy the day. I can't wait to hear all about it when you bring Aaron home." With that Connie hugged her son and then threw them all a kiss as they went through the door.

A short time later Lily pulled up in a parking space and they all piled out of the car, picked up their music and Aaron's guitar from the trunk, and headed in to Legacy Productions. Paul met them at the door and ushered them into a room where there was a piano, a desk and chairs.

"We'll start out here. We may get into the sound room later today, but first let's pull out your music and lay it out on the table. Then we'll make some notes and do a little practicing. Around that corner there you'll find the ladies' room and men's room, and across the hall there is a snack room where there are drinks and sandwiches and treats of all kinds."

Lily had to restrain her youngest. "Let's work a little, Susie, before you go check out the goodies, okay?"

"Actually, Lily, you and I and Aaron will be busier than the girls are for a while, so let them go and check out the snack room if they would like. We'll call them when we are ready for them," Paul smiled at the girls who quickly made their escape.

"Now, Aaron and Lily, let's go through your music and make a list of the songs you have here. After we do that we will make another list, a tentative list of the numbers you would like to have on your CD, which ones are your favorites and you feel would be the most pleasing to an audience. We will want to have a combination of fast and slow music, and all varieties such as gospel, western, jazz, classical, etc."

For the next couple of hours Paul, Lily and Aaron were so caught up in what they were doing that they weren't aware of the passage of time. Lily's daughters had found the snack room and had also found the television. They were engrossed in watching a movie, and with the snacks, they were also unaware of the time until Lily finally came in to check on them.

"I see that you girls have made yourselves at home. I am going to take a few of these sandwiches in for us if you girls are all right for a while longer."

"We're good, Mom. We're watching a movie, and we want to see how it turns out. Don't worry, Mom, its G-rated."

Lily laughed. "All right then. Come and find us when the movie is finished, and maybe it will be time to practice a song or two in the sound room, okay?"

Paul spoke to Aaron, "Now that we have picked out your solo numbers, you could come over here on your own time to record those numbers. Lily and the girls would not need to be here then. After we are done today, work with my secretary on the times you are free from your shift at the hospital. We will schedule you and Lily and the girls together, and also schedule a separate time for you, and then plan a time for just Lily. Hope all that makes sense.

"Now, I see that the girls are through with their movie, so let's pick up two or three of the songs you are going to be singing together on your CD and take them into the sound studio and work on them for a couple of hours. After that, the girls will undoubtedly be tired and ready to be done for the day."

Paul ushered them down the hall and into the sound studio. Once again, Paul sat behind his system of knobs and buttons. Lily sat down at the piano. "What song shall we work on first, Paul?"

"Let's work on something upbeat, Lily."

Lily picked up a piece of music and began playing. "Yeah, I like that one," Paul said. "Okay, sing it the way you are used to doing it. Aaron, you play with Lily, and all of you sing it as you have done it before."

For the next two hours, they practiced their music together. Paul would stop them and have them go back over a verse or chorus of the music. He would ask Bonnie and Susie to sing a bit louder on some parts. When he was satisfied with the piece, he recorded it. "This may not be the last taping of the song, but it also may. It sounds really good." Paul was pleased.

"Well, I think that is enough for today. Let's go out to the secretary's desk and work out a schedule for the next couple of weeks. I imagine you, Lily, and your daughters are fairly free until school starts again, right?"

Lily replied, "Yes, that's right. We will work around Aaron's work schedule."

After the scheduling was done and written down by all concerned, Lily and Aaron and the girls said their goodbyes to Paul Strong and went out the door.

Lily pulled up in front of Aaron's, and she and the children got out to visit with Connie for a few minutes before heading home. Connie was waiting for them with great anticipation.

"Tell me, tell me," she said as soon as the door closed behind them. They filled her in on the day. It had been tiring but very enjoyable. They all agreed that they couldn't wait to work on the CD again when their scheduled time came. They told her about the one number they had worked on and recorded.

"We think it's a keeper," Rose spoke for all of them.

The time sped by for the next couple of weeks. Between practicing their music, doing household chores, and working in the garden, there was little time for anything else. They spent Sundays at church and with family, had Family Home Evenings on Monday nights, and on most other evenings when Lily and the girls came home from the studio, they were so tired that after dinner, they curled up in front of the television and watched a movie until it was time to go to bed, often falling asleep before the movie had finished.

The work of making a CD was exhausting. Often, they went over the music several times before Paul felt it was ready to be recorded. The first two or three times singing the same song wasn't so bad, but stopping and starting over and over again took its toll on Susie and even Bonnie. Sometimes the frustration led to tears, even some stubborn retorts. Paul was solicitous of the girls' feelings, and when he could tell that they needed a break, he called a halt and sent them to the snack room for a snack or a drink of soda.

By the end of the two weeks, they had managed to record half a dozen songs with Aaron, and Aaron had recorded two of the songs he was to sing alone. These were two of his own songs, and Paul planned to have all three on the CD before it was finished. Lily still had to record her piano solos, and there were still several more to be recorded with Lily and the girls alone and then with Aaron.

Paul said, "We have made amazing progress. I am very pleased. I think we should take a few days off now and start again in a week. That will give you young ladies a chance to have some fun before summer is over. We'll meet here again next Wednesday as usual."

"Yes, Paul, I think a little time off would do us all good. We'll keep practicing the songs we haven't recorded yet, and I'll continue to work on my piano solos," Lily said. "Do you think we will be done by the time school starts again?"

"Let's see. Tomorrow is August 1, and your school begins the last week in August. Is that right?"

"Yes, August 25."

Paul shook his head. "That doesn't give us much time. There is still a lot to be done. We'll have about two more weeks after you come back from your break. I really think it is going to take another month of hard work before the music portion is all wrapped up."

Aaron spoke, "I can tell the hospital that I want to cut my hours back to maybe one other day besides Saturday. That will give us some extra time to work together."

"If you don't mind doing that, Aaron. That will work out well, and maybe we can get all or most of the music recorded by the end of August, a few days after school starts."

"Sounds good, then, we'll see you next Wednesday, Paul," Lily commented.

On the way home after Lily dropped Aaron off, Susie asked, "What are we going to do for fun, Mom?

"Let's go camping," Rose suggested.

"Yeah, let's go camping with the Greens. That would be just like old times, wouldn't it?" This was Bonnie.

"Let me give them a call, girls, and if they want to do some camping, we'll plan it together. I think it might be fun. Hope Bill can get away for a few days."

As soon as they arrived home, Lily called the Greens. Mary answered. "Mary, the girls and I have a little time off from our recording sessions. Paul Strong is giving us some R & R time. The girls and I want to know if your family is up to going camping for a few days."

"Let me get back to you. I'll talk it over with Bill and see if he can clear his schedule. The kids and I could go if Bill can. I'll call you tomorrow morning."

"I'll look forward to your call, Mary. Bye."

As Lily hung up the phone, she smiled to herself as she thought, *There is something I have to do tomorrow morning, bright and early. I intend to solve a mystery.*

CHAPTER TWENTY-TWO

The alarm went off at 5:30 a.m. As soon as Lily heard it, she jumped out of bed, dressed quickly, and headed to the kitchen for a glass of orange juice. As she headed out the back door, she grabbed the newspaper. It was still dark, so reading was clearly not a choice. Why she picked up the newspaper, thinking she could pass the time reading it was silly. *Oh, well, maybe I'll run back in and get my iPod.*

A few minutes later, Lily was sitting in an inconspicuous spot in the yard. She had also picked up a light sweater as it was a bit cool there in the garden. She slowly sipped on her orange juice, listened to music, and enjoyed the sweet fragrance of the flowers in the cool morning air.

As she waited, she reminisced the happy times she had spent with her precious Samuel. So many wonderful memories. As she sat dreaming, she began to drift off toward sleep, when suddenly a movement caught her eye. Someone had entered the garden. Someone dressed in dark clothing moved softly toward the flower bed. It was starting to get light and, to Lily, the shadow seemed familiar. Just as he placed something in the flower bed, she recognized him. "You!"

Jacob Manning nearly jumped out of his skin. He turned to see Lily standing in the glow of the early-rising sun. She had on white slacks and a white sweater. He caught his breath. It was as if she was surrounded by a halo. Jacob Manning thought it was the most beautiful sight he had ever seen.

"Lily, you caught me. Now I have to confess, don't I?" Jacob laughed. "By the way, I thought you were an angel. The sun cast a halo around you as you were standing there. You are beautiful, do you know that?"

"Well, Mr. Manning, you are not so bad-looking yourself," Lily countered, smiling. "Now, a confession is definitely in order. Let's go sit over in the comfortable chairs. I am very anxious to hear why someone of your stature would be slinking around in my garden practically in the dead of night."

"I guess you figured out when I would be coming back by making note of the other two times I was here. Pretty smart of you. And you can drop the 'Mr. Manning' nonsense now that we are conspiracy buddies."

Jacob got up and went over to the flower bed and retrieved the coin he had placed there. He put it in Lily's hand.

"There is someone whom I work for who is very interested in one Lily Langston and her beautiful daughters. He has followed your career from the time you and Samuel first began to sing and perform together. He was devastated when Samuel was killed. You and your family are very special to him, and he wanted to let you know just how very much he values you. Your family has brought joy to so many people with your music. I can tell by how your lovely face lit up just now that you know who I am talking about."

Lily nodded. "It's Carson Hunter, isn't it? I should have guessed. He is legendary for his good and charitable works in this state. And Kay is right there with him. I should have guessed," Lily repeated. Lily went on, "Did he tell you what he hoped I would do with the coins?"

Jacob said, "Well, you know how he likes to surprise people. Some of them guess who is behind the good deed. Some never find out. He wanted you to know. He told me to hide a coin each month. There are ten of them. After I had given you all ten, I was supposed to let you know who had given them to you and find out what you did with them. He really didn't care what you did with them, he just thought it would be fun to find out. He enjoys playing these little guessing games with people. If you wanted to just keep them, he would not have minded, but he knew you well enough to know that you would want to do something special with them. Now that you have caught me, I am going to give you the other seven. Do you have any idea what you might like to do with them now that you will have them all?"

Lily smiled. "With the first two coins, the Green family and my family and Aaron painted the inside of the Turner's home. It was in pretty bad shape. Bill Green fixed what needed to be fixed, and we all painted. Then we put up her pictures that they had stored in the attic. It really pleased Connie.

"The outside of the house also needs a lot of work. The roof is missing quite a few shingles and needs to be replaced. Then it badly needs a coat of paint. Aaron wants it painted the same color it is now, and then he wants the outside doors and window frames painted red. He thinks that would look nice. I think it would too."

"That would be great, Lily."

"With whatever money is left over, we could give their landscaping a makeover," Lily added.

"Walk to the car with me, Lily, and I will give you the coins. Let me know what I can do to help. I'd like to be a part of the renovations, if you will let me. My son, James, would also like to help. He is ten. He is autistic but can be a lot of help if the task is explained to him carefully."

"That would be nice, Jacob. I would like to meet your son."

Jacob reached into the car, took out the bag of coins, and placed them in Lily's hands. "There you are, Lily. Carson Hunter will be very pleased to get my report." With that, Jacob leaned over from his six-foot-two height and planted a kiss on Lily's forehead. Lily looked up and saw Jacob grinning at her. "That's for luck, Lily Langston." Jacob got into his black Lexus, smiled, waved at her, and drove off.

Lily slowly turned and went back in the house. "What just happened?" she asked herself softly. It was difficult to separate the feelings swirling around inside her. She looked down and felt the heaviness of the coins in her hands. Carson Hunter had clearly wanted her to do something special with the coins he had given her. They were not meant to be stashed away in her safe. She felt very strongly that he would approve of her plans to finish fixing and painting the Turner's house.

She touched the spot on her forehead where Jacob had kissed her. She thought of Samuel, *Samuel, has it only been five months since you left us? Jacob was just being nice, I'm sure. But it was a sweet gesture. I liked it.*

It was still early, so Lily sat down at the piano and began to play Polonaise in A Flat Major by Frederick Chopin softly so she wouldn't wake up the girls. It was her favorite Chopin piece. She planned to play it on the CD. As she played, she felt a warm sensation around her shoulders like someone had placed an arm around her. She knew it was Samuel. He was letting her know that he loved her and that everything was going to be all right.

After Lily finished the music, she rose and went into the kitchen to begin to fix ham and eggs for breakfast for the children. The smell of the cooking food awoke her youngsters, and soon they were dressed and sitting at the table.

"Susie, will you bless the food, honey?"

"Sure, Mom."

After the blessing, they were soon eating and discussing the proposed camping trip. Several spots were suggested.

"We never miss church, but maybe this one Sunday, we will just have our church out in nature. What do you girls think about that?" Lily asked them between bites of egg.

"Could we? That would give us a few more days to camp," Rose said.

"I'll have to get someone to teach my class on Sunday. And it will also depend on the Greens, whether they are tied up in their church meetings, or if they can get substitutes too. We will have to figure all that out before we can make final plans," Lily told her daughters.

Bonnie said, "Is it too early to call them, Mom?"

"Let's finish breakfast and clean up, and then it will be all right to call. They should be up and able to conference with us on the phone by then."

Soon, Lily and the girls were talking to Mary, Bill, and the kids on a conference call. They asked how they felt about taking Sunday as part of their camping days so that they would have more time to enjoy the outdoors. It was now Thursday morning, and they would not have to be back before Tuesday evening. Wednesday, they would need to be back in Paul Strong's studio to resume their work on the CD. That would give them five days if they left that afternoon.

"Give us a couple of hours to make arrangements to have our classes covered, and we'll get back to you guys, okay?" Bill asked.

"Good, I need to cover my lesson too," Lily told them. "Where do we want to go this time?"

"How about going north and following I-89 up past Logan into the Wasatch-Cache National Forest. There are a lot of camping areas, and the forest will be a nice place to relax in. How does that sound?" Bill suggested. "By the way, Lily, Tom will drive your motor home so you won't have to."

"Wonderful, thank Tom for me. That will be a great help."

"That's settled then. We'll call you back as soon as we have lessons squared away. In the meantime, let's begin to get our stuff packed and ready to go so we can get out on the trail by this evening, if at all possible."

After Lily made her call to arrange to have someone teach her Sunday school lesson, she set about organizing the motor home. Rose took clean sheets and pillowcases out and changed the bedding. Bonnie and Susie swept and mopped the floor and cleaned the kitchen and bathroom.

Lily got the food together and made sandwiches and some cookies for their meal with the Greens when they camped for the evening. She filled the water tank. The first stop they would make when they got going was for gas. Then they would be ready to head out. They would buy what groceries they would need as they passed through Logan tomorrow.

CHAPTER TWENTY-THREE

They were nearly finished with their tasks when Bill Green called and told them all was in readiness. A half hour later, the Greens pulled up in their motor home. Lily and the girls locked the doors to their home and got into their motor home, and Tom got behind the wheel.

Bill stepped over to Lily's rolled-down window and said, "We'll stop down the street at the Chevron station and fill the tanks, and then we'll be off. Since its now just after 4:00 p.m., lets plan to camp near Willard Bay. That's about a two-hour drive from here. I know of a nice campground near there. Then tomorrow morning, we'll head up the canyon toward Logan, okay?"

"Sounds good, Bill. Give us just a few minutes for a prayer, and then we'll follow you to the gas station." Lily moved over to sit next to her girls at the table, and Tom came over to stand beside her. Lily then said a prayer of thanksgiving and asked for safety for themselves and their dear friends, the Greens, and a blessing on their homes.

After they gassed up at the Chevron station, Tom followed his family's motor home as they merged with the traffic onto I-15 going north. It was a lovely warm afternoon. Lily sat in the front passenger seat next to Tom. The girls sat around the table and talked and laughed together. They were going on a little vacation, and they were clearly ecstatic about it.

Lily and Tom didn't talk as he carefully maneuvered the vehicle through the traffic and attempted to keep up with his dad. The traffic at this time of the day north out of Salt Lake City was very heavy. Lily was relieved at how careful a driver he was at just seventeen. Tom was a serious young man, a fine role model for her daughters.

North of Ogden, the traffic cleared up somewhat, and Lily asked Tom about his future plans. "As you know, I will be a senior this year. Then I am thinking of going to BYU-Idaho the following year to study architecture. After my mission, I plan to finish my college degree at Brigham Young University in Provo. Those are my plans right now, anyway."

"Those are good choices, Tom. Now that we are passed the worst part of the traffic, can we get you something to drink? We have some soda in the fridge. We have almost anything you would like." Lily smiled at Tom.

"I'll have a Dr. Pepper."

"One Dr. Pepper coming up." Rose got up and carefully worked her way to the fridge and, after opening it for him, handed Tom the drink. Tom took a sip and placed it in the cupholder between the seats.

Rose sat back down. The rest of them would have to wait till they stopped at the campground for their drinks. She knew it was not wise to move around too much in a moving vehicle. After another two hours, both motor homes pulled into the campground at Willard Bay. It was just before 7:00 p.m. After getting their vehicles situated in camping spots, they took the sandwiches and cookies out and put them on the picnic table between the campers that they had covered with a tablecloth. Mary and her children brought out some salads and drinks. Paper plates and cups and utensils were placed on the table, and drinks poured all around.

"Boy, I'm starving," Susie said. "Let's eat."

"First, the blessing, then we eat," Bill told her. The blessing was said, and the group filled their plates and dug in.

"Ouch," Bonnie cried as she slapped a mosquito.

"Guess we had better get the mosquito repellent out," Mary commented. "I'm pretty sure we have some in the camper." She got up and went inside for the repellent. "We had better finish eating before we spray this stuff, or we will be eating tainted food. It won't taste too good."

After they were finished, and everything was cleared away, the bug spray was generously applied to all present. After that, chairs were pulled over under the trees, and the two families played games and talked and laughed the evening away. No one was in a hurry to go to bed, and so they stayed up long past the coming out of the stars in the night sky. It was an idyllic evening. As they sat there, Lily, Bill, and Mary made a game with their children of guessing the names of the different constellations of stars. Finally, about midnight, it was time to call it a day.

After a round of hugs, the families went to their own motor homes for a good night's rest. Prayers were said, and Lily tucked her girls in their bunks and then stretched out on her own. *What a lovely day this has been,* she thought, *I am so glad we decided to go camping.* Almost immediately, Lily was asleep.

The next day, the two families drove up Highway 89 in the northeast section of the state of Utah. They stopped in Logan to shop for the food they would need for the rest of the trip. Bug spray and sunscreen were high on their lists, along with a generous amount of their favorite treats and drinks.

That night, they stopped and camped in Garden City on the shore of scenic Bear Lake. They camped at the KOA Campground. It was decided by the group that they could spend Saturday and part of Sunday at Bear Lake before heading over to Evanston, Wyoming.

Fun in the water was the order of the day. Bill and Mary's children—Tom, Josh, Margaret, and Lucy—along with Rose, Bonnie, and Susie spent all Saturday playing on the lovely sandy beach. They had covered themselves with a generous layer of Deet and sunscreen, and each wore a hat, at their parents' insistence.

They stopped their play when they got hungry or thirsty and were back at it again after these basic needs were satisfied. The volleyball net was put up, and other kids on the beach were invited to come and play with them. It turned out to be a wonderful day.

Later, after dinner, the children spent the evening in the KOA swimming pool. They mingled with their new friends around the pool. After the pool closed at 10:00 p.m., the Langstons and the Greens sat under the trees and again looked up into the night sky to enjoy the stars.

"Look, there's the Space Station," Bill cried out excitedly. The station was easily distinguishable from the stars as it emitted a pulsating light as it slowly crossed the dark sky. "Wow, this is the first time I've witnessed it. What a treat."

For the next several minutes, they were all awed at the site of the space vehicle traveling across the dark sky from the northwest to the southeast. "What a perfect ending to a perfect day," Lily said. They all chimed in in agreement. It had been a fantastic day.

"Time for bed," Mary told her children. "Tomorrow morning, let's have breakfast together in our camper and then have our own little Sunday school meeting. I don't think we should play on the beach, as it is Sunday."

Bill agreed. "How about a meeting where we each tell what we are most thankful for. And we'll sing some of the church hymns. We have several hymn books we keep in the camper."

"We have some in our camper too. We'll bring them over tomorrow morning. Why don't we make eggs and bacon in our camper, and you fill in toast, juice, and milk, Mary," Lily offered. "Then we'll bring them over here. What else do you want us to do?"

"That will be fine, Lily. Let's not get up too early. How about we get together for breakfast at 10:00 a.m.?"

"Or later?" Bonnie pleaded.

"How about ten-thirty?" Bill compromised with a laugh.

The next morning, Lily made the bacon and eggs for the breakfast. It had been nice to sleep in for a change. After they were dressed, Rose carried the pan of food, and Bonnie and Susie carried the hymn books over to the Green's camper.

Since there was not enough room for all to sit around the table, the parents sat on the sofa across from the table. Bill had hymns playing softly on his CD player in the background. Even though the kids were squished in beside one another tightly, they didn't mind a bit.

After breakfast and dishes cleared, washed, and put away, everyone sat down, and Bill led their meeting. "Tom, will you please say the opening prayer?"

After Tom was finished, hymn books were opened, and they all sang "Count Your Many Blessings." Bill then got up from the sofa and said, "I'll start out by telling you what I am most thankful for. We'll go oldest to youngest, okay? I am most thankful for the Gospel of Jesus Christ in my life, for the privilege of being alive today in the fullness of times. I am thankful for my family and for my dear friends. Now, Mary, it's your turn."

Mary stood up. "It goes without saying that I too am thankful for the same things Bill has mentioned. I will add that I am thankful to live in this blessed country where we are free to worship as we see fit."

Then Lily spoke, "I will add that I am thankful for the Holy Spirit. Without His comfort over the past several months since Samuel died, I don't know how I could have gotten through it. And He continues to bring me comfort. I am so thankful for Him." Lily wiped tears from her eyes. Mary got up to embrace her dear friend.

After a pause, Tom cleared his throat and spoke, "We all love you, Lily, and you, Rose and Bonnie and Susie. You are dear friends. And that is what I am thankful for: you, our dear friends."

"I guess I'm next," fifteen-year-old Josh said. "Well, I agree with all of you. Those are my blessings too. Let's see, I am thankful for Mom and Dad, for Tom and Margaret and Lucy, and I am thankful for my job cutting the lawns for the Langstons. They pay good."

Everyone laughed. Then Margaret, thirteen, added, "You know I agree too. with all the blessings you have mentioned, that is, except for the mowing part. And I am thankful for my dance lessons."

Now it was twelve-year-old Rose's turn to speak. "This is really hard for me. I miss my dad so much." She wiped away tears and continued, "I am thankful that we will be together again some day. I guess, besides all the blessings that you have mentioned, my greatest blessing is that we will be together again, that we are a 'forever family'."

Lily commented, "Isn't it great that we have that wonderful knowledge, Rose? It doesn't make the loss any less painful, but it does give us peace and comfort to know that we will all be together again in the Celestial Kingdom if we are worthy and endure to the end. It certainly makes keeping the commandments and enduring to the end worth it, doesn't it?"

They all nodded their heads in agreement. Eleven-year-old Lucy spoke up, "I am thankful for all the blessings you all have mentioned, and I am thankful that we could come on this trip. Next time, I hope it can be longer."

"You probably aren't expecting this one, but I am thankful for Aaron Turner. I know that sounds crazy because he…he is the one who…well, you know…" Bonnie started sobbing quietly.

"It's okay, honey. We have all grown very fond of Aaron and also of Connie. Someday, we'll understand why your father died and his passing brought Aaron and his mother into our lives. Somehow, someday it will all make sense, Bonnie. For now, we need to be strong and do whatever our Heavenly Father wants us to do and be faithful to the values we all hold so dear." Lily comforted her daughter. She would have hugged her, but she was sitting in the back of the table, and Lily couldn't get to her right then. She would hug her as soon as she could.

"It's my turn now," Susie exclaimed. "I am thankful for all those blessings too, and I am also happy we are making a CD. And I think it is great that Aaron is performing with us on it. I like Aaron too." And then she laughed. "And I like all of you too."

"Thanks, everyone, for your participation in our meeting. You all did great. Now, how about we close with 'I Stand All Amazed'? I think that would be a very fitting conclusion. Then, Josh, will you say the closing prayer?" Bill asked.

After the song was sung and the prayer was said, Bill spoke again, "We are about an hour-and-a-half away from Evanston, Wyoming, our next stop before we head home. So shall we pack up and drive there and spend the rest of Sunday there? I don't think it would be wise to play on the beach today because it is the Sabbath. Anyway, it is almost noon, and our checkout time is 1:00 p.m. When we get to Evanston, we could see the sights around there and maybe play some fun church games after dinner. What say you?"

"Okay, give us about an hour, and we will be ready to go." Lily got up and hustled her daughters out of Green's motor home. "It was a great meeting. See you in an hour, ready to drive."

Lily and the girls straightened up the camper and got ready to move out of the campground. With Tom at the wheel once again and prayers for safety uttered, the two motor homes pulled out of their campsites and were soon on the highway leading to Evanston, Wyoming.

They drove to Sage Junction past Laketown on Highway 30 and then traveled south on Highway 16 to Evanston. When they got to Evanston, they stopped at a park to have lunch and to decide on what they would do for the rest of the day. It was still early afternoon on Sunday. Bill suggested they drive east the short distance over Highway 80 to Fort Bridger, Wyoming, which is a historic site.

Bill turned to his family, "Do you remember the Family Home Evening we had a few weeks ago when we discussed how the US government sent an army west to Utah to go against our church? Fort Bridger area is where the Mormons took a stand against the US Army. Let's drive over there and see how much of that history the guides at the monument can tell us."

"We'd better fill up with gas before we go," Tom said. "Lily's tank is about a quarter full."

After filling up with gas, the two vehicles headed out on the highway leading to Bridger Historic Monument. The jaunt over to Fort Bridger was under thirty miles. When they arrived, they parked the campers near the site and went in search of a guide.

Their guide, a white-haired man by the name of John, led the families into the Traders Store, and there began to tell the visitors the story of Fort Bridger. "Fort Bridger was established in 1843 by famous mountain men Jim Bridger and Louis Vasquez. It was one of the most important stops on the Oregon Trail. It was used as a trading post and a stop for outfitting emigrants along the overland route. In 1855, the fort was purchased by Mormons who were the ones using the trail the most at the time.

"Shortly thereafter, the Mormons conflicted with the US government, and the fort and what buildings were not burned were taken over by US troops. It was rebuilt in 1858 and then became a military post to help control the Indians who were robbing and plundering at the time. During the 1860s, it became a stage stop for the Pony Express and Overland Stage routes. Today, a number of original buildings from 1858 through 1890 are still standing. Many have been restored and are open to the public, including a museum and the first schoolhouse in Wyoming.

"This original Traders Store was erected in 1867, the commissary provided soldiers with the necessary food, candles, stationery, pens, etc., for a successful operation. Authorized civilians could also be supplied. By 1884, a new commissary had been built, and this structure's days as commissary storehouse were over. Well, that includes my presentation. Do any of you have any questions or comments?"

Joshua spoke up, "This year, 2010, is the 150th anniversary of the Pony Express. Did you know that, John?"

"I did, young man, but thank you for reminding me." The guide then walked over to a desk and came back holding a pamphlet. "Since you brought up the Pony Express, I think it might be fun to see how much you young people know about its history. Who's game for a quiz?"

Tom, Joshua, and Margaret raised their hands. "We studied about the Pony Express in our Family Home Evening about a month ago. We also studied the history of this area and the US Army coming against the Mormon people back then. Also, a lot has been in the paper lately about the Pony Express," Tom said.

"Good. Before we start our quiz, let's go around the room and have you tell me your names and your ages. I see some more people have come to listen. There are chairs here for you. Why don't you come and join us?"

Several other families came into the trading post and quickly found chairs to sit on. One by one, every one present spoke his name and where they lived, and the youngsters gave their ages.

"Thank you. We are going to have a little test to see how much these young people know about the history of the Pony Express and Fort Bridger. Their histories are linked, as you will see." John looked down at his notes.

"Who knows when the Pony Express was first organized?"

Tom answered, "April 3, 1860. Oh, and it continued until late October 1861, when the telegraph was finished and working."

"Very good, Tom. Now who knows where in the east it originated?"

"St. Joseph, Missouri. And it ended in Sacramento, California," Margaret said, clearly pleased with herself.

John smiled at them. "You clearly know your history. Okay, here's a tricky question: how many riders ultimately rode the Pony Express line, and what was the average age of the riders?"

Joshua hesitated then put his hand up. "The average age was around twenty, I think, but I don't know how many total riders there were."

"Let me help you out, Joshua. There were 183 altogether who made the journey across the continent. These were very brave men. They were willing to risk death to take the job. Their average weight was 120 lbs. They rode day and night, summer and winter. The riders rode both east to west and west to east, and they traveled once or twice a week, depending on the time of year. Do any of you know how far a rider averaged on his turn to ride?" After a pause, John told them, "Between seventy-five and one hundred miles. A horse averaged ten miles per hour, and fresh horses were provided every ten to fifteen miles. Who knows how many stations were set up along the way to provide fresh horses and supplies and to expedite mail across the nation?"

"I know, I know," Josh answered. "There were 165 all together."

"That's correct, Josh. Tom, can you tell me which modern-day states the Pony Express traveled through?"

"Yes, I believe so. There was Kansas, Nebraska, the northeast corner of Colorado, Wyoming, across Utah, Nevada to California, and then back the other way."

"Very good. Now I have a question for one of you moms or dads. The Pony Express didn't last very long because the telegraph came on line, but it is credited with some successes. Can any of you tell me how it might have been a positive in the history of the West?"

Bill Green got up and went to the front of the group. "My family has always been fascinated with the Pony Express and how it got started, and if John will permit me, I will take a little time and tell you some of the history of this area."

John nodded to Bill. "Terrific, take as much time as you need. If anyone in the group needs to leave, just walk out, and we'll excuse you. Please proceed, Bill."

"First, I will answer your question. The Pony Express improved east-west communication. It also captured the hearts and imagination of people all over the world. Here we are, 150 years later, and we are still intrigued by what those brave men did so many years ago. Also, it proved that a central route could be traveled all winter through our great country. You may be asking yourself: how and why did the Pony Express get started? That is an interesting question. For the answer, we have to go back to the year 1855. At that time, the US government was suspicious of the members of the Church of Jesus Christ of Latter-day Saints, of which I and my family and the Langstons here are members. We are called Mormons, as you know. The church had settled in the Salt Lake area, arriving there beginning in 1847.

"The church purchased this property, where we sit, in 1855. They were the ones who were using the trail the most at the time. However, US president Franklin Pierce sent Albert Sidney Johnston with his army to go into the valley of the Great Salt Lake to remove then-governor Brigham Young from office and replace him with one Alfred Cumming, who would then become governor of the Utah territory. The army's orders were to support the installment of the new governor, using force as necessary if there was resistance. The history of the Mormon Church is one of persecution by the US government for many years.

"Brigham Young, prophet and leader of the Mormon Church at the time hoped to delay the army from coming into the Salt Lake Valley where the church's headquarters were situated, so he sent a gentleman by the name of Lot Smith to carry this out. Lot Smith and a group of Nauvoo Legion rangers traveled east across Wyoming along the stretch where the California, Oregon, and Mormon Trails merge. Eventually, he found the Union wagon train and destroyed several wagons. Lot Smith and his rangers held off the federal soldiers in the cold weather. He did so without his troops harming any soldiers on the federal side. For many Mormons, Lot Smith and his men are considered heroes."

Bill paused briefly and then continued, "This is where the story intersects with the history of the Pony Express. The owners of the destroyed wagons, Russell, Majors, and Waddell, were never reimbursed by the government, and in 1860, they formed the Pony Express to stave off bankruptcy with a new government mail contract. Lot Smith's efforts delayed the US forces from reaching Utah in 1857, forcing them to winter here at Fort Bridger, Wyoming.

"As an interesting ending to this so-called Utah War, Brigham Young was replaced as governor of the territory. A full pardon for charges of sedition and treason was issued to the citizens of the Utah territory by President James Buchanan on the condition that they accept US federal authority, which the Mormons did. Thank you, John, for letting me speak today."

The guide stood up and shook hands with Bill Green. "Thank you, Bill, I really enjoyed that, as I am sure everyone here did."

All present clapped. Several in the group came and shook Bill's hand and then went to shake John's hand. While Bill and John continued to visit together, the children looked at the exhibits in the building.

It was now time to find a camping spot. John pointed to a nice one on the map on the wall that was just a short distance away from the trading post. After saying their goodbyes, they headed out the door and to their motor homes.

Soon they were situated in the campground and ready to get something to eat. The families got their food ready and once again sat out around the table between the campers. Again, after the dinner was finished and the dishes were cleaned up and everything put away, the two families sat under the trees in the campground and enjoyed the lovely evening breeze, watched the sun go down behind the hills, and the night sky glow with stars.

Rose began to sing softly "Now the Day Is Over." One by one, her sisters and then her mother joined, "Night is drawing nigh; Shadows of the evening steal across the sky."

"Do you know the second verse?" Mary asked.

Lily and the girls then sang:

"Jesus, give the weary
Calm and sweet repose;
With thy tend'rest blessing
May our eyelids close."

"Wow, that was beautiful. Your harmony is incredible," Bill commented. "Sing another song for us."

"We'll sing one more, and then you join us on one, okay?" Lily said.

"Okay."

Lily and the girls decided on "Abide with Me; 'Tis Eventide."

After their song, the Greens all clapped. They then all joined in singing "Love One Another."

By now it was close to midnight. Although they had sung their music as quietly as possible, they didn't want to further disturb the other campers. It was time to say good night.

"Tomorrow we need to head home, but we don't have to get up early. Let's eat breakfast out here at, say, ten-thirty. How does that sound, Susie?" Mary asked.

"I'm pretty sure I can make it up by then." Susie laughed.

After hugs and good nights, the friends headed to their respective campers. Lily and her daughters got ready for bed then said their prayers. Lily kissed and hugged each one. "I love you so much," she whispered as she turned out the lights.

The next day after they were ready, they headed home. They went back to Evanston, Wyoming along Interstate 80. They stopped to have lunch just after 2:00 p.m. at a place called Castle Rock on the Utah side.

While they were eating, Bill remarked, "This stretch of Highway 80 is named after a very famous person. Did you happen to notice the name on the side of the highway back a ways?"

"Dwight D. Eisenhower," Tom answered.

"Very good. Now who can tell me something about him?"

Tom spoke up again, "Wasn't he our thirty-fourth president? And I think he was a general in WWII, if I remember correctly."

"Yes, he was the most famous US Army general during World War II. And he was indeed our thirty-fourth president. He was also instrumental in the creation of our interstate system of paved highways all across America. We have him to thank for our beautiful highway system all through our great nation.

"Another interesting bit of history is that President George H. W. Bush signed the law that honored President Eisenhower by naming a highway after him. Bush signed the document one hundred years and one day after Eisenhower's birth. Also, President George H. W. Bush's father, Senator Prescott Bush (R-CT), was one of the chief boosters of President Eisenhower's proposal for financing the Interstate Highway System. That would be President George W. Bush's grandfather. This stretch of highway we are now traveling was named after a great statesman."

Lily said, "Thanks for that bit of history, Bill. I learned something new today. Actually, I have learned a lot of history on this trip. I love learning about our great country."

"Me toos," were all around.

After everything was cleaned up, the families headed to their campers and off they went, continuing along Highway 80 to the west, and then south on Interstate 15, until they returned home to Salt Lake City. The Greens followed the Langston motor home until Tom parked it in its spot in the Langston yard. After heartfelt thanks and hugs, the Greens said their goodbyes and were gone.

Lily and the girls unpacked their clothes and what was left of the food. They would clean out the camper in the morning before heading to Paul Strong's studio. Lily called her parents and Samuel's parents as soon as she got in the house and was able to sit down for a few minutes. They were interested in hearing about the trip. Lily's enthusiasm came through in her conversations with her parents and her in-laws.

"You needed that trip, Lily dear," her mother commented. "I'm so glad you and the girls had a great time."

"We really did, Mom. The Greens are wonderful traveling companions and friends to us. We loved being with them. The children get along so well together. Well, tomorrow we work on our CD again with Paul Strong. I'll call you soon. I love you, Mom. Give Dad my love, okay?"

CHAPTER TWENTY-FOUR

The next morning, Lily and the children cleaned out the motor home and then got ready and headed for Paul Strong's studio. They picked up Aaron, whom they greeted warmly. After visiting with Connie for a few minutes, they were off for the studio.

The day went well. They were able to record several of the songs that Aaron and the Langstons were to do together. Paul was pleased. "We have nearly half of the music recorded now. There will be some do-overs, I suspect, but it is going well."

"It is time for me and my staff to start putting out promotions for the CD to drum up enthusiasm for its coming release."

"Lily, for the next few days, let's concentrate on getting your piano solos recorded. Do you need more time to practice, or do you feel you are ready?"

"Well, we just got back from camping, so I haven't touched my music in the past four or five days. Give me a day or two to brush them up, Paul," Lily answered.

"Fine, come back Friday ready to record them. Will that give you enough time?" Paul asked.

"That should be good. I'll see you then." Lily and the girls and Aaron said goodbye.

After Lily dropped Aaron off, she and the girls drove home. They were tired but felt good about their day.

Over the next two days, Lily worked on her piano pieces. She also took two more of the coins to the dealer to sell. She felt that would give her the money they would need to paint the outside of the Turner's house and do the fix-ups. The other coins she would put in the safe for now. After she sold the coins, she went to the bank and deposited the money in the special account she had opened with the first two coins. The money would cover the painting on the outside of Connie and Aaron's house and the needed repairs to the roof.

When she arrived home, Lily got on the phone and arranged to get bids from three reputable roofing companies to replace the Turner's roof. She then called Connie to let her know that the companies were coming to bid on the work to be done on the roof, and as soon as the decision was made as to who would get the contract, the work would be done.

"Thank you so much," Connie told her. "We have needed a new roof for a long time. We have had it patched a time or two when the rain has come in on us, but it needed to be replaced each time. I can't begin to tell you how much we appreciate all you are doing for us. How can we ever repay you?"

Lily laughed, "Connie, we are getting help from a very special source. When we are all finished, I will tell you who it is, and then you can thank them yourself. Also, getting to know you and Aaron is payment enough. You have become like family to us."

"I feel the same way, Lily. God wanted us to find each other, but the cost for you and your family was far too great. Oh, I wish it didn't have to come at such a price," Connie stammered. "I am so sorry."

"Connie, we can't change what has happened. We can only live in the present and have hope, faith, and trust that the future will be good for us. Someday, we will understand why Samuel was taken. It probably won't be in this life, but we will know the whys of everything, I'm sure of it. In the meantime, don't be sad for us, Connie. The Lord is blessing us every day."

"You are a precious person, Lily. Thank you for your friendship. And I love those darling daughters of yours. So does Aaron," Connie added.

After Lily hung up, she turned to her girls who were listening attentively. Bonnie asked her mother, "When do you think we will be able to paint the outside of Connie and Aaron's house, Mom?"

"Let's get the new roof done, and then we'll get as many people as we can from the Turner's ward to work on the painting. That should make the work go quickly. We'll see how many can help, and when the best time would be for them to come paint together. If we can't get it done before school starts, then maybe they will be willing to do the work on Labor Day weekend, which is the first weekend in September."

Lily continued, "Jacob Manning told me he wanted to help and that he wanted his son James to come and help too. I think we will have several who will be willing to come work. James is your age, Bonnie, ten. He is autistic. Jacob said he likes to help even though he has to be given simple tasks to do."

Susie asked, "What is that word you said, Mom, *autistic*?"

"Good question, Susie. I know little about the condition, but I'll tell you what I do know. Then Jacob can explain a lot more about the illness when we see him."

Lily walked over to the couch and sat down with her daughters. "Autism occurs in approximately one out of every seventy births here in Utah. Most of the time, it shows up in infancy. The experts say that no two children with autism will act the same way. When a child is born autistic, his brain doesn't always work the way it should. This is why these children do things that may cause harm to themselves or others. They are impulsive and cannot stop themselves from behavior that you girls know instinctively is wrong. They don't react to situations as normal children do in many cases.

"I don't want to frighten you. There is no need to be worried about James, I am sure. He is supervised by his father, grandparents who live with them, and by his teachers and friends and neighbors. When we get a chance to talk to Jacob about James, we can ask him a lot of questions. There may be some special signals that Jacob and others have to let James know he is loved or steers him from doing something that will hurt others or himself. Mr. Manning can teach you girls and me and probably Aaron and Connie some of the things to watch out for and how to interact with James. I know that supervision is the key to protecting these children. We'll learn all we can so we can be James's friends too."

"I'm going to be James's friend, Mom," Susie said.

"We all will," Bonnie told her little sister. "We can be great friends and help him whenever he needs us. We'll play with him. And maybe we can teach him some of our songs too."

"Great idea, Bonnie. And just maybe, he can teach us a thing or two." Lily smiled at her daughters.

"Now, Rose, will you and Bonnie and Susie get the table set, and I'll warm up the soup and get the dinner rolls out of the oven. The buzzer just went off, so they must be ready. And we'll have ice cream for dessert."

After dinner dishes were cleaned up, Lily went over her songs again. The girls got out a game and played until it was time to go get ready for bed.

The following morning, Lily left for the studio to record her piano pieces. Her daughters went over to the neighbor's to play with their friends until their mother came home to retrieve them.

CHAPTER TWENTY-FIVE

Aaron kissed his mother goodbye and left for the hospital. It was Saturday morning once again. Lily had called him the night before to tell him that her piano pieces had been recorded. Paul Strong wanted him back in his studio Monday morning to finish recording his solo work.

Also, she told him that the bids on the roof had come back, and she had chosen a roofer to do the work. He would start on the roof the following Tuesday and planned to be finished in a week.

After the roof was completed, Lily would arrange to have people come and help paint the outside of the house the way he had suggested doing it—brown with red trim on the windows and red doors. He liked that idea. She was working on getting a lot of people together on Labor Day weekend. Hopefully, everyone wouldn't be going away for the holiday.

Let's see, Aaron thought to himself, *next week is the last week before school starts again. Then I will be in school one week, and then it will be Labor Day weekend. My birthday is next week. Yeah, I'll be sixteen. I wonder if we could have the Langstons over for a party. I'll ask Mom if we can.*

Aaron went to work mopping floors as usual. He greeted the staff members he met and stopped to talk to a few of the doctors and nurses as they greeted him in the hall. The day went quickly, and it was soon time for his miniconcert once again.

He had become something of a legend in the hospital now. Everyone who knew him knew of the recording he was making with the Langstons. They kept asking him when he expected it to be ready for sale. Everyone wanted to have a copy. Aaron was very excited about the CD now that it was close to being finished. He still had two of his songs to be recorded as solos, and then there were three or four of the songs to be recorded of him and the Langstons together. Paul Strong and his staff would do whatever the studio needed to do to get it in marketable condition, and then it would be out in the music stores for sale.

Today, the concert was to be held on the geriatrics floor. The elderly patients were gathered in their wheelchairs or beds in the main visitors' area. Everything was set up and ready to go. When Aaron walked into the room, nurses and patients clapped. There were even three doctors who were on their breaks who had come to enjoy Aaron's music. Some of the nurses had finished their shifts but stayed to listen to the songs.

Aaron sat down and strummed his guitar, making sure it was tuned. He started off with some old western music, some of the classics by Roy Orbison, Roy Rogers, Hank Williams, and one or two of Gene Autry's hits. Then he changed and sang some hymns about faith and God. When he was finished, there was hardly a dry eye in the room. All who came to hear Aaron sing and play his guitar were deeply touched by the beauty of the music. They didn't want the concert to end. He played longer than his allotted time, but finally, he stood up and walked over to each patient and either shook their hands or, for the ladies, he leaned over and kissed their foreheads.

"Thank you," they said if they could or gave him a smile or a little nod. He stayed and waved goodbye to each one as they left the room.

"Young man," one of the doctors approached him, "you have a remarkable voice. And your ability on that guitar of yours is really something. I am looking forward to getting your CD when it comes out. Thanks for performing for the patients. You are a blessing to this hospital, son."

"Thank you, Doctor..."

"Its Dr. Smith."

"Thank you, Doctor Smith. You're very kind. I love the opportunity to sing for the patients and for the staff. And it's an honor to have you doctors come when you can," Aaron told him.

After Doctor Smith shook Aaron's hand and left the room, Aaron put his guitar away and left the hospital. Others waved warmly as he walked out the door. He strapped his guitar on his back, got on his bike, and rode home.

CHAPTER TWENTY-SIX

Connie got on the telephone and talked to the men in their church congregation and asked them to make an announcement in church tomorrow, Sunday, about painting the outside of her home on the Saturday of Labor Day weekend. Lily had asked her to do that, and she had obliged, somewhat hesitantly. Asking people to come and paint her house was not something she was comfortable doing. She didn't like to be a bother to people any more than her disability already made her. But Lily had requested she make the calls, and she would do anything to help Lily, who had become very dear to her.

Connie thought, *I would do anything to help Lily. Who was trying to help us? What a silly statement. Anyway, as absurd as that statement is, that is exactly what I am doing, helping Lily help me.* Connie chuckled at the absurdity of the thought.

The men quickly agreed to make the announcements and also told Connie that they and their older children would like to come help too.

Connie called Lily back to tell her what the men had told her. Lily was pleased.

CHAPTER TWENTY-SEVEN

Getting the paint and anything else they didn't have would have to wait until the rest of the songs were recorded.

Aaron had talked to his mother about having Lily and the children over Friday evening for his sixteenth birthday party, and she was delighted to say yes. Bonnie and Susie looked forward to the party. Rose said emphatically that she wouldn't go. Nothing Lily said would persuade her to change her mind.

Lily and the girls and Aaron worked hard over the following week to record the rest of the music. Finally, by Thursday evening, Paul Strong clapped his hands as the last note of the last song was taped.

"I think we are finally done, people. And it sounds great. Next Monday, my staff and I will start putting the music together in the order I think it should be on the CD and get it ready for sale. I'll let you know if there will be any do-overs. Right now I don't think there will be, but as we start putting everything together, there may be one or two spots that will need to be worked on a little more. I'll let you know. Good work, everyone. And you girls, wow, you were great."

"Thank you, Mr. Strong," Rose said, "for giving us this opportunity."

"We have started to advertise. You probably have heard the commercials for the CD. Have you?" Paul asked.

"Yes, we have," Lily replied.

"The people I work with at the hospital are anxious to get a copy of it when it is ready for sale," Aaron said. "I think we will sell a lot of copies to the doctors and nurses and even to some of the patients."

"Great," Paul told Aaron. "What proceeds you earn from copies you are able to sell at the hospital are yours to keep, Aaron. It will be like selling them after your miniconcerts. That is the agreement."

"I'll split the money with the Langstons."

"That isn't necessary, Aaron. You take the money and put it in an account for your mother's medical needs. You told us there is a possibility she may be able to walk again one day. Save the money for that day, Aaron."

"Thanks, Lily, and thank you, Rose, Bonnie, and Susie."

"You are very welcome, Aaron," Bonnie said. Rose just made a face. Lily looked sternly at her daughter, but Rose just turned and walked away.

CHAPTER TWENTY-EIGHT

Connie called Lily with exciting news, "Lily, there are fifty people from our ward who have signed up to come Saturday morning to help paint the house."

"Wow, good news, Connie," Lily commented. "That means with them and Aaron and Jacob and James and my girls and me, there will be almost sixty people there to help. Now that we are through recording the CD, I'll pick up Aaron, and we'll go get the paint and enough rollers and pans and paintbrushes for those who are helping. Do you think you and Aaron could figure out how much paint we will need? I believe that if Aaron measures the length and height of the outside walls, the store can figure out how much paint we will need. We will buy extra just in case. Also, I need the total number of windows you have and the sizes of them for the red paint, plus the back and front doors, of course."

"I'm pretty sure we can get our neighbors to come measure everything for us. I'll call you back as soon as I have the measurements, Lily."

"Thanks, Connie. Bye for now."

Friday evening came, and it was time to go to the Turners for Aaron's party. Lily, Bonnie, and Susie had purchased a gift certificate at a music store so that Aaron could choose whatever he wanted. They had also purchased some snacks and treats to have at the party. Connie and Aaron greeted the Langstons warmly at the door. Susie stepped up to Aaron and gave him a big bear hug. He hugged her back.

"Rose didn't come?" Aaron asked. "Is there anything I can do to make things right?" He murmured, "I'll do anything."

Lily placed her hand on his arm. "She just needs time, Aaron." Lily smiled. "Actually, I could tell she really wanted to come. She is probably sitting right now on her bed wishing she had come. Just give her time. She'll come around."

"Okay, I will give her all the time she needs. I just want her to forgive me. I hope she can someday." Aaron then pointed to the yard and said, "It is such a lovely evening, we decided to eat outdoors on the patio. I have fired up the barbecue, and it is all ready for the wieners and hamburgers. The table is all set out there, and everything is ready except for the meat," Aaron told them. He led the way. Lily helped Connie with her wheelchair.

While Aaron cooked the hamburger and wieners, Connie faced Lily and the girls and said, "I got a call from the Relief Society president this afternoon. She told me that the sisters will bring food in on the Saturday the men and boys come over to paint the house. That would be one week from tomorrow. Isn't that great?"

"That's wonderful, Connie. We'll be able to keep everyone busy who can possibly stay for the day without worrying about food. I have a couple of large water jugs that we can keep ice water in, maybe water in one and punch in the other. I'll bring them over that morning with lots of ice, and plenty of cups too."

A few minutes later, the meat was cooked, and the families sat down to eat. Bonnie gave the blessing on the food. They laughed and visited together as they enjoyed the meal. Afterward, Aaron went into the house and brought out the birthday cake Connie had made and decorated. On the top in colored frosting, it had a male figure holding a guitar. Connie had put her whole heart and soul into the decorations, and she felt they had turned out very well. The others agreed she had done herself proud.

"Happy birthday" was sung, and the cake cut and passed out. With the cake, they also had ice cream. After giving Aaron the gift certificate, Lily passed out the treats she had brought—miniature guitars and tiny male figures. These she had purchased at the same store where they bought the gift certificate. They were very cute, and Aaron was pleased.

For the next hour, Bonnie, Susie, and Aaron played croquet on the grass. Aaron had rummaged through the outdoor closet and had found the dusty game. After the wickets were set out in their places, he showed the girls how to play. It wasn't long before the sisters were ganging up on Aaron and knocking his ball out of bounds.

"Hey, you're not supposed to treat your host this way. Quit ganging up on me. No fair," Aaron commented with a laugh.

They were having such a good time that Lily and Connie sat and watched them without saying much.

When Connie spoke finally, she had tears in her eyes, "Lily, Aaron hasn't had much time in his young life to make many friends. Most of the time, he has gone to school and comes home right after to take care of me."

"You and your girls are giving him a life he really has never had before. Watching him laugh with them and tease them, well, it's very special to me."

"I am glad that they are good friends too, Connie. When we were on our trip with our friends, the Greens, last week, we each told of what we are thankful for. The girls said one of their most important blessings has been getting to know you and Aaron. Isn't it interesting how things work out in life?" Lily put her arm around Connie's shoulders.

"Oh, yes. The Lord brings people into our lives when we need them the most, of that I am sure," Connie said softly. "I just wish it hadn't had to be at such a price."

"Everything happens for a reason, Connie. We won't know the whys and the wherefores while we are here on earth, but I believe we were meant to be friends, soul mates even. So, dear Connie, we won't dwell on the negative. We'll just count our many blessings each day from now on. That's what the Lord would have us do, count our many blessings."

"Bless you, Lily."

CHAPTER TWENTY-NINE

The week before Labor Day was filled with a flurry of to-dos. With arms full of school supplies, Lily got her daughters into their respective grades. She met their teachers and got them settled in as best she could.

Then, with the measurements of Connie and Aaron's house, including the number of windows and their sizes and the two doors and their sizes, Lily headed over to the hardware store not far from their home. Aaron was now back at school and would not be able to be with her to get the supplies. The clerks, however, were very helpful and worked with her to get everything she would need to have fifty-plus individuals paint. She remembered to buy some extension poles for the rollers so the painting could be done without having to stand on ladders.

The trim at the very top of the walls under the eaves would have to be done by some standing on ladders, but hopefully that was all. Some of the men agreed to go to the house and do the high areas on Friday so they would not be in the way of the other painters. They would bring their own ladders with them.

The roofers were almost done. They would be done tomorrow, Tuesday. *If all goes well,* Lily thought, *everything should be done by Saturday evening. Oh, dear Lord, please bless that no one will be hurt and that all will go very well.* With that fervent silent prayer on her lips, she watched as the clerks filled her car to capacity with her purchases.

After Monday's classes, Aaron rode his bike over to the hospital to let them know that he would not be able to work on the coming

Saturday, as he would be helping paint his house. He reassured the staff there that he would be back the following Saturday to fulfill his duties and to play for the patients at the usual time.

As the week went by, the girls and Aaron got settled in at their respective schools. Lily worked in the yard. She called to let Jacob Manning know the time they would all be over to Turners on Saturday to begin painting. She told him how many were planning to come and that the Relief Society sisters in Connie's ward were going to bring over a meal at noon.

"Jacob, my daughters have a great many questions to ask you about James. They want to know about autism. I know something about it, but not a lot. I have questions too," Lily commented.

"Do you think we could have a family home evening together, say next Monday, and talk about it? Is James comfortable about having people talk about it in front of him?"

"Lily, James knows he has autism. We tell him he is a very special child, one of God's chosen children. I think he will be fine with it. And we would love to have family home evening together with you. Shall we have it at your house or mine?"

"Let's have it here, Jacob. How does seven o'clock sound to you?"

"That would be great, Lily," Jacob said. "How about if James and I stop on the way over and pick up a couple of pizzas. What kind do your girls like?"

"Thanks, Jacob. They like pepperoni the best."

"Okay, pepperoni it is. James and I will see you at the Turners Saturday at nine in the morning, ready to work. Bye for now."

CHAPTER THIRTY

Lily, Rose, Bonnie, and Susie got dressed in their grubbiest clothes to paint. Lily made sure they piled their hair up on top of their heads and insisted they wear hats. This time, maybe, they could avoid getting paint in their hair.

Lily and her daughters arrived at Connie and Aaron's house a half hour before the others were to arrive. Aaron came out to help Lily with the supplies.

"When everyone gets here, let's divide them into groups, Aaron. We'll choose a leader or captain for each of the four sides of the house and have him take his group and paint one side of the house. They can pick up what they and their group will need and go and get started."

"Good idea, Lily."

They laid out the brushes and pans and extension poles and stirred the brown paint so it would be all ready.

Next they put up a table and set the jugs of ice water and juice on it, along with the cups.

Soon everyone was there and anxious to get started. Jacob Manning was chosen to head up one group, and three other captains were quickly chosen. After the groups were formed, Lily asked Aaron if he would say a prayer for the Lord's guidance and safety in their endeavors.

Before Jacob took his team over to the east side of the house, he turned to James and said, "Son, we have a very important assignment for you. You will be in charge of handing out the water when these folks get thirsty. Will you do that for us, James?"

"Yes, Dad, I can do that."

Susie looked at her mother. "Mom, would it be all right if I helped James with the drinks?"

"What a great idea, honey, if that is all right with James."

Susie walked over to James. "My name is Susie. Would it be all right if I help you with the drinks, James?"

"I think so. Dad, would it be all right if Susie help me?"

Jacob smiled at Susie and then at James. "Thank you, Susie, that would be very helpful."

Lily and her other two daughters followed Jacob to the east side of the house. From her vantage point, she could keep an eye on Susie and James. She would go from time to time around the house to see who was thirsty and then direct the children with their water and punch to wherever it was needed. The day was sunny and expected to be in the 90s, so people would indeed get thirsty.

Altogether, there were approximately twelve on each side to work. It took a few minutes to arrange everyone and give them their assignments. Soon they were hard at work scraping, wiping, sanding where it was needed. The younger men got the long poles and attached the paint rollers to the ends. With these, they were able to reach high enough on the walls to cover the tops of the walls completely. The men who had come the day before had done a nice job of painting the trim at the top of the wall and down a ways so that the young men had no trouble nicely finishing painting the tops of the walls. After they were done, the others could paint the middle and bottom parts of the walls.

At noon, the ladies from their ward came and set up their luncheon. They brought fried chicken, potato and green salads, rolls and butter. The jugs were refilled with punch and ice water. All the workers washed their hands at the outside tap and sat down to enjoy their meal.

Jacob found Lily and sat down beside her and the children. The tables were set up in the shade of an old oak tree on the Turner's property. The shade was a very welcome change after standing in the warm sunshine all morning.

Lily spoke to James and Susie, "You kids are doing a great job with those drinks. I am very proud of you."

"With all these folks here," Jacob noted, "we will be done with the brown paint in about two hours or so. Then another couple of hours for the doors and the trim around the windows. We should be done by five or five-thirty. Do you think, Lily?"

She looked at the house and then at Jacob. "There are some who have to leave soon. I hope we can get all the walls painted before they have to leave, then those who are left can work on the trim around the windows and paint the two doors. If all goes well, we should be finished as you said, Jacob."

After everyone had eaten, the Relief Society sisters cleaned up and put everything away. Most of the sisters then left, but a few stayed to visit with Connie as she watched the painting from her wheelchair situated under the old oak. She thought it wise to stay out of everyone's way. Every once in a while, Susie and James came over to give her and her companions something to drink. They were being very serious about their assignment, hardly ever stopping to play. Connie enjoyed watching them as they worked at their duties.

Just as everything seemed to be going so well, James gave a yelp from the farthest area away from where Lily and Jacob were painting. They quickly put down their brushes and ran to where the sound came from.

"What happened, young man?" Jacob asked his son. James's arm was being held by a stern-looking older gentleman. In James's hand was the telltale culprit, a brush dripping with brown paint. Susie was standing just behind them with a surprised look on her face. Her right arm had been sloshed with the paint.

James started to cry. "I'm sorry, I'm sorry." Jacob went to his son. He knew exactly what had happened. With his tendency to be compulsive, James had wanted to find out what would happen if he did a little painting himself. Susie got in the way. Before the boy could do any more damage, the man had quickly grabbed his arm.

Jacob turned to the man and introduced himself. "Thank you very much. I really appreciate your intervening before this got too far out of hand. James is autistic. He does things compulsively. He always feels badly afterward."

"That's okay. By the way, my name is Ted. I am glad I was where I could help this young lady." He pointed to Susie and smiled encouragement.

Lily said, "I'll take Susie in the house and clean off the paint. She'll be as good as new. Come, Susie."

Susie followed her mother into the house. Lily washed her arm and settled her down. "I'm sure Jacob is talking with James right now, honey. James is very sorry for what he did. I don't think he can help himself, so we need to be very patient with him. Can you do that, Susie?"

"Yes, Mom, I'll try to be patient with him."

"Good girl."

Jacob took James over to some chairs and sat down with him. "James, do you know what you could have done to not get into trouble?"

"Yes, Dad. I could have asked that man if I could have painted a little bit while he was watching. I just wanted to do some painting." James started to cry again. "He put the paintbrush down to take a drink of water, and I just grabbed it. Then I turned and got paint on Susie. Is she mad at me?"

"Let's go find out."

"Susie," Jacob called to her as she and Lily came out of the house, "James wants to know if you are angry with him. He is very sorry."

"No, James, I'm okay. We can still be friends."

Jacob then took his son over to the side of the house where the painting was nearly completed. Jacob handed his son his brush and then guided him to dip it into the paint and brush the paint on the wall. After a few minutes, James had had enough of the exercise.

"Let's go see if anyone wants a drink, James," Susie said. Off they went to do their assignment once again. All was forgiven.

When the walls were nearly finished, some of the men started on the red trim around the windows where the brown paint had dried. Two men took off the doors and set them up on blocks to be painted by some of the women who were there to help. After the doors were painted and dried, they were rehung. The painting was all finished. The workers cleaned everything up, washed out the brushes and rollers, and then walked around the house and admired their handiwork. Everyone agreed that a very good job was done. It was just after five o'clock.

Lily asked one of the men who was a painter by trade if he would take the brushes, rollers, and pans and store them. "You are welcome to use anything you can," Lily told him. What was left of the paint was stored in Turner's garage to use for brushups, if need be.

"Well, Jacob, you were right on with the time we would be finished."

"It looks great, doesn't it?" Jacob turned to Connie. "The roof looks good, and these folks here did a superb job, don't you think?"

Connie grabbed Jacob's hand. "It looks wonderful. How am I ever going to be able to thank everyone? I took down all the names of everyone who came while I was sitting over there watching, and I will send out thank-you notes. But that doesn't seem to be enough. I appreciate this so much."

Lily put her hand on Connie's shoulder. "There is still some money left over, and so we were wondering about freshening up the landscaping a bit. Would that be okay, Connie?"

"That would be lovely. You can see we have a few dead spots in our lawn, so, yes, we'd like that. You told me, Lily, that you would let me know who is behind all this, remember?"

"Let us say goodbye to the folks who are leaving, and then we will be back to tell you the story."

Lily turned and walked over to where people were beginning to get into their cars. She went to each one and thanked them for their hard work. They all told her that they were happy to have been able to help. They all loved Connie. Lily could tell that in the way they spoke of her. It made them feel good to know they could do something like this that would please both her and Aaron.

After Lily said the last goodbye, she and Jacob walked over to where Connie sat. Aaron and Lily's daughters were sitting beside her drinking some punch. Jacob began to tell Connie about Carson Hunter and the ten gold coins. Connie sat in rapt attention as he told the story, and she chuckled when he got to the part where Lily had caught him hiding one of the coins in her garden early that morning, just over a month ago now. When he had asked Lily what she planned to do with the coins, she quickly told him she wanted to paint Connie and Aaron's house for them and have a new roof put on.

"So, Connie and Aaron, this you see before you is the result of our secret scheming and planning," Jacob said, smiling.

Connie laughed. "Thanks for telling me the story, Jacob. I will add Mr. Hunter to my list of thank yous to do. What a kind man he is. I have always admired him and the unselfish work he has done for this community."

"I think we all have much to thank him for. The cancer hospital where Aaron works and plays and sings for the patients is there because of Mr. Hunter. And he has done so much more, much of which is done in secret so the recipients never find out the many kindnesses done for the people of this community, and I expect his philanthropy reaches far beyond our state. In fact, I know it does," Jacob said, smiling.

"Well, Connie and Aaron, I am going to take my daughters home and get some of this paint off them and me. I'll call you next week." Lily promised.

Jacob and James followed the Langstons, waving at Connie and Aaron as Lily and her girls got ready to get into their car. Jacob turned to Lily.

"I would take you girls out to dinner if you wanted to go," Jacob hinted.

"I don't think we want to be seen in public right now, thanks anyway." Lily laughed. "We'll see you two Monday night, seven sharp, okay?"

"Okay. See you Monday, Susie," James called.

"I think you have a boyfriend, Susie." Bonnie teased her sister as Jacob and James walked away.

"James is really nice. We had fun giving out the water and punch, at least until he swung that paintbrush at me. But I still like James," Susie said.

"Good for you. It's nice to have friends. I hope you and James will always be friends. I want him to be my friend too," Bonnie told her sister.

CHAPTER THIRTY-ONE

Sunday morning, Lily and the girls went to their church meetings as usual. Lily taught her Sunday school class. She was now teaching Rose's class, the twelve and thirteen-year-olds. Rose loved having her mother for her teacher. And Lily loved having her in her class.

After their church services, they drove over to spend the lunch hour with Samuel's parents. Lily and the girls told the Langstons that their CD was finished now and in the hands of Paul Strong's staff. They were not sure when it would be ready to sell.

"We painted Aaron and Connie Turner's house yesterday," Bonnie said. "There were a whole lot of people there."

"We painted it brown, with red doors and red trim around the windows. It looks really nice," Rose added.

"I helped James Manning give the people drinks," Susie told her grandparents. "It was a very important job. Lots of people got thirsty, so we were always busy." Then Susie added shyly, "He got paint on me on accident. But I still like James."

Lily had already told her in-laws about the ten gold coins that Carson Hunter had bequeathed to her and the story behind her finding Jacob Manning in her garden, so she concluded with, "There is still a little over five hundred dollars left from the funds I received after selling four of the coins, so we are going to have a landscaper go over and work with Connie and Aaron to plan what landscaping they want to do to brighten up their yard. Then that project will be finished."

Dallas Langston looked lovingly at her daughter-in-law and said, "You have grown very fond of the Turners, haven't you, Lily? I sense a real bond there."

"Yes, Connie is very special. She does not dwell on her disability, ever. She is always upbeat and kind. And Aaron, he is precious. The girls and I went over to their home for Aaron's sixteenth birthday party. Yes, Dallas, we have become very close friends."

Matt Langston remarked, "I am anxious to get a copy of your CD. Was it hard work making it?"

"It took a lot of time, Grandpa," Bonnie said. "We had to do some of the songs over and over again until Paul Strong thought they were good enough to record. It was tiring, but we really enjoyed it, especially working with Aaron. He is really, really good."

"Mr. Strong has a room in his building where he keeps snacks and all kinds of drinks. He also has a television. When we weren't practicing our songs or recording, we spent a lot of time in there," Rose added.

"I liked the snacks," Susie chimed in.

"All in all, it was a very rewarding experience," Lily told her in-laws. "But we will have to wait and see how successful it was when the CD is released."

After a while, Lily and her daughters said their goodbyes with hugs and kisses. Soon they were at Lily's parent's home to spend the supper hour with them. The conversation went much as it had at the Langstons.

It had been a lovely Sunday, and when they got ready for bed that evening, their prayers were prayers of thanksgiving. Lily knew the Lord was blessing them. She felt it in so many ways.

As she fell asleep, she thought of the last six gold coins she still had in the safe. *I wonder what we should do with the rest of them.*

CHAPTER THIRTY-TWO

Monday morning, Jacob walked into Carson Hunter's office. After a warm greeting and handshake, Jacob sat down opposite his friend.

Smiling, Carson asked Jacob how Lily Langston and her family were doing, and if she had said anything about the gold coins to him. For the next half hour or so, Jacob told him about how he had placed a coin in Lily's flower beds at the first of every month, starting in June.

"When I placed the second coin in her garden on the first day of July at the same time in the morning, Lily figured out my routine. She was waiting in her garden on August 1. It was very early and still quite dark. She nearly scared me to death." Jacob chuckled. "She was wearing a white sweater and white pair of slacks, and she looked like an angel standing there with the sunlight behind her. Carson, I have never seen anything so beautiful." Jacob paused and then continued, "After she caught me in the act of placing another coin in her garden, there was nothing to do but to give her the rest of the coins. I then asked her what she had done with the first two coins and what she might want to do with the other eight, now that she had them.

"She didn't hesitate. She told me that the first two coins had already been spent painting the inside of the Turner's house, which they did along with Bill Green and his family. The Greens and the Langstons are good friends. Bill Green fixed some door hinges and did some other little jobs that were needed around the Turner house also.

"Then this last Saturday, several people in Turner's ward and some of their neighbors came over to the Turner house, and they and Lily's family and my son, James, and I painted the outside of the house. Lily still has some of the money left over from the four coins she sold, so she is hiring a landscaper to spruce up the Turner's yard for them. I don't know what she has in mind for the other six coins, or whether she plans on just keeping them for now."

Carson Hunter spoke, "Jacob, that's a great story. Well done. You know I have been fond of Lily and her family for a long time. I sense that you are becoming quite attached to them yourself. Am I sensing something special here?"

"You are very perceptive, Carson. Yes, Lily is someone like no one else I have ever known. And those girls of hers…they are very much like their mother. I am becoming very fond of all of them."

Carson, with a twinkle in his eye, smiled. "I'll be watching, Jacob."

CHAPTER THIRTY-THREE

Lily got the girls off to school and then called the landscaper who had worked on their yard over the years. He agreed to call Connie and work with her and Aaron on their landscaping. Then Lily called Connie and let her know to expect a call that morning about the yard work.

After hanging up, Lily called the school district to see what her assignments would be for the school year as far as substitute teaching was concerned. She told them she wanted to work only once or twice a week, if possible. They told her they had added her to the list of substitute teachers and would put an asterisk beside her name and a note to call her to work no more than two days a week.

In spite of herself, Lily looked forward to their family home evening that night with Jacob and James Manning. The day dragged by as she tried to stay busy. She washed some clothes and tidied up the house and did some reading. When the girls got home, she helped them with their homework.

They had been asked to sing in Sacrament Meeting the following Sunday, and so they spent an hour deciding on what to sing and practicing the number.

At seven o'clock sharp, the doorbell rang. Susie ran to open the door for Jacob and James. "Hi, James," Susie said. "Welcome to our home."

Jacob handed the pizzas to Susie. "Can you carry that okay?" Jacob asked.

"Barely," Susie answered, carrying them carefully over to the table that had already been set.

Lily put a tossed salad together, and Rose mixed up some fruit punch. After the blessing on the food, they ate and visited. After the dinner was over and the clean-up was finished, the two families retired to the family room to have their Family Home Evening.

Bonnie gave the opening prayer. Rose read a scripture and then a song was sung. It was one of Susie's favorite primary songs, "We are a Happy Family."

Jacob then spoke, "Your mother told me you had some questions about James's disability. You can ask us anything you wish. Susie?"

"Is autism catching?"

"No, it isn't, Susie. When a person has autism, his brain doesn't always work the way it should. And no two children with autism think the same way or do the same things."

Bonnie asked Jacob, "What causes autism?"

"Good question, Bonnie. The experts are still trying to figure that one out. It could be a combination of genetics and the environment. Genetics is what is passed down through a family. The environment means something outside of our bodies may be contributing. Some people believe immunization shots babies and young children receive may cause autism, though this has not in any way been proven. There are ongoing studies, but they are not conclusive as yet. No one really knows for sure."

"Can it be cured, Jacob?" asked Rose.

"No, there is as yet no cure. There are some medications that help with the symptoms, but no, there is no cure yet."

"How early can a child be diagnosed?"

"Young babies who do not babble or point by age one, do not speak single words or two-word phrases by age two, do not respond to their names, have poor eye contact. That means they won't look at you when you speak to them. They may have poor language or social skills. These are some of the early signs of autism."

"Did you know early on that James had autism, Jacob?" Lily questioned.

"My wife, Trudy, and I suspected something was wrong very early on," Jacob said. "We were in the process of having him tested when Trudy was killed."

"I'm so sorry, Jacob. That must have been very difficult, losing your wife like that and knowing that your precious son had a serious problem too."

"My parents moved in with James and me. Without them, I could not have gotten through those terrible years." Jacob turned to his son and smiled. "My parents saved my sanity in so many ways, and James adores them, don't you, James?"

"I love Grandma and Grandpa. They play with me and read me stories. Then when Dad comes home, we all play together, don't we, Dad?" James said.

"Yes, we do, son."

Jacob continued, "One of the symptoms James has is panic attacks. Just imagine, for instance, that a big bus is speeding toward you as you step into a crosswalk to go across the street, and when it is just a few feet away from hitting you, you step out of the way and are safe. After a few minutes, you realize that you are fine, and the feeling of fear leaves you. But for James, it doesn't go away. He relives it over and over in his mind. That is what autism does to you. Because James's brain doesn't work like a normal child, if he gets the urge to do something bad, like maybe push a child down, he is not being mean. It is just that he has a hard time stopping himself. What happened the other day at the Turner home when we were all there painting is a very good example. James got the urge to paint and grabbed Ted's paintbrush, and just before Ted was able to stop him, he got paint on Susie. Then, of course, he feels badly about what he did." Jacob continued, "Also, he doesn't like noise, and he avoids being touched."

"Is there anything my girls and I can do to help him?" Lily asked.

"I am glad you asked, Lily. There are some things James and I do to understand each other. Right, son?"

"We sing a song. Do you want me to sing it for you?" James stood up and began to sing in a slightly off-key voice,

I'm STRONG. I'm SMART. I'm a CHILD OF GOD.
I'm STRONG. I'm SMART. I'm a CHILD OF GOD.
I'm STRONG. I'm SMART. I'm a CHILD OF GOD.
So I can OVERCOME anything!

As he sang, he signed with his fingers to the words. Jacob said, "When James is afraid, he will sing and sign this little song. It is meant to let him know that Heavenly Father is with him always and will keep him safe. Would you like to learn the signs so you can sing along with James?"

"Yes," Susie jumped up. "Teach us the signs, okay, James?"

For several minutes, Jacob and James taught the signs to Lily and her daughters. They were soon singing and signing as good as James could do it.

"Now, there is another thing we do. Because James and most all autistic children do not like to be touched, we have devised a greeting that says, 'Hi, I love you.' James, will you show Lily and the girls the sign we use?"

James got up and made the sign of "I love you." This consists of holding out the thumb, the pointer finger, and the pinky finger while holding down the middle and ring fingers.

"This means 'I love you'," said James.

Jacob said, "Now, Susie, make the sign and press the thumb, forefinger, and little finger to James's thumb, forefinger, and little finger. That is the greeting we give each other. That means, 'I'm glad to see you, and I love you, James.' Good, Susie, now you other girls can try it. It works great, doesn't it? Whenever you see James, you can give him that special greeting. He'll like that."

"There is one more thing that my parents and I have devised to help James know when he is not to do something he shouldn't, when he needs to be reminded to stop and think about the consequences of his actions before he acts. We have placed a large stop sign on our refrigerator. The red circle reads STOP, the yellow reads THINK, and the green reads REACT. We have hand signals for these words also. Then, whenever James is feeling the urge to do something he shouldn't, say and sign with him STOP, THINK, REACT. The signs will help him redirect his energy and encourage him to think before he acts."

For the next half hour, Jacob and James taught Lily and her daughters the hand signs for stop, think, and react. They also went over the other signs again to make sure they had them solidly in their minds.

"That was fun," Susie said. Her sisters agreed wholeheartedly with her.

Lily smiled and said, "Let's have our dessert now. The girls made cookies for us. We hope you like chocolate chip cookies, James."

"Yes, I do. I like lots of kinds of cookies. Thank you for making the cookies."

"You're welcome, James," Rose told him.

After the dessert was served and eaten, Lily, her daughters, and Jacob and James knelt around the sofa. Lily gave the prayer, a heartfelt prayer of thanks for the wonderful evening they had spent together, for their many blessings, for great friends. She finished with a plea for continuing health and strength.

"It was a very special evening, Jacob. Thanks for teaching us your special signs and your song, James," Lily made the sign for "I love you" and placed her fingers up for James to touch. James was pleased. He then went around and did the same for the girls and his father.

"Jacob, before you and James leave, will you think about what we should do with the other gold coins I still have? It might be nice to give each one to a family who is struggling somehow. Wait, I just thought of an idea. Aaron has a lot of contacts with families who are struggling with health issues. He could help us find families who need a little boost, a little brightness in their sea of troubles. What do you think?"

"Lily, that would be fantastic. You have six left. You could give them out to six needy families. I could help Aaron find the right families. Is that what you would like to do with them, Lily?"

Lily looked at her daughters. "What do you think, girls? Would that be a good way to use the last of the gold coins?"

"Yes," they all chimed in at once.

"All right, then. That is settled." Lily smiled. "I'll call Aaron, and you and he can figure out the families to give them to."

"Good night, everyone." James waved as he went out the door. Jacob held Lily's hand for a moment and then waved goodbye to the girls.

Later, when the girls were ready for bed and Lily was ready to call it a night, Rose asked her mother, "Why would Heavenly Father have babies and little children be born with illnesses like what James has? It seems cruel, don't you think?"

Lily had her daughters come and sit on her bed with her and then answered Rose's question as well as she could, knowing that the spirit was guiding her answer.

"A long, long time ago, before any of us were born, we each counseled with our Father in heaven and, with His help, made some very important decisions about what our lives on earth would be like and what challenges we would be willing to take on. I'm certain that our Father, who knows us so well and loves us so much, gave us advice and told us what He thought we should do. But He left the final decisions up to us. We knew our life here on earth would not be easy, that we would be faced with tough challenges. For instance, some of us would be born in a poor country, or have to live through a great calamity, like a flood or an earthquake, or be born with a disability.

"However, we also understood that if we accepted the difficult challenges, we would grow faster and become stronger than we would without them. So we had some really tough decisions to make. Should we take the easier road, on which life wouldn't be quite so difficult or frightening, or should we take the hard one, the one that would make us stronger? It is obvious that James chose the hard one. And I believe that Jacob and Jacob's parents agreed to care for him on earth. They will all be stronger and very much blessed for taking on the challenge of a handicapped child.

"And James is automatically heir to the celestial kingdom, as are all children under the age of eight or who are handicapped and can't process the concept of right from wrong. Heavenly Father sends angels to help others who have special needs. Besides James's father and grandparents, other angels were placed on earth to help him and comfort him when he is afraid and to remind him of his strength." Lily smiled at her daughters. "Some of those angels could be named Rose, and Bonnie, and Susie, and even Lily."

"I like being an angel," Susie said. "I am going to be a very good angel too."

Lily smiled at her youngest daughter. "I am sure you will, Susie. We will all do the very best we can to be good angels. James is a very special boy. I think he and Jacob will become our very good friends. Now, girls, it's time for bed."

Lily tucked her daughters in their beds and kissed them good night. It had been a lovely evening, indeed.

CHAPTER THIRTY-FOUR

During the rest of the week, the girls went to school. They were enjoying their new classes and teachers. When they came home each day, they were full of stories to tell their mother about new friends they had made. They sat at the table doing their homework and teasing each other about the boys in their classes.

Lily substituted Wednesday and Friday that week. She too was enjoying the interaction with the students she had met. On the days she didn't teach, she worked in the yard, getting it ready for the fall, which would shortly be there.

Paul Strong had called to tell them that the CD would likely be ready by the middle of October. "It is coming together nicely so far," he told the Langstons.

On Sunday during Sacrament Meeting, the Langstons got up between the speakers to sing the music they had practiced for the occasion. After Lily was seated at the piano, the girls stepped up to the pulpit. Rose spoke to the congregation, "For our musical number today, we are going to sing 'The Light Divine'."

The bishop had placed a microphone by the piano so that Lily could sing with her daughters while she also accompanied them. The song was lovely. After the meeting ended, several of the congregation came up to congratulate them.

That afternoon, as was now a habit, Lily and her girls spent time with both the Langstons and the Wrights. After they got home from visiting with Lily's parents, the phone rang. "Lily, this is Jacob Manning. How has your day been?"

"Really great, Jacob. The girls and I sang in Sacrament Meeting, then later we visited both sets of grandparents. How was yours?

"It was nice too. James and I were wondering if you and the girls would be able to accompany us to the Salt Lake County Fair one day next week? What day would be best for you all?"

"We would like to go with you and James to the fair, Jacob. Susie has been asking me when we can get together again with you and James." Lily laughed as she added, "Especially James. The girls have piano lessons after school on Tuesday, so how about Wednesday?" Lily answered.

"Wednesday it is, then. James was quite persistent that I call you. He wants to hang out with Susie again, so it looks like the feeling between those two tykes is mutual. We'll come by and pick you all up at 6:00 p.m., okay?"

"That'll be fine, Jacob. See you then, bye."

"Looks like we have a date Wednesday evening, girls." Lily smiled at her daughters. "It should be fun going to the fair with Jacob and James." With that, Lily gave Susie a squeeze.

"Yes." Susie jumped up and down. "Maybe James will go on some rides with me. Do you think he will want to go on some rides with me, Mom?"

"I'm sure he will, honey."

CHAPTER THIRTY-FIVE

"Hi, Mom." Aaron walked into the house, set down his books, and gave Connie a hug and kiss on her forehead. "I was in the hallway today, and the music director for the high school walked up to me and told me he wanted to visit with me after school. After classes, I went in to talk to him in the choir room. Mom, he wants me to be in the choir. He suggested I come home and talk to you about it. He has been watching me and my career, as he puts it, and says he knows what I can do. He wants me to be not only in the choir, but perhaps do some solo and small-group work.

"I am supposed to let him know tomorrow. It would mean spending some nights at the school working on special music or performing at various functions. What do you think, Mom, would it be doable?"

Connie didn't say anything for a few minutes. Then tears filled her eyes. Aaron looked at his mother and waited for her to say something. He knew how much she wanted him to be engaged in school activities. But, at first, he thought this much time away from her in her condition would just be too much for her.

"Oh, Aaron." She grabbed his hands and held them to her face. Her tears spilled over his hands. "I have been praying hard for this, for you to be able to be involved in the high school's music program. Heavenly Father is blessing us every day." She took his hands from her face and squeezed them in hers before letting them go.

"Somebody needs to be here when I'm not, especially in the evenings, Mom."

"I know, son. My neighbor and friend Helen will spend what time she can. And I do have other friends who will come in and stay with me. Then the Relief Society sisters told me they would take turns coming in. I'll be just fine. I'll have Helen get in touch with the ladies in the ward and set up a schedule for them to come on the nights you will be at the school or wherever you will be performing. It's all going to work out, I know it will, son. Have your music director give you a schedule of when you will be gone at night. That will help."

Aaron said, "The CD should be ready by the middle of October, Paul Strong told me. When I go to the hospital to work and sing for the patients on Saturday, I'll have the staff make a list of those who want a copy. I don't know how many Paul will turn out at first, but that will give him an idea of how many to make in the first batch."

"I can hardly wait 'til it's ready, Aaron," Connie said. "I know my friends will all want one."

The next day, when Aaron got to school, a little early on purpose, he found Steven Black in the choir room. "My mother is fine with me being in the high school choir, Mr. Black. In fact, she has been praying that I would get involved more in school activities. She says anything you want me to do in the music field would be fine with her. She has friends who will stay with her in the evenings when I can't be there."

Steven Black, like Aaron, had red hair and brown eyes. And, like Aaron, he too was tall and slender. It was uncanny how much the two resembled each other.

And his name, Turner.... No, it couldn't be.

"You are definitely going to be my good-luck charm, Aaron." Steven Black grabbed Aaron's hand and shook it vigorously. "We are going to have a great year."

"If you have a schedule ready, could you give me a copy to give to my mother? That way, she can anticipate the times she will need to have someone come and stay with her."

"I don't have one yet, Aaron, but as soon as I do, I will give you a copy."

"That will be great, Mr. Black." Aaron continued, "Well, I better go to class now or I'll be late. Bye now."

Steven Black watched Aaron as he left the room. *My child would be Aaron's age. Oh, that's silly*, he thought. He put his hand up to his forehead and brushed his red hair back as if to expel the thought that was nagging at him. *I will have to find out what Aaron's mother's name is, or I'll never rest.*

CHAPTER THIRTY-SIX

"Let's go find out what time the sea lion show is on. It's supposed to be great," Jacob told the children.

After they found out that the show would start in forty-five minutes, Lily suggested they go get something to eat. "The girls didn't eat much before you and James came to pick us up. They were too excited. There were several food booths at the fair. Each one found their favorite food, and then they sat down at the tables arranged in front of the food booths."

"This hamburger is really good," Rose said.

Bonnie agreed, taking a big bite of hers and nodding so she wouldn't have to talk with her mouth full.

"I like my pizza. James and I got the same thing. Do you like yours, James?" Susie asked him.

"Yes, it's good. I want some ice cream. Is that all right, Dad?"

"Of course, son, but let's have dessert after we go visit the sea lions. And after that, we will go on some rides. Who dares to go on that giant Ferris wheel over there?" Jacob asked them.

"I do," said Susie. The others all chimed in that they wanted to ride it too.

"I think I will pass on the rides, Jacob," Lily said. "My stomach isn't made for all that motion. It'll be fun to watch, though."

After they had finished eating, it was time to go see the sea lion show. They were reminded to get there early to be guaranteed good seats.

The sea lions were a hoot. The children watched and laughed with the others in the audience at their antics. After the show was over, the sea lions posed with each one so they could get pictures.

"That was the best show. I wish we could see it again," Susie said.

"Me too," James echoed his friend. "Is it on again, Dad?"

"Not today," Jacob told his son. "That was the last show. So now who is up for a ride on the Ferris wheel?"

"Me," said Susie, waving her hand in the air.

"We all are. Let's go." Rose led the way over to the Ferris wheel. After about a ten-minute wait in line, the children were seated on the Ferris wheel. Jacob and Lily watched as it went up and around and back down. The youngsters were clearly enjoying it. Susie and James were seated together, and when they got to the top of the wheel, they raised their arms and squealed.

"That was fun," James told his dad and Lily. "Let's do it again, okay, Susie?"

"Can we, Mom?" Lily looked toward Jacob who nodded his head.

Up and down they went again, Rose and Bonnie watching from the sidelines this time.

After the Ferris wheel, there were other rides to enjoy. When the crowds and the noise became too much for James to handle, his dad took him to a quiet place. There his son put his jacket over his head and lay quietly on the bench until he was calm and ready to join the others again.

Before the evening was over, James reminded his dad about the promised ice cream. Finally, four very tired but happy children agreed it was time to leave the fair. It had been a wonderful outing. When Lily and her daughters got home, they thanked Jacob and James for a great evening.

Susie lifted her hand and with the sign of "I love you" pressed her thumb, forefinger, and pinky finger to James's hand as they had learned. Rose and Bonnie followed, and then Lily.

As the girls turned to go into the house, Jacob caught Lily's hands between his and lifted them up to his lips. "Thank you for coming with us tonight. I had a great time, Lily. Would it be all right if I called you again soon?"

"We'd like that, Jacob." She emphasized the *we*, which he understood to mean that she would agree to group dates.

"I'm totally fine with group dating for now, Lily. I'll call you soon."

CHAPTER THIRTY-SEVEN

Steven Black stepped up to the counter in the office at the high school. "May I see Aaron Turner's records for a minute, Beth. He is going to be my assistant in the music program, and I wanted to get his address and phone number in case I need to pick him up some night for a concert."

"Why don't you just ask him?"

"Well, um, now that I am here, I'll just get what I need now, okay?"

Beth turned and went over to the file cabinet marked "m to z" and came back with Aaron's file. She handed it to Mr. Black.

Steven Black opened the file and quickly wrote down the address and telephone number. He didn't really come to look for that information but wanted to find out who Aaron's mother was, and if she was married and had other children.

There it was, her name: Connie. Connie Turner, single and one child, Aaron Turner, sixteen years old.

"Thank you, Beth. You were very helpful." Mr. Black turned and left the office. *Aaron is my son. I need to sit down, or I am going to fall down right here in the hallway with dozens of students staring at me.*

Steven Black made it to the music room just as four students passed him as he was coming through the door. "Hi, Mr. Black," they said as he held the door for them.

He sat down at his desk and put his head in his hands. *Now what?* He agonized. *What a pickle I'm in.*

He stood up and walked across to the window. He watched as the students began to walk home or step onto the waiting school buses.

He had seen Aaron for the first time about a month before when he was singing and playing his guitar at the hospital. Steven had gone to visit a friend who was a patient there. Aaron happened to be singing for the patients on the same floor where his friend was a patient. His friend had told Steven about Aaron and how talented he was and had invited him to stay for the miniconcert that afternoon, which was shortly to begin.

Steven was so impressed with Aaron that he began to ask questions about him. How old was he, and what high school did he attend? When he found out he would attend the same high school at which he taught, Steven Black was ecstatic. He had to convince Aaron to join the choir, but also he had other projects he wanted Aaron to be part of.

Now he had a serious dilemma. He knew he had to face Connie and beg her forgiveness. Almost every day of his life since the day Connie had thrown him out, he had regretted his decision to ask her to abort the baby. He should have stood by her. After all, he loved her then and still had feelings for her. The thought of a baby when they were both in high school and so young had frightened him.

Connie, he thought, *if you only knew how many times I tried to call you, to ask your forgiveness. After you told me you wanted nothing to do with me, I quit school. I left Salt Lake City and joined the Navy. If I tell Aaron I am his father, how will he react? He probably would not want to have anything to do with me. If I tell you, Connie, will you be able to forgive me? Will you want Aaron to stay away from me? One thing I do know, I cannot start out my career here in this high school living a lie. Connie and Aaron will have to know about me. If they will forgive me and look past my failings, then there is hope that I can be in my son's life, something I would cherish more than life itself. It will be better to talk to Connie first before anything is said to Aaron. I'll get Aaron and the other students settled in for a few days and then find a way to get together with Connie. That will work unless Aaron lets my name slip before I talk to her. Today is Thursday. I'll drive over to Connie and Aaron's house on Saturday morning. I think Aaron will be working at the hospital, and Connie and I can talk. Oh, I pray she will forgive me.*

CHAPTER THIRTY-EIGHT

Saturday morning, Connie had just finished with her breakfast and was cleaning up in the kitchen when the doorbell rang. She glanced at the clock. It was just 9:00 a.m. Aaron had been gone about half an hour. Connie wheeled herself over to the door and opened it.

"Steven?" She sat there staring at him in the doorway.

"Hi, Connie. May I please come in?" He was surprised to see her in a wheelchair. She wheeled herself out of the way so that Steven Black could step into the room.

"Why are you here, Steven?"

"I've come to talk to you about Aaron. I just found out he is my son. It is important that I talk to you about him, Connie."

"I guess that's all right. Some part of me knew this day would come. Come and sit down." Connie wheeled herself over to the couch and motioned for him to sit. "It's quite a shock to see you after all these years. Your parents told me you had joined the Navy. I haven't had any contact with them since Aaron was born. I don't think they even knew I was pregnant with your child. I thought it best since you wanted nothing to do with him."

"Well, Connie. That's not quite true. I tried to call you several times after you told me to leave. I wanted to tell you I made a terrible mistake. I was wrong to suggest an abortion. But you wouldn't speak to me, remember?"

Connie stared at Steven for a long moment before speaking. "I was so hurt by what you said that I just wanted you out of my life."

"We were so young, Connie. I have regretted my words all these years. I should have stayed and faced up to my responsibilities, but I was angry and stubborn. It's the red hair, I suppose. Aren't redheads supposed to be stubborn?" With that, Steven managed a weak smile. He continued, "I wrote you many letters."

"I never got any of them."

"I tore them up."

"Why do you want to talk to me about Aaron now, Steven?"

"A month or so ago, I was visiting a friend in the Hunter Cancer Clinic, and he invited me to attend a miniconcert there at the hospital. He told me about this young man who sang and played guitar for the patients every Saturday afternoon. He wanted me to hear him. I have been hired as music director at the same school this young man attends. I found out his name is Aaron Turner. Of course, I thoroughly enjoyed his performance, and after finding out where he would be going to school, I made it a point to invite him to join the choir. I also want him to do some solo work and some ensemble work.

"When he came in to talk to me at the school, I couldn't help but notice how much he looked like me. And with the last name of Turner, well, I did some snooping in the records and found out his mother's name is Connie. Then I knew for sure who he was."

"Have you said anything to him about this?"

"No, of course not. I had to talk to you first. I am not sure he will want to have anything to do with me when he finds out."

"How long have you been back in town, Steven? You haven't kept track of me or him over the years. Is that right?"

"Connie, you told me you never wanted to see me again, and after trying several times to call you, I finally got the message. I joined the Navy and never looked back. Actually, I thought about you every day. And I wondered whether you had a boy or girl. The Navy put me through school. I didn't come back to Utah until a month ago. I wasn't sure I should look you up, even though I wanted to very much. But when I saw Aaron and figured out who he was, I just had to come and talk to you about the situation."

Connie hesitated and then spoke, "Aaron will have to know. Then he can make up his own mind. He is a wonderful young man, Steven. He means everything to me. Since my accident, he has waited on me hand and foot. I was hoping that he could get involved in the music program at the high school. It sure is strange how things happen, isn't it?"

"Tell me about the accident, Connie. What happened to you?"

"My parents were wonderful. They took care of me, and after the baby was born, they helped raise him. They both worked and managed to work their schedules around, so at least one of them could be with Aaron each day while I finished school. Of course, I didn't have any time for extracurricular activities, but one day, they suggested I go skiing with some of my friends. I was so excited to go. It had been a long time since I had really had any fun. My friends and I went up to Alta to ski. Remember, that was the favorite place you and I had to go skiing. Anyway, I was coming down a rather steep hill and lost my footing. I was kind of careless. I should not have tried to do so much as I was pretty rusty on skis, not having been on them for a few years. I fell, got twisted around and hit a tree backward. It injured my spine. My parents had to take care of me and Aaron, and work, taking turns caring for us. It was very hard on them, Steven. They are both gone now."

"I am so sorry I wasn't here to help you," Steven said. "Perhaps, if I had not run away—"

"One thing I have learned, Steven, is that some things happen for a reason. I know that my life has been blessed in countless ways. I have wonderful neighbors and friends who help all they can. And Aaron is the very best thing that has ever happened to me."

"Should we tell Aaron together, Connie?"

"Yes, I think that would be best. There is so much more I need to tell you. I need to tell you about Lily Langston and her children. They have become a very big part of our lives. But I will save that for when we get together with Aaron. By the way, Steven, are you married? Do you have any other children?"

"No. I had no interest in marrying after I left Salt Lake City. I loved you. I guess I never got over you in all these years."

"I never married either. After the accident and finding myself bedridden or able to get around only in a wheelchair, I guess I just didn't think I was marriage material. Who would want an invalid for a wife anyway?"

Steven let the question go by. To himself, he thought, *I would, Connie*. "When should we tell Aaron, Connie?"

"I think the sooner, the better. Come back tonight. Aaron gets home about 6:00 p.m. We both need to pray about this, Steven. However, I have a strong feeling that everything will be all right. He has gone through some tough times in the past several months. I think his wisdom and his maturity will surprise you."

"Good," Steven answered. "I'll be back. Shall we go out to dinner and have our talk there?"

"Okay, good, that would be nice. We'll go to a restaurant where we can have privacy. There's one not far from here. I'll see you at six then, Steven."

Steven Black turned and waved back at Connie as he closed the door.

CHAPTER THIRTY-NINE

"Aaron, I met your music director today. He is coming to take us to dinner. He'll be here in half an hour."

"You mean Steven Black, Mom?"

"Yes."

"How come he is coming to take us to dinner?"

"He is very interested in you, Aaron. Both of us have something we need to tell you, dear," Connie told him.

"Can you tell me now?"

"I could, but I want him to be here so we can both tell you. Is that okay?"

"I suppose I'll just have to be patient, Mom, won't I?"

Half an hour later, the doorbell rang. Aaron opened the door and motioned for Steven Black to step into the room.

"Hello, Mr. Black. Mom tells me you and she have something to tell me. I suppose you're going to make me wait until we get to the restaurant?"

"Yes, let's talk about what we want to discuss with you then."

Aaron and Steven helped Connie down the ramp and into Steven's car. The restaurant was just a few blocks from their house, so they were soon there, seated in the farthest booth from the entrance. After they had each placed their orders, Aaron looked at his mother impatiently. "Okay, now tell me what this is all about."

"Aaron, there is no easy way to say this, so I am going to come right out and introduce you to your father. Steven Black is your father, honey."

Aaron turned to look at Steven Black. He didn't know whether to be angry or if he should just laugh it off. He stared at his father. He said nothing. He saw the resemblance. Actually, he had noticed that the resemblance was striking.

"Aaron," Steven began, "I have only been back in Salt Lake City for about a month. After your mother sent me away, I joined the Navy. They put me through school. I have been working back east, and then I got this wonderful opportunity to teach in my hometown. I jumped on it. I wanted to be a part of my child's life, but your mother made it very plain she wanted nothing to do with me. To tell you the truth, Aaron, I don't blame her.

"You see, when she told me she was pregnant, I told her to get an abortion. We argued about it. She absolutely refused. I got all huffy and left her, banging the door behind me. Later, when I had cooled down, I called her. She refused to talk to me. I called a few more times after that. She wouldn't take my calls. So I left Salt Lake City and joined the Navy, as I said. I always wanted to come back. I never forgot her, and I never ceased to wonder if I would ever know my son or daughter. Then I got the opportunity to be head of the music department at your high school. I believe I was meant to come back here, to be a part of your life, if you will let me, son."

Just then, their meals were served. For a few minutes, no one spoke, and then Connie reached for her son's hand.

"Aaron, Steven and I both made some bad decisions. We knew better than to get too close as a couple of young high school kids. The church teaches us that we should group-date until we are old enough to date responsibly. We made a mistake, just that one night, but it changed our lives. The best and most wonderful outcome was you, Aaron. You are the light of my life. I want you to give Steven a chance to be part of your life too.

"I was wrong to shut him out. I never gave him a chance to explain or to make amends. My pride and hurt and anger got in the way. We all have to grow up, honey. Some of us have to come through the school of hard knocks before we learn. I did. I acted stupidly. Now, I am hoping that you will give him a chance. He wants to be in your life. I hope you will not shut him out like I did."

Aaron turned to Steven and extended his hand. With a smile, he asked, "What shall I call you? Do you want me to call you Mr. Black, Steven, or Dad?"

Happily, Steven clutched his son's hand. "If it wouldn't be too much to ask, would you call me Dad? I would be so honored to have you call me Dad."

"Dad, it is. So, Dad, are you picking up the tab for this great dinner?"

Connie looked at her son and then at Steven. Tears had filled her eyes and were falling down her cheeks. "There is so much we need to tell you, Steven. Aaron, I think you should tell your dad about Lily Langston and her family."

"Lily Langston and her family have become very close and dear to us. By all that is reasonable, they should hate me. I was driving late one night last April. It was raining. I hit and killed Lily Langston's husband, Samuel. It was an accident, but it shouldn't have happened. I was driving too fast. I was only fifteen and should not have been driving at night. Then I took a wrong turn and ran right into him. He didn't have a chance—"

Connie added, "We had broken my bottle of medicine. It fell and shattered on the linoleum floor. I had to have the medicine. We could have called a neighbor to go pick it up for me, but Aaron thought he would be okay. It wasn't that far. It was a terrible night." Connie sighed.

"The Langstons met with the police captain and my attorney and told them they didn't want me to have to do jail time. They were okay with me getting a suspended sentence and doing community service." Aaron paused and then continued, "I mop floors at the Hunter Cancer Clinic on Saturdays while I am in school. After my shift as part of my service, I get to sing and play my guitar for the patients. I don't mind the work, and I love singing and playing for the patients. The Langstons are the best, Dad. Their oldest daughter, Rose, hasn't forgiven me. I hope she will one day. Her mother keeps reassuring me that she will come around one day." Tears clouded Aaron's brown eyes.

Steven looked at his son, then at Connie who was wiping her eyes on her napkin. "Thanks for telling me. I can't wait to meet them. How old is Rose, Aaron?"

"She is probably thirteen by now."

"There's more, Steven. Aaron and the Langstons have been working on a CD together. It should be coming out soon, the middle of October. Lily found out one night when they came over to our house to meet me that Aaron is very talented. They got together and practiced singing a couple of songs to sing as a surprise for Carson Hunter when he had a big dinner and program for medical big-wigs from other countries. They were a hit. Then one of the gentlemen at the shindig came up and wanted them to record a CD. They worked with him, and now it is finished and will soon be ready to go on the market."

"That pretty much brings us up to date with what has been going on in our lives, Steven. Just one more thing, my doctor wants to use me as a 'guinea pig' to try out some medical procedures to see if there is a possibility I'll be able to walk again. There is some interesting work being done in the area of spinal cord injuries. If Aaron and the Langston's CD does well, we may be able to get enough money together to have an operation to fix me. In the meantime, it won't cost anything for me to be part of a test study that is soon to be started at the clinic that does work on spinal cord injuries."

"That's great news, Connie."

"Well, it may not be successful, so I am trying not to get my hopes up too high."

"It's probably time to get you two home. It's getting late. Can you believe it is almost ten o'clock?" Steven commented. "What a great evening this has been. Thank you both. I have never been happier than I am at this minute." Steven reached over and took Connie's hand and then patted Aaron's arm with his free hand. "Coming back to Salt Lake City was the wisest decision I have ever made. I know the Lord directed me here."

With that, Steven got up and went to the counter and paid the bill. He returned and put a tip on the table. Then he and Aaron helped Connie out to the car and put her safely in the back seat. Aaron sat beside Steven as he drove them home.

Once Connie and Aaron were back home, Steven shook Connie's hand and then Aaron's. "I will see you bright and early on Monday morning, Aaron. I'll call you next week, Connie, if that is all right with you."

"Do that, Steven. Bye for now."

After Steven had left, Aaron turned to his mother and smiled at her. "Well, mother dear, has life come full circle? Do I get the sense that we are going to be a family at last, the three of us?"

"Well, honey, I am going to take it slow and easy, one day at a time. But it sure is an interesting turn of events, don't you think?"

"Yes, I think." Aaron wheeled his mother into the bedroom and helped her get ready for bed. When he had her settled, he bent over and kissed her and said good night. He then locked the outside doors and turned out the lights.

CHAPTER FORTY

Connie couldn't wait to call Lily. As soon as she thought Lily and her girls would be home from their church meetings, she called.

"Lily," Connie said excitedly. "Lily, Aaron's father has come back to Salt Lake City. He is the music director at Aaron's high school. Do you believe in coincidences, Lily? I don't. I believe everything happens for a reason. I believe Steven was meant to come into our lives again at this time."

"Connie, slow down. Tell me what happened."

Connie took a deep breath and then proceeded to tell Lily all that had happened, how he had found out about Aaron. She told Lily everything, just as Steven had told her.

"I have to admit, I was startled when I opened the door and saw Steven standing there, like a ghost from the past. But I soon realized I was happy to see him."

"How did Aaron take meeting his father like that?"

"At first, he was stunned. But when Steven and I told the story of how I had told Steven to leave and then didn't give him a chance to come back or make amends, and then when Steven told him how he had wanted badly to know his child and be in his life again, he seemed to be all right with it. Of course, Lily, time will tell. They will be working together in the music program at the school, so they will get to know each other. It all feels so right, so good."

"This is incredible news, Connie. When do we get to meet him?"

"When he calls next week, I'll set up a time for us all to get together. I'll call you then."

"Good. Bye for now then." Lily hung up the phone and turned to tell her daughters.

"Aaron has found his father. Actually, his father found him." Lily then proceeded to tell the girls what Connie had told her. "When Steven Black calls Connie next week, they will set up a time when we can meet him."

Susie said, "Mom, I think Jacob and James should be there too."

"Jacob is Aaron's attorney, so he should be there to meet Aaron's father. Of course, James should be there too." Bonnie teased her little sister. "At least for Susie's sake."

CHAPTER FORTY-ONE

It was Wednesday evening at the Turner's house. It was decided to have an open house and introduce Steven Black to everyone who knew and was interested in the Turner family. That included close friends, family, neighbors, and ward members.

At the last minute, Rose decided to come with them. Lily surmised that Rose, for all her stubbornness, did not really want to be left home sulking while everyone was at the Turners having a good time. Rose would just avoid being anywhere near Aaron, she told her mother. Lily just smiled at her daughter.

Several of their neighbors brought food for a pot club dinner. Lily brought a tossed salad and rolls.

At 7:00 p.m., the guests started coming to welcome Steven and get to know him. One big surprise of the evening was when Carson Hunter and his wife, Kay, walked in. Jacob Manning had mentioned the open house to the Hunters, and they said they would be there for sure. They had grown very fond of the Turners and wanted to welcome Aaron's father into the fold, so to speak.

James and Susie were inseparable. They kept asking the guests if they could get them drinks or take their plates, anything they could do to be a part of the festivities.

After the last guest had closed the door, Steven turned to Connie and, with a big smile, said, "Connie, that was the second-best thing that has happened to me in a long, long time. Being back in your life and getting to know my son was the best," Steven chuckled. "And this is right next to that. Everyone was so kind. Thank you for doing this for me, for Aaron and me."

"You're welcome, Steven. I enjoyed it very much too."

Aaron stood beside his father. "I feel good about tonight too. Thanks, Mom."

CHAPTER FORTY-TWO

The CD had just come out. It was now the third week in October, just when Paul Strong said it would be ready. Aaron had grabbed a box full of them to take with him to the hospital.

"Hi, Aaron," the receptionist hailed him. "What have you got there?"

"My CDs. How many do you want?"

"I wrote down I wanted five copies. Will you have enough to sell me five copies?"

"You bet."

After that transaction was completed, Aaron took the box and dropped it off at the main office. The staff had promised Aaron they would handle them for him and gather the money.

He went into the janitor's room and got the broom, bucket, and mop he would need to mop the floors and then got going doing his job. As he worked, staff members and patients alike waved the CD they had purchased to let him know that they had gotten their copies.

"Paul," Aaron spoke into the phone, "this is Aaron Turner. We've sold the box of CDs I brought over to the hospital this morning. We have several people who didn't get theirs. Is there someone in your office who could bring us another box or two?"

"I'll send over two more boxes, Aaron. My receptionist can bring them over now. She is just leaving to go to lunch. I'll have her drop them off to you very soon. She can call you on your cell phone, and you can come out and help her take the boxes in, if you will."

"Thanks, Paul. Are the stores going to be carrying the CD?"

"Yes, we are in the process right now of putting them in the retail outlets. They should be on the shelves by the end of the week."

"Great. Thanks, Paul. I'm just finishing my lunch break. I'll go out and wait for Margie on the front steps of the hospital. Bye now, and thanks again."

After Aaron and Margie, Paul Strong's cute blond receptionist took the boxes of CDs in. Aaron got back to work finishing mopping the upper floors. He then cleaned himself up once again and went to sing and play for the patients and staff.

This day, he would be singing on the children's floor. He had become attached to the patients on all the floors, but the children were his favorites. As he sat down with his guitar in front of the patients and members of the staff, he looked around the room to see who was still there as patients whom he knew. He greeted them, and everyone else warmly.

As he started to sing, he noticed two little boys sitting in wheelchairs that were way too big for their small frames—two little boys exactly alike, blond blue-eyed identical twins. They looked to be about five years old. He asked them for their names.

"My name is Patrick."

"I'm Derek. We have leukemia."

The twins' mother, a tall slender blonde woman, added, "They are in remission now. The doctors are doing some tests on them to make sure everything is good."

"I am glad to hear they are doing well. What song would you boys like to hear me sing first?"

"'Popcorn Popping On the Apricot Tree'. Do you know that one, Aaron? Our mommy told us your name is Aaron. Do you know that one?" Derek asked again.

"Yes, I do. Will you sing it with me? Everyone join in and sing with us if you would like."

After the popcorn song, Aaron continued to take requests. It was enjoyable to be back with the children. After the miniconcert, Aaron answered questions and then said his goodbyes all around.

The twin's mother came up to him and introduced herself. "I'm Rebecca Hall."

"Nice to meet you, Rebecca. You have fine boys there. I hope and pray that they will grow up healthy."

"Thanks, Aaron. They have been in remission for a year now. The doctors are very optimistic about their complete recovery. I would say hope to see you again and hear you sing and play for us, but under the circumstances, I hope we don't have to meet here again. Perhaps we'll run into you in a place where people aren't sick."

"I understand. Just a minute, I have something I want to give you and the twins." Aaron went over to his jacket and pulled out a CD. "Here, I would like you to have this. It has just been released. Hope you and the boys will enjoy it."

"I am sure we will. It's nice to have gotten to meet you, Aaron, and to hear your lovely voice," Rebecca shook hands with Aaron and then escorted her children out of the room.

CHAPTER FORTY-THREE

"Lily, hi, Jacob here. How is everything going since I last saw you?"

"Good, Jacob, busy as usual. I've been substituting in school this week. My gardening is all done now, so I am concentrating on working on some new piano pieces. The girls are all excited about what they are going to wear for Halloween."

"Your CD is doing very well, I understand. I was in Walmart yesterday, and there were several people waiting to check out who had copies to buy. It is definitely going to be a hit."

"That would be wonderful, Jacob. I am getting calls from ward members and friends telling me they are buying them for Christmas presents. Imagine, for Christmas presents. There aren't even any Christmas songs on it," Lily said.

"Next year, you will have to be sure and put out a Christmas CD. I bought several of them to give for gifts also." Jacob laughed. He continued, "Lily, James, and I want to take you and the girls to a Halloween party Carson and Kay Hunter are having in their home. It's this coming Saturday. Will you come?"

Lily made a face, though Jacob couldn't see it, of course. "Jacob, I don't enjoy dressing up in costume. Is everyone who is going to be there expected to be in costume?"

Jacob chuckled. "Everyone will be in costume, Lily. If we get together on what to wear, perhaps you will warm up to the idea."

"Well, I guess that would be all right. I will agree to dressing up but very reluctantly. And you say this get-together is for the whole family?"

"Yes, otherwise I would have turned Hunters down. I remember our agreement, Lily, group dating only. So are you game to dress up with me and the kids for it?"

"Okay, you talked me into it. Who shall we go as, the king and queen of England? Or, maybe, clowns or chimney sweeps?"

"Let's take the children and go to some of the Deseret Industries stores and see what they have. That will be fun. Then we can plan our costumes around what we find there."

"We better do it right away while there are still some choices left. We're almost too late for getting good stuff already."

Jacob agreed, "Yes, can you and the girls be ready when they get home from school tomorrow, say, four o'clock?"

"Sure, we'll see you and James then."

The next day, the girls and Lily were sitting on the front steps waiting when Jacob pulled up.

"Come and sit by me, Susie," James called.

After they were all piled in the car, they started out for the nearest Deseret Industries store. After looking through all the clothes there, they began to formulate a plan for their Halloween costumes.

As Lily had suggested to Jacob on the phone, they would go as chimney sweeps like they had seen in the movie *Mary Poppins*. There were plenty of black clothes in all their sizes. They even found some old hats and shoes they could paint black. "Now we need some black paint to paint the shoes and hats, and then some black face paint to make us look all dirty like we have been cleaning chimneys. Also, we will black out some of our teeth. This is going to be fun." Lily was getting into the mood of the moment in spite of herself.

James and Susie had to be reined in a little bit. Their exuberance was causing the other shoppers to stop and stare at them.

"Quiet down, kids," Jacob admonished. "We don't want to be thrown out of the store. In fact, we may well be the first ones to ever be thrown out of a DI."

James giggled, "Will they pick us up like bags of trash, Dad, and throw us out the door?"

"I would certainly hope not, son. Just quiet down a little, okay?"

"Okay, Dad."

CHAPTER FORTY-FOUR

The October night was chilly. Susie stood at the window watching for Jacob and James to come. "They're here, everybody," she called out.

The doorbell rang, and Susie quickly opened the door to find James all dressed up in his black clothes, floppy hat, and oversized shoes. His face was streaked in "dirt." He grinned at Susie, and she couldn't help laughing. His teeth were mostly blacked out.

"You look great, James. Just great." She then held out her hand in their greeting sign and smiled back in her toothless smile. "Oh, I can't wait 'til everyone sees us."

Soon they were at the Hunters. As they walked in the door, they carried brooms like the chimney sweeps carry. They had found them in a hardware store and had painted them black too. James and Susie had smaller brooms than the others. What a picture they all made as they walked in the door.

Everyone turned to watch them walk in. Then they clapped wildly. There were kings and queens, brides and grooms, Frankenstein and his monster, ladies in old-fashioned ball gowns, and men in tuxedos. Carson and Kay Hunter were dressed as Napoleon Bonaparte and Josephine. As they came up to Jacob and Lily, they extended their hands in a warm greeting and bowed. Then Jacob and Lily bowed in return and then smiled. At the sight of their toothless grins, the Hunters laughed. The children then all smiled to show their toothless grins. It was a great moment. The Langstons and the Mannings were the hit of the evening.

While the grown-ups danced and visited together, the children played games and laughed, clearly enjoying themselves. There were all kinds of food, and it was set around buffet style so that one could go and help himself at any time. It was such a fun party that the time went far too quickly.

At last, the evening was over, and Jacob escorted Lily and her daughters to their doorstep. After the girls went into the house, Jacob bent over and kissed Lily. "I know that was not allowed, Lily dear, but it just happened, and I am not going to say I'm sorry. I have wanted to do that for some time. You must know I am falling in love with you."

Lily looked up into Jacob's dark eyes and smiled. "Be patient, Jacob, it's too soon. Be my…our friend. That's best for now, okay?"

"Okay, Lily. But just to let you know, I've waited for someone to come along for a long time now, that special someone—you. You are an incredible person. I can't imagine life without you."

Lily put her finger to her own lips and then to Jacob's. "I like you, I like you very, very much. I am just not ready to declare anything more right now, Jacob. Let's just take things easy for now. Tonight was marvelous. We all had so much fun."

Lily then laughed at the sheer nonsense of their silly costumes. "Everyone there was dressed up in their best finery, and we come in all black and dirty and toothless, and we were the hit of the party. How great is that?"

"It was terrific." Jacob reached for her hand. "I'll call you soon, Lily. I had better get James home now. He is asleep in the back seat. Bye, sweet Lily."

With that, Lily went inside. She was deep in thought as she showered and got ready for bed. She then went in to kiss her sleeping daughters. Afterward, she knelt down by her bed and thanked Heavenly Father for her many blessings. He was blessing her. In spite of her deep sorrow at losing Samuel, she knew that the Lord had a plan for her, and she also knew that whatever it was, she would embrace it fully.

CHAPTER FORTY-FIVE

It was now the month of November. Lily kept busy doing her substitute teaching. The girls were doing well in school. Two days ago, Connie had called Lily to see if she would be with her when she went in to the hospital to begin the clinical study she was invited to be a part of on spinal cord injuries.

"I'm really nervous about it, Lily. I would sure like to have you with me, at least this first time."

"I would be happy to go with you, Connie. What day do you go in, and what time do you want me to pick you up?" Lily asked.

"It begins next Monday. They want me at the clinic at 9:00 a.m. Could you come and pick me up at eight-thirty?"

"Of course, Connie. I'll be there. How are things going with Aaron and his father? Are they enjoying working together at the high school?"

"It's only been a few weeks, but everything seems to be going well. The choir is getting ready to sing for the whole school's Thanksgiving program. Also, they are working on Christmas music. Steven has Aaron accompany some of the pieces along with the piano accompaniment. He is really enjoying it."

"How is he doing on his other school classes?"

"Very good. He loves learning."

"Has the landscaper finished on your property?" Lily asked.

"He has done all he can do now, he said. He will be back in the spring to finish. He is going to put in a whole new lawn. He told me it will not cost you any more than just patching the dead spots. He is a very nice young man, Lily. When he gets done, our yard is going to be a showplace."

"That's great, Connie."

"Are your daughters enjoying their school classes?"

"They are. They are busy with their homework, piano practicing, and our singing practices. Anyway, Connie, I'll be there next Monday morning, eight-thirty sharp. Bye."

A few moments later, Lily called Connie back. "Connie, would it be all right with you if I invited Jacob to come on Monday with me? If he is available, he would be great support."

"Of course, dear. Call him and then call me back and tell me what he says. Bye."

"Jacob, it's Lily. Are you busy next Monday morning? Connie Turner has asked me if I would accompany her to the clinic where her doctor wants her to begin initial tests to determine if she would be a good candidate to join a clinical study on some new treatments for her spinal cord injury. She is a small person, but I may have trouble getting her in and out of the car. Anyway, that is not my only reason for asking you. It would be nice to have you with us, you know, for moral support."

Jacob chuckled at that. "Well, let's see. I have my calendar right here. I have a client coming in, but I can reschedule him for Tuesday. He won't mind. It's for a will and living trust. He has put it off for years, I guess one more day won't hurt. What time should I pick you up, Lily?"

"We need to be over at Connie's to pick her up at eight-thirty. Would shortly after eight be too early? I can have the girls out on their way to school by then."

"Eight o'clock it is. James's special bus picks him up at eight, so I will be there a few minutes after that. Even though his grandparents could put him on the bus, I like to see him off myself. He likes me to be there when he leaves for school."

"Thanks, Jacob. I'll see you then."

After Lily hung up, she called Connie to tell her she and Jacob would be there on time Monday, as planned.

CHAPTER FORTY-SIX

Jacob and Lily helped Connie get seated in Jacob's car and then drove to the other side of Salt Lake City where the rehabilitation clinic was located near the University of Utah.

As they were seated in the clinic's waiting room, a nurse came up to Connie with some paperwork for her to complete. "Today, we are mainly going to focus on preliminary testing, Mrs. Turner. We will take a sample of your blood, urine, take your blood pressure, heart rate, and temperature. Also, we will weigh you and get your height measurement. We will need a list of any medicines you are taking. Also, we are going to take the measurement of the electrical activity of your heart. That test is known as an ECG. Your friends can wait here in the waiting room, or we can call them when you are finished. After the testing is complete, your friends can accompany you in to visit with the doctor."

Jacob asked how long the tests would take. He was told about an hour.

"Why don't I give you my cell phone number, and then you can call us when Connie is ready to visit with the doctor? Would that be all right, Connie, or would you prefer we wait for you? We would be glad to."

"I'll be fine, Jacob. The nurse can call you when the doctor is ready to visit with me."

"We'll wait here with you until you finish your paperwork and the nurse is ready for you," Lily told her.

Fifteen minutes later, the nurse came back and ushered Connie into the lab. Connie waved back at them. "So, Lily, what shall we do for an hour up here on the University of Utah campus? Got any ideas?"

"Shall we just drive around and see what's new up here since I visited this campus about, maybe fifteen years ago? I think it's been that long since Samuel and I came up here to a BYU-Utah football game. As I remember, BYU won. We were ecstatic."

"I did my schooling back east, so I didn't get involved in the BYU-Utah rivalry until ten years ago when Trudy and I came back to live in Utah. Since then, I have been a U of U fan. Oh, oh, is that going to be a sticking point in our friendship, Lily dear?"

"Not if you change your affiliation, Jacob." Lily laughed. "Actually, I root for both teams unless they are playing each other. Then we might have a problem."

"So far, this year, both teams are doing well. Do you like basketball too?" Jacob asked.

"Of course. I used to play basketball whenever I could. My ward had a basketball team, and we were really good. For a while there, we won every game we played. Then I met Samuel. Basketball didn't seem so important after that."

"I know what you mean, Lily."

After a pause, Lily changed the subject. "When are we going to start giving the gold coins away, Jacob? It has been a while since we last talked about it."

"Actually, dear lady, I have spoken to Aaron about who he might like to give some of the coins to. He immediately mentioned little Grace's family. They are still grieving over the loss of their little daughter. He thought he would like to give them the first one. Would that be all right?"

Lily smiled at Jacob when she answered, "Oh, that's a marvelous idea."

"Also, there were a couple of boys, identical twins, who have leukemia, but their mother says they are in remission. He would like to give that family one also."

Lily replied, "When you take me home, Jacob, I will give you two of the gold coins to give to Aaron, and he can see that the two families each get one. They should probably be told that they are from Carson and Kay Hunter, don't you think?"

"I do, honey."

For a while, they were silent, as they toured around the campus and around the expensive homes on the hills close to the school. When Jacob's phone rang, they drove back to the clinic. As they walked in the door, the nurse met them and ushered them into the patient room where Connie and the doctor were seated.

The doctor stood, and Jacob and Lily introduced themselves. The doctor spoke, "What we are trying to determine is if Connie is a candidate for one or more of the clinical studies that are about to begin at this hospital. Her vital signs are good. In a week or so, we will get the results back on the ECG test we just took and on the blood work. At that time, we will decide what study to enter her in and find out at that time if she really wants to participate. She can take home the literature we have on each study, and if and when she is cleared to join, she will know what she wants to do. How does that sound, Connie?" Without waiting for her to answer, the doctor continued, "Let me explain the two clinical studies that are about to begin to kind of give you all an overview right now. One study will be testing new medicines which, hopefully, will prove helpful in regenerating the nerves in the spinal cord. This may entail one drug or a combination of drugs.

"The other involves electrical muscle stimulation, or electrotherapy. This is used for relaxation of muscle spasms, increase of local blood circulation, muscle rehabilitation, and reeducation electrical muscle stimulation, etc. There may be a crossover in which medicines are used along with the electrical stimulation. The studies will involve some period of time. I don't know how long. Spinal cord injuries are complicated. But there are hopeful signs that Connie can get movement in her legs. Time will tell.

"One more thing, we will want Connie to stay at the clinic while the studies are being conducted. This is so we can monitor her twenty-four hours a day. We are not sure exactly how long we will want to keep you here, Connie, but it may be as long as a month. Please take that into consideration as you contemplate your decision. Thanks for coming in, Mr. Manning and Mrs. Langston, with Connie. She will need a lot of support and encouragement. We will call her in a week or so with the results of her tests." After shaking hands with each one, the doctor walked out of the room. The nurse returned and ushered them to the door. "Good luck, Connie." She smiled as they walked out.

As they drove Connie home, Connie remarked that she had a lot of studying to do. "It's pretty complicated, I think. And I can't help about the future costs. Even with the funds coming in from the sale of your CD, I am not sure if I'll be able to afford the treatments, even if they prove to be promising."

Lily answered, "Connie, don't worry about the money. Just read the literature, and we'll see where this all leads. Your initial studies won't cost you anything. I think there will be some compensation for time and travel. Let's just see what happens. Things have a way of working out for the best."

"You are such a dear, Lily."

"You've noticed too, Connie?" Jacob jabbed his finger gently in Lily's arm. They all chuckled.

Jacob and Lily helped Connie wheel her chair into the house and got her situated before saying goodbye. Connie smiled a big thank you and waved to them as they closed the door behind them.

At Lily's home, they went inside, and Lily opened the safe and gave Jacob two of the gold coins. As they walked over to the outside door to say goodbye, Jacob planted a kiss firmly on the tip of Lily's nose.

CHAPTER FORTY-SEVEN

"I'm home, Mom," Aaron called to his mother as he came through the door. "How did your appointment go today at the clinic?"

Connie was seated in her wheelchair next to the kitchen table reading from some papers. "Good, dear. I have a lot of reading to do. These papers are what the clinic gave me so I would be informed on the clinical trials that are set to begin right after Thanksgiving."

"Do you know if you are going to be eligible to participate, Mom?"

"Not yet. It will take a few days to get the results of the tests they took. In the meantime, I am to read this information so that when they call me, I can let them know if I am interested in continuing with the program. If they accept me, and I agree that I want to do it, I have to go into the clinic and plan to stay there for thirty days. I am wondering how you are going to manage, Aaron."

"Mom, I'll be fine."

"You've never been alone before. I know when you get to be sixteen, you think you can do anything, but it will get very lonely here for a whole month. I've been thinking about Steven and was wondering how you and he are getting along. Are you enjoying your association with him, or has it become a strain? Are you having second thoughts about wanting him in your life, dear?"

"The more I am with him, the more I admire him. He is a very good man, Mom. I am glad he is in my life. Every day we have so much to talk about. After class, he spends a few minutes with me before we both have to be to our next class. He has been telling me about his time in the Navy and about his schooling. He asks me all kinds of questions too. He asks me all about you too. He still loves you, you know?"

"Aaron, I don't want to dwell on the past. I should never have sent him away. But that part of my life is over. I can't go back and change anything, but I can make sure I do what is right now. I just want more than anything for you to be happy, and I want him to be happy too. Having you in each other's lives seems to be working out well. Wonderful. If it works out that I can be a part of his life also, then it is meant to be. I was wondering if Steven might like to come and spend that month with you here. I would feel better knowing that you are not alone, and it would give you two more time to bond. You wouldn't have to get acquainted in bits of time here and there. What do you think, do you want to ask him if he would be interested?"

"I'll ask him tomorrow, Mom. I think it is a wonderful idea. We could work on some musical numbers together."

Aaron added, "I got a call from Paul Strong on my cell phone at lunch today. It was good to hear from him. He said the CD is flying off the shelves at the big stores. If this keeps up, his expenses will be paid by Christmas, and we can start making some money on each sale made after that."

Connie clapped her hands together. "That is great. How much have you made from the sales at the hospital? Do you know offhand, dear?"

"I have deposited close to $8,000 in my savings account altogether. I am so happy the CD is doing well. The money will go to help in your treatments, whatever they will be, Mom. Also, I was talking with Lily, and we are thinking that as soon as we find out what procedure your doctor is going to be interested in your doing, and what the approximate cost will be, we will put on a benefit concert. Dad said he would like to help in any way he can. He's a good man, Mom," Aaron repeated.

"What is he having you do with him in your music class, son? I know you are working on a Thanksgiving program for the students at your school. Is he having you play your guitar with any of the music?"

"He is. He is also having me sing a couple of solo parts, just short ones. He is going out of his way not to show favoritism, so others in the group will also have solos. And some of the other students play instruments, so he has written in parts in the music for them to solo in. It is going to be a great concert. The students all love him, Mom. They want to make him proud of them, so they are working hard."

"That is wonderful, Aaron. I am really looking forward to coming to the concert. I hope you will invite Lily and her children and Jacob and James. What about Lily's parents and Samuel's parents?"

"Lily and Jacob and the kids already know they are invited and have said they will be there. I will remind them to bring their parents, Jacob's parents too. Also, I think Carson Hunter and Kay will be there also. You know I have been keeping in touch with little Grace's family. I am going to call them and invite them to come to the choir's Thanksgiving concert too. They are still having a pretty rough go of it. Perhaps coming to the concert will give them some solace.

"Jacob Manning brought me two of the gold coins that Lily got from Carson Hunter. One of them will be for Grace's family, and the other for the family of the twin boys I told you about whose leukemia is in remission. I'll give the Summers theirs at the concert, and then in the next few days, I'll see that the other family gets the other one."

"It must be so hard losing a child. I am glad you have been keeping in touch with them," Connie said. "And giving those two families each a gold coin should certainly help to boost their spirits."

"Now, Aaron, what shall we fix for dinner tonight?"

"I am thinking about opening a can of tomato soup and warming it up with a can of milk. For some reason, I am hungry for a cup of tomato soup and some of that French bread we have. We also have some fruit salad in the fridge left over from last night," Aaron said.

"That sounds delicious. Afterward, Aaron my dear, will you entertain me with some of the new songs you are working on for the concert?"

CHAPTER FORTY-EIGHT

Steven Black was just getting ready to begin his first class of the day when Aaron motioned him from the doorway. Steven excused himself from the students and walked to the door. "Hi, Aaron. Is everything all right?"

"I just had to see you first thing this morning. Mom has suggested that I ask you if you would be willing to come and stay with me when she goes into the clinic for the clinical study she will be involved in, if they accept her. Would you?"

"I would love to, Aaron. Do you know the dates yet?"

"If they take her, and she is willing, it will be after Thanksgiving and goes to just before the Christmas holidays."

"That's great. We'll talk about it after your class this afternoon, son. You better get to class now." With that, he gave his son a high five.

"Okay, Dad, I'll see you this afternoon. Bye." Aaron waved and ran down the hall to his class.

As Steven taught, he couldn't help but feel a sense of anticipation at the prospect of spending a whole month with Aaron, a whole month to be with this special young man, his son whom he never would have known if he had not come back to Salt Lake City. He knew that he had been guided back to his hometown. And it was not a coincidence that he had found Aaron. He knew that with his whole being. The spirit had guided him. *I'm a grown man, and the tears won't be denied.* He smiled to himself. *I have got to get hold of myself or my students will think I'm a crybaby.*

In the two months since he had found Aaron and Connie, he had never been happier. He had begun to go back to church. Now with Aaron and Connie in his life, with the gospel he felt complete. He wasn't sure what the future would bring for his relationship with Connie, but for now, just having her in his life was enough.

He loved teaching. His students were trying hard to learn the music, and it was beginning to sound wonderful. There were just two more weeks until the concert.

He smiled as the young people walked through the door to begin the second class of the morning. As they sat down at their desks, they got out their music. Steven sat down at the piano and began to play one of the songs they would be singing for the concert. "Let's go over the chorus. There is one rough spot in the second stanza at the top of page three. Do you see where I mean?" He then played through the music at the trouble spot, and after hitting a chord to give them each their notes, they began working on the spot. Soon, Steven was satisfied, and they began at the beginning and played and sang the song through a few times before they went on to their other pieces.

Later in the day when Aaron's class time came, Steven stood at the door to welcome the students. He gave Aaron a special smile and hug as he entered the classroom.

After class, Aaron picked up his books and walked up to his father. "I can tell that you are as excited about our spending a month together as I am, Dad. I can't wait. It will be so fun to hang out together."

"Aaron, I kind of had a hard time keeping my emotions in check during my classes today. I am so happy to have you and your mother in my life. There I go tearing up again. Men aren't supposed to get so emotional, are they?"

"It's okay, Dad. All the years since I was a little boy, I wondered what you were like. Mom never talked about you at all until recently when I finally asked her to tell me what she could. In the last couple of years, I have laid awake sometimes thinking about what it would be like to have my father in my life. I was planning to look for you when I turned eighteen. And here you are. How great is that?" Now they were both tearing up and laughing. Aaron said, "I guess we're both big babies."

"Well, Aaron, you have another class now, so you better dry your eyes and get going." Then Steven added, "I love you, son."

"I love you too, Dad. I love you too." Aaron put his arms around his father in a big bear hug. With a wave to his dad, Aaron wiped a tear from his cheek and walked out of the classroom.

CHAPTER FORTY-NINE

The ringing of the telephone caused Connie to jump. She answered and was greeted with a big hello from her doctor. "Connie, good news. You have been cleared to join the clinical study. It begins the Monday after Thanksgiving. That will be November 28. Your tests showed that you are a prime candidate for the study. So, dear lady, are you willing to participate?"

"Yes I am, Doctor. What time should I be at the clinic on the twenty-eighth, and what do I need to bring?"

"I will be sending you all the information you will need to prepare for the study, including what you should bring with you. We will want you there at 7:00 a.m. In the meantime, Connie, have a great Thanksgiving, and we will see you on Monday, the twenty-eighth. Bye now."

After hanging up, the first one she called was Lily. "Lily, the clinic has okayed me to take part in the clinical study they are going to do. It begins November 28."

"Fantastic, Connie. What can we do to help? Will you need a ride?"

"I'll let you know if I will need a ride, Lily. It's early enough in the morning at 7:00 a.m. that Steven may be able to drive me there before he and Aaron go to school. Steven is going to stay here with Aaron while I am in the hospital for that month. They are both very much looking forward to being here together. It will be good for them both, I am sure."

"Please let me know if there is anything I can do to help you prepare. Also, my girls and I are looking forward to the concert at the high school. My parents and Samuel's parents will be there. Jacob and James and Jacob's parents will also be going. We are looking forward to it. It will be a great concert I am sure."

"Steven and Aaron and the other students have been working hard on their numbers. I have been praying for it to be as marvelous as I think it will be."

"Connie, how would you and Aaron and Steven feel about coming here for Thanksgiving dinner. We would love to have you. We are planning to have Jacob and James and Jacob's parents and my parents and Samuel's parents. We would be happy if you would come and join us."

"Oh, Lily, we would love to, but won't that be too much for you?"

"Connie, I haven't felt much like celebrating anything since Samuel's death. But, lately, I feel the time is just right to get back into the swing of things. You know, show my appreciation for all of the Lord's blessings and His love. He has surely poured out His blessings on me and my family, and I want Him to know how much I appreciate His love by sharing this special Thanksgiving with my dear friends and family. I can't think of anything more fitting than having you and Aaron and Steven join us. Please say you will come?"

"Yes, of course we will come. Please let me know what I can bring. I love making rolls. Why don't I bring the rolls and butter?"

"That would be lovely, Connie. I'll plan on that. Dinner will be at 1:00 p.m. on the twenty-fourth. The high school concert is on Wednesday the twenty-third, so that week is going to be very busy. I look forward to it. I'll talk to you again soon, Connie, dear. Bye."

Connie couldn't wait until Aaron came home from school to tell him that she had been accepted to take part in the clinical study. Aaron called his father to tell him the good news. He also told him about the Thanksgiving invitation to dinner at the Langstons.

CHAPTER FIFTY

The school choir was seated in their places in their scarlet choir robes. They made a lovely picture. Lily was seated with her daughters, and James on one side of her. James insisted on sitting next to Susie. Their parents admonished them to sit still and not talk. Jacob sat next to Lily. Behind them sat Jacob's parents and Lily and Samuel's parents. On the other side of Jacob sat Connie in her wheelchair.

Aaron looked carefully over the crowd to see who had come whom he knew. He smiled at Lily and Jacob and their families. He watched as the Hunters walked in. He greeted them with a wave. And then he saw Hannah and Peter Summers, Grace's parents. And with them were their two children, Bobby and Jennie. Jennie was carrying Grace's doll, Hope, tightly in her small arms. They smiled and waved to Aaron who threw a big kiss back at them.

The pianist came in and sat at the piano to polite applause. Then Steven Black walked in and bowed to the audience, as they clapped for him.

"Good evening, ladies and gentlemen. Tonight you are in for a treat. The choir has worked very hard for you, and I think you will be very pleased with the result. Our student pianist is Marnie Edwards. Please give her a nice round of applause." Marnie stood up and bowed to the audience. "And I am Steven Black, choir director. We will begin our concert this evening with the lovely 'Bless This House'." Steven then turned to the choir and with a nod to Marnie began to wave his baton. The choir responded with the opening notes, and the audience settled down to a lovely evening of spectacular music.

One by one, the numbers were wonderful. Several of the students had solo parts, including Aaron. He also got to play his guitar on one of the numbers. One of the students who played the flute had a solo also.

"For the closing number, we are going to sing for you 'How Great Thou Art'. We would like all of you in the congregation to join us in singing the chorus after the fourth and last verse. I'm sure you all know the words." When it was time, Steven turned to the audience who then joined in singing the last chorus:

> Then sings my soul
> My Savior God, to thee,
> How great thou art!
> How great thou art!
> Then sings my soul
> My Savior God, to thee,
> How great thou art!
> How great thou art!

The audience then stood as one and clapped and cheered the choir. Steven Black raised his hand toward the choir who bowed in unison to the audience.

"Wow, that was amazing," Jacob Manning said. He turned to his parents. "What a lovely evening. Aren't you glad you came?"

No one in their group was in a hurry to leave. Aaron went over to the Summers and hugged each one of them. "Come and meet my family and friends." Aaron took Hannah's arm and ushered her and her family to where his mother and friends stood. "Hannah and Peter, this is my mother, Connie, and these are my friends, Lily Langston and her children Rose, Bonnie, and Susie. And these are Lily's parents, Fred and Julie Wright, and her late husband's parents, Matt and Dallas Langston. This is Jacob Manning, my attorney and friend, and his son, James. And here is Jacob's parents, Mary and John Manning. Hannah and Peter are the parents of my little friend, Grace, who died of leukemia a few months ago. These are their children, Bobby and Jennie."

As they greeted each other, the Hunters came up to visit. "What a wonderful concert, Aaron. Thank you for inviting us."

Carson and Kay Hunter were introduced all around, and as they talked together, Steven Black came up to them. "This is my father, Steven Black, everyone." Aaron smiled as the group acknowledged the tall redhead. "We have been getting to know each other. He is going to be staying with me while my mother is in the hospital taking part in the clinical study on spinal cord injuries. She will be there for a month. The study starts next Monday. It will be great having my dad stay with me. We are making lots of plans to do stuff together."

As Aaron spoke, Jennie came up and hugged his leg with one arm as she held her doll with the other. Aaron acknowledged her by hugging her and planting a kiss on the top of her head.

They continued visiting for several more minutes and then, as they noticed the chairs were being folded and stacked neatly on the side walls of the auditorium, Lily spoke, smiling, "I think they are telling us that the evening is over. It has been so special. Thank you, Steven, it was really terrific."

All joined in to congratulate him on the fine evening. Lily spoke again, "Remember, 1:00 p.m. at our home tomorrow for Thanksgiving dinner. Hannah and Peter, do you and your family have plans for Thanksgiving dinner tomorrow? If not, we would love it if you would join us?"

"Thank you, Lily," Hannah answered. "We are going to our parents' for dinner." She turned to Aaron. "It was a great evening, Aaron. Thanks, it is just what we needed."

Aaron took Hannah's hand in his. "I'll walk to the door with you guys. I have something for you." When they got to the door, Aaron reached in his coat pocket and pulled out a gold coin and placed it in Hannah's hand. Both Hannah and Peter stared at it in disbelief. Then they looked up at Aaron who had a big grin on his face. He told them how he had come into possession of the coin. "Jacob Manning and Lily Langston both agreed you were to have this coin. It was given to Lily by Carson Hunter. She could do whatever she wanted with them, and she wanted me to give you this one."

"Thank you all so much," Peter said. Hannah couldn't speak as she was crying softly and hugging her children to her. He and Hannah turned to Lily and Jacob and whispered their thanks before they quietly closed the door behind them.

After saying a warm goodbye to the Hunters, the group dispersed to their cars. "See you tomorrow everyone." Aaron and Steven got Connie into the car and waved to Hannah and Peter and the others as they and the Summers drove away. Jacob opened the car door for Lily as the youngsters piled in the back.

"Good night, James." At their front door, the girls and then Lily held up their hands in the "I love you" signal and pressed them against James's fingers. "You and Susie were very well behaved tonight," Lily told him. "I am very proud of you both."

James said, "You were good too, Lily. I was proud of you too."

Lily laughed. The others joined in. They were getting used to his charming precociousness. They were continually being surprised at the comments that came out of James. He could be a real charmer. Jacob kissed Lily on her forehead, waved to the girls, and he and James said goodbye, telling them they would be back the next day before 1:00 p.m.

CHAPTER FIFTY-ONE

All the guests were bringing some part of the dinner, so Lily and the girls only had to stuff and cook the turkey and get the table all ready. After the tables were set with their best china and the turkey was baking, Lily suggested they sing some songs. "Let's take turns and suggest what songs to sing," Lily told her daughters. "I'll go first. I choose 'Love at Home.' For the next half hour, their voices blended to the music of the hymns each in turn chose to sing. When the doorbell rang, they quickly ran to the door to see who was first to come."

"It's Jacob and James," Susie squealed. She grabbed James and took him to show him where they both would be sitting during dinner.

"Here I come bearing gifts." Jacob laughed as he handed Lily a covered dish.

"It smells wonderful, Jacob." She placed the candied yams on the main table. "Did you make those yourself?"

"Of course, who else could have made such a perfectly delicious and tasty dish. I am really quite a cook." Jacob smiled teasingly at Lily.

Jacob's parents were right behind him and were soon climbing the stairs to the front door. Dallas Manning was also carrying a bowl, which her husband took out of her hands as she got out of the car.

She had cooked baked potatoes and had brought butter, sour cream, and chives to top them with. These too were placed on the main table. "Thank you," Lily told them.

After them came Lily and Samuel's parents. They were followed soon after by Aaron, Connie, and Steven. Each had brought a dish for the dinner, a fruit salad, a tossed salad, and Connie's famous homemade rolls and butter.

Rose took her grandparents and sat them down at the head table. Jacob's parents were seated opposite the Langstons and the Wrights. Lily, Jacob, and Connie sat at an adjoining table with Aaron and Steven. The children were seated at a third table. All were in readiness for their Thanksgiving feast.

"Dad." Lily turned to her father. "Will you please give the blessing on the food?"

"Of course, honey." His prayer was a prayer of thanksgiving for all the blessings so abundantly showered on each and every one seated there on that special occasion. As he sat back down in his chair, he noticed that the guests were wiping at their eyes. It truly was a day of thanksgiving for each one in that gathering that day.

After the meal was over, Fred Wright got up again and cleared his throat. "I am thankful to be here in Lily's home to enjoy the company of all you special people of whom we have become very fond. I think it would be nice if each one of us would share a thought about what we are most thankful for." He turned to his wife. "Julie and I have been married for forty-five years. I am thankful for her, for my precious daughter, Lily, and my grandchildren, Rose, Bonnie, and Susie. And I am thankful for the gospel of Jesus Christ. All my blessings come from Him, the Savior of all."

Julie Wright then spoke to echo what her husband had said. She reached over and caught his hand in hers as she spoke.

The Langstons got on their feet together. Matt spoke for both of them when he acknowledged his love for his wife. "We miss Samuel. It is still hard to think of him not being with us. It has been a difficult time for the Langston and Wright families. We all miss him so much. We know that he is busy in the spirit world doing missionary work. And we know that he is happy. We also know that someday, we will be together again as a family. We want Lily to know how much we love her and admire her as a woman of great strength and courage. And you, young ones, we love you. You are the light that keeps us going every day. And we have grown very fond of Jacob and James and your parents. Thank you for being part of our world. Connie, we wish you great success in your upcoming clinical studies. May the Lord be with you every day. Aaron, you are a wonderful, talented young man. You have obviously inherited your musical talent from your father. We are glad to know you all. Thank you." With that, Matt and Karen Langston returned to their seat.

Jacob was next. "I, too, am thankful for the many gifts my Heavenly Father has poured upon my head. He gave me James. I love you, James. And I love my parents. Thank you for all you do for James and me. I am so thankful for my siblings. I don't get to see them as often as I would like because they live quite a ways away. But we talk on the phone often. They are good people. I want Aaron to know how much I love and admire him. He is truly a remarkable young man. Connie, he has much to thank you for his being so special. He gets that from you. Steven hasn't been in his life very long, but I believe you will be the father he has always wanted, and you will make each other very proud, I am sure. And, Lily, you know how much you mean to me. I have never known anyone like you. Like your in-laws said, you are strong and wise in so many ways and very talented. I love your girls too. We can all see where they get their good looks and talent from."

Steven Black got up and thanked everyone. "I just want you all to know that my coming back to Salt Lake City has got to be the greatest blessing in my life. I have found the dearest of friends. And I have a family, something I never thought I would ever have." With that, the tears rolled down Steven's cheeks. He wiped them away with the back of his hand. "I love Aaron and Connie so much." Not being able to say more, Steven sat back down. Connie leaned over from her wheelchair to squeeze Steven's hand. Aaron got up to put his arm around his dad. He too was crying.

"I am grateful that my dad found me. I just know that it was meant to be. Thank you, everybody, for being my friends. I have been blessed in so many ways. Lily and her family forgave me for the accident that took Samuel's life. Bless you all. You have brought so much joy into my life. And I love singing and playing for the patients and staff at the Hunter Cancer Clinic every Saturday. That has been such a blessing to me, even though it came in such a painful way for all of you in Samuel's family. I love you all so much." Aaron sat down.

Connie, who was wiping away tears, spoke, "Thank you all for being there for me and Aaron. Thank you for fixing up my house. I love being in it every day. It's so pretty with its new paint and pictures on the walls. And thank you for befriending Aaron in the most trying and painful time in his life. You are truly God's precious children in every way. Whatever happens with the clinical study, I will accept. It would be wonderful to be able to walk again, but I know it is in God's hands."

Lily stood up. "I want to thank my parents and Samuel's parents for all you have done for my girls and me. You are truly precious, and I love you very much. And, Mom and Dad, thank you for making me practice the piano when I wanted to be outside playing with my friends. I thought you were very hard taskmasters, but I truly thank you that you made me stick to practicing. Aaron's and our CD is doing surprisingly well. Paul Strong said all the up-front charges will be paid by Christmas, and then we will get our share of the proceeds.

"I want to tell Connie and Aaron that having you come into our lives has been truly a blessing. Thank you for your friendship. And I am looking forward to getting to know you, Steven. I am thankful for my girls. I love you so, so much. Also, thank you, Jacob, for your friendship." Lily smiled and winked at him. He smiled back at her. "And, James, I love you too, honey. You are truly a light in our lives. And, Mary and John, thank you for raising such a fine son."

As Lily sat down, Rose stood up. "Thank you, everybody, for coming today. This is really fun having you here for Thanksgiving. After we clean up the dishes, could we get together and sing some songs? Mom and Bonnie and Susie and I sang before you came. It was fun." Rose hesitated for a brief moment and then added, "And Aaron could play and sing for us too." The last remark brought a happy grin to Aaron's face.

"What a wonderful idea," Grandpa Wright said. "We were going to ask you if you would sing and play for us after dinner. Before we start clearing the dishes, Bonnie and Susie and James, do you wish to add your thoughts to those that have been uttered here today?"

Susie got up. "I am thankful that you all came today. And I am thankful for all my blessings."

Bonnie echoed her sister, "Me too."

Jacob asked James if he wanted to say anything. "What's for dessert?"

Lily and the others laughed, but Jacob looked sternly at his son. "Aren't you thankful for your blessings, James? Your grandparents have been wonderful to you, and everyone else here has too."

"Thank you, everyone, for being my friends. I love you." With that, James held up his hand in the "I love you" sign. "Now, can we have dessert?"

Lily smiled at James. "Can you wait a little while, dear? Let's clear up and then have our little concert. After that, we will have dessert. Will you be all right until then?"

"Okay, I guess," James went over to stand by Susie.

After the dinner dishes were washed and put away, the floor swept and everything back in place, the families gathered together to sing the music of Thanksgiving. Aaron sang a couple of his own songs, including the one he wrote for his mother.

Susie asked her mother if she could play her latest piano piece for the guests. She was given permission and sat down and played a simple arrangement of "Families Can Be Together Forever."

"That was very good, Susie. Bonnie, do you want to play one of the piano selections you've been working on?" Lily asked. "Play that Chopin piece you've been practicing."

Bonnie replied, "Okay, Mom, but it still needs some work." She sat down at the piano and played the piece with only a couple of mistakes. Everyone clapped.

Rose then sat at the piano and played the latest piece she was working on. It too was a Chopin piece. Again, everyone clapped.

"You girls are getting good on the piano," Jacob commented. "It won't be long 'til you're as good as your mother."

"Not hardly, Jacob," Rose answered. "She is light-years ahead of us."

"But keep practicing hard, and one day you will be as proficient as she is. The secret is hard work and sticking to it every day."

"That is sure the secret of success," Lily said. "Now, how about that dessert we promised you, James?"

"What is it?" James asked.

"Do you like pumpkin pie and ice cream?"

"Yes. Can I have a big piece and a big scoop of ice cream, Lily?"

"Of course, James, if it's all right with your father."

Jacob smiled at his son, "Why don't you show Lily how big a slice you want. But remember the rule, son, you have to eat every spoonful you take."

The pie and ice cream was all dished up, and James picked out the piece he wanted and went to sit by Susie and Rose and Bonnie. After dessert was eaten and conversation wound up, everyone said their goodbyes. What a wonderful day it had been.

"Connie, we will be praying for you, dear lady. We will find out what the visiting hours are going to be at the clinic and come and visit you every day." Lily reached over to give her a hug and kiss her cheek. The rest of the group all came forward with their well-wishes.

"Steven, are you taking Connie to the clinic Monday morning as you had planned? Do you need any help?"

"We'll be fine, Lily. Thanks for asking. I'm taking Monday off to get Connie settled."

"Good, well, good night then. Let us know when the visiting hours will be, Steven."

"I will."

"Good night, everyone." As each family member walked out the door, there were hugs and kisses. Soon, Lily and her daughters and Jacob and James were standing at the door getting ready to bid each other farewell. James made the round of "I love yous," while Jacob said his goodbyes. This time, he kissed Lily lightly on the lips. She didn't resist.

CHAPTER FIFTY-TWO

Steven Black handed the nurse at the clinic Connie's suitcase. "Right this way, please," she commanded them to follow her down the hall. They turned into a small hospital room. At the last minute, Connie had agreed to having Aaron accompany her and Steven to the clinic. She knew her son wanted very much to be there to see her settled in, and she wanted him to be there too. His missing one day of school wouldn't hurt.

"This will be Mrs. Turner's room for the next month," the nurse said. Connie was pleased to see that the room was more like her bedroom at home than one a person would find in a hospital. The bed was queen-sized and looked quite comfortable. There was an end table that held a lamp and some reading material. There were two padded chairs also. There was a 50" TV screen opposite the bed. Connie could lay in her bed to watch TV or sit in her wheelchair. Pretty white-lace curtains framed the window.

There was a private bathroom, and over the bed was hanging a series of pulleys and cords for what, Connie had no idea. However, she knew she would undoubtedly soon find out.

"Please sit down. The doctor will come in soon to talk to you." The nurse walked out into the hall.

Steven and Aaron took the chairs as Connie sat in her wheelchair. "After we get you settled in to begin your treatment," Steven said, "Aaron and I will go over to my place and pack up my things to take over to your house. Do you have everything you need, Connie?"

"I followed the directions that were given me, so I think I got everything. If I have forgotten anything, you could bring it tonight if you are coming back."

Just then, the doctor walked through the door. "Mrs. Turner, I am Mark Hill. I will be overseeing your treatment while you are here in the clinic." Dr. Hill was of medium build, sandy-haired, in his middle fifties.

"This is my son, Aaron, and Steven Black."

The doctor shook hands with the two men. He then went to the door and asked the nurse to bring in another chair.

After sitting down, Dr. Hill began to talk to them about what would be happening during the thirty days Connie would be hospitalized. "There are six patients who are taking part in this clinical study. You will meet them all tomorrow. There are three men and two other women besides you, Ms. Turner. I see your name is Connie. May I call you Connie?" Dr. Hill asked.

"Of course, Doctor. I would prefer to be called by my first name."

"Good, then Connie it is. We will be doing a number of procedures on you and your team members. In the material we sent home with you to read was the information on what is known as Functional Electrical Stimulation or FES for short. You will exercise on an FES bicycle three times a week. This technology allows a person with little or no voluntary leg movement to pedal a stationary leg-cycle called an ergometer. Computer-generated, low-level electrical pulses are transmitted through surface electrodes to the leg muscles. This causes coordinated contractions and the pedaling motion.

"These bikes have been on the market for over twenty years. If these exercises prove helpful, and you wish to have one in your home at the end of the treatment here, they cost approximately $15,000. There are some of these bikes that are set up in health clubs and rehab centers in the city so they would be available in one of those places. Right now, we won't concern ourselves with what needs to be done after you leave here, Connie. There will be plenty of time for that later.

"We will also do some locomotor training. Another name for this is treadmill training. You will be suspended in a harness above a treadmill. This reduces the weight the legs will have to bear. As the treadmill begins to move, therapists will move your legs in a walking pattern. The theory that drives the work is that paralysis causes 'learned nonuse' of muscles. The theory behind this is that when a paralyzed person is retrained to walk, both the brain and spinal cord figure out new ways to do it. Many people with paralysis, regardless of time elapsed since onset, have improved their walking after receiving locomotor training. The level of recovery is different for each person, so there is great hope we will be successful in your case, Connie.

"Aquatherapy is another treatment you will be involved in. The effects of gravity are greatly reduced in water so that small body movements can be more easily detected, and therapists can determine a person's maximum ability to move without the full resistance of gravity. When people are beginning to recover movement, water makes practice easier. We will be giving you medicine to help make your bones stronger. When people can't exercise, they tend to lose bone density and develop osteoporosis, so the drugs we will be giving you will help with that.

"One more thing is the system of pulleys and cords above your bed. I hope they haven't made you nervous. We want you to get plenty of rest, of course. But for a few minutes each day, we want you to exercise the upper part of your body. A good time to do this is when you are watching television. Upper body strength will greatly help in your recovery. If we need to use further treatments, then upper-body strength will be essential. I am referring to a locomotor system called a Lokomat. The device is described as an exoskeleton (an external skeleton) with robotic joints at the hip and knee to guide the user's legs as they step along the treadmill. There are exciting new innovations coming out, such as the exoskeleton that will be available soon. Do either of you have questions you wish to ask me?"

Steven asked, "What about visiting hours, Doctor?"

"There are visiting hours scheduled every evening from 6:00 p.m. until 8:00 p.m. During the day, we want our patients to rest in between the treatments, so we are asking visitors to come after dinner and not during the day. That way, we can have an uninterrupted workday. Now, Connie, say your goodbyes to your visitors. Lunch will be served in about an hour, and then we'll get to work. It's good to meet you, Mr. Black, and you, Aaron."

"Thank you, Doctor."

"Well, Aaron, are you up to helping me pack my things and taking them over to your house? Then we will go to some place for lunch, perhaps some pizza place."

Aaron reached over to hug and kiss his mother. Steven hugged her and told her they would be back at six. Steven followed Aaron out the door.

CHAPTER FIFTY-THREE

After Aaron and Steven filled their plates with food, they sat down at a table near the window. They had decided to go to a place that served food, buffet style. They arrived there after picking up Steven's clothes, his keyboard, and other items from his apartment.

"Let's make a list of groceries we need to get while your mother is in the clinic, Aaron. Then after we are finished eating, we can go shopping. Do you know what all we will need?"

Aaron pulled a slip of paper out of his pocket. "Well, Dad, I just happen to have the list right here. Mom insisted that I write down things we will probably run out of, like detergent and paper towels, etc. So you will just need to add some of your favorite foods, and we'll be set." Aaron handed the paper to Steven who proceeded to add a few items to the list.

After they finished their leisurely lunch, they stopped at Walmart to purchase supplies and then headed to Aaron and Connie's house. When they arrived, Steven's things were hauled into the house, and then they both spent the next few hours getting Steven settled in and the groceries put away. After eating a light supper and watching the five o'clock news, Steven and Aaron headed back to the hospital. On the way, Aaron called Lily to tell her that Connie was settled in at the clinic and when the visiting hours were.

*****

"How did your first afternoon go, Connie?" Steven asked.

"It went well. Mostly, the nurse took me around and showed me the equipment and got me acquainted with all the staff. I know it's going to be challenging, but I intend to keep a positive attitude."

"Good, Mom, that will sure help."

"Lily called to say she and her daughters would be here in a while. It will be nice to see them."

About a half hour later, Lily, Rose, Bonnie, and Susie came in to the hospital room to visit with Connie.

"This is cool. It looks like my bedroom at home," Rose said.

"I like it too, Rose," Connie told her. "It helps to make me feel like I am at home, not in a hospital."

"The lace curtains are a nice touch," Lily added. "That picture of the Wasatch Mountains on the wall there is lovely too."

At eight o'clock, Connie's guests were ushered out with hugs and well-wishes. Connie sat in her chair and watched television until the nurse came in to get her settled in bed. As she lay there waiting for sleep, Connie prayed to her Father in heaven for the strength to stay positive through the coming ordeal. She told Him how thankful she was for this opportunity, and that she would accept the outcome with dignity and grace, whatever it might be. She thanked him for Aaron and for Steven coming into their lives. She finished with thanks for her wonderful friends and ended in the name of Jesus Christ, amen.

CHAPTER FIFTY-FOUR

As Connie spent the next four weeks in the clinic, life continued to be somewhat of a whirl in the Langston home. The girls went to school every weekday, came home to do their homework, practiced the piano, and helped getting dinner and cleaning up after. After the practicing, homework and chores were done, the girls were allowed to watch television for a while before going to bed.

Lily taught school two days a week as a substitute teacher, practiced her piano for several hours each day, and helped the girls with their homework in the evenings. They had family home evening on Mondays, as usual. Every evening, they spent a few minutes with Connie at the clinic.

Jacob and James were often invited to come join Lily and her girls for dinner. About once a week, Jacob and Lily and the children went out to dinner at some of their favorite restaurants. They would pile in Jacob's car and head to the clinic for a brief visit and then to eat.

*****

The first snowfall happened the first weekend in December. Great snowflakes filled the cold winter air in a fairy-tale setting. Jacob and Lily bundled up the kids, and then they walked around the neighborhood. It was magical.

"Mom, when I look up, I feel like I'm floating in the air," Susie commented. "It's fun."

"Let's go skiing this weekend if the ski resorts are open," Jacob suggested.

"Can we, Mom?" Bonnie asked.

"Of course, I'd like that," Lily answered. "It may be another week before the ski resorts are open, though. But we'll go when they are. Shall we go up to Alta, then?" Lily asked Jacob.

"Yes, Alta Ski Resort it is. If it isn't open until the weekend after this, then that is when we will go. We'll spend the whole day up there, all right?"

James squealed, "Susie and I get to ride the lift together, don't we?"

"We'll see, James. I think for a few times you will need either Lily or I to go on the lift with you. It will be safer for you to have an adult with you."

"Okay, Dad."

"Let's see if Aaron and Steven want to join us," Lily said.

"Good idea. When we know when we will be going up the mountain, we'll check and see if they can go with us," Jacob told her.

CHAPTER FIFTY-FIVE

"Jacob and Lily want us to go skiing with them," Aaron told his father as he hung up the phone. "Have you ever been on skis, Dad?"

"I learned to ski after I got out of the Navy. I got to be quite good, if I do say so myself. When do they want to go?"

"Alta Ski Resort is opening this weekend. They want to make a day of it. But I have to work at the cancer clinic like I do every Saturday. Then I have my miniconcert later in the day. I won't be able to go, but you could, Dad. Why don't you go with them? It would be a good time to get to know them and for them to get to know you better."

"I wish there was some way you could go too, Aaron?"

"It's okay, Dad. If I had known ahead of time, I probably could have made up the work hours during the week after school. There'll be another time, I'm sure."

"All right, I'll call Lily and tell her I would like to go with them."

*****

Saturday morning, Jacob and James arrived at the Langston home to take Lily and her daughters skiing. After getting everyone settled in his parents' suburban and the skis stowed on the top in the ski rack, Jacob headed over to the Turner house to pick up Steven. The vehicle Jacob had borrowed from his parents had three seats to accommodate the four children and three adults. They drove to the area at the bottom of the mountain where they could park the car and take the ski bus up the mountain to the ski area.

Earlier, Steven had driven Aaron to work at the cancer hospital. Snow was falling, and Steven didn't want Aaron to have to ride his bicycle. Later, he would pick him up, get some dinner, and head over to the clinic to visit with Connie.

After they arrived at the parking area, they all piled out of the car, grabbed their skis, and climbed into the ski bus, with several others, to ride up the mountain for their day of skiing. The snow had stopped falling when they arrived at the ski run, and it was a bright, crisp sunny day that greeted them as they rode the ski lift to the landing at the top. Jacob and Lily made sure the youngsters were bundled up and ready before they headed down the slope. They had decided to ski the easier run the first time, but as they day wore on, they were going down the intermediate runs.

At lunchtime, they skied to the lodge, removed their skis and gloves, and went in to have lunch together. "James, you are getting good on those skis of yours," Jacob told him. This pleased James, especially when the others told him the same thing.

"I like to ski," he answered. "Now I am going to have a hamburger and some French fries. I'm very hungry."

"So am I," Susie said. "And I want what James is having. And I want a chocolate milk shake, okay, Mom?"

"Wouldn't you rather have hot chocolate, Susie?"

"Nope, a milk shake."

"Me too," James said.

"I'll have a bowl of clam chowder with my hamburger, thank you," Rose told her mother and Jacob.

"That sounds good," Bonnie said. "But I want a slice of pepperoni pizza instead of a hamburger. I'll have a bowl of clam chowder and a piece of pizza and a large Sprite, thank you."

Steven said, "That sounds good, Bonnie. I'll have what she is having," he told the waitress.

The waitress took their orders, and as they waited, they talked about their morning together. "You all did so well this morning," Lily said. "It is really fun having you with us, Steven. We all wish Aaron could have come too. He has been very conscientious in his probation assignment. He is very special. We all have grown very fond of him."

"He is a wonderful young man. We are having a great time living together while Connie is in the clinic. We play music every night, get dinner together, watch television. We like the same shows, and we like to watch sports games. It has been great so far. I wish it wouldn't have to come to an end," Steven finished on a wistful note.

A few minutes later, their dinners arrived. Jacob had ordered a steak and all the trimmings, and Lily had ordered a crab salad. An hour later, they were again on the slopes. Under the watchful eye of their parents, James and Susie were allowed to ride the ski lift together. "No funny stuff, all right? That means you have to sit still."

"We will, Mom," Susie called to her mother.

The rest of the day went as the morning had. When they piled back on the ski bus for the ride down the mountain from the Alta Ski Resort, they were very tired but happy. It had been a great day. Later, they would get showers, dress, and go visit Connie for a little while.

*****

Connie greeted them all with a huge smile. "Tell me all about your day," she demanded. "Oh, I wish I could have been there."

"One day you will be riding down the slopes with the best of them," Lily told her. "We will all be there to cheer you on."

"That is sure something to work toward," Connie said. "This is very difficult, what they are putting me through. But I will keep that goal in mind. I have been praying for the strength to endure this. During the breaks in between the procedures, I lie here and mostly sleep. Now I know why I can't have visitors during the day. All this is very exhausting."

"We are all praying for you," Lily remarked.

Just then, Aaron and Steven walked through the door. Aaron went to his mother and gave her a big hug and kiss.

After asking her about her day, he turned to Lily and her daughters and Jacob and James. "I had my little concert at the hospital today again after my shift. It was on the third floor for the children.

I love playing for the children, they are so innocent and sweet, and so loving."

Steven added, "I got to the hospital just as Aaron was beginning to play and sing. The room was packed. The doctors and nurses come in to listen to him too. If they are not needed during that hour, they all come in to hear him. It is quite the scene." Steven continued, "There are as many or more staff members there as there are patients. Aaron is so good. Several of the staff came up to me and told me how much they appreciate Aaron, not only for his skills as a janitor"—Steven laughed at that—"but his musical skills as well. They all told me they have purchased several copies of his and Lily's family's CD for Christmas gifts. I am sure proud of him."

"Thanks, Dad. The staff has been great to support me in every way they can. If mother can benefit from using one of those bicycles at home they are using for her treatment here in the hospital, you know, the ones with the Functional Electrical Stimulation capabilities, I think we will have the $15,000 to pay for one after the first of the new year. I have about $10,000 saved already from the sales from the CDs here at the hospital."

"We, our family, would be happy to help with the rest of the money, Aaron," Lily told him.

"That would be great, Lily. You are truly amazing. We may not need financial help, but if we do, we will gladly accept your generous offer," Connie told to her friend.

Susie came and stood next to Connie's wheelchair. "Are you really going to be able to walk someday, Connie?"

"If it is God's will, Susie. The doctors and nurses and I are working very hard to get my nerves to respond to messages from my brain. We are doing everything that we can. With God's help, anything is possible. I truly believe that."

"So do I, Connie."

"Me too," James echoed. Everyone nodded their agreement as they chuckled at James's response.

"Mom, Dad is putting together a Christmas concert for the school. It is going to be held on December 22, the day after you get out of the clinic. He has asked Lily and her girls and me to sing together. We will sing as an ensemble group with the high school choir in the background. We are to sing two numbers together. One will be 'What Child is This.' You will be able to be there. Isn't that great?"

Connie clapped her hands together. "Steven, how wonderful. It is something I can look forward to for the next two and a half weeks of hard labor." She laughed and continued, "What is the other song you will be singing together?"

Lily said, "We have been thinking of doing, 'Oh Holy Night.' Do you have another song you would prefer us to do, Connie?"

"Oh no. That is my all-time favorite Christmas carol. Oh, I am so happy. God is blessing us so very much. I can hardly wait."

"Every day after school from now until the concert, Lily will pick up her girls from their schools and bring them over to the high school for practices. They will rehearse with the choir and Aaron for about an hour every week night except Monday night," Steven told the group. "Then when we are finished practicing, we will get dinner and come and visit here at the clinic," Lily said.

Jacob stood up and took Connie's hand. "Just keep working, Connie. And we will keep praying for success." He then bent down and kissed her forward. Connie patted his hand and said, "I will, Jacob. I will."

CHAPTER FIFTY-SIX

The next two and a half weeks were a whirl of activity. The time went so fast that it seemed to pass with lightning speed.

Lily and the girls managed here and there to get their home decorated for the holidays, and the Christmas tree up and lighted. They had the lights on timers so that every evening when they got home from the clinic after visiting with Connie, the twinkling lights would greet them. Lily would park the car in the garage, close the door, and then run outside with her daughters to walk around on the sidewalk, looking up and admiring the lights on the tree in the front, on the fence around their property, in the windows. Some of the lights would twinkle off and on, and some were steady. Beside the giant lighted tree, they had placed a snowman. The snowman moved on a swivel stand and seemed to mimic their movements as they walked back and forth.

"Mom, it's a fairyland," Bonnie said. The snow began to fall as they stood gazing at the yard. "I wish we could keep the lights on for another month."

"Believe me, Bonnie, after the New Year, you will be anxious to get the lights down and be done with them for another year." Lily laughed. "Well, let's go in. You still have homework to do."

"Are James and Jacob coming over tonight, Mom?" Susie asked.

"Not tonight, honey. They need to spend some time with their family. They are putting up their tree, and then Jacob's siblings and their families are coming to spend a few days with them before Christmas. They invited us over whenever we have the time. I just don't know when that will be, girls. We are so tied up with getting ready for the Christmas concert and going and visiting Connie nearly every day. Then on Sundays, we go to visit your grandparents. The concert is only three days away now. They will be with us that night, for sure, and I have invited all of Jacob's family to come to the concert. They are very excited to come, Jacob tells me.

"Also, we will see Jacob and James on Christmas day. And we are going to get together during the holidays and go skiing as often as we can. Aaron and Steven will join us too. Also, I think I will invite the Greens to go skiing with us. That would be fun, don't you think?"

"Yes, it's been too long since we have done anything with the Greens. I have missed them," Rose said. "I have texted Josh and Margaret nearly every day, but it would be nice to do something with them. It was great going camping with them in the summer."

"We'll call them, I promise," Lily told her girls.

CHAPTER FIFTY-SEVEN

Jacob and James sat with Jacob's parents and his siblings and their families. The concert was about to begin. Lily and her daughters had met them as they walked into the hall. They greeted each other with warm handshakes, and then the Langston family ushered them to the seats they had been saving for them next to Connie.

"We have to sit up there by the choir," Lily said. "We'll see you after, okay?"

Jacob hugged her. "Go knock 'em dead, honey," he teased her. James gave each one of Lily's girls their special "I love you" sign, and then Lily too.

After they all sat down, Steven Black stood up and acknowledged the cheering crowd. Once again, the high school choir outdid themselves. Steven had worked his magic on the group. They sang carols that were old favorites mixed in with some lesser-known works. They were all sung beautifully.

When Lily sat down at the piano, her daughters stood in front of the baby grand. Aaron came to stand on the other side of Rose. They sang "What Child Is This." The choir sang with them on certain passages. When they were finished singing, the large crowd cheered wildly. Lily, her daughters, and Aaron bowed in acknowledgment.

After their number, Steven had the choir sing some fun Christmas music such as "I Saw Mommy Kissing Santa Claus" and "The Twelve Days of Christmas," which members of the choir acted out.

Then, for the last number of the evening, Lily again sat at the piano with her girls and Aaron in front of her. They then played and sang the beloved "Oh, Holy Night." The choir came in on the last two verses, humming behind Lily and her daughters and Aaron on the second verse and then singing the words softly with them on the last verse, building up to a glorious crescendo at the end.

When the last note was sung, the crowd stood on their feet and cheered loudly. Steven pointed to Lily and her family and Aaron and then to the choir. The crowd loved the music and kept cheering for several minutes. It had been a spectacular evening. Steven wished the large crowd a very merry Christmas. Lily and the girls and Aaron were thanked over and over again. The choir members circled them and told them how lovely their music had been. Lily's family and Aaron graciously returned the compliment.

As the crowd was leaving, Connie asked Lily if she and her daughters and their other close friends would stay for a few minutes. She wanted to show them something. As they huddled around her in great anticipation, Connie motioned to Aaron. Aaron came and knelt by his mother and gently removed one of her shoes. As he lifted her foot, she wiggled her toes.

"I couldn't do that before. All that hard work is paying off. The doctor and nurses were thrilled. I couldn't wait to surprise all of you," Connie commented, tears streaming down her cheeks.

"Oh, Connie, how wonderful." Lily put her arms around her friend and gave her a big hug. Her daughters came and hugged her too. Everyone there was happy for her.

"How did the others in your test group do?" Jacob asked.

"There were six of us all together," Connie explained. "All but two of them showed marked improvement. The doctor is not giving up on any of them. There are great advances in the area of spinal cord injuries. The doctors will be trying other treatments on them shortly, I am sure."

"Wiggle your toes, again, Connie," Susie said.

James came forward to watch closely as she moved her toes again. "Can you walk yet?" James asked.

"No, dear, I am a long way from being able to walk. But now I know that it is very possible, even likely, if I work hard over the next months, that I will be able to walk."

Steven came to stand behind Connie's wheelchair. "Connie and Aaron have asked me to stay with them. If I do, I will be able to help with her exercises. We have ordered one of those bicycles, you know, the Functional Electrical Stimulation thingies. Connie will need Aaron and I to help her every day."

"We have plenty of room for Dad to stay with us. We have an extra bedroom, and Dad and I can share the second bathroom. It is going to be great." All present could see the excitement in Aaron's eyes.

"Well, this is cause for a celebration, don't you think?" Jacob asked. Everyone agreed. "Let's meet at that little restaurant down the street south of here, say in about twenty minutes."

Shortly thereafter, their group was seated at one large table that had been arranged by putting several small tables together. As Lily sat there, she realized what a special time this was. Connie very likely going to be able to walk again. The Lord was blessing her, there was no doubt about it.

Lily glanced around the table, looking at each person sitting there. Jacob and James sat on one side of her. Next to them sat Jacob's parents, the Mannings, and then Jacob's sister and brothers and their families. Next to her on the right side were her own sweet daughters. Next to them were Aaron, Steven, and Connie in her wheelchair.

As she looked at Jacob's family, she mused, *These people could be my family if Jacob and I marry. How would I manage with an autistic stepchild? Well, that's a no-brainer. He is very special, and my girls and I love him dearly. James already feels like he belongs.* Lily tucked her hand in Jacob's under the table. He smiled and squeezed her hand as if he understood what she was thinking.

As they were about to leave the restaurant, Lily walked up to Steven and tucked something in his hand. With her other hand, she motioned with a finger to her lips to let him know to show it to no one right then. He understood, smiled, and winked at her, and stuffed the paper in his pocket.

Later, when Connie and Aaron and Steven were back in their home, Steven pulled the paper out of his pocket. It was a check for $5,000. Lily had written on the bottom: "To help with that special bicycle, love, Lily and daughters."

CHAPTER FIFTY-EIGHT

The doorbell rang. Susie flew to the door to open it. "We've been waiting for you. We've been up for hours." Susie exaggerated, as she grabbed James by the sleeve and pulled him over to the Christmas tree. "Hi, Jacob," she added as an afterthought.

"Well, hello to you too, Susie." Jacob laughed. "I can tell I am not the one you have been waiting for." He winked at Lily.

Rose and Bonnie came over to Jacob and grabbed his arms and escorted him over to the couch to sit by Lily. "Merry Christmas, Jacob and James."

"Rose, you and Bonnie bring the Christmas punch in from the kitchen and pass it around, and then we will open presents, youngest to oldest. How does that sound?"

"Great, I'm first," Susie squealed. "Then James."

The gifts were passed out one by one. Susie got the new Barbie doll; James, games for his Nintendo. Bonnie received a new DVD-CD player of her very own. Rose, now a big thirteen-year-old, received an iPad electronic gadget. These gifts were from Santa Claus. They also received clothes and books and new bicycles.

Jacob gave Lily a diamond necklace. He wanted to give her an engagement ring and ask her to marry him. *The time is not right yet, be patient,* he cautioned himself.

Lily gave Jacob a signed copy of Carson Hunter's autobiography, bound in leather. She knew how much Jacob admired Carson. She took the book and had Mr. Hunter write a personal note in it for him. Jacob was clearly moved when he read what his friend had written:

To my dear friend, Jacob Manning,
Who has always been by my side,
In joyous times, and hard times.
May you know how much you mean
To Kay and me. We love you, *Carson Hunter.*

"Thank you, Lily, you could not have given me a better present." Jacob bent down and kissed her. She kissed him back.

"Now, let's get everything cleared up and put away, and then we will have brunch. Jacob and James need to be with their family members, and we need to go visit your grandparents. I wish we could spend all day together, but we have extended family members we all need to visit," Lily told them.

"When are we going skiing, Mom?" Rose asked.

"Tomorrow is the big day, December 26. We have invited the Greens to accompany us. That should be fun."

After brunch, Jacob and James left to visit with their families, and Lily and her daughters visited with each set of grandparents. They took with them their presents, all except their bikes, to show their grandparents.

CHAPTER FIFTY-NINE

The Langstons, Greens, and Mannings stood at the bottom of the ski lift waiting for their turn to go to the top of the hill.

"Let's pair off," Tom Green suggested. New snowflakes were gently falling on the group as they stood there. Soon-to-be eighteen-year-old Tom looked down on the other children.

"Tom, I think you have grown a foot since we saw you last," Lily exclaimed.

"Well, about eight inches, actually," Tom's dark hair had turned white as snowflakes clung to it. "I'm six feet four inches tall now."

"And very handsome, I might add," Lily said. "You'd better cover your head, or you'll catch cold."

Tom lifted his parka hood over his head and tied the strings.

"I'll pair up with Lucy," Bonnie said.

"James and I will ride up together," Susie told the families.

"Of course." Rose laughed. "I wonder how we all knew that. Margaret, will you join me on the lift?"

Josh asked his brother if he wanted to pair with him. Tom said, "Let's do it, bro."

After the children were on the ski lift, Bill and Mary Green got the next lift, and Jacob and Lily brought up the rear.

The snow continued falling all day, but nobody seemed to mind. A lot of people had come up to Alta to go skiing, so there was some waiting at the bottom of the ski lift each time they went up the hill, but, again, no one seemed to mind. The day was about friends and family, the joy of togetherness. The beauty of the mountain and the valleys in the gently falling snow was indescribable.

Jacob remarked to Lily as they were about to get on the ski lift for about the umpteenth time, "This is about as close to heaven as a person can get on earth."

"Oh, yes, it is. It is wonderful being up here." Jacob put his arms around her and hugged her tightly. "The snow suits you very well, Lily." He gently touched her soft upturned cheek with his gloved finger. "You are very lovely in the snow, sweet lady." Lily rewarded him with a smile.

When it was dark and the ski area was closing down, the employees who had been working at the top of the mountain came skiing down, one after another, with lighted torches. It was a magical end to a magical day.

CHAPTER SIXTY

"Where are we going to put this FES bicycle, Connie? Do you want it in your bedroom or in the living room?" Steven asked as the deliverymen carried the big box into the house.

"Let's put it in the living room for now, Steven. We can always move it later if I change my mind and want it in by the bed. If I put it by the bed, it just might keep me awake at night if I have to look at it and know all the hard work it is going to make me do." Connie surveyed the living room. "Put it over in that area." She motioned to the deliverymen. They obediently set it up where Connie had pointed.

After the men left, Aaron and Steven helped Connie get up onto the bike. They set the controls to slow at first and strapped her on it so she couldn't fall. Then they stood on either side of her as the machine moved her legs up and down.

"How is that, Connie. Is it too slow or about right?"

"It's okay for now. The doctor said I should stay on it for about fifteen minutes at a time and gradually work up to staying on longer as time goes on. As soon as my fifteen minutes are up, we'll go in and get some supper."

"Mom, don't try to get on it before we get home from school. Right now, while it is still the Christmas holidays, we can put you on whenever you want to use it, but when school starts, you have to wait until we get home so we can help you. At least until we know you are able to work it on your own. Okay?"

"Okay, son. I won't try any funny stuff." Connie laughed. "I also have to do my upper body exercises. Those I can do while you are at school. Upper body strength will help me maneuver myself on and off the bicycle. But, for now, I won't try to climb on it without you two. Now help me off and let's go get supper."

CHAPTER SIXTY-ONE

It was now early on New Year's Eve day. "Let's go ice skating at the Gallivan Center. Who's up for skating up town? Anyone?"

Susie squealed, "Me. I do. James, do you want to go skating?"

Jacob turned to his son. "James, do you want to go skating? There are also going to be lots of entertainers tonight. Salt Lake City has a great New Year's Eve party up town. Several places have entertainment and lots of food. I borrowed my dad's suburban again, so there is room for all of us. Now, who wants to go?"

Lily said, "Jacob, are you kidding? Look at all those smiles. Everyone wants to go. Girls, go find your skates. And get your ski togs. It will be cold."

After much rummaging, skates were found and ski clothes assembled. They soon had the first layers of coats and pants on and were piled in the car. They would wait until they actually got to the skating rink before outer layers of clothing would be added against the cold. It was a clear but very cold night. They could see each other's breath as they laughed and talked.

Music was playing loudly from the various loudspeakers set up around the outdoor rink. Jacob helped James put on his skates and then helped where the girls needed a little nudge here and there. As the children held hands and began to skate, Jacob tied Lily's skates for her and then bent down and finished fastening his own. "I guess I didn't ask you if you could skate, Lily, did I?"

"No, you didn't, Jacob. But watch me!" Lily stood up and glided into a perfect double axel.

"I should have known. You do everything else so well."

Jacob too glided onto the rink and immediately tripped and fell on his behind. "No laughing allowed!" Lily stifled a giggle. He managed to get to his feet and wobble over to the side of the rink so he could hold on. James and Susie skated over to Jacob.

"We'll help you, Dad." James then took hold of his left hand and Susie his right. Jacob was carefully maneuvered back onto the rink. With Lily skating behind the three, they managed to make a circle of the rink.

"You kids take him around a couple more times, and then it's my turn," Lily told them.

For another hour, they all skated. It was so much fun. Jacob was soon feeling at home on the ice, and holding hands, he and Lily made several more circles around the rink.

After skating, they removed their skates and stowed them back in the suburban. Now it was time to go around to the different venues set up around Salt Lake's downtown area. Music greeted them everywhere. They munched on hot dogs and popcorn and soda pop. The last place they visited before midnight was Temple Square. Each tree branch was covered with lights. Music from the famed Mormon Tabernacle Choir was piped in to the square and filled the air with songs of angels singing about the newborn baby Jesus born in Bethlehem so many years ago. Next to the tabernacle, a lovely crèche was set up with animals and shepherds and Mary and Joseph and baby Jesus.

As the hymns were sung by the choir, Lily and her daughters joined in and sang quietly with them. "What lovely voices you have," a middle-aged lady standing not far from them came over to talk to them. "It is obvious you sing together as a group. What are your names?"

Lily said, "My name is Lily Langston, and these are my daughters, Rose, Bonnie, and Susie. We do sing together. Thank you for noticing."

"My dear"—the lady held out her hand to Lily—"we bought your CD. We love it. We also bought one for each of our children. How wonderful to meet you." As she shook Lily's hand, she said, "My name is Jenny Jameson. I sing with the Tabernacle Choir."

"How wonderful to meet you, Jenny. These are our dear friends, Jacob and James Manning."

"This is my husband, Tom," Jenny told them. Lily and then Jacob shook Tom's hand. They were a handsome couple: Jenny with her reddish-blonde hair, and Tom with his dark hair. Both had dark brown eyes.

They talked together for a few more minutes, and then Lily told Jenny she would be watching for her when they watched the choir sing the following Sunday. They all waved goodbye and walked slowly out of temple square and back to their automobile.

On the way home, they continued to sing carols. Christmas was over, but they weren't quite ready to say goodbye to the season yet. It had been glorious.

"Thank you for the wonderful, wonderful evening, Jacob. We are so glad you thought of coming up town tonight. We all had a great time," Lily told him.

"It was special, wasn't it?" Jacob said. "I love you, Lily Langston. I'm being patient. I'll wait as long as it takes."

"I know, Jacob. Thank you for being so special. Good night." Then Lily did something she had not done before. She raised up on her toes and initiated a kiss on Jacob's welcoming lips. "Good night, my dearest friend."

CHAPTER SIXTY-TWO

Aaron looked down at the gold coin in his hand. It was the coin he wanted to give the Hall family, the family of the twin boys who had gone to get physicals at the Hunter Cancer Clinic a few months ago. They had gone there so the doctors could make sure they were still in remission. It was time to go to their home and give it to them.

"Dad," Aaron called, "I wonder if you would be able to go with me on an errand this afternoon after school."

"Of course, son. What do you have in mind?"

"Lily Langston gave me two gold coins to give to special families that I had in mind. I gave the first one to Grace Summers's family. I want to give the other one to Rebecca Hall and her twins, Patrick and Derek. They have been battling leukemia but are, as far as I know, still in remission. She is a single mother. I think the coin will give her life a much-needed boost."

"Do you have her address? Did you want to call her and tell her we are coming or just surprise her?"

"I already called her and asked her if we might come over for a little while to see the twins and to see how she is holding up. They will be expecting us between five and five-thirty. I let her know we would be bringing something to eat. She told me the boys like pizza, pepperoni. We'll stop and get it and drinks on our way over to their house."

Steven asked, "Aaron, how old are the Hall twins?"

"They are five years old, blond blue-eyed, curly-haired angels."

*****

Aaron and his father knocked on the Hall door. It was just after five-thirty. They had the pizza and soda in hand as Rebecca Hall answered the door, "Come in, Aaron. And this must be your father."

Aaron replied, "Indeed it is, Rebecca. His name is Steven Black." Rebecca stepped aside so that the two men could come inside. They set the pizza and the drinks on the table which was only a few steps in from the door.

"I'm happy to meet you, Mr. Black. We are all in love with Aaron. Aren't we, boys?" Patrick was clinging to Aaron's left leg, Derek the other.

"Yes, it seems to be obvious." Steven laughed.

The apartment was small but cozy. The table occupied one end of the room, a couch the other. It was open to a small kitchen. Rebecca had lovely landscapes on the walls and a few plants placed here and there. Pictures of her sons had been placed in tasteful frames and hung beside the landscapes. The boys' toys were neatly placed in a toy box in a corner by the sofa. A small television hung on a wall, well placed for easy watching from the sofa. Aaron could picture in his mind the many evenings that Rebecca and her small boys watched cartoons or other kid-friendly movies. He also could imagine her with a boy on each side, reading them bedtime stories. It was obvious that love reigned in this little home.

Rebecca took her boys' hands in her own as they sat at the table to begin their meal. The boys reached out to hold Steven and Aaron's hands in theirs. Father and son held each other's hands as they completed the circle. Rebecca then gave the blessing on the food, after which her twins said loud amens. Aaron and his father added theirs, smiling at the boys' enthusiasm.

In answer to Aaron and Steven's questions, Rebecca told them that in the mornings before going to her job as an accountant in a law firm, she took them to their kindergarten. Her parents picked them up after school and kept them at their home until Rebecca came to pick them up.

"It's been working very well. My parents are wonderful. The twins adore them. Most nights, we stay for dinner there before I bring the boys home. They don't live that far from here. Patrick and

Derek were delighted to hear you were coming to visit. Thank you so much. They are happy boys, as you can see."

"Are they still in remission? They sure look healthy."

"The doctor tells me that if they do not have a recurrence of the disease for five years, we can consider them cured. Isn't that marvelous?" Rebecca smiled as tears filled her eyes.

Aaron cleared his throat. "We have something we want to give you, Rebecca. It is not from us but from Carson Hunter. I am sure you know of him."

"Of course. It is his clinic where the twins got their chemo."

Aaron pulled the gold coin out of his pocket and handed it to her. She and the boys stared at it. They each took turns holding it. The boys were wide-eyed. Aaron proceeded to tell them about Lily Langston and how she had obtained the coins from Mr. Hunter. "He gave her ten gold coins. She used the first four to fix up my home, inside and out. It was in need of a lot of repairs and painting. She even had a landscaper come and beautify the lawns and put shrubs in to make it really lovely. She had six coins left. It was not in her nature to keep them tucked away, so she asked me if I would be able to find a couple of special families to give them to. I was happy to oblige her. I thought of you and the boys immediately, and here we are."

"Oh, Aaron and Steven. How wonderful. Thank you so much. We will treasure it. I will write a letter to Mr. Hunter and one to Lily Langston, thanking them for their great kindness."

Steven Black said, "Rebecca, gold is going through the roof right now, if you need to sell it."

"Oh, no, sir. This is a keeper. My sons and I will treasure it always, won't we boys?"

The children nodded their heads in agreement.

Aaron and then Steven stooped down to give each boy a hug, and then Rebecca, who was still wiping tears from her eyes. Aaron also wiped a tear from his eye as he and Steven waved goodbye at the door.

CHAPTER SIXTY-THREE

The months of January, February, and March came and left, snow-filled months. The children were back in their respective schools. Lily continued to substitute teach two days a week and sometimes more if they needed her and couldn't find someone else for a specific teaching assignment who was as qualified as she was. She loved the students, and they loved her.

On Sundays, they spent the major part of the Sabbath after their own block of meetings with the grandparents. Sunday evenings were spent either at Jacob and James's home with Jacob's parents or with Lily and the girls at their home.

Mondays were Family Home Evening days, spent together by Jacob and Lily and the children. They took turns giving the lessons and making dessert.

The weekends were special times for family get-togethers. Often, Saturdays were spent up on the mountains. They took turns going to the several different ski areas around Salt Lake City. There was Brighton and Alta, Deer Valley Resort and Snowbird, Solitude and the Canyons in the Park City area. Sometimes the Greens went with them, sometimes Steven. Once in a while, Aaron was able to make arrangements so that he too could accompany them on their day of skiing.

Connie continued to work on her bicycle and exercise her upper body to strengthen it. Soon she was able to get on the bicycle by herself. The strength in her upper body allowed her to easily maneuver onto the seat. With her arms, she was able to lift her right leg over to the other side until she was straddled on it like she was riding a horse.

She then secured the straps around her so that she couldn't fall off. She was able to turn up the speed a little at a time as she progressed.

One day she would try to stand up but knew that when that time came, she would need Steven and Aaron by her side. *If I try to stand on my own and fall, I will have to lie there all day until Steven and Aaron come home.* Connie always made sure she had her cell phone with her to call for help if she got into trouble.

Aaron continued to do his janitorial work at the hospital on Saturdays and performed his miniconcerts in the afternoon. He was doing well in school. He had all As. He and his father were together every available minute of each day. Aaron was a great help to Steven with the choirs and any other things associated with the music department. Aaron helped Steven with song arrangements and often accompanied on his guitar.

Aaron kept in touch with Grace's family. He called them every week. Once in a while, they came to listen in on Aaron's miniconcerts. Whenever little Jennie saw Aaron, she ran up to him and hugged his leg. She always had the doll, Hope, with her. Hannah Summers laughed. "She carries that doll everywhere, Aaron. She sleeps with it and sits it beside her when she eats her meals. I have had to mend it a few times." Jennie showed Aaron where the doll had been mended and then she tucked it under her arm again.

Jennie's brother, Bobby, was not to be forgotten. He usually brought a favorite toy with him to show Aaron. He would show it off and tell Aaron all the special things it could do. After the concert was over and Aaron had said goodbye to each of the patients, he would sit and hold Bobby and Jenny for a few minutes and visit with them and Hannah and their father, Peter, if he was with them.

CHAPTER SIXTY-FOUR

The busy winter months came and went. It was now April—April 15 in fact. Lily woke up, thinking, *One year ago tomorrow, Samuel was killed.* She rose and went to the window. Buds were beginning to form on the trees, and she could see purple crocuses pushing their heads through a light sprinkling of snow on the ground.

She thought back over the events that had turned her world upside down just one year ago. *I didn't even notice the buds on the trees last year, or the crocuses, or anything about the spring. My world had turned dark and painful. I still miss you, Samuel, I miss you so much.*

She thought of Aaron. She and Bonnie and Susie had grown to love Aaron and Connie and now, Steven. Rose too was not as hostile as she was at first, though she still made a point of avoiding Aaron whenever she could. Lily suspected she liked Aaron more than she let on. She clearly was fond of Connie, and now Steven.

There was something she wanted to do and had thought about for some time. She had discussed it with her daughters who gave her a big thumbs-up. She was anxious to talk to Jacob about her idea. He and James would be over soon. She and the girls would discuss it with him then.

After she and her daughters got dressed and had their breakfast, and after Jacob and James came to pick them up, they were going to the cemetery to put flowers on Samuel's grave, and then they were going to a buffet-type restaurant in uptown Salt Lake City for an early lunch.

Bonnie answered the door and ushered Jacob and James in. James raised his hand in his "I love you" hand greeting. Bonnie held her hand up and touched his. Susie was next, followed by Rose and Lily.

"Good morning, James." Susie giggled. "Hi, Jacob."

"Hello to you, Susie. I see you are all ready for our outing today. You look very pretty in your pink sweater and pink bow in your curly blonde hair," Jacob said as he gave her a hug.

"You look good," James echoed.

With that, the group left the house and piled into the suburban. Jacob laughed. "I'll have to buy this vehicle from my dad. I use it more than he does."

After putting flowers on Samuel's grave, they lingered awhile. The families had others buried in this same graveyard, so they walked around pointing out ancestors here and there to each other. When they had finished looking at headstones and telling the histories of their loved ones to each other, they left and went to the restaurant. As they were coming to the end of their luncheon, Lily began, "Jacob, the girls and I have something we would like to discuss with you. It's about Aaron. Bonnie, would you fill Jacob in on our idea?"

"I would love to, Mom. Jacob, we think Aaron has been on probation long enough. It has been a year almost since he was sentenced to work at the hospital. He worked several more days each week during the summer months. Now that he has been reunited with his father, we think it would be great if you would go before the sentencing judge on Aaron's behalf and ask that his probation period be terminated."

"He has served faithfully, as you know." Lily continued, "He is a great help to his mother as he has always been, and now he works with Steven with the high school music department. It would be wonderful if he could concentrate on his responsibilities in those areas and not have to worry about having probation hanging over his head for another four or five years."

Jacob took Lily's hand in his and smiled at her. He looked around the table at the girls whose upturned faces were glowing with anticipation. "You are a very special family, you Langstons. You have just been putting flowers on your father's grave, and now you are asking me to go to the judge and ask him for leniency on behalf of the young man who put your father there."

"This is why I love you all so much, and why James loves you too." James vigorously nodded his head. "Tomorrow I will call the district attorney and talk to him about getting Aaron's probation terminated. If he agrees, we will all petition the court to vacate the probation. Will tomorrow be soon enough, Susie?"

Susie clapped her hands together. "When can we tell Aaron, Mom?"

"Not yet, honey. It needs to be finalized by the court. We won't tell Aaron yet. We will surprise him. If the judge won't do it, we don't want to disappoint Aaron and his mother and Steven. If the judge agrees to what we are asking, then it will be a wonderful surprise for them. So nobody say a word to anyone about this, okay?"

"Okay, Mom," the girls agreed.

*****

The district attorney's secretary answered the phone. "District Attorney, Joseph Bird's office, this is Marlon speaking, may I help you?"

"This is Jacob Manning, Marlon. Is Joe in his office this morning?"

"Hi, Jacob, it's good to speak to you. Yes, he is here. Do you want to talk to him by telephone, or do you wish to come in and see him in person?"

"I would love to come in and chat with him about a matter that has come up, if he has the time."

"How about ten o'clock, Jacob. He has a few minutes before he has to be at a meeting at ten-thirty. Would that fit into your schedule?"

"That would be great, Marlon. I'll see you then."

Jacob entered Joe Bird's office just before ten. "Hi, Joe." They shook hands warmly, and then Joseph Bird motioned to Jacob to sit in one of the comfortable chairs in front of his desk. "Well, Jacob, what can I do for you today?"

"Do you remember the Samuel Langston case? It was just a year ago that he was hit by Aaron Turner and killed?"

Joe lifted the intercom and asked Marlon to bring in the file on Samuel's case. She knocked on the door and then entered, handing her boss the file he had asked for. Joe opened it and spent a few minutes going through the pages. "The judge in the case was William Thomas. Looks like Aaron Turner was given probation until age twenty-one. He is now sixteen. What can I do for you, Jacob?"

"Lily Langston, Samuel's widow, and her three daughters have become very close to Aaron Turner and his mother, Connie. They have asked me to find out if it is possible to have his probation vacated. He has been faithful in his responsibilities for the past year. Also, during the summer months, he worked several days a week to fulfill his assignment."

Joseph Bird glanced at the file again. "I see that he entertains at the hospital every Saturday afternoon after he is through with his janitorial work. There are some very positive notations here in the file by his probation officer. What do you think of Aaron, Jacob? Have you stayed in touch with him?"

"We see him every week. He is a very nice young man, serious and dedicated. His father is in his life now and is a very positive influence on Aaron. Aaron's mother is doing physical therapy now in the hopes of being able to walk sometime in the future. Aaron is a fine musician. He and the Langston family have recorded a CD that is on the market. It is doing very well. His father, Steven, is the music director at the high school Aaron attends. Aaron does a lot of arranging of the music for the choir with his father. They have become very close. The incident that took Samuel Langston's life was an accident, Joe, and I think it would be a very good gesture on your part if you would help me get this matter closed."

"Let me see what I can do, Jacob. I will review the file closely, and then I will talk to Aaron's probation officer, and if I agree that this has merit, I'll talk to Judge Thomas. I'll be in touch. Does Aaron know you and the Langstons are doing this?"

"No, we thought it best not to get his hopes up if it doesn't happen."

"Good idea. I'll get back to you in a few days. Well, it's time for my meeting. It was very good to see you. I think we can make this happen, Jacob."

CHAPTER SIXTY-FIVE

"Lily, I went in to see District Attorney Bird this morning. We discussed ending Aaron's probation as soon as possible. We had a nice visit about it. He is going to review the matter, talk with Aaron's probation officer, and if he feels that it is in the best interest of justice, he will take the matter to the judge who handled the case."

"Thanks, Jacob. The girls and I feel very strongly that this is the right thing to do. It will free up Aaron's Saturdays to help Connie with her therapy and to help him have the life of a normal teenager, something he has never been able to have in the past, what with taking care of his mother every day from a very young age." Lily reminded Jacob, though unnecessarily, about coming over at seven that evening.

After Lily hung up the phone, she turned to her daughters and told them of Jacob's visit with the DA. "It will probably be several days before we hear back," Jacob said.

The girls were sitting around the kitchen table working on their homework. Lily was helping where she was needed.

Bonnie stopped working on her assignment and remarked, "I hope Aaron will continue to entertain the patients at the Hunter Cancer Clinic. They look forward to hearing him sing and play every Saturday. Do you think he will continue to do that, Mom?"

"I think that is just what he will do. It is so like Aaron to continue to be of service where he can," Lily said. "He loves the patients there, especially the little ones, and they love him. I don't think he will want to give that up for anything."

"Mom, I'm done with my homework now," Susie said. "May I go over to Mary's house to play with her until suppertime?"

Mary lived two doors down the street from the Langstons. "Yes, you may, Susie. Let Mary's mother know you need to be home by five-thirty. We will eat, and then Jacob and James are coming over to have Family Home Evening with us, remember?"

Susie walked over to the Family Home Evening calendar and pointed to her name. "I have the opening prayer and the scripture reading. I picked out the scripture already. I'll be home at five-thirty, Mom." Susie gave her mother a quick kiss and ran out the door, slamming the door behind her. A few seconds later, she was back, opened the door, and said, "Oh, sorry," and gently closed the door.

"At least she remembered, Mom, a little after the fact." Rose laughed.

After a meal of pot roast, baked potatoes and sour cream, green beans and pudding, the dishes were put in the dishwasher and washed, the floor was swept, and the room tidied. At 7:00 p.m., the doorbell rang and in walked Jacob and James. James greeted everyone with his special handshake, and Jacob hugged the girls and kissed Lily.

*****

After Family Home Evening was over, Lily remarked, "We still have four gold coins to give away. Does anyone have an idea as to what we should do with them?"

Rose spoke up, "There is a little girl in my school class whose family is struggling. Her dad was just laid off from his job. Her name is Carla Jones. Could we give one to their family, Mom?"

Lily was about to answer her in the affirmative when Bonnie said, "Let's each of us kids pick some family to give one to. There's a crippled boy in my class. He has a lame leg. He walks with a cane. I would love to give one to his family. His name is Johnny Elliott."

"What a great idea, girls. Susie, can you think of any of your classmates who might need a little help, a ray of sunshine?"

"Yes, yes. My friend, Nancy, has been sick at home for the past several days. Teacher told us she has pneumonia. She is recovering, but I don't think her family has much money, Mom. She wears the same clothes to school nearly every day. Could we give them one? Her last name is Thompson."

Jacob smiled at the girls. "I'll tell you what. Let me see what I can find out about each of those families you mentioned. James and I will think of a family we can give the fourth coin to, okay, James? Then we will get together one evening and distribute the coins. We'll make a fun evening of it."

"Great idea, Jacob." At the door, Lily and the girls said a fond farewell to their dear friends.

CHAPTER SIXTY-SIX

Two weeks later, Jacob called to ask Lily and her daughters to come to the courthouse the following afternoon at four. "Judge Thomas wanted to visit with them and give them his decision regarding Aaron."

It was May 1. It was a lovely spring day when Lily, Rose, Bonnie, and Susie walked into the judge's chambers behind Jacob.

"Mrs. Langston, it's good to see you again. And it is nice to see you, girls. You have grown taller since you were last in my courtroom. I trust this will be a much happier occasion for you. Come sit down over here," the judge motioned toward some chairs placed in front of his desk. "Jacob, you can sit over here by me."

Judge Thomas opened the file that lay before him. "I have gone over the records of Aaron's history and probation, and I must say, I am very impressed with him. He is quite the gifted young man, and he has been conscientious in his assignment for the court. Jacob tells me that you have become very close friends with him. He even tells me that you sing together. Someday I would like to hear you perform. Jacob, let me know the next time they perform together out in public."

"I certainly will, Judge. You are in for a treat."

"Now, Susie, tell me what you think I should do about Aaron Turner?"

Susie stood up before the judge and in a very serious tone said, "Mr. Judge, I think you should let him be done with his probation. We want him to be done."

Judge Thomas smiled. "Thank you, Susie. Now, Bonnie, do you feel the same way?"

"Yes, sir, I do. So does Rose."

"Rose?"

Rose looked toward her mother. She saw the pleading look in her eyes and noticed the almost-imperceptible nod Lily gave her daughter.

"Yeah, I do too." Lily breathed a sigh of relief.

Judge Thomas took out of the file a document and signed his name on the bottom. "I have reviewed this matter carefully with District Attorney Bird and with Aaron's probation officer. Also, I called and talked to the person in charge of the janitorial staff at the Hunter Cancer Clinic. I let him know that Aaron is no longer on probation, and he will have to find someone else to do the mopping of the floors at his clinic. He told me what a fine worker Aaron had been and that he would miss him. He also told me he hoped that Aaron would be able to continue to come in once a week or so to entertain the patients. I told him I would talk to you and have you ask Aaron and, if he is willing, have him get in touch with the hospital staff to set up times he can go sing and play for the patients." The judge then handed the document to Jacob.

Judge Thomas stood up and walked around his desk, "Now, does that take care of our business together?"

Susie ran up to the judge, put her arms around him, and gave him a big hug. "Oh, thank you, Mr. Judge, thank you so much. Mom, Jacob, let's go tell Aaron right now, can we?"

"Thank you, Judge Thomas. Thank you very much." Lily shook the judge's hand warmly. Rose and Bonnie and then Jacob also shook hands with him. As they turned and left the judge's chambers, Susie said again, "Can we go tell Aaron right now?"

Lily looked at Jacob. "I think that is a fine idea, Susie," Jacob answered.

A few minutes later, Jacob and the Langstons stood on the doorstep ringing the bell at the Turners. Aaron and Steven had just arrived home after staying at the school doing some arranging work on some special music the high school choir would be singing.

"Well, hello there. Come in, please," Aaron greeted them. "We just got home." Connie came toward them in her wheelchair. She grasped Lily's hand warmly, and then Jacob's. She smiled at Susie and then pointed to her own cheek, on which Susie obediently planted a big juicy kiss. Rose and Bonnie followed with somewhat less messy ones.

"We have something to tell you, Aaron." Susie couldn't hide her excitement. "Can I tell him, Mom?"

"Yes, of course, honey. But let's all sit down first, okay?"

"Okay," Susie replied as she ran and sat down on one end of the couch. After everyone was seated, Susie jumped up and blurted out, "You don't have to do probation any more, Aaron. Mr. Judge signed a paper. Jacob has the paper."

Jacob handed Aaron the document. Aaron stared down at it. "How did this come about?" he asked no one in particular.

Jacob answered him, "Lily called me a few weeks ago and asked me if I would intercede with the judge, Judge Thomas, and see if he would be willing to vacate your sentence. He did some checking, talked to your probation officer, and agreed with us that you were a model young man in every way and deserving of being taken off the list, so to speak. So here we are, paper in hand, to let you know that you are finished with your probation. We are very pleased to be able to give you the judge's ruling, Aaron."

Aaron still seemed to be in shock. His father put his arm around him and smiled broadly at their guests. "What a wonderful thing you have done for Aaron. You are very special people. Thank you. Thank you so much."

"Aaron, the judge talked to the head of the janitorial staff at the hospital and told them you were done. They said they would miss you and that you have been a stellar employee. The hospital staff hopes that you will continue to entertain the patients, and if you agree, they want you to talk to them about setting up a schedule for your miniconcerts. They don't have to be on Saturdays, but they can be. It is up to you."

With his eyes wet with tears, Aaron finally spoke, "Of course, I want to keep playing and singing for the patients. Oh, Lily and

Jacob, this is wonderful. I don't know how to thank you. You have been so wonderful to me and my mother. This is just incredible." He looked down at the document in his hands and repeated, "This is incredible." He turned to his dad and said, "Do you know what this means, Dad? You and Mom and I can have time to do stuff on Saturdays, special family things." Aaron handed the paper to his mother.

"I will go visit with the hospital staff after school tomorrow and work out a schedule for my concerts."

"I'll go with you," Steven told him.

Connie was crying and laughing at the same time. Through her happy tears, she looked at the blurred words on the paper. She wiped her eyes to be able to see better what was there in black and white. "Thank you. That's all I can think to say to all of you. Thank you." With that, Connie burst into tears again.

Lily went over and hugged her friend close to her. "You are very welcome, Connie dear. It was time. I felt it, and so did the girls. Jacob made it happen."

Jacob walked over and took Connie's hand in his. "Now, Connie, what is left is for you to get out of that wheelchair and walk for us? How is your rehabilitation coming along?"

Connie removed the blanket that covered her legs. She then moved her right leg ever so slightly. Everyone cheered. "See, it is going well. I exercise every day on the bike several times. I am making progress. One of these days, with the help of Aaron and Steven, I am going to try to stand up. My doctors are pleased. So am I." With that, she put the blanket back over her legs. "This is definitely a good day."

CHAPTER SIXTY-SEVEN

The following day, Aaron and Steven walked into the cancer clinic and down the hallway to the main offices at the hospital. They were expecting them.

"Come in, Aaron. Thank you for coming." Timothy Trower, head of staff at the Hunter Cancer Hospital, came up and shook their hands warmly. "Please, come and sit down." He ushered them to a corner of his office where there were comfortable armchairs arranged in a semicircle. "My assistant will get you something to drink. What kind of soda would you like?"

Steven said, "I'll have a Diet Coke, please."

"I will too, thank you," Aaron told them.

"Good, make that three, John."

A few minutes later, the assistant came back with glasses of ice and three cans of Coke on a tray. After filling the glasses from the cans and getting seated comfortably in their chairs, Mr. Trower spoke, "Well, Aaron, I guess we have lost your services. We will miss you. You have been a beacon of light to this hospital. I personally want to thank you for all you have done for us. It has been great to work with you."

"Thank you, Mr. Trower. Judge Thomas told Jacob Manning that you still wanted me to do the miniconcerts. Is that correct?"

"Absolutely, Aaron. Our patients look forward to them. It helps in their recovery as I know you have noticed, those that will recover, that is. And those who don't are still comforted by the music. They tell the nurses and the staff all the time how much they love your music. We hope you will be able to continue as long as you are able to, Aaron."

"That is what I want too. You have met my father haven't you?"

"Yes, of course. It's nice to see you again, Mr. Black. May I call you Steven?"

"Please do."

"My father and I have been talking about the miniconcerts and figuring out when we could do them. My dad is the high school music director, and I work with him a lot on arranging music and even doing some songwriting. He would like to be involved in the miniconcerts with me. Would that be all right with you?"

"That would be terrific, Aaron."

"Could we change the concerts from Saturday afternoon to, say, Monday evenings? It would be like having a family home evening here each Monday with the patients."

"What time do you want to start, Aaron? And we should probably continue doing them one floor at a time. It would be impossible to have them any other way, of course." Timothy Trower chuckled at himself.

"The patients are usually done with their meals about 5:00 p.m. Why don't we start at six o'clock. That will give them and the nurses plenty of time to get everything cleared up and the patients settled in the visiting area. Would 6:00 p.m. be all right? We get done at school usually about four so that would give us time to go home and grab something to eat and be here in plenty of time to set up for the concert. My dad plays the piano and will do some solo work too."

"Great. This is Wednesday. So we will expect you around five-forty-five next Monday evening. Let's see now, you performed your music on the first floor of the clinic last Saturday, so it will be the second floor patients who will have the concert next Monday. Is that right, Aaron? I will let the staff and patients know that the concert will not be this coming Saturday afternoon but the following Monday instead."

"Yes, that will be good." They stood up and shook hands.

Mr. Trower ushered them out of the room with a "goodbye and thank you, and we'll see you next Monday."

"While we're here, Dad, could we run up to the third floor and visit the kids for a few minutes?"

"Sure, why not?"

For the next half hour, they visited the children. Some faces were new to them, but those who were there for his last concert squealed with delight to see Aaron. Aaron talked to them and hugged those he could who weren't hooked up to a lot of tubes and monitors. It always affected him greatly seeing the children so sick. But he was always cheered by the love that he was shown. They were angels, these little ones. He and his father were deeply moved by their sweet spirits and the gentle care given them by their nurses.

CHAPTER SIXTY-EIGHT

"Mom," Aaron said as he finished chewing a bite of steak, "Dad and I are going to be entertaining the patients at the Hunter Cancer Clinic on Monday evenings now instead of Saturday afternoons. That will free up our Saturdays so we can do things together as a family."

Steven added, "We'll be able to take you on drives up the mountains. Would you like that, Connie?"

"Oh, yes, that would be wonderful. It has been a long time since I have been able to go on scenic drives. I would love that, Steven."

Steven took Connie's hand in his and responded, "We'll go visit the national parks here in Utah. I haven't been to see any of them since coming back here to live. Utah is full of wondrous scenery. Let's plan on getting to as many parks as we can this very summer coming up."

As they continued their supper of steak, potato casserole, green beans, tossed salad, and apple pie, Connie told them she had some news. "My doctor called me today. He told me of a wonderful new product that is in the early stages of clinical testing. It is in the area of robotic technology. A company by the name of Berkeley Bionics has invented something called E-Legs exoskeleton technology. It consists of electronic leg braces. The patient wears a backpack computer and sensors in the crutches the patient is holding to tell the computer how to move the battery-powered legs. The sensors detect arm movements, which guides the person forward one step at a time.

"He told me of a lady who had been paralyzed for eighteen years from a skiing accident. After just twelve hours of training, she has been able to maneuver the E-leg equipment that she is using and is walking. She is just walking a step at a time, but she is walking. The medical community is very excited about this new invention. My accident was not as long ago as hers. I fell skiing fourteen years ago. Before this, it was thought to be impossible for a paraplegic to ever walk again after this many years, but now they are very hopeful.

"There are some limitations. One has to have upper body strength and mobility. I have to be able to lift myself out of my wheelchair. And I have to have a range of motion in my legs. I am working hard to build up my upper body strength, and the work I am doing on my FES bicycle is helping me get some movement in my legs, as you have seen. I am going to keep working on these exercises and maybe, just maybe, with the help of the E-leg technology, I really will be able to walk again."

Aaron and Steven got up and came over to Connie and hugged her.

"Do you have any idea how much the E-legs will cost, Mom? I am just curious. Whatever the cost, we will find a way to get them, won't we, Dad?"

"We sure will. We may have to have some fund-raisers, but we will do whatever it takes, honey." Steven bent down and kissed Connie's cheek.

"You are both so good to me. I heard that it will be in the range of $100,000." Connie looked from Aaron to Steven. "That seems to be an insurmountable sum. I wonder if we will ever be able to raise that much money."

Steven bent down and hugged her. "Well, Connie, we'll give it the very best effort we can, you can be very sure of that."

Connie squeezed his hand and reached for Aaron's. "In the meantime, let's get the dishes done. I want to hear you two play and sing for me afterward, okay? I'll get on the bike and exercise a while as you perform for me."

CHAPTER SIXTY-NINE

It was Monday evening. Lily's family and Jacob and James were seated in the Langston living room. Jacob had just finished giving a lesson on service. Earlier, they had eaten a lovely dinner of fried chicken, rice, broccoli, and homemade chocolate chip cookies for dessert.

Lily spoke, "Tonight we are going to decide how we want to present the four remaining gold coins to the families we have picked out." She read from a sheet of paper she had in her hand. "Jacob, you were going to find out about each of the families and get a feel for how they might receive the coins. I have the names right here. They are Carla Jones, Johnny Elliott, and Nancy Thompson. James was going to pick out one of the children in his class to give a coin to. Who did you decide you wanted to give one of the coins to, James?"

"Sammy, Sammy Ellis. He is my friend. We play together at recess. I like Sammy."

Jacob smiled at his young son. "Sammy has autism as James does. His family have been very kind to James. They are a good choice.

"The other families too are very special. I think they would appreciate getting the coin. I was impressed with all of them."

Lily looked at her girls and then at James. "Do any of you have an idea how we can present the coins to the families?"

After some discussion, Rose responded, "Let's have a barbecue and invite them all to come. Let's make it next Monday evening. The yard is looking good, and we have not had a party out there since Dad died. It would be fun."

Jacob and Lily looked at each other and then, almost in unison, said, "What a great idea." They both laughed. Susie jumped up and down. James mimicked her. They were clearly happy about the idea.

"Okay. Tomorrow each one of you will get on the telephone and call the family of your friend and invite them to come for a barbecue party next Monday. Then, if they say yes, I want you to make a special invitation to send them in the mail. Agreed?"

"It's not late right now, only 8:00 p.m. Let's call them tonight, and then we can make the invitations after they accept. What do you think about that, Mom?" Bonnie asked.

"Good. I have the phone numbers right here, except for Sammy Ellis's number. Do you have that, Jacob?"

"I do. James can call him on my cell phone right now."

For the next fifteen minutes, the girls used their home phone and their mother's cell phone and called the families of the friends they wished to invite. All of them were happy to say yes. They were told an invitation would be following in the mail.

James talked to Sammy, and then Jacob got on the phone and spoke to his father. The response was positive. While the phone calls were being made, Lily got card stock for the invitations. She rounded up scissors, crayons, colored pencils, and envelopes. For the next hour, each child made a special invitation for the family he had invited. Lily had written all the pertinent information on a blackboard, which the girls and James copied, with a little help from Jacob and Lily for the younger ones.

When they were finished, envelopes were addressed and stamped, and return addresses placed in the corners. The children had each made a fine work of art and were complimented on them. Jacob put the cards in his pocket to mail the following day.

Lily said, "Let's clean up now and then say our closing prayer. This was really fun. I am looking forward to next Monday night when we get to meet your friends and their families.

*****

The week went by quickly. Monday evening at six-thirty, the families were all in the Langston's backyard, admiring the spring flowers. "What a lovely backyard you have, Mrs. Langston," Johnny Elliott's father remarked.

"Thank you. Please call me Lily." Johnny's father was a short stocky man. He had sandy colored hair and wore glasses. "My name is Marv, and my wife's name is Judy. These are Johnny's siblings: Petey and Annie. They are five and three." The children had brown hair and brown eyes like Johnny.

"How very nice to meet you," Lily said. She went to the other families and introduced herself to them. She introduced her daughters and then Jacob and James. Soon they were all visiting together and enjoying each other's company.

Jacob and Rose and Bonnie barbecued chicken, ribs, and wieners. The tables were all set. They had been placed as close together as they could be and still be able to move around them.

Lily had made a big tossed salad. There were also French fries, sliced tomatoes, garlic bread and hot dog buns and ketchup, mustard, and mayonnaise. Rose and Bonnie had made a fruit salad. Drinks were soda, water, or milk. The meal was topped off with ice cream sundaes.

After the meal was over, Rose and Bonnie took the children to one end of the yard and played games with them. Lily and Jacob sat with the parents and visited with them until it was time for them all to say good night. It had been a wonderful evening. Lily called to the children and asked them to come back to the tables. When everyone was gathered together again, Lily said, "We have something we want each family to have." She reached into a coin purse sitting on the table next to her. "These coins were given to me by our dear friend, Carson Hunter. As most of you know, he is a very special man who has done much for this community. He gave me ten gold coins and told me that I could do anything I wanted with them. We have these four left. My girls and James have picked out your families to each receive a coin. They are, of course, pure gold."

"James, will you take this one and give it to Sammy and his family?" James walked very carefully over to Sammy and handed it to him. Sammy gave him the "I love you" sign. James was pleased.

In turn, each of Lily's daughters took a coin to give to her special friend. They were thrilled. There in the dusk, their eyes sparkled with happy tears. The families came up and hugged Lily and Jacob and the children. They were clearly moved by the special gift they had been given.

"We will send Carson Hunter our thanks, Lily," Marv Elliott told her. "We will treasure our coin."

"You are welcome to sell them if you should need the money at some time. Gold is selling very well right now, as I am sure you know."

Each of them assured Lily and Jacob they had no intention of selling the coins.

After saying fond goodbyes to their new friends, Lily and her girls and Jacob and James cleaned up. It was late, but Jacob did not want to leave Lily and the girls to clean up by themselves, so he and James pitched in to put everything in order. James carried the black trash bag, and the girls placed the paper plates and other throw-away items in it. He was clearly pleased with himself.

Finally, when all was done, Lily and the girls said their goodbyes. Jacob kissed Lily lightly on the cheek as he held her hand. "Good night, angels," he called as he closed the door.

CHAPTER SEVENTY

"Jacob, this is Carson Hunter. Will you stop by my office tomorrow when you get a minute? I have been thinking a lot about putting on a citywide celebration next July 4. Come in so we can discuss the particulars."

"I will be there just after lunch, about 1:00 p.m. Will that work for you, Carson?"

"That will be great. See you then."

The next afternoon, promptly at one o'clock, Jacob opened the door to Mr. Hunter's office and was motioned to sit down in his usual chair.

"Jacob, before we get started on your new assignment"—Carson smiled—"I have something here in my pocket I want to show you." Out of his pocket, Carson Hunter pulled some pieces of paper, neatly folded. "There are six letters there, six thank-you notes. Read them."

Jacob read each one silently and then looked up at Carson. "Well, my friend, you told me to tell Lily she could do anything she wanted with the coins."

Carson cleared his throat. "What a blessing that dear lady is. I was so pleased to get the first letter, which was from the Summers. But, then, receiving five more, well, I…I couldn't be happier with the outcome."

"Read the letter from Hannah Summers to me, will you please, Jacob?"

"Of course.

Dear Mr. Hunter,

With heartfelt appreciation, I write this letter to you to thank you for the gold coin. Aaron Turner presented it to Peter and me and the children after the concert last weekend.

As you know, our precious little Grace died some months ago. Aaron had become very attached to Grace and spent all the time he could at her bedside. Grace loved him, and he her. He was as devastated as we were at her loss.

Not long after she died, my husband Peter lost his job. He was a night watchman at a company that went out of business because of the slowing economy. The company was forced to close some of its stores, and Peter's was one of them.

Peter fell into a deep depression. We had some savings, and the church has helped us out. Peter looked for work every week since he lost his job. But being as depressed as he was, he just couldn't seem to present a happy face in his interviews. He was passed over every time he was interviewed.

He had an interview for a job the very next working day after the concert, but he was not hopeful. Then Aaron gave us the gold coin. Peter's whole outlook changed. He became upbeat and hopeful. The interview went very well. He was hired on the spot. The interviewer told Peter that he appreciated his positive attitude and knew he would make a fine employee.

He started his job a week ago and loves it. The bosses like him and told him they are pleased with his work.

We know the story of how you gave Lily Langston the coins. Thank you from the bottom of our hearts for the ray of hope, of sunshine we received. It has led us to happier times. Bless you and Lily.

With much affection,
Hannah and Peter Summers

"I received that letter some time ago. Then, just in the last few days, I received the others." Carson cleared his throat again. "Every letter is special. I can't begin to tell you how they have affected both Kay and me. I will treasure them always."

Carson Hunter stood up from his chair and came to sit on his desk in front of where Jacob was sitting. "Now, to the business I wish to discuss with you. Jacob, my wife, and I have been discussing doing a big Salt Lake City-wide celebration of our Constitution and the great Founding Fathers who made it all possible. We have been getting the feeling that as a people who have been enormously blessed to live in this great land, we have been getting away from appreciating what we have. This year July 4 falls on Sunday. I have talked to the producers of the 'Stadium of Fire' which is held in Provo each year, as you know, and they tell me they will be having it on the third. Let's plan our big event for Friday, July 2.

"I have talked to the schedulers at the University of Utah, and they have told me that we can have the celebration in the football stadium there on that Friday. They were just as excited as I was when I talked to them. Rice-Eccles Stadium holds approximately forty-five thousand in the stands, and I believe we can more than fill it. I want you to spearhead the event with the help of my assistant, Mona Thompson. I would also like Lily Langston and her daughters involved, and Aaron and his father, Steven Black, and anyone else you would like to recruit. I would like to have the high school choirs from throughout the city be involved. That would mean that they would need to start on the music shortly and work on it while school is still in session. This is the first part of May, so they will just get started learning it before school is through for the year. It will entail getting the young people together often during June for practices together. I think Steven could pull that together, don't you Jacob?"

"He is very capable. He would do a fine job of it, I am sure," Jacob answered.

"Great. Would you call the people who you will want to work together with you on the celebration and set up a time and let me know? Kay and I would like to be there for the first meeting."

"I'll get back to you as soon as I have a chance to talk to everybody. It is a very good idea, Carson. I believe it will be a great occasion. Thanks for asking me to be in charge. I am honored." Jacob stood up and grasped his friend's hand warmly with both of his.

*****

"Lily, Carson Hunter has asked me to spearhead a big celebration for the Fourth of July this year. He wants it to be held in the University of Utah Rice-Eccles stadium on Friday, July 2. He wants you and your daughters, Steven Black, and Aaron Turner to help us. He has asked that we all get together for a planning meeting. How do you feel about being a part of it, honey, as if I don't already know the answer to that question?"

"Oh, Jacob, how wonderful." Lily laughed. "Of course, we would love to do it. Have you decided on a date and time for the meeting?"

"We only have just over six weeks to pull this program together, so what do you think about getting together tomorrow evening, say six, at Carson's offices? He and Kay want to be there for the first meeting, so his office would be the perfect place for the get-together. I'll call Aaron and Steven, and you talk to your daughters. We will want them to be there for the meeting to get their input."

"Of course, Jacob. Bring James to the meeting too. It would be terrific if he could take part in the program in some way, don't you think?" Lily asked.

"What a wonderful idea, Lily. We could possibly get several handicapped children to participate. Good thinking, dear. I'll see you then. Bye."

When Lily hung up the phone, she turned to her daughters and told them of her conversation with Jacob. They were clearly excited. Susie jumped up and down and hugged her mother.

"What will we be able to do on the program, Mom? Will we be able to sing?"

"Of course, silly," Bonnie chided her sister. "We always get to sing, don't we, Mom?"

"We will be planning the program at the meeting tomorrow night. We'll know more then. Now get your homework done, and we'll eat. The macaroni and cheese and hot dogs are just about ready. I just have to put together a salad."

When Jacob got home that evening, he hugged his parents and then told them and James about the big celebration he was to be in charge of. When Jacob told James that he would have a part in the program, he clapped his hands together.

"Will Susie be in it too, Dad?" He was assured that she would be. He clapped his hands again. Jacob had earlier called Steven and Aaron and had gotten their okay to work with him. They were also very excited to help. Jacob told Steven of Carson Hunter's desire to have the school choirs participate together and asked him to be in charge of making that happen.

"I'll bring my patriotic music to the meeting, Jacob. Aaron and I will be there, and thank you very much for the opportunity to be a part of such a glorious occasion."

"Steven, it was Carson's idea to ask you, though I would have done so anyway." Jacob laughed. "This great occasion needs both you and Aaron."

CHAPTER SEVENTY-ONE

The next evening, promptly at 6:00 p.m., Jacob, James, Lily and her daughters, Aaron and Steven walked into Carson Hunter's office. Kay Hunter stood up from her chair and walked toward the group. After her husband's warm handshakes, Kay grasped each hand in her own. "It is so good to see you all again. We think this occasion we are planning will be great for Salt Lake City. We certainly have the right people to put it together." Kay Hunter, still lovely in her middle sixties with her graying hair held back at the nape of her neck in a diamond clasp, walked back to her chair and sat down, motioning the others to join her.

As soon as they were all seated, the door opened, and Carson's assistant, Mona Thompson, entered the room. It was clear that she would be taking charge of the meeting. Her blonde hair was tied up in a ponytail. The wispy curls that had escaped were framing her pretty face. She carried a pad and pen with her and quickly opened the meeting with a warm greeting.

"Thank you for coming. Carson and Kay and I are very excited to have all of you here. We want this to be a spectacular celebration of the founding of this great country. We want those who attend to be so impressed, they will never forget it. It will be one of the greatest events ever to take place here in this great city. At least, since the 2002 Winter Olympics." Mona amended with a laugh. "So let's get down to the planning of this superb event. Jacob, we want you to be liaison between the different members of our team. You will be checking to make sure all is going smoothly and report back to Carson or me. Will you agree to taking on this very important calling?"

"Of course, Mona." With that, he nodded toward Carson Hunter who responded with a warm smile and a nod of his own head.

"Lily, will you work side by side with Jacob? We want you and your girls to sing one or two songs with Aaron. This is where Mr. Black, Steven, you come in. Will you take charge of the music, the singing part of the program? That would entail getting the choir directors of the various high school choirs together and get them the music and enough copies to give to each student. If you want to be the chorister for the event, that is fine. However, you might want to have a couple of the other choir directors working with you and divide the directing of the music between you."

"That would be great, Mona. I brought my file of patriotic music with me, so we can pick out the pieces we want to have the choirs sing," Steven said.

"Mr. Hunter and Kay will fund whatever expenses are needed to make this presentation perfect. He has set up an account at his credit union and will give each of you a credit card to use to purchase supplies with."

Lily raised her hand to get Mona's attention. "My girls and I would be happy to help in whatever way we can. May I make a suggestion, Mona?"

"Please do, Lily. We want all the input we can get."

"Several months ago, Rose's teacher gave her class an assignment to do a paper on one of the Founding Fathers. Rose picked Benjamin Franklin. Her report garnered her an A++ from her teacher. Why couldn't we have Rose's teacher pick out four or five of the best papers and have the young authors present their papers at the celebration? With this much time, I'm sure they could be memorized."

"Oh, could we, Mona? I'd love to tell what I learned about Benjamin Franklin," Rose asked excitedly.

"What a wonderful idea, Lily. They could be presented with background songs of the period of time in which our founders lived. I like that idea a lot. Lily, talk to Rose's teacher and have her work with you on it.

"Now, James, would you like to help in our production? You wouldn't be too scared, would you?" Mona smiled at him.

"Can I, Dad, can I be in the program? I promise I wouldn't be too scared."

"What did you have in mind?" Jacob asked Mona.

Carson Hunter answered, "Jacob, I understand that James goes to a special school. Is this correct?"

"Yes, he does. Are you thinking what I am thinking?"

"Yes, I think I am." Mr. Hunter smiled. "Talk to the principal of James's school and see what he thinks about having the students participate in our program. I am thinking of having them recite something important in the founding of our country, like maybe Abraham Lincoln's Gettysburg Address. Each child could memorize a line, or they could recite it together. In the background, a screen would flash the line as the child recited it. You and the principal and the teachers could work out the logistics and get the children working on it," Carson finished.

"I'll get right on it, Carson. Would you like to work with your class on performing, James?" Jacob asked his son.

"Yes, yes, Dad." James jumped up and down, clapping his hands. Susie went up to James and held up her hand in their "I love you" signal. He proceeded to go around the circle repeating the signal with each one present, laughing as he did so. They all reciprocated warmly to his enthusiasm.

"Now we need music behind the choirs and the talks. Got any suggestions?"

Both Lily and Aaron held up their hands at the same time. Lily spoke first, "Paul Strong, of Legacy Productions, who did our CD, would be perfect for the job, I think. He has all the equipment to pull off a big production like this. He would have to have it all set up in the stadium. He would have to hire some technical assistants to help him, but I am thinking he would do it very well. Is that who you were thinking of, Aaron?"

"Yes, I was. I was very impressed with his production skills. He could put a team together and do a great job."

"Very well, Jacob, you and Lily and Aaron approach him and see if he has the time and if he would be willing to do this for us."

Mona turned her attention to Steven. "You brought some patriotic music with you, you said. Share with us what you have with you, Steven."

"I have the music to Francis Scott Key's 'The Star-Spangled Banner,' to 'Battle Hymn of the Republic,' 'My Country 'tis of Thee' by Samuel F. Smith, 'America the Beautiful' by Katherine Lee Bates, Lee Greenwood's 'God Bless the USA,' Irving Berlin's 'God Bless America,' 'The Stars and Stripes Forever' by John Philip Sousa, 'The Marine Hymn,' and 'Yankee Doodle'."

"Those will do fine. Find out what the other school's choir directors have when you meet with them. You will need to order enough of the pieces for each student so they can learn them by heart. There aren't many weeks left before the celebration, so meet as quickly as you can with them, Steven, and get the music ordered. The choirs will need to get practicing the music as soon as you can get it."

"Will do, Mona, and thank you for this opportunity."

"You are very welcome." Mona continued, "I talked to the people in charge of scheduling events for the University of Utah, and they are willing to handle such things as the selling of refreshments and ticket sales. They will also produce the programs for the event. They will give us a bill for the cost for their expenses so the school will not be out anything financially. Carson, Kay, and I are thinking about using the money from the ticket sales to fund scholarships at the various colleges and universities in the area, for studies in the area of United States history. So many Americans do not know our history as well as they should. And some of it has been distorted or many important facts left out. We want to change this if we can. This would be a good starting place, we think."

The Hunters stood up. Carson said, "Thank you all so much for agreeing to work with us. We think this will be a sensational program. With your gracious help, we know it will be. You all have your assignments. Keep Jacob informed of your progress, and he will get back to us."

One by one, the Hunters walked around the room shaking each individual's hand as they left the room. Outside, the friends wished each other well and proceeded to their vehicles. Jacob and Lily and the children walked together. "This is quite an undertaking Carson and Kay have given us. It should culminate in a marvelous production," Jacob told the others. "How would you all like to go out for pizza?"

With a resounding Yes from the youngsters, Lily and Jacob agreed on the nearest pizza place and took off in their separate cars to meet shortly at their designated meeting place. The work would begin the very next morning on the celebration, but tonight they would relax and enjoy being together.

CHAPTER SEVENTY-TWO

The next morning, Thursday, Steven and Aaron arrived at the high school earlier than usual. Steven went to the office and got a list of all the high schools in the Salt Lake City area and their choir directors. In between classes, Aaron helped Steven call the schools and talk to their music people. Most of them agreed to meet at their high school after classes were over for the day. Those who couldn't make it were told on the phone what Carson and Kay Hunter wanted them to be a part of. They all thought it was a wonderful idea and asked to be filled in on what transpired at the meeting.

After school, the other directors came in to the music room one by one until they were all present. Steven called out the names and had them raise their hands to acknowledge their presence. All in all, there were twenty present. Several of the high schools had two persons representing them. They were all curious about why Steven Black had asked them to come. Even some of the assistant directors wanted to be there and were welcomed warmly.

Steven began by telling the group about the great Fourth of July production that would be taking place on July 2 of that year. "You are all familiar with Carson and Kay Hunter, I believe. They are well-known for their philanthropic works in the area. Of course, you know of the hospital they started, the Hunter Cancer Hospital?" They all nodded their heads. "The Hunters want to have a big celebration this year because they believe, as do I, that we need to be reminded of what our great country stands for, how it was founded, and the sacrifices that have been given by not only our great Founding Fathers, but also the men and women who have fought for our freedoms. It is to remind us that because of the bravery of these great and valiant souls, we have all the blessings we have. They want the high school choirs to do the bulk of the music. All of you who are in favor of this undertaking, please raise your hands."

Everyone present raised his or her hand.

"Good, now there are only three weeks left of school, so we need to get working on the music as soon as possible. On the blackboard, I made a list of the music that I have here at the school that I want to begin working on, starting Monday. How many of you have all the pieces mentioned?"

A few hands went up. "Okay, let's do it this way. Aaron, give each person here a piece of paper. Do you all have something to write with? Good. Now I want you to put your name and your school at the top of the page and your personal phone number. Then write down the names of the pieces you do not have or do not have enough of for each of your choir members. We want each choir member who plans to participate to memorize the song and their part in it, so they will each need to have a copy. Please write down the number of copies you will need by each song so that every one of your students can be given a copy.

"After you have finished your tallies, Aaron and I will gather them up and be able to order what copies we will still need. We have already spoken to the music store we like to order from, and they assured me that they can get enough copies of these pieces by next Tuesday. He will just need a total to call the order in to the manufacturer by tomorrow." It took about twenty minutes for the directors to make the lists and hand them in.

"Thank you," Steven told them. "Is there going to be any problem that any of you can foresee to working hard on these pieces?"

One gentleman raised his hand. "What are the plans for after-school is out to get all the choirs together, and who is going to lead the choirs at the celebration? Also, what kind of background music are you planning to use?"

"Thank you, John. It is John, isn't it? We are going to try and get Paul Strong of Legacy Productions to handle all the music. Jacob Manning and Lily Langston and my son, Aaron, here, are in charge of arranging that end. In the meantime, your pianists will work with you and the choirs. As far as getting the choirs together after school is out, we will find a place where we can all fit in and practice together. I'll get back to you on that.

"The Hunters have asked me to be in charge, but if any of you would like to help in the leading of the choirs at the celebration, I would be more than happy to have you. Is there any of you in this group who would be interested in helping lead the choirs, both for practices and for the main event?"

The man called John raised his hand, as did five others, three women and two men.

"Excellent, I welcome your help. Let's see." Steven picked up the papers. "I'll make a note on your paper. John, Audrey, Tracy, Martha, Hugh, and you are…Tom, is that correct?"

Tom nodded his head.

"Thanks very much for coming on such short notice, people. Aaron and I will go through your papers and tally up the number of each piece we need. As soon as they come in, we will get them to you, hopefully no later than Tuesday."

Steven had written on the blackboard his and Aaron's full names and cell phone numbers so that those who were there could contact them with any questions or comments.

"Aaron and I will contact those who are not here. There were only a couple who couldn't make it. We will get their lists also and get the numbers to the music store. It is going to be great working with all of you. Thanks again for coming."

Later, when they were home with Connie, they sat around the kitchen table and tallied up the sheets they received. Connie worked the calculator. After Steven called the directors who were not able to attend the meeting and got their enthusiastic remarks and the number of pieces of the sheet music they would need for their school choirs, the numbers were added to the total.

The next morning, Steven called the music store and gave them the names of the musical numbers and the total number they would need of each. The store promised the music would be there on the following Tuesday.

On Monday, Aaron and Steven drove to the Hunter Cancer Hospital and performed for the patients there that afternoon as they had promised. After they played and sang the music they had prepared, they asked the patients for requests. They went well past the hour that was set aside for them, but no one seemed to mind. As Aaron and Steven got up to leave, they were hugged and congratulated on a wonderful miniconcert. Some of the patients had tears in their eyes as they said their goodbyes. As father and son walked down the corridor and out the door to their automobile, they were silent. Each was reflecting on what had just transpired.

As they drove home, Aaron broke the silence. "Dad, I am so happy to have you in my life. And to be able to come and sing and play together for so many who are sick—it was just unbelievable." He choked out the last word.

Steven was struggling with his own emotions. "Son, I love you, you know, don't you? And I love your mother. I too am so very happy that we are together again. I am so blessed. You are precious to me beyond words. I want to ask your mother to marry me if she will have me. Then we can be a real family as we should have been all along these past years. Would that be all right with you?"

"Would it?" Aaron laughed. "I have mentioned it in my prayers every night since you came back into our lives. I know that is what Mom wants too, though she hasn't said it in so many words."

"When we get home, let's ask her." Steven reached over and gave Aaron's hand a pat.

Shortly after, Steven parked the car, and he and Aaron walked into the house. Connie had the dinner table set, and the food was ready to be put on the table.

"You are home just in time. Dinner is ready. Let's get it on the table, and then you can tell me all about your day." Connie smiled and was about to wheel her chair into the kitchen, but Steven stopped her.

"You go sit at your place there, and Aaron and I will serve up the food." With that, father and son soon had everything on the table and quickly sat down. After the blessing on the food, they filled Connie in on their experiences at the cancer clinic. As they ate roast beef, mashed potatoes, whole kernel corn, and fruit salad, Aaron and Steven filled her in on their miniconcert. She noticed that it had been a very emotional experience for the two of them. As they spoke to her, she felt a warm feeling come over her. Father and son together after all the years since she had sent Steven away. She refused to think about what might have been had she not impulsively pushed him out of her life.

Right now is all that matters, she thought to herself, *I love them both so much.*

"I can tell from what you are saying and the way you are saying it that you have had a very special experience together this afternoon. Thank you for letting me share it with you, every detail. I can truly imagine how lovely it must have been."

"Mom, Steven has something he wants to ask you." Aaron turned to his father. "Dad?"

"Connie"—Steven stood up and went to kneel beside her wheelchair—"Aaron and I would like to know if you would marry me. Will you marry me, Connie?"

"Don't you want to wait until I can walk again, Steven?"

"I want to marry you as soon as we can arrange it, Connie. Then we will work to get you walking again. Will you marry me, dearest?"

"Yes, I will marry you, Steven. Nothing would make me happier."

"Me too." Aaron laughed as he walked over and hugged them both. "Me too."

CHAPTER SEVENTY-THREE

Lily dropped in on Rose's school class one morning before the lessons were to begin. As Rose found her desk, Lily approached the teacher. Her name was Joan Taylor. Mrs. Taylor was a gray-haired woman in her late fifties, smallish with a kind smile.

She walked toward Lily and smiled warmly as they shook hands. "It is very nice to meet you, Mrs. Langston. I have enjoyed your performances when you and your daughters have sung in various programs throughout the valley. And I bought your CD that my family and I are enjoying very much. Come and sit down, please." She turned to the class and said, "Get your history books and turn to page 150. Read to yourself for the next five or ten minutes while I visit with Mrs. Langston, and then we will discuss the pages you have read."

Mrs. Taylor turned to Lily. "Now you mentioned on the phone that you had something to talk to me about, something about a big program you want some of my students to be involved in. Is that correct?"

"Thank you for giving me this time, Mrs. Taylor. I am delighted you moved up with your students this year so that Rose could continue in your class. She really enjoys you as a teacher. I am sure you remember last year you had your students do papers on some of our Founding Fathers. Rose did hers on Benjamin Franklin. You gave her an A++, which she was thrilled to get.

"Carson and Kay Hunter are putting together a big July 4 celebration this year. It will be held in the Rice-Eccles Stadium at the University of Utah on Friday, July 2. I suggested that we have some of your students tell about their favorite Founding Father. We will showcase them as part of the program to be put on during the celebration. We were hoping that you would pick four or five or maybe six of your students having the best papers to memorize them and participate in the program. It is going to be big, very big. The high school choirs are singing together, and several other things are in the works to make it a never-to-be-forgotten program for the ages." Lily laughed at the words. "Will you help us, and may I call you Joan?"

"I would love to be of help. Of course, Rose will be asked to do her speech on Benjamin Franklin."

Lily stood up. "Thank you, Joan. I'll let you get back to your class now." Lily handed the teacher her card. "Let me know who you choose and keep me informed on their progress. We will have some practices with all the participants after school is out so we can get everything working well together. I'll talk to you soon." Lily waved at Rose as she left the room.

Next, Lily drove over to Legacy Productions where she and Jacob had a scheduled meeting with Paul Strong. Just as she parked her car, Jacob pulled up beside her. He got out and came over and opened the door for her. "Hi, honey, we have exquisite timing, don't you agree?"

"Yes, we do." Lily laughed. As they walked into the studio, Lily filled Jacob in on the conversation she'd had with Rose's teacher. "She seemed very excited to help, Jacob."

"That's great. Let's hope Paul Strong will be just as excited. It is going to be an enormous job for him. I hope he feels up to it."

Paul greeted them at the door and welcomed them into his studio. "What can I do for you people." Paul smiled at them. "Please come and sit down." He motioned for his assistant to bring them Diet Cokes. "I seem to remember that is your drink of choice." They both nodded. Soon the man was back with the drinks.

Jacob was the first to speak. "Paul, we have a huge favor to ask of you, and we are hoping you will say yes. Carson and Kay Hunter are spearheading a big Fourth of July celebration to help to bring the citizens of our great community back to a remembrance of what a marvelous blessing it is to be able to live in this great land. So many brave men and women are responsible for the freedoms we enjoy. They feel that we are more and more taking them for granted. They want to bring us back to what made and still makes our country such a great place to live.

"As a big part of the celebration, he has asked the high school choirs to get together and sing as one unit. They have all agreed to do it, and Steven Black, Aaron Turner's father, will be in charge of making it all happen. We want you to do the background music and to accompany the choirs and to do whatever else will be needed. The Hunters have also asked Lily, her daughters, and Aaron to perform a couple of numbers. They will want you to use your talents to play background for them also. We know it is a huge undertaking we are asking you to take on. Do you want some time to think about it, check your schedule, and then get back to us?"

"That won't be necessary, Jacob. I happen to be very fond of the Hunters. They helped me get started in this business. It would be an honor to fulfill this request. I will get in touch with Steven Black and get going on doing whatever it takes to make everything happen smoothly. By the way, Lily, I have a check for you and Aaron. Your CD is still selling well. My secretary will hand it to you on your way out."

"Thanks, Paul."

"After the big Fourth of July celebration, let's get together and start on a Christmas CD. What do you say about that, Lily?"

"That would be wonderful. After we are through with this program, we'd like to do it." Lily continued, "The girls and I will let you know what numbers we will be doing with Aaron on the Fourth of July program. Thank you so much for saying yes."

The check was for just under $6,000. It was made out to Lily on behalf of both herself and Aaron. Lily would deposit the check and send half of it to Aaron and Connie.

"I talked to James's teacher this morning," Jacob told Lily as he escorted her to her car. "She thinks James's class could memorize something with a patriotic theme. She too is excited to work with us on this project."

"That is great, Jacob. So far, everyone we have talked to is happy to be asked to work on it. It is going to turn out great. I can just feel it."

Jacob kissed Lily as Lily continued, "My girls are making pasta tonight, and they want you and James to come over and eat with us."

"What time, Lily?"

"Come over at six. We have a new game we want to play with you and James."

"See you at six then." Jacob smiled and waved as he shut his car door.

CHAPTER SEVENTY-FOUR

"Lily, this is Connie. Steven and Aaron and I have something to tell you." Lily and Jacob had just finished clearing off the table, and the girls were busy in the kitchen putting the food away and filling the dishwasher.

"Please, tell us. Jacob and James are here too. What do you want to tell us?"

"Steven has asked me to marry him, and I told him yes. Aaron is ecstatic about it. We wanted you and Jacob to be the first to know."

"Connie, that is so wonderful. Just a minute. I want to put Jacob on the extension." Lily motioned to Jacob to pick up the phone. "Now tell us again so Jacob can hear."

Connie repeated what she had said. Jacob was clearly pleased. "We want you two to be our witnesses."

"We would be honored," Lily said as she saw Jacob's head nod up and down. "We would be pleased to stand up with you. Have you got a date and time yet?"

"We called our bishop and set it up for two weeks tomorrow. That would be Saturday, May 29. It will be in the evening, probably 7:00 p.m."

"Do you have a special color you want me to wear?" Lily asked.

"I am thinking royal blue would be nice."

"Okay, let me see what I can find in that color, dear Connie. Is there anything we can do to help you get ready?"

"No, but I would like you and the girls to sing something romantic for us. Will you?"

"Of course, dear. We'd love to."

"I'll talk to you soon then, and thanks again, Lily," Connie said before hanging up.

"Well, girls, we have to practice a song to sing for Connie and Steven's wedding. It will be on the twenty-ninth. I think we probably already have some music that would be appropriate."

"That is the day after school gets out for the summer. Yay!" said Susie. "It's going to be fun getting to be part of Connie and Steven's wedding."

"Tomorrow morning, we'll do the chores around the house, and then we'll get our music and pick a number to sing. We also need to start working on a couple of patriotic songs to sing for the Fourth of July celebration."

Bonnie coaxed everyone to sit back down around the table so they could begin to play their game.

CHAPTER SEVENTY-FIVE

Monday afternoon, the music store called Steven to let him know the music he ordered had just been delivered by UPS. As soon as school was over, he and Aaron drove uptown and picked it up. They then delivered it to the various high schools that were participating in the Fourth of July celebration. Some of the music directors were still at their schools and gladly received the music, ready to start on it first thing Tuesday morning. Those who had gone home would pick up theirs in the schools' front offices the next morning. "We'll see that they get it as soon as they come in tomorrow morning," the office staffs all promised. It was clear that there was a lot of interest in the upcoming festivities.

*****

As Jacob walked through the front door of his home, he was greeted by a very excited James. "Dad, our teacher gave each of us our assignment that our class is going to be doing for the big party, you know, the one we talked about at that meeting we went to."

He handed his dad the sheet of paper he had brought home from school. On it was Abraham Lincoln's Gettysburg Address. "There's my line there. It's underlined. Teacher told me that I was to say my line right after Billy says his. Will you help me learn it, Dad?"

"Of course, son." Jacob looked at his mother who had a puzzled look on her face. "It's okay, Mom. On large screens that will be set up in several places in the stadium, the words will be scrolled so that everyone present will see them while the children are saying them. We have plenty of time to practice the words. I know that James will learn them and do great, won't you, son?" Jacob put his hand up to James's in their special "I love you" sign.

"I already know the first five words, Dad." James then repeated them. "The world will little note.... But I don't know what that means."

"It means that the people will not pay much attention to what Abraham Lincoln said when he gave that speech, but it was such an incredible speech that people have remembered it. It is one of the greatest speeches ever given before the world. And, my dear son, you get to be part of your school class to recite it before a great big audience. That is really special."

"I'm glad I get to say the words. I like that I can say the words."

Jacob smiled at his son. Then turning to his mother, he asked if there was anything he could do to help with dinner.

"It's all ready, Jacob, but you and James can set the table for us. We are having spaghetti and tossed salad and garlic bread, and ice cream for dessert. James, go tell your grandfather dinner is ready. He's in the study, dear."

*****

Lily and the girls had decided on the music they would sing for Connie and Steven's wedding. They would sing "We've Only Just Begun" by the Carpenters and written by Paul Williams. Lily sat at the piano and played it through. They had sung it before, so it would not take much to brush it up for them to perform.

After going through the song twice, they turned to the music they would sing for the patriotic celebration. They decided on Allie Wrubel's "My Own America." Aaron would join them on it. They needed to pick out another piece. Rose suggested Woody Guthrie's "This Land is Your Land." They had the music for that piece too, so for the next hour, they practiced together.

"Has your teacher decided on who will be doing the other recitations from your class, Rose?"

"She has, Mom. There will be five of us, two boys and three girls. She wants us to memorize our essays so that we won't have to look at notes. I am so excited to do it. I nearly have my essay on

Benjamin Franklin memorized already. Next week, she is going to have us say them to her after class, one of us each day. She will then critique them."

"What does critique mean?" Susie asked.

"She will let us know what we still need to work on to make our talks really good. She'll give us pointers about how we should present ourselves and the material. After she is satisfied, she will have us give them before the class. During the final assembly of the school year, we will be doing our presentations before the whole school. I am excited but nervous too."

"You will do wonderfully, Rose. I know you will." Lily hugged her oldest daughter.

"The principal will have the choir sing their numbers at the assembly too to give them a good practice. You are going to be there, aren't you, Mom?"

"I wouldn't miss it. When will it be, do you know?"

"It will be on Wednesday, May 26, at one o'clock in the afternoon."

"Good. I'll be there."

*****

Carson and Kay Hunter sat in the office of the director of operations at Hill Air Force Base, some miles north of Salt Lake City. Carson and the director were old friends.

"I hear you have a special request, my friend. We will be happy to accommodate you in any way we can. Just name it, and we will see what we can do."

"On the telephone I told you about what we are planning for the Fourth of July. Actually, since the Fourth is Sunday, and the Stadium of Fire will be held in Provo on the third, we are going to have our special festivities on July 2 in the Rice-Eccles Stadium at the University of Utah. What we would like is a flyby by some of your jet fighters. Is that even possible, Frank?"

"I think that can be arranged. Let's see, that is a Friday evening, right? What time would you like them to fly over the stadium? Do you know yet?"

"The program will begin at 8:00 p.m., Frank. Could you make it for 8:05? I want it to be a surprise. It will be a marvelous way to get the evening started."

Frank stood up and walked over to the Hunters who had also stood up. "We will get it done, Carson. It's great to see you again. And, Kay, you are as lovely as ever."

"Oh, Frank, you flatterer." Kay laughed. "It is great to see you again too. It's been too long."

"Carson, I just had a thought. Would you have a section of the bleachers there at the stadium for our servicemen and women. I am sure they would like to be there en masse, if it can be arranged."

"Absolutely. It will be our great honor to have them there. Thanks, Frank. And please tell the servicemen and women we will be delighted to welcome them with open arms.

"Goodbye, Carson and Kay. We'll see you on the second of July, if not before."

CHAPTER SEVENTY-SIX

Jacob checked with the University of Utah special events director and found out that the students in the art department were working on flyers to hand out to all the businesses in the city and surrounding areas. They would be distributed close to the middle of June. The director asked Jacob to supply a copy of the program for the evening as soon as possible so that it could be produced by those same students.

The events director told Jacob that the university had stored a lot of patriotic banners and such and that they would put them up in the stadium for the event.

After he hung up the phone, he received a call from Carson Hunter. "Jacob, Kay, and I have just returned from Hill Air Force Base. My friend, Frank Hoover, who is director of operations out there, has agreed to a fly-over of jet fighters. This is for your ears only. It will be a surprise. They will be flying over at 8:05, just as the program is about to begin. Also, reserve a section for the men and women of the armed forces. We will honor them that night."

"That is great, sir. You must carry a lot of clout with those guys out there. I am not sure they would do a fly-over for just anyone." Jacob laughed.

"Frank Hoover and I go way back. He is a great friend. He thinks our project is a good one and wants to help make it special in any way he can." Carson chuckled too.

After Mr. Hunter hung up, Jacob called the special events director at the U of U again and asked him to set up an area on the bleachers for the men and women of the armed services. "Make it the best seats available. We want to honor them." He received a "will do" from the director.

Jacob sat in his office looking over his notes regarding the celebration. *Let's see now, we contacted Paul Strong, and he is getting his staff working on what he needs to set up the sound system at the U and working on the arrangements of the numbers we gave him. He and Steven Black will work closely together to coordinate the music with the choirs. They will work with the University of Utah to set up the sound system. They will set up the practices for after school is out.*

Lily is working on her numbers with her girls and with Aaron. She also talked to Rose's teacher, and they are working on the talks about the Founding Fathers. James's class is working on the Gettysburg Address. I think they will do a great job. James is very excited. The teacher tells me that every morning, the kids want to practice their lines. They will be fine. I talked to the university people about setting up the screens in strategic places in the stadium so that everyone can see the words when the children say them.

I arranged to have a lovely display of fireworks after the program is through. I asked the same people who are doing them for the Stadium of Fire festivities the following night. They said they would, so that has been taken care of. The university will handle the refreshments with the various vendors and are working on flyers to be given out at every venue possible throughout the city. The radio stations will begin advertising the event shortly after June 1, two weeks from now. The Salt Lake Tribune *and* the Deseret News *will carry articles leading up to the event.*

Now, is there anything I have left out? The weather—may the weather be spectacular that evening. We can't have any rain and, please, no wind. That's your department, Lord, if you please. Jacob closed his eyes and gave a silent prayer.

Jacob reached in his pocket and pulled out a little box. He gently opened it. It contained a beautiful engagement ring. It sparkled in the light. He planned on asking Lily to marry him after the celebration. *Dear Lord, bless her and please help her say yes.*

CHAPTER SEVENTY-SEVEN

Connie and Steven's wedding was about to begin. It was Saturday, May 29. The bishop stood before the small audience and motioned the wedding couple forward. Aaron stood beside them as best man. Jacob and Lily stood beside them as witnesses.

The ceremony was short and sweet. Friends and neighbors and relatives came forward to congratulate them. Afterward, all were ushered into the recreation hall for refreshments. While the guests ate, Aaron entertained the group, and then Lily and her daughters sang their special song for Connie and Steven.

After the luncheon was over, Connie addressed the group from her wheelchair. "Thank you all so very much for coming. Steven and I are very happy." She held Steven's hand tightly in hers. "Aaron will say a few words now."

Aaron stood up and looked over the well-wishers. He estimated there were about forty people in attendance. He thanked them for coming. "I am so happy that Mom and Dad have taken this step. Now we are truly a family." He wiped a tear from his eyes. "I have dreamed of this ever since my dad came back into our lives. This is a wonderful day. Mom has a surprise to show all of you, and what better time to show you than on her wedding day."

With that, Steven stood on one side of Connie, and Aaron on the other. Connie gripped their hands and slowly stood up. Everyone gasped, and then a big cheer arose. Then with Steven and Aaron's help, she walked two steps. "That is all I can manage for now," she told her friends.

"We have been told by my doctor that there is going to be a clinic set up here in Salt Lake where I can go and work with their E-legs, exoskeleton apparatus. This is a very exciting innovation to help paraplegics walk." Connie explained what it was and how it works. "To own one would cost in the neighborhood of $100,000, so that is out of our range, but Steven's insurance will pick up an exercise program at the clinic for me. I have been exercising on my special bike at home and strengthening my upper body muscles. I know now that I will walk again. I just know it." Connie beamed as she said the words.

Everyone present came up to her and hugged her and Steven and Aaron. It was truly a joyous occasion.

The next morning, Steven and Connie left for their honeymoon. Steven took Connie on the promised road trip around the state of Utah to see and enjoy the wonders that this great state has to offer. They couldn't take a long honeymoon trip because Steven needed to have the choirs begin practicing all together. It was a large undertaking, but he was looking forward to it. He would have a lot of help from the other music directors who had agreed to help him. Even though their trip lasted only a few days, they were glorious, happy days.

CHAPTER SEVENTY-EIGHT

On the following Monday after his mother and dad's wedding, Aaron took the elevator to the third floor of the Hunter Cancer Clinic and entered the visitors' area. The patients and a few of the doctors and nurses were also there to attend his concert. He greeted them warmly, strapped on his guitar, and began to play some of their favorite songs. The children, who could, sang along with him.

"My dad can't be with us today," Aaron told the children. "He will be back next week for sure. Now, do any of you have a special song you would like me to do?"

Several hands went up. For the next hour and a half, he entertained his special audience and, then when it was time to go, he stood up and walked over and said goodbye to each of the patients. One by one he greeted them. Just as he got to the last patient, he recognized him. He had been sitting in a wheelchair somewhat obscured by another patient. Aaron hadn't noticed him as he was performing, but as he went from bed to bed or wheelchair to wheelchair he saw him. He felt an odd shiver go through his body at the sight of the young man.

"Matthew, I didn't see you there."

"That's because I didn't want you to see me," Matthew replied. He practically spit out the words. Again, Aaron felt a shiver go through him. The last time he had seen Matthew, he had been more than a little afraid.

"I heard about your little concerts, Aaron. Now I get to see you in person. Who knew that little Aaron would grow up to be such a big star. We should have taken care of you years ago," Matthew scowled at Aaron.

Aaron was struck by the anger in Matthew's voice. After a few moments, Aaron managed to tear himself away and say a personal goodbye to the doctors and nurses. As he picked up his guitar and was about to leave the room, Dr. Smith came up to Aaron and asked him if he could speak with him out in the hall.

Aaron followed the doctor, and when they were a safe distance away from the visitors' area, Dr. Smith asked Aaron how he knew Matthew Trujillo.

"Matthew was in my social studies class last year, Doctor. He tried to recruit me for his gang. Every time he had a chance, he would grab me in the hall and warn me that if I didn't go along and join his gang of thugs, they would beat me up. I would have nothing to do with them. Finally, I had no choice but to go to the principal. I guess the principal warned him to leave me alone because he didn't bother me after that. However, I avoided him as much as I could. Once in a while when we happened to meet, he looked at me like he wanted to do something to me. It really scared me. I didn't tell anyone else about it, not even my mother. What is Matthew in the hospital for, Doctor Smith?"

"He and some of his thugs, as you call them, tried to rob a bank a couple of days ago. He was shot in the thigh by a cop. I took the bullet out, and he should be fine and able to go home in a few days. He and his gang members will have to serve some jail time, I am sure. Right now, they are in the custody of their parents. What I noticed is how he looked at you as you walked into the visitors' area. He obviously harbors some ill will toward you, Aaron. Please be careful."

"Thank you, Doctor." Aaron and the doctor shook hands. Aaron left the hospital, got on his bicycle, and rode toward home. He was about two blocks from the hospital when he noticed a car coming fast toward him. He tried to get out of the way. Then everything went dark.

*****

"Aaron, Aaron, I am so sorry. Please forgive me."

He recognized Rose's voice, but her face kept swimming around like it was somehow detached. He tried to focus on what she was saying. "Rose?"

"Do you remember what happened, Aaron?" Rose asked him.

"I saw a car. I swerved. I don't remember anything after that."

Just then, another voice was heard. It was a male voice. Aaron tried to locate a face to go with the voice but it too was distorted. Aaron shut his eyes and then opened them again. Still, the faces swam around like fish in a tank.

"You are a very lucky young man, Aaron," the voice addressed him. "I am Doctor Shilling. You have a broken leg and some cuts and bruises. You're going to be all right, son. We will get your leg set as soon as an operating room is available. It will be just a few minutes."

"My eyes won't focus, Doctor. I can't see you very well."

"You have a slight concussion, Aaron. Hopefully, your eyes should clear up on their own. If not, we will have to do a scan to see if there is some bleeding. In the meantime, try not to worry."

"My mother, where's my mother? Does she know?"

"I'm here, son."

"Mom, it was a friend of Matthew Trujillo who ran me down. I know it. Matthew must have called him from the hospital."

Connie wheeled her chair as close as she could to the bed. Aaron tried to focus his eyes on her face. However, she had two faces, and they kept dancing in front of him. He closed his eyes. Connie took his hand in hers and kissed it. "We were on our way home from our honeymoon when Lily called me with the news. We were so scared. Lily told us the doctors thought you would be all right, but we still were worried. Oh, what if you had been killed," Connie's started to cry. Other voices tried to calm her. He heard his father, and Lily, and Rose.

"Rose?"

Rose came over to clutch Aaron's hand. "I am so sorry for being such a nerd. I am not mad at you. I know that my father died because of an accident. I want you to know I…I love you, Aaron Turner. You are like a brother to me. Please, please get well. I promise I will be a better friend to you." She started to cry.

"It's all right, Rose. I am going to get better, you'll see. Everything is going to be all right."

Rose bent down and kissed Aaron's forehead. He was clearly pleased. Soon, an operating room became available, and all were ushered into the waiting room near the surgical wing. Lily and Rose, Connie and Steven sat mostly silent as they waited. Lily had called Jacob, and he was soon there with the others.

Finally, two hours later, Aaron was wheeled into his room. Dr. Shilling came over to talk with them for a few moments. "Aaron is heavily sedated. The operation went well, but we had to put a couple of pins in the leg to hold everything together. He won't be able to do much for several weeks while his leg heals. Then we will have him do physical therapy and get him all better. He should have no lasting effects from the break. You might as well go home and get some rest." The doctor shook each person's hand and waved goodbye as he walked out the door.

CHAPTER SEVENTY-NINE

Two days after Aaron's surgery, the police came to visit him in the hospital. By now, his eyes had cleared, and he could see as well as ever. He was very grateful that he would not need a brain scan to see if there was bleeding in his brain.

The policemen introduced themselves. "I am Peter Evans, and my partner is Tom Wood." They shook Aaron's hand. Chairs were placed by the bed for the two officers. "Tell us what you remember about the accident, Aaron."

"It was no accident, Officers. I was riding my bicycle home from the Hunter Cancer Hospital. I sing and play for the patients on Monday afternoon. On my way home, a car came right at me. I swerved my bike, but it knocked me down. I don't remember anything after that until I woke up in the hospital."

"You say it was no accident, Aaron? What makes you think it was done on purpose?"

Aaron proceeded to tell the officers about seeing Matthew Trujillo in the hospital.

"You know Matthew Trujillo?" Officer Wood queried. "That young man is in serious trouble."

"Yes, and I think he called one of his goons to run me down." Aaron told the policemen all about his run-ins with Matthew in school the year before. He told them how he had threatened him and how he had to go to the principal to get the harassment stopped. "He has it in for me because I refused to join his gang, and then I went and tattled on him because he kept grabbing me or pinning me up against the wall at school. Even after he quit bothering me, he would look at me with a menacing look, like he wanted to hurt me. I mostly stayed as far away from him as I could. He scared me."

The officers stood up and thanked Aaron for the information. "We will let you know what we find out. In the meantime, young man, we hope you have a speedy recovery." The officers waved as they left the room.

*****

Aaron stayed in the hospital two more days before he was allowed to go home. Steven asked Jacob to come and help him get Aaron home. His leg was broken below the knee, so he was able to sit in a wheelchair without too much trouble. Steven tried to make light of the situation by pointing out that he now had two patients in wheelchairs. "What fun!"

One day, a few days later, Police Officer Peter Evans called and asked to speak to Aaron. "Hello, this is Aaron."

"Hi, Aaron. Just wanted to let you know that we did some checking on your mishap. We know now, as you said, it was no accident. Matthew Trujillo did not have a cell phone in the hospital. He wasn't allowed to have one. When we checked with the other patients, we found that he had borrowed a phone from one of the other patients. The patient was just a young boy who didn't know Matthew wasn't to make any calls. We were able to trace the calls made on the phone and found one that was made while you were still entertaining the children. One of his gang, a kid by the name of Paul, Paul Shotts, took the call. We went to his house and, right there in his driveway, was his banged-up car. I wish all our cases were this easy, Aaron.

"We arrested him and took him to a juvenile facility. We have also arrested Matthew. He had left the hospital, so we went to his home and placed him in juvenile detention too. They will be going away for some time, what with the attempted bank holdup and the attempt made on your life. Paul Shotts confessed everything. Now, you get well Aaron so you can go sing for the patients soon. I understand you are the star of the hospital."

"Thank you, Officer, for the news. I am very glad you caught them both. And I'll be performing again as soon as I can. Thanks again." Aaron hung up, a big grin on his face.

"They caught the kid who hit me, Dad, and he confessed that Matthew Trujillo put him up to it."

"That is great, son. Now how about some dinner. I made a delicious vegetable beef soup. Well, actually, I just opened a couple of cans." Steven chuckled as Connie grinned at him.

"I'll get the bread and butter." Connie wheeled over to the fridge. "I think we have some fruit salad. Oh, yes, here it is. Aaron, let's see how good you are at setting the table from your wheelchair."

"You both know, of course, that I am going to have to be gone a great deal over the next few weeks, don't you? Those choirs still need their head director. Will you be all right, the two of you?"

"Don't worry, Steven, we will get along just fine. It is going to be quite a fine challenge trying to keep out of each other's way, but we'll manage. Right, son?"

"Of course, Mom, we will be fine. By the way, what happened to my guitar. I suppose it got smashed to smithereens."

Steven walked into Aaron's bedroom and came out with the guitar. "Sorry, Aaron, it's toast. I am going to find out if that kid had insurance. His insurance should pay all your hospital bills and get you a brand-new guitar."

"You better hurry. I have to practice my songs for the celebration. I am way behind on getting them ready."

"Do you think you still want to try to play and sing for the event, son?" Connie asked. "You are pretty banged-up."

"I want so much to be a part of it, Mom. I just have to sing and play for it." Aaron looked up at his mother with such resolve that she just nodded her head.

"Let's eat," Steven said. "I'm hungry."

CHAPTER EIGHTY

The month of June flew by. There was great excitement in the city. University of Utah was engaged in all the workings to make it the most memorable celebration since the 2002 Winter Olympics.

The choirs were practicing together every week. A venue had been found for them to use. The teenagers were working hard on their music so they could sing it without having to hold the music before them.

The Greens called Lily and offered their help, which was greatly appreciated. Their oldest son, Tom, had graduated in May from high school but still participated in his choir. Also, now sixteen-year-old Josh was singing in his school choir too.

The weeks were full of activity. Lily and the girls worked in the garden every chance they could. They practiced their music every day until they were sure they knew every note and word by heart. Aaron came over every day to practice with them. His father brought him over when he could, but usually, Lily and the girls drove over to the Turners to get him. They gently maneuvered him into the back seat and then folded up the wheelchair and placed it in the trunk of the car. Rose insisted she be the one to slide in next to Aaron. Aaron smiled at her as she sat beside him. He felt happy and relieved that she was no longer angry at him.

Paul Shotts's attorney and the negotiators for the insurance on the Shotts's car were working together with the Turners to come up with a settlement that would pay for all of Aaron's medical bills as well as compensation for pain and suffering. They willingly paid for a new guitar for Aaron.

Jacob kept tabs on everything that was going on. They had scheduled one dress rehearsal for one week before the second of July, but it had been rained out. Thank goodness, the weather forecast was for good weather over the weekend.

Lily, her daughters, Jacob, James and their parents, Aaron, Connie, and Steven got together the night the rehearsal was rained out and held hands and prayed that the weather would be great so that they could get a rehearsal in before the second and that the day of the second would be perfect, and that everything would go as planned.

On June 30, they were able to have the dress rehearsal that had been rained out a few days before. There were a few hitches, but they were solved during the practice. At the end of the practice, Carson Hunter stood up and addressed the crowd: "From the bottom of my heart, I want you to know how much I appreciate what you are doing to bring to Salt Lake City this glorious celebration. If everything goes well, it will be remembered as one of the best celebrations this city, this state has ever witnessed. On July 2, we ask that you are all in your places no later than 7:30 p.m. I have asked my assistant, Mona Thompson, to give a prayer for a successful undertaking. Mona?"

Mona stepped up to the microphone and gave a heartfelt prayer to the Lord for his great goodness and love. She thanked him for the opportunity to put on this program about patriotism and appreciation for all who have blessed and served this great land. She asked the Lord to bless each and every one who would be participating and asked that the weather would be perfect for the occasion. Then she closed in the name of Jesus Christ, amen.

Carson Hunter stepped up to the mike and thanked Mona and then waved to the crowd. "See you all Friday evening." All who were there clapped and cheered loudly.

CHAPTER EIGHTY-ONE

It was 7:55 p.m. Everyone was in their seat. The program was about to begin. The bleachers were full, all except the area roped off for the servicemen and women. On a cue given by their commander, they marched in full-dress uniforms, in perfect formation, climbed the bleachers, and stood by their seats. The crowd stood as one to cheer and clap for them. They acknowledged by smartly saluting the crowd before they sat down all at the same time. It was a glorious sight to witness.

Carson Hunter stepped up to the microphone to deadening applause. He acknowledged the applause and then raised his arms to quiet the huge crowd. "Thank you all for coming." Just as he said the words, there was a great roar above the stadium. The jet fighters from Hill Air Force Base flew in perfect formation across the evening sky. The crowd stood and yelled and cheered.

When the people had settled down, Mr. Hunter spoke, "We would like to acknowledge the men and women in uniform who are with us here today. Let's give them a hand of appreciation." When the audience finished clapping and returned to their seats, Mr. Hunter continued, "Now all of you in this audience who have served in any of the armed services for our great country, will you please stand up and let us acknowledge your service." Many men and women in the crowd stood up, and the rest loudly cheered.

Carson Hunter said, "Please stand for the posting of our flag and our national anthem." All stood as the flag was carried into the bleachers by several Eagle Scouts who gently placed it in its stand. They stood back and placed their hands on their hearts as they and the audience sang our national anthem. They then walked in formation to their seats.

"You were all given a program of tonight's celebration. Let the show begin."

Steven and the other music directors stepped out before the choirs, and at a signal, Paul Strong and his team began the music through the loudspeakers situated throughout the stadium. The choirs and the great crowd stood up and sang the national anthem.

Following the national anthem, the choirs sang Irving Berlin's "God Bless America" and followed it with Lee Greenwood's "God Bless the U.S.A."

The crowd hushed as James and his class walked on to the stage. When they were all in place, their teacher stood beside them. Flashed on the screens were the words from Abraham Lincoln's Gettysburg Address. One by one, the children spoke their lines loud and clear.

> Four score and seven years ago our fathers brought forth on this continent, a new nation, conceived in Liberty, and dedicated to the proposition that all men are created equal.
>
> Now we are engaged in a great civil war, testing whether that nation, or any nation so conceived and so dedicated, can long endure. We are met on a great battle-field of that war. We have come to dedicate a portion of that field, as a final resting place for those who here gave their lives that that nation might live. It is altogether fitting and proper that we should do this.
>
> But, in a larger sense, we cannot dedicate – we can not consecrate – we cannot hallow – this ground. The brave men, living and dead, who struggled here, have consecrated it, far above our poor power to add or detract. The world will little note, nor long remember what we say here, but it can never forget what they did here. It is for us the living, rather, to be dedicated here to

> the unfinished work which they who fought here have thus far so nobly advanced.
>
> It is rather for us to be here dedicated to the great task remaining before us – that from these honored dead we take increased devotion to that cause for which they gave the last full measure of devotion – that we here highly resolve that these dead shall not have died in vain – that this nation, under God, shall have a new birth of freedom – and that government of the people, by the people, for the people, shall not perish from the earth.

The young students then bowed to the vast audience who gave them thunderous applause.

The choir then sang "Yankee Doodle" and John Philip Sousa's "The Stars and Stripes Forever."

It was time for Rose and her classmates to give their essays on the Founding Fathers. One by one they stood before the microphone. Each child said his name and then told about their special Founding Father. They told of George Washington, Thomas Jefferson, John Adams, and James Madison. The last one to speak was Rose. "I am Rose Langston. I am going to tell you about my favorite Founding Father, Benjamin Franklin." In a clear, sweet voice, she spoke the words she had memorized about this great man, the words from her essay she had written several months before and given for her family's Family Home Evening.

As the five students finished they too bowed to appreciative applause. The choirs then stood and sang "The Marine's Hymn" and Samuel F. Smith's "America."

It was now Lily and her daughters' turn. Lily came forward and sat at the piano. She was lovely in her red chiffon dress. She had a red flower in her dark hair that cascaded in curls to her shoulders. Her daughters were dressed in white chiffon dresses and had red, white, and blue flowers arranged in corsages on their shoulders. They made a stunning picture. The girls stood in front of the piano, each with her own mike. Lily played the introduction, and then they sang "My Own America."

After the number was finished and the applause had died down a little, Lily spoke into the microphone, "The next number we are going to do is Woody Guthrie's 'This Land is Your Land.' Aaron Turner will sing and play with us."

The applause was loud. Aaron's father stepped off the stage and walked over to where Aaron was sitting in his wheelchair. He hugged his son and then pushed his wheelchair onto the stage. The crowd stood and clapped and shouted as Aaron was placed beside Lily and her girls. He bowed and acknowledged the audience. He was dressed in a tuxedo and had a small red, white, and blue ribbon tucked in his breast pocket. Aaron was very handsome with his red hair and fine facial features. Steven then walked back to sit in his place in front of the high school choirs.

Aaron played his new guitar, and Lily accompanied on the piano, and together they sang, as the audience stood and clapped in rhythm to the music. After their performance, the crowd cheered for several moments.

When all was quiet once again, Carson Hunter got up and acknowledged and thanked all who had participated. The crowd cheered again. "We are coming to the end of our program. I hope you all feel a renewed love for your country and to God for placing the right people in the right place at the right time to fight for our inspired system of government. This is truly the greatest country the world has ever known. May God bless us to keep it free and a safe place to raise our families. May we always value our Constitution and live by its principles. We will close with the choirs singing 'America the Beautiful,' a favorite of mine, and I am sure yours also. All of you who wish to join in singing, please do so. The words are on your program. After we finish singing, please stand for the retiring of the colors by the Eagle Scouts. After the music, stay in your seats for the fireworks. Thank you all for coming."

CHAPTER EIGHTY-TWO

After the fireworks were over, the audience slowly left the bleachers and headed for the exits and their cars. Jacob and Lily were in no hurry to leave. They continued to sit in their seats watching the crowd as it dispersed. Jacob put his arm around Lily's shoulders and hugged her. He would wait a little while before he asked her the important question.

First, they needed to walk over and talk to Steven and Aaron. Then they wished to visit a few moments with the Hunters, and Jacob supposed there would be others who would want to visit with them.

They began to mingle with the crowd, receiving accolades and well-wishes from several. Kay and Carson Hunter walked over to where Lily and Jacob were standing. "What did you think of the evening. Do you think it will be remembered favorably?"

"Absolutely," Jacob answered.

"It was wonderful," Lily echoed.

Carson Hunter gave Lily a big hug. Just then, the girls came forward, and each received a hug. James's teacher brought him to Jacob. On his face was a great big grin.

"I did my part good, didn't I, Dad?" With that, he held up his hand and went around the circle giving everyone his "I love you" sign. Steven came forward with Aaron and Connie in their wheelchairs. They approached just in time to be included in James's "I love you" sign.

"It has been a marvelous evening. I will relive it in my mind and heart for a long, long time," Carson Hunter said. Kay echoed what he said. She gave his arm a squeeze.

As they stood there visiting, many people came up to them and thanked them for the inspirational evening. Lily's parents and in-laws came up to congratulate them.

Finally, as the lights were about to be turned off in the stadium, they moved toward the exits. It was time to end this most special evening.

Jacob piled everyone in the suburban. His parents had taken his car and left the bigger one so he could fit everyone in. First, he drove to his place and took James in to his parents. "I'll be back soon, son. Your grandmother and grandfather will tuck you into bed. You did a fine job tonight, son. I am very proud of you." With that, Jacob gave him the "I love you" sign and then waved goodbye.

Next, he stopped at Lily's and hugged the girls and told them good night, "Lily, I need to go home for a few minutes, and then I'll be back. Will you wait for me?"

"Yes. I'll get the girls ready for bed. See you when you get back." Lily waved and walked into the house.

Jacob walked into his house and up the stairs to James's bedroom. James was undressing. He folded his clothes carefully and placed them in the dirty clothes hamper. Then he put on his pajamas, right leg and right arm first, as always. Jacob tucked him in bed. "James, there is something I need to ask you. Will you try to look at me while I ask you? It is very important." James stared at the ceiling. "James, how would you feel about having Susie and her sisters as part of our family? I want to ask Lily to marry me. Would that be all right, James?"

James continued to stare at the ceiling. After a long pause, he said, "Dad, did you know there are 979 stars on my ceiling?"

"What?"

"I'll show you. Turn off the big light."

Jacob walked over and turned off the ceiling light. Now only the night-light glimmered softly, along with some light coming through the window from the street lamp on the corner. Jacob lay down by his son, and he too stared up at the ceiling. There in the semidarkness, shiny specks glowed in the ceiling tiles.

"Wow, James, that is lovely. I didn't know that those little flecks in the tile would glow like that."

"I'd like that, Dad."

At first, Jacob wasn't sure what James was referring to. And then he understood. James was telling him it was fine for him to ask Lily to marry him.

"Thank you, son. I love you so much."

"I like Susie. She will make a fun sister. Yes, and I like Bonnie and Rose. And I like Lily too."

Jacob reached over and touched James's "I love you" sign with his own.

"Good night, son," Jacob said as he softly closed the door.

*****

"Let's go out into the garden, Lily. Remember the first time we met? You scared the living daylights out of me then. I was putting the gold coin in the garden, and you came up and asked me what I was doing. In the early sunshine, you looked like an angel greeting me. Do you remember?"

"I'll never forget it, Jacob."

"You were the most beautiful woman I had ever seen, there with the sun peeking over the horizon. It glowed all around you. You are beautiful, Lily." With those words, Jacob reached into his pocket and pulled out a little box.

"It has been fifteen months since Samuel was killed. I hope it isn't too soon to ask you, dear, but…will you marry me, Lily?"

Lily looked up into Jacob's handsome face, his dark eyes looking down into her blue ones. "Yes, Jacob, I will marry you." She reached up and kissed him. With that, he opened the little box and placed the diamond ring on her finger. In the moonlight, it sparkled.

"Let's go tell the girls."

Jacob held Lily close as he pointed toward the house. There, standing at the sliding glass door peering out at them, were Lily's daughters. Jacob laughed. "I think they already know."

ABOUT THE AUTHOR

Doreen Hatton was born Lucy Doreen Lyons in Lethbridge, Alberta, Canada. Her parents, Ilene Betts and George Lyons, were the parents of thirteen children. In 1960, Doreen married Max F. Parrish. They had six children. Max passed away in 1986. In 1990, she married Lynn Harold Hatton. Lynn passed away on 2013. Doreen is a grandmother of thirty-four grandchildren and several great-grandchildren.